and the Munch and Krüger series:

'As clever and twisty as his hugely successful debut *I'm Travelling Alone*.'

Sunday Times

'Another ice-cool slice of gruesome goings-on featuring detective duo Munch and Krüger to delight Scandi-noir fans . . . fabulously suspenseful.'

Sunday Mirror

'Icy landscapes, mysterious clues, a messed up heroine . . . Nordic noir at its delicious best.'

Sarah Hilary, author of *Someone Else's Skin*

'Tense, thrilling and genuinely scary.'

Heat

'The latest Norwegian crime-writing sensation.'

Sunday Times

'The characters are completely believable, the plot is scalpel sharp and, as the hunt escalates, it will frighten the wits out of you in an utterly brilliant way.'

Sunday Mirror

'Mesmerising fare.'

Independent

'Compelling . . . with plenty of intrigue.'

Guardian

Samuel Bjork is the pen name of Norwegian novelist, playwright and singer/songwriter Frode Sander Øien. *The Boy in the Headlights* is the third in his Munch and Krüger series: *I'm Travelling Alone* and *The Owl Always Hunts at Night* were the first two. All three have been bestsellers across Scandinavia and the rest of Europe.

Also by Samuel Bjork

I'm Travelling Alone
The Owl Always Hunts at Night

and published by Corgi Books

SAMUEL BJORK

The boy in the head lights

Translated from the Norwegian by Charlotte Barslund

CORGI BOOKS

TRANSWORLD PUBLISHERS
61–63 Uxbridge Road, London W5 5SA
www.penguin.co.uk

Transworld is part of the Penguin Random House group of companies
whose addresses can be found at global.penguinrandomhouse.com

Penguin
Random House
UK

First published in Great Britain in 2019 by Doubleday
an imprint of Transworld Publishers
Published by agreement with Ahlander Agency
Corgi edition published 2019

A CIP catalogue record for this book is available from the British Library.

ISBN
9780552170925 (B format)
9780552176644 (A format)

Typeset in 10.34/13pt Sabon
by Integra Software Services Pvt. Ltd, Pondicherry.

Printed and bound in Great Britain by Clays Ltd, Elcograf S.p.A.

Penguin Random House is committed to a sustainable future for
our business, our readers and our planet. This book is made
from Forest Stewardship Council® certified paper.

MIX
Paper from
responsible sources
FSC® C018179

1 3 5 7 9 10 8 6 4 2

The boy in the headlights

On Christmas Day 1996 a man was driving across the mountains on his way home from Oslo. He was seventy-one years old, a widower, and he had spent Christmas with his daughter. He usually loved this road, for two reasons. Firstly, he didn't care much for the city, though it always did him good to be with younger people and their constant activity. The second reason was being surrounded by this magnificent landscape. Forests, wide expanses, mountaintops, lakes; every season was equally breathtaking. Norway at her best. True beauty as far as the eye could see. Winter had come early this year and, once the magical snow had settled, it was like driving through a quiet and enchanting postcard. Usually. The old man's eyesight was poor and he had tried desperately to leave early in order to enjoy the drive home. In the daylight. Only this time he hadn't left early enough. The darkness. He didn't like it. Sitting at home in front of the fireplace was fine – then he didn't mind at all that the world was spinning on its axis and that now it was his turn to be surrounded by night, not at all; at times it could even be cosy. He would pour himself a tipple. Snuggle up on the sofa under a blanket while the nocturnal wildlife woke up outside and the cold took a hold so strong that the thick timber walls creaked. But being out on the roads? This far from home? No, he didn't like that. The old man slowed down and moved his face even closer to the windscreen. He had bought extra-bright driving lights for the car for emergencies like this one and he switched them on as the clouds in the sky blocked out the last of the faint moonlight. An icy, silencing darkness descended upon the landscape. The old man took a deep breath and briefly considered pulling over and sitting it out. Madness, of course. It was almost minus 20°C outside, and he was miles from any populated areas. There was only one thing for it and that was to keep going. Do the best he could. The old man was about to turn on the radio to find a station that would keep him awake when his headlights caught something which made him slam both feet against the floor.

Good heavens!

There was a creature on the road ahead.

What the . . .?

Fifty metres.

Twenty metres.

Ten metres.

He pressed the brake pedal frantically, feeling his heart leap into his throat, his knuckles whitening on the steering wheel, the world almost imploding in front of his eyes before the car finally stopped.

The man gasped for breath.

What the hell?

A small boy was standing on the road in front of him.

He didn't move.

His lips were blue.

And he had antlers on his head.

ONE

APRIL 2013

Chapter 1

The boy with the curly hair sat on the back thwart in the small dinghy, trying to be very quiet. He glanced furtively at his father, who had the oars, and felt flushed with happiness. He was seeing his dad again. Finally. It had been a while since the last time, since his mum had found out what had happened during that trip. In his dad's house deep in the forest – in the mountains, practically – the house his mum called a shack. The boy had tried to explain to her that it was OK that his dad didn't make the kind of dinners she cooked for him, and that he smoked inside and kept a gun in the living room, because it was for shooting grouse, not people, but his mum had refused to listen to him. No more visits; she had even called the police, or maybe not the police, but someone who had come to their home and spoken to him at the kitchen table and written things down in a notebook, and after that he hadn't been allowed to see his dad. Until now.

The boy wanted to tell his dad that he had read books since his last visit. About fishing. At the library. That he had learned the names of many fish – whitefish, char, blenny, trout, salmon – and that he now knew there wouldn't be pike in a lake like this because pike liked hiding in the reeds. There were no reeds here, just bog straight to the water's edge, but he said nothing because he had learned not to. When you went fishing, you weren't supposed to talk; only in a very soft voice and only if his father spoke first.

'First trip to Svarttjønn this year,' his father whispered, and smiled to him through his beard.

'And it's special every time,' the boy whispered back, and felt once more the wonderful rush of love that flooded over him whenever his father looked at him.

The boy had tried explaining this to his mum over and over. About his dad. How much he liked being up here. The birds outside the window. The smell of the trees. That money wasn't the only thing that mattered, that it wasn't his dad's fault no one wanted to buy his drawings, that it was OK to eat your dinner without washing your hands first, without a tablecloth, but she refused to listen and sometimes the words were so hard to find that in the end he had given up trying.

To be with his dad.

He raised his eyes to the clouds and hoped they would soon disappear and make way for the stars. Then the fish would come. He shifted his gaze to his father once more, towards his strong arms, which quietly pulled the oars through the almost pitch-black water, and was tempted to tell him that he, too, had been working out and would soon be able to row the boat himself, but he said nothing. He didn't go to the gym where his mum went – children weren't allowed and he was only ten years old – but he had worked out at home in his room, push-ups and sit-ups practically every afternoon for almost six months now. He had studied himself in the mirror several times, but his muscles hadn't grown very much. Never mind, at least he was trying. Next summer, perhaps. By then, the training might have made a difference. The boy with the curly hair had tried to imagine what it would be like. He would walk through the gate with his rucksack, maybe wearing one of the T-shirts the men at his mum's gym wore, men with big arms, big muscles, who could easily row the boat, and then his dad could sit on the thwart at the back while his son pulled the oars through the water.

'It's not a proper fishing trip without a beer.' His father winked at him while he reached between his legs and opened yet another of the green cans at the bottom of the boat.

The boy nodded back, although he knew this was one of the things his mum had discussed with the visitors, how his dad drank too much and that it was irresponsible. Lake Svarttjønn. The lovely, remote

6

mountain lake which few people knew about, and now the two of them were finally out on it together and so he tried hard not to think about it any more. That his mum had said there wouldn't be a next time. No more visits to his dad. That this might be the last one.

'First cast?' his father whispered, putting the oars in the boat.

'Fly or spinner?' the boy whispered back, knowing that this was important, although he had yet to work out why.

His father took another swig of his beer and glanced up at the clouds, then looked across the dark water.

'What do you think?'

'Spinner?' the boy ventured, somewhat hesitantly at first, but he felt his cheeks tingle with happiness when his father nodded and smiled at him and opened the bait box beside him on the thwart.

'Too dark for a fly, wouldn't you say?'

'Yes,' the boy nodded; he looked up at the clouds and pretended for a moment that he hadn't noticed the sky wasn't as starry as it ought to be.

'Here you go,' his father said, when he had attached the colourful hook to the end of the fishing line.

It was a solemn moment when the boy took the rod his father was passing to him and, although he knew what his father would say next, he pretended he was learning something new when his father said in a low voice:

'Keep it short so we don't hit the bottom, OK?'

'OK,' the boy said, and swung the rod over the gunwale.

Hold on tight. Lift the rod. Pull back. Let go at just the right moment. The boy with the curly hair felt flushed with love once more when he saw his father's eyes, which told him he had done everything right as the colourful hook flew through the air and hit the black water with an almost silent plop.

'Not too much,' his father murmured, opening another beer. 'Easy does it.'

The boy did as his father told him and suddenly felt a strong urge to tell his mum that she was wrong. About the boat. And the lake. He wanted to be with his dad. No matter what the people with the notebooks said. Perhaps he could even move here? Feed the birds?

7

Help his dad fix the roof? Repair the flagstones on the steps, the loose ones? He was so immersed in his thoughts of how wonderful it would be that he nearly forgot he was holding the fishing rod.

'Bite!'

'Eh?'

'You have a bite!'

The boy snapped out of his reverie when he realized that the rod had started to bend. He tried to reel in the line, but he could barely move the handle.

'It's a big one!' the boy burst out, completely forgetting that he was supposed to be quiet.

'Shit,' his father said, moving to the back thwart. 'Your first throw – are you sure you didn't catch something on the bank?'

'I . . . don't . . . think . . . so . . .' the boy said, reeling in his catch as best he could. It was so heavy it pulled the boat closer to the shore.

'Here it comes,' his father said, then grinned and swung his arms over the gunwale. 'Oh, Jesus!' he exclaimed.

'What is it?'

'Don't look, Thomas,' his father cried out as their catch neared the boat.

'Dad?'

'Lie down in the bottom of the boat. Don't look!'

He so desperately wanted to listen, but his ears weren't working.

'Dad?'

'Get down, Thomas, don't look!'

But he looked anyway.

At the girl lying in the water below them.

Her blue-and-white face.

Her open eyes.

Her floating, wet clothing; clothing completely unsuitable for being out in the forest.

'Dad?'

'Lie down, Thomas! For fuck's sake.'

The little boy didn't manage to see anything more before his father lunged across the thwart.

And pressed him against the bottom of the boat.

Chapter 2

It wasn't true that Karoline Berg was afraid of flying. It was just an excuse. The truth was that she was scared of going anywhere at all. She preferred being at home. She liked her routines – no, she *needed* her routines.

'Please come and visit me, Mum?'

'I would love to, Vivian, but you know how I hate flying . . .'

'So take the train.'

'And be stuck in a hermetically sealed box for sixteen hours with total strangers?'

'No, I get it, only I would so love you to see me dance.'

'But I've seen you dance, Vivian. Many times.'

'I know, but we're not talking about Bodø Arts Centre. This is the Oslo Opera, Mum. The Opera! Did I tell you that I've been accepted into Alexander Ekman's ensemble? I'll be dancing *Swan Lake. Swan Lake!* How amazing is that?'

'Vivian, that's wonderful. Congratulations, sweetheart.'

'You're growing old before your time, up there all on your own, Mum. Please come to Oslo. We could go out for dinner. Have you heard of Maaemo? It's in the Michelin Guide and everything. We could . . .'

Of course she wanted to see her daughter dance.

Dear God, there was nothing she wanted more.

'I'll see you the next time you come home. Can't we leave it at that?'

'Of course, Mum. Listen, I've got to run, we have a rehearsal. Are you all right?'

'I'm fine, Vivian. Don't worry about me.'

9

'OK, Mum, speak soon.'

'That'd be good.'

Dear God, when had it become like this?

The days just coming and going.

What had happened to her life?

The life she had dreamed of?

She was forty-two years old, but she felt like a hundred. Eating her prawn sandwich for lunch down at Sydvest every Saturday; no one ever said it out loud, but she knew they were laughing at her. Her friends. The same old friends she had always had. They had been at school together and she had had so many plans. Travelling to India. To Africa. Picking apples in Guatemala. Playing the guitar in a street in Amsterdam. The others, no, they had no plans beyond marriage, children, a job with the council or at the local supermarket – they were definitely never leaving Bodø – but now it seemed as if everyone had been round the world: everyone except her.

Vivian had travelled to Oslo to audition one spring, two years ago. Strong, lovely Vivian, who had arrived unexpectedly, practically out of nowhere. Bodø Airport, where planes flew from all over the world; NATO soldiers came here for exercises. Karoline Berg had been twenty years old and without a care in the world. He was an Englishman who left her with a big belly and no address.

Was it his fault?

Luke Moore from Leeds, the handsome pilot with the dark curls.

That you never went anywhere, Karoline?

No, you only have yourself to blame.

She lived in a small apartment a stone's throw from the airport, but she had never been to it.

Or anywhere.

You must go to Alicante. It's just lovely, it really is.

Said Mette.

Who had been one of her best friends once, but not any more, now she had a husband, children, a big house in Hundstad and went on holiday every summer to places far away from Bodø.

10

I mean, Key West. I'd heard it was great, but seriously?

Said Synnøve.

Who had struggled at school but had later managed to land a businessman from Harstad who liked yachting and investing in foreign property.

They laughed at her, yes, that was exactly what they did.

Whenever they walked through the doors of the Co-op.

Not out loud, but she could tell from their faces.

'Would you like a receipt? Do you need a bag?'

God, how she hated that noise.

Wholemeal loaf.

Beep.

Milk.

Beep.

Four cans of Coke, special offer.

Beep.

You're ugly.

Beep.

You'll never make anything of yourself.

Beep.

But then, in all secrecy – oh, if only they had known! – she had called a number she had found on the Internet. She had drunk several glasses of red wine to summon up the courage. And yes, she had rung off the first few times without saying anything at all, her palms sweaty, but finally, on her third attempt, she had dared to open her mouth.

A psychologist.

Christ, more grist to the gossip mill, yet another reason to laugh at her, but she had made the call anyway.

Thank God.

Bodø Airport.

She had lived near it for almost thirty-five years but had never set foot inside its doors.

Karoline Berg pulled the big new red suitcase the last stretch to the entrance then stopped to get her breath back.

Now what was it the psychologist had said?

Baby steps.

OK, you can do this, Karoline.

She could see her reflection in the shiny sliding doors. She could almost touch them now, and yet it felt as if they were on another planet. She had bought new clothes. She had been to the hairdresser's. Once she had finally managed to make that call, she had done everything he said. Not immediately; no, initially she had been consumed with self-loathing. As if filth were pouring from her mouth whenever she opened it. He had asked her so many personal questions. Things she had never even thought about. What was your relationship with your father? How did you and your mother get on? She had been dizzy, nauseous; distressing thoughts and feelings she hadn't known she had kept her awake at night. But then, after several weeks, something seemed to loosen up. It was like an avalanche. Once she began to open up, she couldn't stop.

She smiled to her reflection.

How nice you look, Karoline.

You're doing really well, Karoline.

New coat, Karoline? It suits you.

He had given her homework.

You need to learn to love yourself.

Oslo?

The capital.

She had wanted to go there for so long.

See the royal palace. Parliament. Karl Johans gate. The National Theatre. The statues in Frogner Park. And, last but not least, the Opera.

She took a deep breath and forced herself to walk the last few steps. She moved one foot. And then another. She was inside now. She was in the departure hall. She felt a little giddy, but she didn't stop. *You'll be fine, Karoline. You're nearly there. Check-in is just over there.* A blue screen. SK4111. SAS. Destination Oslo. Departing 12.35.

I'm coming, Vivian.

Mummy is coming to watch you dance!

Chapter 3

Holger Munch felt like an idiot as he stood by the window in his small flat, lighting his fourth cigarette of the day. Spring was coming to Oslo and the trees around Bislett Stadium had started to turn green, but that was the only thing that made him feel slightly better. It had been a difficult winter. *No, it had been a great winter, and that was the very reason he now felt like such a fool.* He had been on compassionate leave. Miriam, his daughter, had been badly injured. He had taken time off work to help her recover. The tragedy had brought his family close again. It was over ten years since he had moved out of the family home in Røa, but during the winter it was as if their past unhappiness had been forgotten, almost as if his divorce from Marianne hadn't happened. To begin with, Miriam had been in hospital, but as she started to improve they had moved her home to Røa. And he had followed suit. His ex-wife's new husband, Rolf, had moved out to make room for Miriam, and Munch had seized the opportunity to take his place. Soon it was almost like the old days. But he should have known that it couldn't last. What an idiot he had been. Dinners around the expensive dining table. The one he and Marianne had bought a long time ago when he was made a homicide investigator and they had finally had a little extra spending money. Friday evenings in front of the TV, like a normal family. He and Marianne together on the sofa with their granddaughter, Marion, between them. They had come so close to losing Miriam and he should have known that was why Marianne had behaved like this. As if it were the old days. As if they were back together.

Nor had she blamed him at any point, although he was the reason their daughter had almost lost her life. Or maybe he wasn't the reason. The special unit had been hunting a twisted killer and Miriam had been his last victim. Or rather, could have been his last victim. Munch took another drag on his cigarette and shook his head at himself. He could feel that he hadn't yet overcome his fear of losing his daughter. What if . . .? What if . . .? But she was recovering. Fortunately. And so he had lulled himself into this fantasy. Him and Marianne. Miriam. And little Marion. He had even started wearing his wedding ring again, like the idiot he was, and he was guessing she had seen it. A few days later she had come outside, where he was smoking.

Listen, Holger, we need to talk . . .

He had seen it in her eyes.

Rolf is moving back tomorrow . . .

He had merely nodded. Packed his few belongings and left the house with his tail between his legs – again.

He was a bloody fool.

Acting like a lovestruck teenager.

What had he been thinking?

Holger Munch stubbed out the half-smoked cigarette in the ashtray by the window and was about to light another when his mobile rang.

The name on the display.

He hadn't seen that one for a long time.

Anette Goli.

The brilliant police lawyer who had kept the special unit going in his absence.

'Yes? Munch speaking.'

'Hi, Holger,' her friendly voice said.

Holger Munch had headed the special unit based in Mariboesgate for just over ten years and during that time he had put together a team of Norway's most talented investigators. Anette Goli was definitely one of them. Admittedly, there were times when his unit and Oslo police headquarters at Grønland locked horns. Munch liked going his own way and not everybody appreciated that. Mikkelson, his boss, was one of those people. Munch was convinced that, if it hadn't been for his team's impeccable clear-up rate, Mikkelson would have moved them all back to police head-quarters so that he could keep an eye on what they were doing. It was all about politics and control, and Anette Goli often acted as the diplomat. The glue that held the two organizations together.

'How are you doing?' Goli said. 'And how is Miriam?'

'She is doing well,' Munch replied, reaching for another cigarette. 'Getting better every day – she's even started talking again. She slurs her words, but that will improve with time.'

'Glad to hear it.' Goli's voice darkened. 'I'm sorry if I'm inter-rupting, but I had to know. I'm also calling to let you know that Mikkelson wants the special unit up and running again. No pres-sure, of course, and only if you're ready to come back.'

'Is it about the girl up in the lake?'

'Yes. You've heard about it?'

Munch had lived in a bubble, a fantasy of his own making, up in Røa, and had tried to keep reality at arm's length, but this mur-der had been impossible to avoid. The media had talked of little else. A young woman wearing a ballet costume had been found dead in the shallows of a remote mountain lake.

'I have,' Munch said. 'Do we know who she is?'

'Vivian Berg, aged twenty-two, a dancer with the Norwegian National Ballet.'

'Right. So she was local?'

'She was originally from Bodø but had been living in Oslo, so Mikkelson wants us to handle the investigation.'

'Had she been reported missing?' Munch asked, feeling his investigative instincts starting to fire up again.

A young woman in a ballet costume?

In a remote mountain lake?

He knew he had been sticking his head in the sand for a long time and that it was pointless to carry on doing so. He was back in his small flat, alone, his wedding ring safely back in the bathroom cabinet.

'No, for some reason she hadn't been.'

'So how do we know who she is?'

'Her mother had flown down from Bodø to pay her a surprise visit and found her flat empty.'

'How awful.'

'Exactly. So what do you think? Are you ready? Shall we start the engine? Get the special unit back on its feet?'

'Who is handling the investigation right now?'

'Kripos, the National Crime Agency, but only for the time being. It's ours if you're ready.'

'Are you at the office right now?'

'Yes.'

'I'll be there in twenty minutes,' Munch said, and rang off.

Chapter 4

Mia Krüger was about to tape up the last cardboard box when Skype pinged on her laptop, which was open on the coffee table in front of her. The thirty-three-year-old woman smiled when she saw who was calling her.

Endless Summer.

Six months on a sailboat in the Caribbean.

She picked up her coffee cup from the floor and made herself comfortable on the sofa, tucking her legs underneath her.

'Hi, Mia, how are you? Booked your plane ticket yet?'

Viktor Vik. An old colleague who had left icy Norway and the police force many years ago to follow his dreams.

'Booked it yesterday,' Mia said. 'I'll be flying via New York, and then south down to you.'

'Great.' The tanned face on the screen smiled. 'When is your plane due in?'

'Next Friday. Will you have reached St Thomas by then?'

A dark-skinned waiter appeared behind Viktor and set down a drink with an umbrella in it on the table.

'No, we're docked in Road Town on Tortola. It's too busy over there.'

'On St Thomas?'

'Yes, it's a cruise port. And it's where all the American tourists touch down.'

'So do you want me to join you on Tortola?'

'No, no,' Viktor Vik said, producing a couple of dollar bills from the pocket of his Hawaiian shirt.

The waiter nodded and disappeared from the table. Mia could see a palm tree in the background. A ceiling fan. A closely embracing couple laughing as they walked past; each was carrying a drink, she wore a white bikini, he was bare-chested.

The Caribbean.

She could hardly believe it was true.

'We'll pick you up. It's no bother. Phew, it's hot today, how about there? Is it still winter in Norway?'

He winked and wiped his forehead with the back of his hand.

'No, it's starting to look like spring here,' Mia said, glancing out of the window.

A faint sun cast soft rays over the almost empty living-room floor. April. Spring in Oslo. 13°C. The dense darkness that had lain over the capital all winter had finally gone, but the weak sunshine was nothing compared to what was awaiting her.

The Virgin Islands.

'It's summer here all year round.' Viktor Vik smiled and took a sip of his drink. 'I'm really pleased that we managed to organize this, Mia. It'll be great to see you again. Will you give me a call when you're boarding your plane, so that I know you're on your way?'

'Definitely. I think I'm due to land on St Thomas about one o'clock on Friday afternoon.'

'Yes, that sounds like the morning plane from New York,' Viktor said. 'I'll let you know if we end up having to dock elsewhere, OK?'

'Sounds great.'

'Endless Summer awaits you.' Viktor Vik smiled again and raised his drink one last time before hitting a key on the keyboard and disappearing.

Mia Krüger switched off the screen and felt giddy with joy.

Six months on a boat.

Why hadn't she thought of this before?

Her father at home in the kitchen in Åsgårdstrand, bent over boat magazines, to which he was a keen subscriber.

'Would you take a look at this, Mia, a J-Class Endeavour? Have you ever seen anything so beautiful?'

18

She had been eight years old. One of the few times she had had him all to herself. Sigrid, her twin sister, had been out doing some activity or other. Ballet. Choir. Horse-riding. They had been so different: Sigrid always active, Mia more reticent, not so comfortable performing. Two girls born at the same time, a lifelong bond, and yet so different.

I'll be Sleeping Beauty and you'll be Snow White.

Why do I always have to be Snow White, Sigrid?

Because you have dark hair and I'm blonde, don't you get it?

No. I'm an idiot.

An idiot? Don't ever say that. You're the smartest person I know, Mia.

Mia Krüger closed her laptop and put her coffee cup back down on the floor.

Don't think about it any more.

It was in the past.

She taped up the flaps of the cardboard box and found her marker pen. Spent some time deciding what to write but ended up with a simple label.

Photos.

Mia carried the box to the smallest bedroom, where it joined the others. Memories. At last she had had the strength to face up to a painful past. The last box had been the worst. One photo album in particular had been hard to look at. *Mia's album.* Her mother had made it just for her. There was a photograph of Mia as a baby in a pram on the cover, alone in a photograph for once, and then several pages followed: *Mia and Sigrid on their second birthday. Sigrid and Mia dancing. Daddy has bought a new car!* Her childhood in Åsgårdstrand documented in the way only a 1980s photo album could. Colourful but faded memories that had triggered an immediate urge to run to the bathroom and twist the lid off one of the pill jars, to ease the pain. But she hadn't done so, of course she hadn't.

Because that, too, was empty.

No more pills.

Every cupboard empty.

No more bottles.

Four months ago it had almost been colder inside her than outside the windows. Alcohol and pills. Numbing herself constantly against a world she couldn't cope with.

Her twin sister, Sigrid, had died from a heroin overdose more than ten years ago. Their grief-stricken parents had died soon afterwards.

Last year Mia had moved to a house on the Trøndelag coast and decided to join them.

To take her own life.

Come, Mia, come.

Sigrid in a white dress, running through a field of yellow wheat, beckoning her to follow.

What an idiot she had been.

She was still ashamed when she thought of it.

Mia took a last look at the cardboard boxes, closed the door behind her and returned to the living room.

A new life.

Six months on a boat.

She smiled to herself again, put the empty coffee cup on the kitchen counter and was about to take a shower when someone rang the doorbell. She went out into the hall and saw a familiar face through the spy-hole. Her neighbour Alexander, a young man in his late twenties, in the company of a blonde girl she guessed must be his sister.

Have you thought about renting out your flat?

While you're away?

She's been having a bit of a hard time . . .

Mia Krüger had considered selling her flat and turning her back on Oslo, but she had always had a soft spot for people in need of help. In that respect, they had also been very different, she and Sigrid. Sigrid had always been much tougher; Mia always sensitive to her surroundings. At times, she felt almost transparent. A police officer. Obviously not a brilliant choice of profession for someone like her. There were times when the evil all around her nearly broke her. She had originally planned to study literature.

20

Ever since she was little, she had escaped into the world of fiction, a sanctuary from all the strong impressions around her. And she had tried – she'd enrolled at Blindern University, attended some lectures but had never sat any exams. It had seemed so pointless. Reading books while Sigrid was homeless and on the street, shooting up in doorways – no, she had to do something practical. So she had applied to the Police Academy almost by chance and, for some strange reason, she had done extremely well there. As though she were born for it. Munch had picked her out for the special unit before she had finished the course. She had loved it right from the start. The support of the team. Highly intelligent and skilled people. A sense of contributing to something. Of becoming a shield against all this misery. But it had proved to be a double-edged sword. She was extremely strong and yet also very frail.

That's what makes you so special, Mia.

That's why you're the best I have.

Holger Munch had been almost like a father to her these past ten years and she was eternally grateful to him, but the time had come.

A fresh start.

Six months' leave.

She felt the joy bubble up inside her again as she opened the door and let in her guests.

Chapter 5

Mia ordered coffee and a Farris mineral water and found a table in a quiet corner of Justisen. A few months ago she would have started off her visit to the pub with a beer and a Jägermeister. That felt like a lifetime away. Now, even the thought of alcohol made her gag. Munch was late, and Mia sat fiddling with the bracelet on her wrist while she waited for him. They had been given one each when they were confirmed. A silver charm bracelet with a heart, an anchor and an initial: M on hers; S on Sigrid's. They had admired them in the light from the window in their shared bedroom after the celebrations were over, and it had been Sigrid's suggestion.

How about you have mine and I have yours?

Mia hadn't been able to take the bracelet off since. The date on her mobile showed 10 April. In eight days it would be the eleventh anniversary of Sigrid's overdose. There was a reason for Mia picking this exact date on which to go abroad. She didn't have the energy to visit her sister's grave. She feared what it would do to her mental health. She had been clean for four months now. She worked out almost every single day. She had never felt better. Seeing the gravestone might drag her back down into the darkness; she simply didn't dare risk it.

Sigrid Krüger
Sister, friend and daughter
Born 11 November 1979. Died 18 April 2002.
Much loved. Deeply missed.

She hadn't been able to put away the bracelet. The photographs and the other things were as much as she could manage.

She took another sip of her mineral water and glanced at the bar, where an old man had just bought himself a nice cold beer. No. Not even tempted. She just didn't fancy it now.

Munch was half an hour late. He took off his beige duffel coat and gave her a hug before sitting down and placing a file on the table between them.

'Have you ordered anything to eat?' he asked, looking towards the bar.

'No, I'm not hungry.'

Munch summoned a waiter and ordered a prawn sandwich and an apple juice.

'Listen, Mia,' he said, leaning towards her. 'I've talked to the boss. Mikkelson completely agrees with me. He's an idiot. Your suspension is lifted. He made a mistake. We need you back at work. OK?'

Mia smiled faintly.

'I'm going away next week, Holger.'

'You've made up your mind?'

'Yes.'

'Are you quite sure?'

Mia nodded.

Munch sighed and scratched his beard.

'I understand. OK, it goes without saying that I would have loved you to be on board for this, but you deserve a break. I'm not going to put pressure on you. Only I had to ask.'

'The special unit is up and running again?'

'Yes.'

'Is it the girl they found in the lake?'

Munch nodded as the waiter brought his order.

'Vivian Berg. A ballet dancer. They found her all dressed up. A little boy and his father out fishing.'

'Where was it?'

'Lake Svarttjønn. It's up near Vassfaret. The lake is high up in the mountains – strange scenario.'

'What do you mean?'

Munch attacked his prawn sandwich and spoke with food in his mouth.

'She disappeared from her flat on Thursday and was found in a lake halfway up a mountain on Saturday, four days ago, wearing a ballet costume. What's not weird about that?'

He put his finger on the file between them. 'It's all in there.'

'I know what you're doing, Holger, but I've made up my mind.'

'I understand.'

'What do you mean by "all dressed up"?'

'Her hair had been put up. She was wearing a dance costume with one of those skirts – a tutu. White tights. And pointe shoes.'

'Pointe shoes? She was wearing them?'

Munch nodded.

'That is strange.'

'Yes, isn't it?'

'How far is the road from the lake?'

'About a forty-five-minute walk through quite steep terrain.'

'She was carried all that way?'

'Who knows?' Munch said with a shrug.

He looked at her across his sandwich, and she could see it in his eyes now.

'What?' she said, and tilted her head.

'What do you mean?'

'What are you not telling me?'

Munch looked at her gravely, then wiped his mouth with a napkin.

'I think she walked,' he said at length.

'What do you mean?'

'The soles of her pointe shoes were ripped and torn. I think she must have walked all that way.'

'You're saying she took her own life?'

'No, definitely not. She was killed with a needle straight into her heart.'

'A syringe?'

'Yes.'

'What was in it?'

'Ethylene glycol.'

'Which is what?'

24

'Antifreeze.'

'God Almighty . . .'

'Exactly. It's lethal and you can buy it at any petrol station.'

'So what makes you think she didn't walk up to the lake and inject herself?'

'Because of the pain,' Munch said, leaning back in his chair. 'Is that how you would have done it?'

A moment's thoughtlessness, and he realized it immediately.

Exactly one year to the day.

A table covered with colourful pills.

Mia alone on an island off the coast of Trøndelag.

Come, Mia, come.

'I'm sorry.' Munch leaned towards her again. 'I obviously didn't mean to—'

'That's quite all right, Holger,' Mia said, holding up her hand.

'How are you, by the way?' Munch went on, still looking mortified. 'I completely forgot to ask. Sorry. You know what it's like.'

'Of course, Holger. I understand. And I'm doing well. Really well, in fact.'

She picked up the bottle of mineral water, waved it and took a symbolic sip.

'Good.' Munch nodded. 'You look great – really great – by the way, if I may say so. It's a long time since I've last seen you so, how shall I put it—?'

'Sober?' Mia smiled.

Munch chuckled.

'That wasn't quite the word I was looking for, but yes, why not? How long has it been now?'

'Four months.'

'Wow, congratulations.'

'You shouldn't have to say that.' Mia sighed. 'I've been a terrible police officer, I really am very sorry.'

'Don't mention it.' Munch snorted and shook his head. 'Without you, who knows what would have happened? I'm frightened to even think about it. You solve cases. And I don't give a damn what you need to consume in order to do it. But, nevertheless, it's good to see you now, so . . . with it.'

Mia smiled. She could feel that he really meant it.

'How is she doing?'

'Miriam? Better every day. She's strong. She's going to make it. She sends her love, by the way. You ought to visit her soon.'

'I'll try to before I leave.'

Munch smiled warmly and stuck his hand into the pocket of his coat.

'Will you keep me company while I have a cigarette?'

Mia smiled and followed him outside under the heating lamps in the back garden. It might be spring in Oslo, but it still wasn't very warm. She hugged herself while Munch lit his cigarette, and his expression darkened again.

Mia pressed her lips together and mulled it over.

A young woman in a ballet costume.

Left on the shores of a mountain lake.

A syringe filled with antifreeze.

'We found several bizarre items at the crime scene.' Munch coughed and gave her that look she had seen so many times before.

There's something strange here, Mia.

'What did you find?'

'I'm not quite sure where to start.' Munch paused. 'He had set up a camera on a tripod.'

'Facing the body?'

Munch nodded gravely and took a deep drag on his cigarette.

'Did it contain any pictures?'

'No, it was empty. There was a slot for a memory card, but if there was one in it, he had taken it with him.'

'Why "he"? You know the killer is male?'

'Footprints in the ground. Size 43.'

'She had been left at the water's edge?'

'Yes.'

'And the camera was pointing directly at her?'

'Yes.'

'How strange,' Mia mumbled to herself.

'I know.'

'Anything else?'

'I'm not sure if this is relevant, but we found a page from a children's book a short distance away.'

'Which book?'

'Astrid Lindgren. *The Brothers Lionheart*. So will you do me a favour and take a look at the file? It would mean a lot to me.'

Munch stubbed out his cigarette.

'Would you be willing to give me seven days?' he ventured.

'I don't know, Holger.'

'A week? That's all.'

Chapter 6

Munch felt a stab of guilt as he stuck a cigarette in his mouth and glanced through the window. A holiday. Getting away from it all, the past and the recent past. God knows there were few people who deserved a holiday more than Mia, but it was just too bad: he needed her now. *A case for Mia.* He had thought so the moment he saw the photos from the crime scene. Holger Munch had worked as a homicide investigator for almost thirty years, and cases like this one were rare. Callous. Calculated. Planned. As if someone had enjoyed every second. Murder. Killing. To normal people it sounded dreadful, of course, and so it was for everyone involved, but usually the why was straightforward. The motives were clear. Jealousy. Hatred. Revenge. Often in combination with too much alcohol or drugs. Human nature. Not hard to explain. Munch could count on one hand the number of cases where he couldn't immediately see what had happened and identify the killer from a list of obvious suspects. It might take time, but his first hunch was usually right. *But this?* He shook his head slightly and took another drag on his cigarette as his mobile vibrated in his coat pocket.

'It's Anette. Is now a good time?'

'Yes, sure, go on.'

'I've finally managed to track down someone at Ullevål Hospital, and it would appear that Karoline Berg is ready to be interviewed now.'

'Good. Have they given us a time?'

'Just let me know when you can get to the hospital and I'll speak to the duty nurse.'

'And what about Vivian Berg's boss at the ballet?'

'Her name is Christiane Spidsøe,' Goli said. 'She's working at the Opera today. She seems distraught but will see you at your convenience.'

'What do we know about the car?'

Kripos had found a grey Mercedes abandoned on the roadside near what looked like the start of a footpath. Crime-scene technicians had found a necklace on the floor under the passenger seat. Vivian Berg's mother had confirmed that it belonged to her daughter. Very strange, all of it. So the killer had driven her there? And she had walked the rest of the way herself? Why had someone left the car doors open? And why leave the car behind in such a remote location?

'The Mercedes was reported stolen on Wednesday by a lawyer called Thomas Lorentzen.'

'Does he have a record?'

'Not as far as I can see, but I've asked Grønlie to make a few calls. I don't trust these new databases.'

'OK, good.' Munch could see Mia shift her position by the table inside.

'How are you getting on?' Goli wanted to know.

'She's looking at the pictures as we speak.'

'Good. I've told the pathologist that you'll be stopping by. Do you want to go there first?'

'I'll do it sometime later today. Did you speak to Ernst Hugo Vik directly?'

'No, I believe he has retired. It's a woman now. Lillian Lund.'

'OK. I think we'll go and see Karoline Berg first, if she's ready to talk to us now.'

'Will you be taking Mia?'

'I hope so.'

'Good luck. I'll call you if anything else turns up,' Goli said, and rang off.

Munch threw his cigarette butt down on the tarmac and went back inside the pub. He cleared his throat and slipped quietly into the chair opposite Mia.

'So what do you think?'

He had seen this look often. Her bright blue eyes might be aimed at him, but they were miles away.

'I think my holiday has just been cancelled,' Mia said, raking a hand through her raven-black hair.

'Are you sure?'

'Looks like it.'

'What are your thoughts?' Munch put his hand tentatively on the file between them.

'Something is missing.'

'What is it?'

'We can't see what the camera saw. Didn't someone take a photo from that angle?'

She flicked through the crime-scene photographs and looked up at him, slightly less remote now.

'Not if it's not included in that file.'

'I . . .' Mia grew distant again.

Munch didn't say anything. He just let her disappear. The special unit with or without Mia Krüger? It was like the difference between night and day. She could have as much time as she needed.

'I'm not sure why he picked this location,' she said at length, looking up at him again.

'Go on?'

'He wanted to be alone with her first – do you think that was it?'

'What do you mean by "first"?'

She tilted her head a little and looked at him.

Munch had seen this before too, many times, this gaze which said: *Do you not see what I'm seeing?*

'He set up the camera. He left her lying in the water without trying to cover her up.'

'Yes . . .?'

'He wanted us to find her,' Mia said, reaching for something on the table and seeming almost surprised to find it wasn't there.

A drink.

Whenever Munch had seen Mia study pictures before, she had always had a bottle nearby and it seemed for a moment as if her body didn't understand that this was no longer the case.

'Do you think so?'

'Don't you?' Mia took a sip of her mineral water.

'I don't know. Talk me through it.'

'They always show signs of regret, don't they? They cover the body to hide from themselves what they've done – that was what you taught me, wasn't it? Oh, hell . . .'

Mia withdrew into herself once more.

'He wanted time alone with her.'

Munch said nothing.

'That was what you wanted, wasn't it?' Mia continued with eyes which were again far away, the words soft between her lips. 'You and her. Alone up there in the forest. You take her there. How did you get her there? Did you know her? Did you walk up there together? Did she trust you?'

'What do you make of the book?' Munch asked.

'What do you mean?' Mia sounded dazed.

'The page from the children's book? Is it relevant?'

'Absolutely.'

Mia opened the file and turned a photograph towards him.

'Do you see it?'

'What am I looking for?'

'She disappeared on Thursday?'

'Yes?'

'It rained last week; this week it didn't. The page hasn't been lying there long. The humidity we can see here must have come from the ground. He left it for us to find.'

Mia leaned back in her chair and ran her hand through her hair again.

'*The Brothers Lionheart*. What do you think that means?'

'It's too soon to say,' Mia said.

'So are you in?'

'Shortest holiday ever,' Mia mumbled, giving him a vaguely resigned smile. 'You said something about her mother?'

'Flew down from Bodø to see her dance. Couldn't find her and contacted the police.'

'Where is she now?'

'She's in shock. Admitted to Ullevål Hospital.'

'But we can talk to her?'

'I've just been given the go-ahead.'

'Give me two minutes,' Mia said, and disappeared off towards the Ladies.

Chapter 7

Police officer Jon Larsen, better known as Curry, had a hangover so severe that he struggled to see through the windscreen. He took a gulp from the water bottle between his legs, narrowed his eyes and couldn't make up his mind whether to be pleased about today's assignment. Surveillance. Not much chance of any action. He glanced up at the flat in Kyrre Greppsgate. They were watching Lotte, a seventeen-year-old junkie. Another wretch at the bottom of the drug food chain and yet for some reason they were keeping an eye on her. It was said that she might lead them to someone higher up. He hadn't paid much attention at the briefing. Keeping his eyes open and his breakfast down had kept him fully occupied. Perhaps he should have picked another pub, but the outcome would have been the same. Beer and whisky. A few rounds of pool. More beer. More whisky. And once again he had woken up in the same bed with a young face on the other pillow and with the hangover from hell.

Luna. What the hell sort of name was that? She was twenty-one years old with dreadlocks and a pierced nose. A tattoo of some figure on her arm that Curry had never heard of. Luna. Who in God's name named their kid that? The observation wasn't lost on him; it was how he thought of her. A kid. A child. OK, no, she wasn't a child, but come on, she was fourteen years his junior and a bartender. *No, it couldn't go on. He had to do something.*

He tried to get his head to work, come up with some sort of plan, but he hadn't got very far when the car door was opened and his partner slipped into the seat next to him. Allan Dahl, his opposite in so many ways. Tall and gangly with a moustache he had grown since the last time Curry was assigned to the Drugs Squad and which had now come back into fashion without his partner seeming to care very much.

'Anything happening?'

'Nothing,' Curry mumbled.

'There aren't any other exits from the block, are there?'

'No, not unless they've built one since the last time we checked.'

Dahl took the coffee from the take-out tray without reacting to Curry's obvious sarcasm.

'Mocha latte for me, black for you, as usual. Sorry it took such a long time. I had to walk all the way down to Kaffegutta in Vogtsgate to get something decent.'

Curry sipped the coffee but, to be honest, it tasted no different to what they served everywhere else.

'So,' Dahl said, turning to him with eager eyes. 'I met your mate last night. I hear she's going travelling?'

'Who?'

'The super-detective. She came to the office to get herself a new passport not long ago. Has she got a job abroad?'

Curry took another sip of his coffee and slowly began to realize who his partner was talking about.

Mia Krüger.

He shook his head very carefully. The super-detective? Really? He had heard her referred to by many strange names, but 'super-detective' was a first; he hadn't heard that one before. There had always been some animosity among his colleagues in the force. Membership of Munch's team was highly prestigious and those who weren't picked for it had a tendency to sulk. Curry had left the Drugs Squad feeling very proud to have been chosen, and he had seen the smug smiles now that he had been temporarily reassigned back there again.

What's that?

The special unit has been closed down – again?

So it didn't work out?

Curry didn't regard himself as the world's brightest or most educated person, but at times he felt that the people around him behaved almost like children. The envy in the corridors, the sniping in all directions, the constant battles for a higher place in the pecking order, as if they were at school or in a chicken coop.

Well, whatever.

Don't get drunk tonight.

He made a vow to himself. Every night this week he had gone to the same bar and ended up in bed with the same young woman. What on earth did she see in him?

'Or perhaps you're not in touch with her these days?'

Dahl was not giving up.

'Oh yes, we speak on the phone from time to time.'

'Was it really self-defence or is it true that she executed the guy?'

Curry pretended to take a sudden interest in what was happening in the flat above them, but it didn't work.

'They say she just cracked. That she's not all there. She did kill him, didn't she? It wasn't Munch?'

Curry sighed.

There had been a major internal investigation some years ago. It was another occasion when Curry had been booted back to police headquarters. Munch and Mia had been following up a lead in the search for a missing girl that had taken them to a campervan up by Lake Tryvann. When they got there, they found someone they hadn't expected to bump into. A well-known drug dealer and junkie, Markus Skog. The ex-boyfriend of Mia's twin sister, Sigrid. Mia had shot him twice in the chest. She had been suspended immediately and, when Munch spoke up in her defence, they had disciplined him too. Reassigned him to somewhere out of town. Closed down the special unit.

'It was self-defence,' Curry said, hoping they could now change the subject.

'But she fired the gun?'

'Yes, she did. Munch didn't enter the campervan until afterwards, I don't think.'

'So how could he defend her?'

Dahl took a sip of his coffee and winked at him.

'Was it the press that gave her that name?'

35

Curry sighed again. So that was going to be the topic of today's conversation. The Tryvann case had been picked up by the media and, overnight, Mia Krüger had become Norway's number-one celebrity. Fair game. The paparazzi's new favourite. Fortunately, it hadn't lasted long – the vultures had flown on to their next victim – but within the police force there were clearly those whose curiosity remained undiminished.

'What name?'

'Mia Moonbeam?'

'No, that name came from her grandmother.'

Curry put down his coffee cup and turned irritably to his partner.

'Because of her jet-black hair and bright blue eyes. She's adopted, by the way. Did you know that?'

'Really? No . . .'

'Yes, they were twins,' Curry continued. 'Adopted at birth. Mia and Sigrid. By a couple from Åsgårdstrand. They're dead now, all of them, buried in the same cemetery. She's the only one left. And she has a scar over one eye. Some guy she was interviewing attacked her – a crackpot – she was lucky not to lose her sight. And she's missing a joint on one finger. A Rottweiler, I think. It sank its teeth right into her hand. I believe she had to shoot it.'

Dahl ran a hand through his thinning hair and gave him a small grin and a nod.

'Yes, and then she has a tattoo, I think, of a butterfly, somewhere on her hip.'

Curry pulled up his jumper.

'Here, I believe.'

'All right, all right,' Dahl muttered. 'I was only asking. Christ, do we have to sit here all day doing sod all.'

'Yes, why do we?' Curry wanted to know. 'The girl is clearly not going anywhere. She's probably floating around on a pink cloud while we're wasting resources that could be better used elsewhere.'

'Orders,' Dahl said in a surly voice, and shrugged. 'What is it with you today? Did you get out of the wrong side of bed?'

Curry shook his head and took another slug of water. Working for the Drugs Squad was just as frustrating as it had always been.

And now Oslo had been flooded with heroin in recent weeks and rumour had it that the product was very strong. The overdose team had been working overtime, and there was no doubt in Curry's mind that something was very wrong in Norway, which was supposedly the best country in the world. Perhaps legalizing the crap was the right thing to do, after all? Get some sort of quality control in place. People had a need to get high, there was no doubt about it, so why not let the state run the whole thing? Not heroin, perhaps, but less serious drugs – cannabis, marijuana; cut people some slack, take away the profits, decriminalize everything? It would make everything so much simpler. Why put a seventeen-year-old junkie under surveillance? Surely her life was hard enough already. What was the point?

Dahl sat silently in the seat next to him; he had clearly got the message.

Put Mia Krüger down?

No way.

Not on his watch.

Jealous bastards.

'So,' Dahl piped up after a while, in an obvious effort to mend fences. 'The woman they found up at the lake? Strange case, don't you think? In a ballet costume? Have you heard anything about it?'

'No.'

'It's odd that we haven't been told anything, don't you think? There should be information posted internally by now, shouldn't there?'

'That's Kripos for you. They always keep their cards close to their chest.'

'Well, I think there's more to it than that.'

'Do you?'

'You didn't hear this from me, but I have a friend in Forensics who told me they'd discovered something strange.'

'What?'

'She didn't tell me what it was – everyone has been muzzled.'

'Really?'

37

'Yes, there's definitely something they're not telling us.' Dahl yawned. 'I'm starving. Do you need a break? I don't mind sitting here alone. Perhaps you could go and get us something to eat?'

'But you only went to get us coffee five minutes ago. Why didn't you get some food at the same time?'

Dahl shrugged and nodded towards the flat as if to indicate that he wanted to miss as little as possible.

Curry sighed.

He was just about to get out of the car when he received a text message on his mobile. Curry couldn't suppress his smile when he read it.

'What's up?'

'You'll have to get your own food.'

'What do you mean?'

'That was Anette Goli. The special unit has been reopened. Good luck with the junkie.'

Curry smiled and gave his partner a friendly pat on the shoulder before getting out of the car and hailing a taxi to take him into town.

Chapter 8

Judging by her eyes, Karoline Berg looked like she had been sedated, but there were no pills in all the world that could disguise the fact that something inside her had died and would never come back to life. She was in her early forties with shoulder-length blonde hair and had insisted on standing up when she met them, though it was clear that her legs could barely support her.

'Like I said, we're so very grateful that you could take the time to talk to us,' Munch said, once the introductions and formalities had been dealt with and Karoline Berg was back in her hospital bed.

Mia had a bad feeling about this. The blonde woman from northern Norway seemed far away, not present in the room, and certainly not ready for an in-depth interview. She was tempted to leave right away.

'I can't believe that she's gone.'

A feeble, squealing voice under a floating gaze.

'I understand,' said Munch, who had taken a seat in a chair near her bed. 'And again we're sorry that we're having to trouble you in this way, but we so very much want to try to find out what happened.'

Meeting the victim's relatives. It always affected her much too deeply. Fortunately, Munch was her direct opposite. She had seen several times how the big teddy bear in him came out and made it possible. There was something calm and paternal about him that made grieving relatives feel that they were in safe hands. She had often thought that if Munch had been religious he would have made an excellent priest.

'I didn't think it was her at first,' Karoline Berg mumbled, and stared out of the window. 'She didn't look like herself. She was always so lively. The essence which was Vivian was no longer there, and so it couldn't be her.'

'I understand.' Munch nodded sympathetically. 'And again, Karoline, if this gets too much for you, just let me know. We will do this at your pace.'

'Those pearl studs,' Karoline Berg continued, as if Munch hadn't said anything at all. 'She would never have worn those. She hated pierced ears. I had offered to pay if she wanted to get them done – all the other girls have them – but no, she refused.'

Munch glanced at Mia and raised his eyebrows discreetly.

'So the earrings were new to you?'

Karoline Berg nodded to herself without taking her eyes off the window.

'I really am very sorry, but we have to ask,' Munch said. 'Can you think of anyone who might have done this to Vivian? Did she ever mention something, well, that something had happened? Did she have any enemies?'

Karoline Berg turned to Munch. It seemed as if her dull eyes still couldn't take in that he was there.

'I don't think that she and Sebastian were a couple. Only friends, as far as I could work out. All Vivian ever wanted to do was dance; she has never been terribly interested in boys.'

Mia cleared her throat and tried to make eye contact with Munch. It was obvious that Karoline Berg wasn't ready for this. She wasn't even replying to their questions.

'Sebastian?' Munch tried cautiously. 'Do you remember his surname?'

'Pearl earrings? No, that wasn't you, Vivian. Did you want to look like Granny? You always said that you didn't like them, that they were silly.'

Karoline chuckled quietly to herself as her eyes half shut again. Mia could see only the whites of her eyes now. The poor woman lay like this for a moment, until she appeared to surface and noticed them again.

'Oh, I'm sorry,' she mumbled, and sat up in the bed.

Munch put his hand carefully on hers.

'That's quite all right, Karoline. Listen, I'm wondering if perhaps we should come back a little later so you can get some rest?'

He glanced briefly at Mia, who nodded and got up.

'Are you leaving so soon? No, no. I want to help, please let me help. She can't lie there all alone, someone has to help her. Vivian, Mummy is coming now.'

Karoline Berg tried to get up, but her hands couldn't find the edge of the duvet.

'It's all right,' Munch reassured her, and pressed the red button by her bed.

'We don't have anything to do with him any more!' Karoline Berg suddenly exclaimed.

'Who?' Munch asked.

'Promise me, Vivian. He's no longer a part of our family!'

Her frail body was trembling now.

The door opened and two nurses entered the side ward. The first put her hand on Karoline Berg's forehead and nodded to Munch.

'I think it would be best if you left.'

'Of course,' Munch said, getting up.

'Karoline? Can you hear me?'

The door opened again and this time a doctor entered.

Shortly afterwards they were back in the car park. It was a long time since Mia had last seen Munch so irate.

'Who the hell gave the green light for this? We should never have been there.'

'Don't ask me,' Mia said, getting into the Audi. 'What are we thinking?'

'About this Sebastian?'

'I was thinking more about the last thing she said.'

'Call the office.' Munch started the car. 'Speak to Gabriel. He was assigned to the Fraud Squad, but I think he's back with us now.'

Mia nodded and took out her mobile from her leather jacket.

'Where are we going?'

'To see Vivian Berg's boss,' Munch said, pulling out on Ullevålsveien.

'OK,' Mia said, and rang Gabriel Mørk's number.

Chapter 9

As Gabriel Mørk pressed the button in the lift, he realized he hadn't felt this tingling sensation for a long time. He had been on assignment to the Fraud Squad. Not a bad job, but it was nothing like this; of course it wasn't.

Mariboesgate number 13.

The special unit was back.

He smiled at his reflection in the lift door and thought about how much his life had changed in such a short space of time. Completely upended. He was a different person now. It was less than a year since Holger Munch had brought him in from a life of hacking in front of lonely screens in a basement and made him a police officer. Now he lived in a new flat in Torshov, he got up in the mornings and went to work. And, last but not least, he had a baby daughter.

Emilie.

In shock, yes, he probably still was. Him a dad? Gabriel Mørk didn't know exactly what he had hoped to get out of his life, but definitely not that. Now he had found serenity. A sense of purpose. Something that was bigger than him. Some nights he would wake up just to watch her. Tiny fingers softly curled into soft palms. He would put his hand on her small stomach simply to feel her breathing.

What are you doing?

I just had to check she is all right.

For God's sake, Gabriel, she's asleep, she's fine.

I know, but . . .

He smiled to himself as the lift doors opened.

Last autumn they had worked on a case which involved Munch's daughter, Miriam. She had barely escaped alive. She had run blindly into a gorge and her injuries had been severe but, fortunately, she had survived. Munch had taken leave to look after her and the special unit had been scattered to the winds. Curry had been reassigned to the Drugs Squad, Ylva to Sexual Crimes and he to the Fraud Squad. Anette Goli and Ludvig Grønlie had kept the special unit going, but Mia – no, he didn't know where Mia had been, but he realized that he was looking forward to seeing her again.

Back.

At last.

He got out of the lift and met a familiar face.

'Oh, if it isn't the new daddy!'

Curry, bullish as always, had come out from the break room and slapped him on the shoulder.

'So is it Mia?'

'Eh?' Gabriel said.

'Leave the boy alone, Curry,' Ludvig Grønlie said. 'Hello, Gabriel, good to see you.'

'I was only asking,' Curry chuckled. 'After all, we have a bet going, haven't we?'

'What do you mean?'

'He's just messing with you,' Grønlie said, and disappeared down the corridor.

'Oh?'

'We were just wondering if you had named her Mia,' the bulldog grinned.

'No,' Gabriel said, having finally worked out what it was all about. 'We named her Emilie.'

'Damn, there goes my money.' Curry winked and slapped Gabriel's shoulder again.

'Ha-ha,' Gabriel said, and went into his office.

It was no secret that Gabriel Mørk was very fond of Mia Krüger. And yes, he had considered naming the baby Mia, but his girlfriend, Tove, had put her foot down. She had hinted on several occasions that it was all very well that he was now working with such incredibly clever people, but did he really have to go on quite so much about one particular colleague? So, no, she hadn't been named Mia.

Emilie.

He smiled as he thought of his baby daughter. He had just sat down at his desk and connected his laptop to the network when his mobile rang.

'Yes?'

'Hi, it's Mia. I need you to check something for us.'

'Sure, what is it?'

'Have Vivian Berg's mobile and laptop come back from Forensics?'

'I don't know, but I can check. Why?'

'It looks like she might have had a boyfriend, but all we have is his first name.'

'Which is?'

'Sebastian. Please would you check?'

'Of course.'

Gabriel wedged his mobile between his ear and his shoulder and typed on the keyboard. He brought up Vivian Berg's Facebook page.

'I've found a Sebastian Falk. They're friends on Facebook, at any rate. Let's see—'

'What do you have on him? Is he a dancer too?'

He could hear Munch grunt in the background now.

'No, it doesn't look like it,' Gabriel said, quickly skimming the page he was on. 'He looks more like one of those guys who do extreme sports. It says here that he's an outdoor instructor, whatever that means.'

A young man on a mountaintop. On an indoor climbing wall. Three men in a pub, each with a beer. A helicopter with something dangling underneath it. A kayak on a foaming river. Gabriel Mørk had always been amazed how much of their private lives people were willing to share on this website.

'Pictures of – well, how can I describe it? – outdoor activities, a link to Extreme Sports Week in Voss, photos of parachute jumps, mountaineering, and so on, there's no mention of them being in a relationship, but that doesn't necessarily mean anything.'

'Do you have an address?'

Gabriel opened another tab and typed in '1881'.

'There's only one Sebastian Falk listed here; if it's the same guy, then he lives in Tøyen. I can give you his number.'

'Give it to Ludvig and tell him to call him straightaway.'

'Sure thing.'

There was silence on the phone for a moment. Gabriel could hear Munch bark something in the background, but he didn't catch what it was.

'And I need something else from you. This is a bit more vague, but we have reason to think that a family member might have been involved in something.'

'Like what?'

'That's what we don't know. Please could you check if anyone in Vivian Berg's family has a criminal record?'

'Will do,' Gabriel said.

'Great,' Mia said. 'And could you text me if you find anything?'

'Sure. So you're not heading over here?'

'No, we're on our way to the Opera,' she said.

'OK, I'll call you if—' Gabriel began, but Mia had already rung off.

Gabriel took off his coat, found a can of cola in his bag and logged on to the system.

During his induction Gabriel had been shocked to learn just how much information the government stored on even ordinary citizens. A year ago he had used the Internet to find backdoors into places like this and now open access was only a keystroke away. To begin with, it had almost felt too easy.

Ten different databases, including the DNA Register, and the Photograph and Fingerprint Register, the Person Identity Register and, last but not least, Indicia, the Criminal Intelligence Register, where the police force could store information not just about people with criminal convictions but also people who were only suspected of wrongdoing, including all their family members, their circle of friends and their colleagues.

Big data.

Big Brother is watching.

His old anarchist hacker friends would probably choke on their microchips if they knew what he was doing these days but, to be honest, their opinion no longer mattered to him. To begin with, it had, when he had been on the receiving end of sarcastic messages in some of the IRC chat rooms he visited.

Changed sides, have we?

Did it still hurt him?

Hell, no.

Six-year-old girls hanging from trees with a sign around their necks. A teenager found naked on a bed of feathers in a circle of candles. Vivian Berg, aged twenty-two, found in a mountain lake, killed with an injection of antifreeze straight to her heart.

They could think whatever they wanted.

He was a police officer now.

As he took a sip of his cola and logged on to the first database, Gabriel realized he felt a huge pride in his job.

Chapter 10

Christiane Spidsøe was a gracious, dark-haired woman in her mid-thirties, and there could be no doubt that she was a former dancer. She moved like a ballerina across the office, pouring coffee into cups as though it were part of a performance, with a smile on her lips and her head held high, but no matter how hard the beautiful woman tried to act as if this were just another meeting, Mia could clearly see how deeply the murder had affected her.

'Milk and sugar?'

The elegant woman reached across the table to a bowl and a jug on a silver plate.

'Nothing for me, thank you,' Munch said.

'What a tragedy,' Spidsøe said, looking briefly at Mia.

'We're sorry for your loss. It must have been a shock.' Munch unbuttoned his duffel coat.

'A terrible shock.' Spidsøe shook her head. 'We can barely believe it. It still hasn't sunk in. Vivian. She was . . . our little ray of sunshine.'

She smiled briefly and raised the coffee cup to her lips.

'I know it sounds silly, but she really was. Vivian wasn't like the others – not so self-obsessed, if you know what I mean?'

'Not really.' Munch coughed and smiled.

'Oh well, you know,' Spidsøe went on. 'Dancers?'

'I still don't follow,' Munch said kindly.

'My sister used to dance,' Mia said.

'Oh? Professionally?'

'No, only when we were little. School productions, and so on.'

'How lovely.' Spidsøe nodded. 'Dance is an art form which is sadly underrated in the cultural canon, but we do our best to make it accessible to the man in the street.'

'Did you know her well?' Munch said, and cleared his throat.

'Vivian? Yes and no.' Spidsøe put down her coffee cup. 'As the artistic director of ballet, I'm responsible for almost sixty dancers, as well as ballet masters, tutors, arts administrators, but I try to get to know everyone personally, as far as that's possible.'

'When was the last time you saw her?' Mia asked.

'Wednesday afternoon. We're in between shows so everyone had Thursday and Friday off. As it happens, Vivian stopped by my office to ask if she could take Monday off as well.'

'She did?'

'I believe she was going away.'

'Did she say where?' Munch asked with interest.

Spidsøe reached towards the silver plate and dropped a sugar lump into her coffee cup.

'Family business, I believe. I'm sorry, my mind was on other things. We've had a budget cut so we've been a bit busy recently.'

'And you said yes?'

Spidsøe nodded.

'Everyone works round the clock during performance periods here, so I don't mind my dancers taking some time off when they can.'

'But you have no idea where she was going?'

'I'm afraid not.'

Mia shifted her gaze out of the window. She could see a sailboat far out on the fjord.

'Such a tragedy. Do you have any idea . . .?'

'Not yet, I'm afraid,' Munch said.

'Did Vivian have pierced ears?' Mia said.

'What do you mean?'

Spidsøe looked oddly at her.

'You know . . .' Mia touched her earlobe.

'Er, I really don't know. Why?'

Mia could see it even more clearly now. That this was only a front. Christiane Spidsøe had put on a brave face to get through the day, but the truth was that she was on the verge of a breakdown. The silver tray under the coffee cup clattered when she returned it to the table with trembling hands.

'I'm sorry, I . . .' Spidsøe smiled feebly as a tear trickled down her cheek. She wiped it away resolutely and straightened her back again.

'We're the ones who should apologize,' Munch said. 'We know how hard this must be for you. We really appreciate you taking the time to help us.'

'Don't mention it.' Spidsøe said as a new tear followed.

Mia was starting to feel unwell.

All this grief.

She was saved by her mobile vibrating in the pocket of her leather jacket.

The display read *Ludvig Grønlie*.

'I have to take this,' she said apologetically, and went out into the corridor.

'Yes?'

'I managed to get hold of him,' Grønlie said. 'Sebastian Falk. He's in Switzerland, on a climbing holiday. Poor bloke, didn't even know that she was dead.'

'How did he react?'

'Total shock,' Ludvig said. 'He was speechless. He had to ring off and then call me back.'

'Did you ask if they were in a relationship?'

'I got the impression that they were very close friends, but that was all. He said he'd get on the next plane.'

'Did you ask him to contact us when he gets back?'

'I asked him to call me. He was very keen to help.'

'Great, thank you, Ludvig,' Mia said, and rang off.

She was about to return to Christiane Spidsøe's office when her mobile rang again.

'Hello,' Gabriel Mørk said. 'Is there a problem with your mobile?'

'Yes, it's behaving strangely. I'll buy a new one when I have a moment. Did you find anything?'

'Definitely,' the young man said, and now she could hear that he was excited. 'It took a while, but I discovered something eventually.'

'What have you got?'

'I found an entry in Indicia on Karoline Berg in connection with a man called Raymond Greger.'

'Karoline Berg has previously been a person of interest to us?' Mia was surprised.

'No, not her, him. However, for some strange reason there was nothing in the file, only the name of the police lawyer in Bodø.'

'The entry provided no details?'

'None, just those names, so I called the police lawyer. Very interesting, if I may say so. Is this a good time?'

'Yes, fire away.'

'It turns out,' Gabriel went on, 'that Raymond Greger was a suspect in a bizarre case some years ago.'

'And what is his link to Vivian?'

'He's her uncle.'

'He's Karoline Berg's brother?'

'Stepbrother.'

'And what was he suspected of?'

'That's where it starts to get interesting,' Gabriel said. 'Six years ago there were two unrelated cases in Bodø of a little girl going missing. The girls turned up again and both told the same peculiar story.'

'Which was?'

'They were picked up by a man who took them to a house outside Bodø.'

'And assaulted them?'

'Er, not exactly. He played with them.'

'Define "play".'

'As in, he played with them. They played with dolls, had a tea party, they dressed up . . .'

'Eh . . .?'

51

'I know, it's the weirdest thing I've heard for a while.'

'So why was there no mention of this in the database?'

'Right, listen to this,' Gabriel said eagerly. 'Both girls identified Raymond Greger, but he was never prosecuted.'

'Why not?'

'I'm not really sure, some kind of technicality. Perhaps Anette can explain it better but, whatever it was, he was released without charge and got a lawyer to make sure that we don't have anything on him in the register.'

'How odd. Did the police lawyer say anything about why?'

'So that he could continue, would be my guess.'

'Continue with what?'

'His job. He's a teacher.'

'You're kidding me?'

'No.'

'In Bodø?'

'No, no. He left town.'

'Do we know where he is now?'

'Oh, yes,' Gabriel said triumphantly. 'I've tracked him down. These days he works at Hedrum School. It's just outside Larvik.'

'Bloody hell.'

'I know. Do you think there might be something in it?'

'Definitely,' Mia said. 'Great work, Gabriel.'

'The police lawyer in Bodø would like to be kept informed.'

'OK. Ask Anette to handle that.'

'Will do.'

Mia put the mobile back in her pocket and returned to the office of the artistic director.

Chapter 11

Thomas Lorentzen was sitting in his office in Gabrielsgate, nervously watching the phone in front of him. He was waiting for the inevitable call. He couldn't believe they wouldn't call. They would; he was certain of it. Shit, how did that happen? His car – the Mercedes – stolen right outside his office less than one week ago. And now it had turned up in a murder investigation.

It made no sense.

The mobile continued to lie silently on the desk in front of him, the dead, black, shiny object mocking him, or so it felt. Tormenting him with its absence of noise. He was sorely tempted to hurl it against the wall. Ring, God damn you. You know you're going to soon, so why keep me waiting? Lorentzen gave the mobile the evil eye, loosened the knot in his tie and got up from the chair. He caught a glimpse of his face in the window as he headed to the drinks cabinet. Did he look exhausted? He didn't feel exhausted. Yes, of course his car being taken was stressful but, for God's sake, he had nothing to do with the murder.

Or did he?

Was it connected to the other thing?

Lorentzen opened the drinks cabinet and poured himself a large whisky in one of the crystal tumblers from the shelf on the wall. He didn't realize until he was back behind the mahogany desk that he had actually run back to it. Bloody mobile. And it wasn't a smart one either. Not like his personal mobile, a gold-plated iPhone he had ordered especially from the UK. He knew he shouldn't flash it about, of course, let on how much money he really had, but he hadn't been able to help himself. Surely he was allowed a few treats, after everything he had done? Christ, didn't they know the risks he ran? He could feel himself starting to get irritable now.

Shit, a dead body? And it wasn't just another dead junkie no one cared about. It had been all over the news. A young woman. A ballet dancer. In a lake. He had frantically trawled his memories to see if he could find a connection, but there was nothing. It had to be a coincidence; it couldn't be anything else. The police had called him earlier that day. An officer called Grønlie.

'Am I speaking to Thomas Lorentzen?'

'Yes?'

'Are you the owner of a grey Mercedes Benz E220, registration number DN 87178?'

'Yes?'

'You're saying the car was stolen?'

'Yes, last Wednesday.'

'And you're sure about that?'

Sure?

Of course he was sure.

The car had been parked right outside. In his private parking space. He was supposed to be protected from such thefts here in the backyard, behind the gate, and yet it was gone.

'You'll call us if you notice or remember anything unusual about the theft, won't you?'

Lorentzen pulled off his tie and realized he was sweating under the armpits.

Remember something?

What would that be?

Had they found out?

Was this all a set-up to catch him?

Was this all . . .?

He stopped himself, slumped backwards in the chair and almost laughed.

He was important, yes, he was. But to imagine that a ballet dancer found dead in a lake had been intended to start this frenzied media circus just to take him down – no, ha-ha, of course not.

Pull yourself together, Thomas.

Relax.

Remember what the doctor said.

Lorentzen found a small box in a drawer and washed down two round, white pills with another gulp of whisky.

The police?

Why were the police calling?

After all, they had a man on the inside.

He was supposed to protect them against things like this, wasn't he?

Lorentzen got up again, keeping his eyes fixed on the mobile on the desk.

Bloody ring, damn you.

He knocked back the whisky and refilled the glass, trying to avoid his reflection in the window this time, while his thoughts returned yet again to a subject whose appeal was growing stronger by the hour. Not just because his car had been stolen, no, but because the moment might have come.

To take the money and run.

Disappear.

He wiped the sweat from his brow.

Why not?

He had plenty of money.

He had had plenty of it for a long time.

It was just that . . .

He collapsed back into the chair and realized how exhausted he was.

They would find him.

No matter where he went, they'd find him, wouldn't they?

They were everywhere.

He had sold his soul to the devil.

Voluntarily.

There was no way out. Wasn't that what they had told him?

Lorentzen shook his head and unbuttoned yet another button on his shirt.

Christ, it was hot in here.

Get a grip, you idiot!

OK, he had to make a plan.

He set down the glass on the desk and opened his laptop. Entered the code and was granted access. The sum on the screen was mind-boggling. It would take an average citizen a hundred years to earn even a fraction of that.

Geneva.

A plan started taking shape in his head now; he could feel the beginnings of a smile at the corners of his mouth.

The next delivery.

His fingers flew across the keyboard; he checked the schedule and the map that had appeared in front of him.

He had contacts, of course he had. Contacts they knew nothing about.

Just go through with this last one, and then . . .

Lorentzen smiled broadly, drained the whisky and staggered across the floor to refill the glass once more.

He ground to a halt with the glass still in his hand.

I'll get out.

Disappear.

He nodded quietly at the window.

It's over now.

He smiled and raised the glass in a toast to himself as the object on the table suddenly started to stir.

His mobile was ringing.

The tumbler slipped out of his hand. He didn't even hear it hit the floor.

Shit.

Thomas Lorentzen stood rigid for a few seconds before he finally picked up the mobile from the desk.

'Hello?'

Chapter 12

The rain was pelting down on the hood of the black Audi. A drenched Munch ran across the square and got in behind the wheel.

'I've changed my mind. We're not driving down there.'

'Why not?' Mia demanded to know.

'Raymond Greger is on sick leave. And he's not answering his mobile. He could be anywhere.'

Mia took a throat lozenge from the pocket of her leather jacket. The intensity of the rain had increased; it sounded like the percussion section of an orchestra now and people were running around like frightened cats, looking for shelter.

'I've dispatched a patrol car. If they get hold of him, we can reassess, but I'm not driving three hours for nothing right now.'

'Larvik police?'

Munch nodded and found his cigarette packet in the pocket of his wet coat.

'What did you make of Spidsøe?'

'She seemed honest enough, don't you think?'

Munch shrugged.

'I got the feeling she wasn't telling us everything, but I can't be sure.'

He lit a cigarette and opened the window a tad. Raindrops were blown into the car and mixed with the grey smoke, but Mia didn't comment on it.

'How does a guy who abducts little girls continue working as a teacher?' Munch said irritably, staring out through the windscreen.

'If we don't have anything on him in the register, then there's nothing to stop him,' Mia said.

Munch shook his head.

'Then there's something seriously wrong with the system,' Munch muttered, and took another drag on his cigarette just as Mia's mobile rang.

'Am I speaking to Mia Krüger?' said a male voice.

'Yes.'

'Hi, my name is Torfinn Nakken. I'm calling from Bislett Building Management and Maintenance. Do you live at number 3 Sofies Plass?'

'I do. What's this about?'

'On the second floor?' the deep voice went on.

'Where did you say you were calling from again?'

'Bislett Building Management and Maintenance. We're responsible for your block. I'm sorry to bother you, but our office has been broken into and we're missing quite a few security keys. Have you noticed anything unusual in your flat?'

Mia waved away the smoke from the cigarette and opened the window on her side.

'Like what?' she asked.

'Like unwanted visitors, things that have gone missing – anything like that?'

'Not that I know of, no.'

'OK, great,' Nakken said, sounding relieved. 'These security keys cost a fortune; we'll have to change the locks in the whole building. We're talking hundreds of thousands of kroner – although the insurance will pick up most of it.'

'Listen, I'm a bit busy now,' Mia said, glancing at Munch, who had just got a text message.

'Yes, of course. I'm sorry, I just had to check. Then I'll make a note here saying, "ALL OK with Krüger, Mia".'

'You do that.' Mia ended the call.

'That was Anette,' Munch said.

'Yes?'

'We have the name of the victim's psychiatrist.'

'What psychiatrist?'

'Didn't I tell you? Sorry. Medication was found in Vivian Berg's flat. Antidepressants prescribed by her GP on the recommendation of this man, I believe.'

Munch held up his mobile so she could read the screen.

'Wolfgang Ritter?'

'Ring any bells?' Munch was clearly pleased with himself.

'No.'

'Seriously? Wolfgang Ritter? Don't you watch the news?'

Mia shook her head and found another lozenge in the pocket of her leather jacket. She had junked her TV long ago and avoided newspapers whenever she could. As a child, watching the news had been obligatory, the family gathered in front of the television in the living room in Åsgårdstrand, but she didn't have the energy for it these days. In the past the media had assumed a kind of collective responsibility to inform the population. Now it was all about ratings. Fear and celebrities in a breathless race for prime time and Internet clicks. She couldn't even be bothered to glance at the front pages of newspapers in the shops.

What's the reason behind the conflict between Israel and Palestine?

What's the name of the author against whom a fatwa was declared by Ayatollah Khomeini?

Why did Chinese students demonstrate in Tiananmen Square?

Her mother, Eva Krüger, had been a teacher at Åsgården School and it had been hugely important to her that her daughters did well at school and were up to speed with current affairs. Sigrid had done better than she had, of course. A grades in everything. Mia had often wondered if that was part of the explanation, that all this perfection had finally become too much, that drugs had become a kind of rebellion, but it didn't ring true. Her father, Kyrre, had sold paint. Adopting the twins had been a gift from heaven for the childless couple. Their mother could be a little brusque at times, but she was never overly strict. A little too much of a teacher at home, perhaps, but no more than that.

Markus Skog.

It was his fault.

'Dr LSD?' Munch again.

'Who?'

'Wolfgang Ritter? The director of Blakstad psychiatric hospital? The psychiatrist who has argued in favour of giving psychedelic drugs to patients with severe mental-health problems?'

'Never heard of him.'

'There was a documentary less than a week ago? On the television.'

'Didn't watch it. I thought people had tried that as far back as the 1970s?'

'Yes, yes, but not these days. Which planet are you on?'

Munch turned in his seat and looked at her.

'Sorry,' Mia said, shrugging off her thoughts. 'I'm back.'

'A seemingly healthy young woman? Our little ray of sunshine? On heavy antidepressants? Don't you think that's just a little bit strange?'

Munch scratched his beard and reached for another cigarette but changed his mind.

'Absolutely. Have we spoken to him yet?'

'We'll need a warrant from a judge first.'

'Patient–doctor confidentiality?'

'Anette is on it. It's a formality, won't take long,' Munch said as his mobile rang again.

'Yes?'

She had shot him.

In the chest. Twice.

Markus Skog.

'And you've been to his house?'

No, stop thinking about it.

'Does Raymond Greger have any family – apart from Karoline Berg? Contact the school and find out if any of his colleagues know anything.'

Memories packed away in boxes in her flat.

'Put a car outside his house. And issue a person-of-interest notice. Yes. He's very important to us. All the resources you have, if possible. Please keep me updated. Fine, thank you.'

Munch ended the call and frowned.

'Was that Larvik police?'

'Yes. They haven't found Raymond Greger. He's not at home. His neighbours haven't seen him for a week.'

'Really?'

'Too much of a coincidence, wouldn't you say?'

'Absolutely. We'll have to visit her again, won't we?'

'Karoline Berg?'

'Yes.'

'I hate the idea of it, but I think we'll have to.'

Munch sighed and drummed his fingers on the steering wheel.

'Are you coming with me to see the pathologist?'

'No, I want to talk to Halvorsen from Forensics. I'd have expected to hear from them by now, it's odd that they haven't been in touch – they must not have found anything yet.'

'OK, I'll drop you off on my way,' Munch said, pulling out from the car park.

'Ask the pathologist about the damage to the victim's mouth,' Mia said when they reached the Kripos building in Brynsalléen.

'What damage?'

'Vivian Berg had sores around her mouth. I don't recall having seen anything like that before.'

'OK.'

'Team briefing later today?'

'Between seven and eight.'

'I'll see you then,' Mia said, and got out of the car.

Chapter 13

Munch rang the bell and waited a little while before a voice answered. The new forensic pathologist. Lillian Lund. He realized that he was looking forward to meeting her.

'Yes?'

'It's Holger Munch.'

'Oh, yes, hello, great. Do come in. I'm in room one. At the far end of the corridor. Just follow the music.'

The music?

Munch didn't understand what she meant until he was inside. The music drifted towards him from a room further down the corridor, a very heartening feature in the otherwise sombre department. He couldn't help smiling when he recognized what it was. Bach. One of his personal favourites. And not just any recording either. The Goldberg Variations. He had the CD at home. He had played it so many times he almost knew it by heart. Glenn Gould performing. A genius, no doubt about it, but also an artist on the verge of insanity. Munch couldn't help thinking of Mia. But she seemed to be doing so much better now.

'Hello?'

Munch knocked on the door of the room the music was coming from and was about to enter when he was stopped by a young man wearing a white plastic apron, a mask and latex gloves.

'Who are you?'

'Munch,' he said, holding up his warrant card. 'Special unit. Mariboesgate. I'm looking for Lillian Lund?'

The music was loud in here. Soft, beautiful notes contrasting with the grey, cool room and especially the body lying on the table just inside it.

'Hello, Munch,' said a woman who emerged from the back room and removed a glove in order to shake his hand.

She was wearing a mask but pulled it down now.

'Lillian Lund.' She smiled as she introduced herself.

Dark hair. Clear, blue eyes. About his own age, if he were asked to guess.

'That's not yours,' she said with a nod to the body on the table. 'She's in room two, I'll just finish up here, then I'll join you.'

'I'll wait in the corridor.'

'Great.' Lillian Lund smiled again and turned to the young man who had stopped Munch. 'Please would you redo those samples I asked you about?'

'Again?'

'I think they must have been contaminated. The values are far too high.'

'Yes, yes, of course,' said the young, blond man, glancing furtively at Munch before he disappeared back the way he had come.

Munch returned to the corridor, found a chair and thought about lighting a cigarette. In the old days it wouldn't have been a problem. Ernst Hugo Vik, the previous pathologist who had been responsible for most of the cases he had investigated, had been eccentric but, more importantly, a chain-smoker who never cared much for rules. Something told Munch that there had been a regime change following the arrival of Lillian Lund, so he decided not to light up.

She joined him a few minutes later.

'Phew, I'm sorry.' Lund flopped down in the chair opposite Munch. 'Four bodies in just as many days. Your girl and three overdoses. It seems like Oslo is flooded at the moment.'

'Overdoses come in here?' Munch was surprised.

'Of course. Why not?'

'Nothing. It's just news to me.'

'New boss. New rules,' Lillian Lund said kindly. 'I want to see everybody. That's as it should be, don't you think?'

'Yes, yes, definitely.' Munch nodded, feeling himself warm to this new pathologist.

On the ball and dedicated. And Glenn Gould on the speakers was an added bonus.

'Would you like to see her? Or is it true what I've been told, that you just want to see pictures?'

'What do you mean?'

'Have I got it wrong? You're not the detective who doesn't need to see the bodies?'

'You're thinking of Mia Krüger,' Munch said with a smile.

'Ah, OK, I'm sorry.'

'Don't apologize. What have you got so far?'

He got up from the chair.

'What do you mean, "so far"?' Lund said. 'You'll find protective clothes in that cupboard over there, by the way.'

Don a white plastic gown in order to view the body? That would never have happened in Vik's day. The Institute of Forensic Medicine was definitely under new management, there could be no doubt about it.

'I mean, you haven't had a lot of time.'

'Oh, it's a myth that everything takes so much time. Sometimes, yes, but in this case the cause of death is straightforward.'

Lund put her mask back on and gestured for him to follow her into the other room. She removed the white sheet from the body that was lying there and pointed to the woman's chest. The incisions made during the autopsy had been so crudely stitched together that Munch had a brief moment of thinking that the body in front of him wasn't real. He had never liked this aspect of his job. On the rare occasions he watched TV series where hardened investigators bent over corpses without changing their expression, he was sorely tempted to phone up and complain. It was making light of a difficult situation. And definitely not realistic.

'There's your needle mark. You saw the report I sent to Kripos? Ethylene glycol?'

Munch nodded.

'I don't remember seeing anything like that before. Do you?'

Munch made no reply. He felt respect was due to the white, cut-up body lying lifeless in front of him. Thirty years as an investigator, but he would never get used to this. Death. A life had ended. Had been reduced to an object of scientific interest on a table in a grey basement at Ullevål Hospital.

'Would you like me to cover her up?' Lund said, looking at him kindly.

'It's fine.'

'I completely understand. I do this all the time, but it's difficult even for me.'

'What did you say again?' Munch said, putting on his professional face once more.

'Have you ever seen this before? Antifreeze?'

'Not like this, no, never. We know of several cases where people were poisoned with it, but always orally and over time. They're usually fine in the end. There's long-term damage, but they survive. You need a large dose to kill someone.'

'I know.' Lund nodded, chewing her lip. 'Pretty callous, don't you think?'

'What do you mean?'

'I'm not an investigator, but it's not everyone who can get right up close to another human being and plunge a needle into their heart . . .'

'It's early days yet.'

'I understand,' Lund said, moving down the white body. 'Vagina. No signs of violent penetration. No semen traces. It doesn't look like the motive was sexual, at least not as far as I can see.'

Munch nodded.

'Nails, hands.' Lund pointed. 'Strangely clean. No traces of anything. It's almost as if someone washed her.'

'Really?'

'Yes.' Lund frowned. 'And the same applies to the rest of her body. There's barely anything there.'

'But then again, she was in the water when she was found.'

'Yes, I know, but even so there should be something. No bruises? No injuries anywhere? Surely she must have . . . fought back a little? I mean, a strong girl like her.'

'We're working on a theory that she walked to the crime scene herself,' Munch said in a low voice.

'Seriously?'

Lund looked surprised.

'I know. That's as far as we've got.'

'You don't have anyone in mind?'

'We're looking into a few people, but there are no actual suspects for now, unfortunately.'

'There's only one thing I can't explain yet,' Lund said, moving to the top of the table.

'What's that?'

'Do you see her mouth?'

'Yes?'

'Taped over at some point, wouldn't you say? I didn't look properly at first, but there was something which . . . do you see these?'

She pointed to the skin around the corners of the victim's mouth.

'That's not normal.'

'What?'

'These blisters. They're almost like burns – do you see them?'

'I do. Mia asked me to ask you about them.'

'Well spotted,' Lund said. 'They're not from the tape. In fact, I don't know what they are, but I'll send some fresh samples off for testing.'

'When do you think we'll find out what they are?'

'It shouldn't take all that long, so sometime tomorrow morning, I would say.'

They were interrupted by the young, blond assistant, who entered the room without knocking. For some reason, he evaded Munch's eyes this time.

'I'm sorry to disturb you, but we have another body coming in.'

'An overdose?' Lund wanted to know.

'Yes.'

'Damn it. Excuse my language, but what is going on in this town?'

She shook her head irritably and headed for the door. Munch followed her out into the corridor.

'I'm sorry, but I'll have to leave you now.'

Lillian Lund took off her glove and her mask and shook his hand.

'Thank you for your help so far.'

'My pleasure. I'll call you once I know something,' the forensic pathologist said, and strode quickly down the corridor towards the music.

Chapter 14

Theo Halvorsen sat hunched over a microscope in the laboratory but quickly got up when he saw her enter.

'Moonbeam!' he cried out, smiling at her. 'It's been too long. Where have you been?'

Mia smiled back. 'Nowhere, sadly.'

'Oh, been suspended again, have you? Was that it?' Halvorsen said, taking off his glasses.

'Is that what people are saying?'

'Depends who you ask.' The affable technician shrugged. 'Some said you had been booted out, others that you were going sailing.'

'The last bit is true, except I didn't get very far. You're dealing with the ballet dancer, am I right?'

'Yes, I'm afraid you are.' Halvorsen sighed. 'Plus a whole heap of other jobs. I never seem to have enough time. Do you think I'll ever catch up?'

The technician threw up his hands and looked around. The long laboratory was stacked with papers and boxes from floor to ceiling. The room had no windows and made Mia feel as if she were in the basement, even though they were on the third floor. She knew that Halvorsen had asked for the windows to be blacked out to avoid distraction.

Theo Halvorsen. Mia had known the fifty-something technician for about ten years and knew that, although he was notorious for whingeing about his workload, there was no one else she would rather go to if she needed an answer. Halvorsen was like a mini-Einstein. He didn't like working with other people, preferring to do everything himself, but his results were always better and more accurate than those that came from the second floor.

'So you haven't been to your cabin?' Mia asked, following him across the room.

'When would I find time for that?' Halvorsen said, putting his spectacles back on.

He found a stool and lifted down a small cardboard box from a shelf.

'And how is Britt?'

'She hasn't left me yet, more fool her.' Halvorsen winked and carried the cardboard box to the microscope.

'Is that mine?' Mia said with a nod at the box.

'What do you mean?'

'That one? Why is a current case stored so far away?'

'Moonbeam.' Halvorsen sighed and shook his head patiently. 'I know you wrap everyone around your little finger and that people allow themselves to be blinded by your Gothic charm, but not me, I do things by the book.'

'So what's this?'

'Teeth,' he said, slipping on a pair of blue latex gloves. 'Not all killings are aesthetically pleasing, my dear, or carried out with intelligence and *joie de vivre*, to be solved by Hercule Poirot or young Krüger exercising their little grey cells and ending up in the history books.'

Halvorsen sighed again and opened the box. 'A young drug dealer beaten to death with a crowbar behind Manglerud shopping centre, and now they want to know if there is any connection to a gangster they found with his mouth bleeding in Sofienberg Park. Tasty, don't you think?'

Halvorsen was known for this, complaining about everything, but Mia liked him all the same. They had worked on several cases where his eagle eyes had found the exact evidence they needed, and she knew that grumpiness was merely a façade he adopted when things didn't go his way.

She waited patiently until the brown teeth he had been studying were back in the box and he had made notes on the laptop on the workstation behind him.

'Right, it's your turn now.'

'Vivian Berg?'

Halvorsen rolled his chair across the floor and came back with a file, which he placed in front of her.

'But we've already seen this,' Mia said, having flicked through a few pages.

'Yes,' the technician said. 'But that's all I've got.'

'This is the report you sent to Kripos, isn't it?'

Halvorsen nodded.

'Yes. And I said the same to them.'

'Which was?'

'That it must be a joke. How am I meant to extract any evidence from that?'

'What do you mean?'

'You haven't read it?'

'Yes, or, that is to say . . . no. What does it say?'

Halvorsen sighed.

'It's a circus, that's what it says.'

'A circus?'

'You really haven't read it? Sometimes I wonder why I even bother doing my job.'

Halvorsen rolled his chair across the floor and returned with a sheet of paper, which he thrust at her.

'Talk me through it,' Mia said, having glanced at it.

'Abundance,' Halvorsen said.

'What do you mean?'

'Someone is messing with you.'

'As in . . .?'

Halvorsen pointed to the list he had given her.

'DNA.'

'Yes?'

'From all of Norway, in one place? How am I supposed to do my job when the car and the crime scene contained more hair and skin samples than the drains of a public swimming pool?'

'This is from the Mercedes?'

'And from Lake Svarttjønn.' The technician nodded and rolled his chair back towards his laptop. 'But seeing as it's you, Moonbeam . . .'

He angled the laptop towards her and opened a document.

'Look at this.'

Mia looked at the screen, but she still did not understand.

'What am I looking at?'

'A mess. Sixty-one hair samples. Forty-nine skin samples. Eight samples of excrement. No DNA match on any of them. According to this, more than a hundred people were present at the crime scene *and* inside the car. How do you imagine I can work with this?'

'So the killer contaminated the crime scenes?'

'That, Sherlock, I think we can say with total accuracy,' Halvorsen declared, letting the glasses fall onto his chest on their string. 'The real question is how the hell did the killer get hold of all this? Hair and skin samples? Excrement? Who does something like that, Mia?

'Oh, and by the way,' Halvorsen added, and abruptly got up.

He disappeared towards the back of the lab and returned with a camera.

'This is what happens when you have too much to do.'

'This is the camera you found at the crime scene?'

'Yes. A Nikon E300. No fingerprints, of course, either on the camera or the tripod, but . . .'

Halvorsen smiled conspiratorially as he passed her the camera.

'Look through the lens.'

Mia held it up towards the light and peered through it.

'Do you see it?'

It took a while, but then she suddenly spotted it.

Scratched into the lens.

'Oh, no,' she mumbled. 'Please tell me it's not true.'

She could see it clearly now.

A number.

'Shit,' she said, and looked a second time to double-check.

'I think it looks like the number four, but you're the detective,' Halvorsen said with a shrug.

Mia could feel her heart beating a little faster under her leather jacket.

A number?

She raised the camera to her eyes again.

Yes, it was there.

'I took a picture,' he said, getting up again.

'Using this camera?'

'Yes, take a look.'

Mia quickly studied the picture. There was no doubt about it.

Four.

Crudely scratched into the lens.

'Can I keep this?'

'Of course.'

'Thank you for this, Theo,' said Mia, slipping the picture into her pocket. 'I mean it.'

'That's what I'm here for, Moonbeam.'

'Tell Britt I say hi. Keep me posted if you find anything else, won't you?'

'Of course.' Halvorsen nodded. 'Just call me if you need anything.'

'I will, Theo. See you soon.'

'Always a pleasure.' The amicable forensic technician smiled and raised a finger to his forehead.

Chapter 15

'We have a lot to get through and not much time, so please could everyone keep it short?' Munch said, standing up by the screen.

Gabriel Mørk put down his cola and had only just taken his place as the light was turned off.

'Was that aimed at me?' Curry piped up.

'If you could save any questions until the end, that would be great, yes,' Munch mumbled, flicking swiftly through the papers on the table next to him.

There was muted laughter in the room, but it soon stopped when the first picture appeared on the screen.

'Vivian Berg, aged twenty-two,' Munch said, clicking through the first series of photographs. 'She went missing from her flat in St Hanshaugen on Thursday afternoon and was found floating in Lake Svarttjønn early on Saturday morning.'

'We're sure about that?' Curry asked.

'Sure about what, Jon?' Munch said with a sigh.

'That she disappeared from her flat last Thursday?'

'Anette?' Munch nodded towards Goli, who stood up.

'We have two witnesses from her apartment block who saw Vivian Berg leave her flat last Thursday afternoon, somewhere between five o'clock and a quarter past five. The video we have just received shows that this could well be true, but—'

'Video?' said Curry, who clearly wasn't up to speed.

They had just received CCTV footage from a corner shop which apparently showed Vivian Berg leaving her flat.

'What did I just say about saving questions for the end?' Munch said.

'I know, but come on . . .'

'For anyone who hasn't heard this,' Anette said in a somewhat weary tone, 'we have now received three videos. The Mercedes heading out on the E18. The Mercedes driving past Sandvika shopping centre, and now this last one that shows Vivian as she leaves her flat, presumably heading towards the Mercedes.'

'According to the pathologist, Vivian had been in the water for less than twenty-four hours when she was found,' Anette went on. 'The last footage from Sandvika shows the car passing the shopping centre on Thursday evening just before seven o'clock, so that gives us a time frame of between twenty-four and thirty-six hours.'

She looked towards Munch, who nodded in agreement.

'And the trip from Sandvika to Lake Svarttjønn takes how long?' asked Ylva.

The young Icelandic woman had joined the team last autumn and as usual no one quite knew where Munch had found her, but she had fitted right in. Gabriel was thrilled to no longer be the youngest member. The more experienced investigators took so many things for granted, but now he had Ylva to ask the questions without him looking like an amateur.

'Two hours, max,' Goli said.

'So she was kept in the car?' Ylva said. 'For more than twenty-four hours?'

'We'll get to this later,' Munch said, nodding to Anette Goli.

'So,' Goli continued, 'Vivian disappears on Thursday afternoon. According to Kripos, it looked as if she left her home in a hurry. She didn't take her mobile. Her laptop was left open on the coffee table. There was food in the oven. It looks like she was in the middle of cooking supper but then she suddenly puts on her coat, goes out into the stairwell, locks the door and calmly leaves the apartment block.'

'Eh?' Curry said, unable to restrain himself. 'She leaves her flat in a hurry without taking anything and yet she leaves calmly?'

'Something else that's worth noticing is that we found prescription drugs in her flat,' Goli went on. 'As you'll all be aware by now, we found both antidepressants and sedatives. There's a lot to suggest that Vivian was unhappy. We have been in contact with her

GP and her psychiatrist and we're currently working on accessing her medical records.'

'Thank you, Anette,' Munch said as Goli sat down.

'Raymond Greger,' Ludvig Grønlie said, getting up. 'Something of an oddball. I can find very little on him. Bodø police wouldn't say much either and it's clear that lawyers have been involved and have apparently threatened them with this, that and the other. Even so, the case against him some years ago, where two little girls went missing, doesn't look like something we can bring him in for or something that could help us in any way. Nevertheless, this is what we have. He's fifty-eight years old. Single. No children. He works as a teacher at Hedrum School near Larvik and is currently on sick leave due to . . .'

Grønlie put on his glasses and flicked through his papers.

'Well, I don't think I found that out but, in any case, we want to talk to him. Larvik police are looking for him and I've made it clear to them that he's our number-one priority right now.'

'His mobile?' Gabriel said, opening his mouth for the first time.

'According to Telenor, it's switched off and has been since Thursday,' Grønlie said, sitting down again.

'Was there anything on her mobile?' Ylva wanted to know.

'Not according to the records I was given,' Gabriel said. 'She hasn't been in touch with her uncle. As for Facebook, no, they weren't friends there either. There's nothing to indicate that they had any contact.'

'As Grønlie just said, Raymond Greger,' confirmed Munch, 'is our absolute priority right now. Larvik police are looking for him, and we'll intensify the hunt for him overnight if he's not found. Mia?'

'A few things.' Mia walked up to the screen.

She nodded towards Munch. A new photograph appeared on the screen, one that Gabriel hadn't seen before.

'This was scratched into the camera lens.'

'What is it?' Ylva asked, pushing her glasses further up her nose.

'A number. The number four,' Mia nodded again to Munch, who clicked onto another picture. This time, they could see it even more clearly.

'At first, I thought that this business with the camera meant, well, that the perpetrator had photographed the murder. That that was his *thing*. That he wanted a visual record. But now I'm not so sure.'

'We know it's a he?' Curry interrupted her.

'The prints around the tripod are a size 43,' Mia said calmly.

'What if it was a woman wearing a man's shoes?'

'Then the prints would be deeper in the middle and lighter around the edges.'

Another photo.

This time the page from the book.

'Notice that the page number here has been scraped away,' Mia continued. 'He's telling us that this number isn't significant.'

'What . . .?' Ylva began, but Mia ignored her and gestured to Munch to click again.

'"Now I come to the evil,"' Mia said, quoting from the book and indicating the page on the screen. '"That which I can't bear to think of. And yet I can't not think of it." It's from *The Brothers Lionheart*. It's the younger brother, Karl Lion, talking about the fire. Karl is sick and needs help, and the hero, his big brother Jonathan, sacrifices his life so that his younger brother can live. Afterwards, everyone wishes that he had died instead.'

There was silence in the room now.

'So we have the number four,' Mia continued. 'That's the first clue. And then we have this book page, which is the second. This is where we need to start.'

'But—' Ylva piped up again but was interrupted a second time.

'And then we need to look at this,' Mia said. 'I think this is very important. The surveillance video we're about to see shows Vivian leaving her flat last Thursday. Now pay attention to her gait. I've known many dancers. They are supple, they move like cats, they control every single muscle in their body.'

'What's your point?' Curry said.

'This woman isn't a dancer,' Mia said softly, nodding to Munch, who pressed the remote control.

'This woman isn't the real Vivian Berg.'

Chapter 16

Kurt Wang had never heard a voice like hers. Recorded, yes, but never in real life. Billie Holiday. Radka Toneff. Amy Winehouse, possibly. When the petite, smiling girl with the long, red hair walked up to the microphone and her soft voice filled the large space, which doubled up as a practice room, it was as if time stood still. As if the clouds had disappeared. As if the cold winter had turned into summer. As if the world outside didn't exist. Kurt didn't know whether it was the voice or the girl herself he was in love with.

Her. Her. Her. Of course, it was her. He couldn't sleep. He couldn't breathe. He could barely lift the saxophone to his mouth.

The Nina Wilkins Quartet.

They had met on the jazz course in Trondheim, Norway's best conservatory for training musicians of this calibre. He got in first time. How many saxophonists had tried to get in? Many. Very many indeed. And who had got in straightaway? Aced all three audition pieces, almost to a standing ovation? He had. Kurt Wang. The gangly, shy boy from Manglerud in Oslo where boys are boys only if they play hockey. Hell, he should be strutting like a peacock! He shouldn't care about a half-Swedish jazz singer – there were so many of them in Trondheim; charming, extremely talented girls who sang – but no, this one was different. The first time Nina Wilkins had opened her mouth, his knees had turned to jelly, and he had felt like a puppy dog ever since. No, not a dog, hell no – he was still his own man – but smitten. Unable to think straight.

She had suggested that they move to Oslo, the whole band, and he had nodded and answered, 'Yes, whatever you say, Nina.'

Even though he had loved living up in Trondheim. His flat in Møllenberg. The bars: The Nine Muses. The Antikvariat. Ramp. Trondheim was a wonderful city with an insanely inspirational jazz scene.

She had suggested replacing Mulle with another drummer, some Portuguese guy he had never even heard of. 'Yes, yes, of course, Nina, whatever you say.'

Even though he and Mulle had always played together. They were like twins; they improvised as if they were two heads on the same body.

She had then suggested that he should start playing more soprano saxophone, put away the tenor for now, go up an octave or two; lighter, more brittle, more frantic, like John Coltrane had done at the end of the Miles Davies period. 'Absolutely. Whatever you say, Nina.' Of course he could play soprano; in fact, he had always wanted to do that, hadn't he?

No, his mother had. Jan Garbarek on vinyl in the living room in Manglerud, though he personally had always preferred the fullness of the tenor.

No, enough was enough, he had to put his foot down now. This had to stop. The Nina Wilkins Quartet. Nina. Nina. Nina. Her voice filled his head. No matter where he was.

Certainly after the Portuguese guy turned up in Oslo. Their new drummer. Fine, absolutely, that wasn't the problem. In theory. Soft. Music in every part of his body, but was he better than Mulle? No, he didn't think so. Oh, what a fool he had been. He should have seen it coming miles away. Nina and the Portuguese drummer. Tangled up on the sofa. Passionate kisses during rehearsals. Walking hand in hand down the street on their way to Blå.

He should have left at that point. Said that enough was enough. Of course he should have. If he had been man enough. But how could he?

That voice.
Wow, what a voice.
Like honey and sandpaper.
Like the answer to a secret.

Every time she opened her mouth.

So he had stayed.

Idiot.

The Nina Wilkins Quartet.

Fortunately, it had paid off. Vossa Jazz Festival last year. They had played on one of the smaller stages but had got the best reviews of anyone. The locals had gone wild. Then Kongsberg Jazz Festival. Same thing again. Sold out. People had fought for the tickets. The plan had been to play just two sets, but the audience had refused to let them leave the stage. Total ecstasy. He had spat blood, been unable to feel his lips for days, but it had been worth it. Of course it had. And now they would be playing in Molde. The most prestigious festival in Norway. And not one of the small stages, oh no, but in the actual Molde Cathedral. If his mother had still been alive, she would have been insanely proud.

'I'm not really feeling it today,' Nina slurred, and walked away from the microphone.

She clutched her throat, glanced furtively at the drums and received a complicit nod in return.

Again.

It was happening more and more, and he didn't like it.

Billie Holiday had done it.

As had Charlie Parker.

Coltrane.

Miles.

What kind of an argument was that?

'It's not as if we're shooting up, Kurt. What the hell is your problem?'

It wasn't the amount or the frequency.

Or whether it was injected or smoked.

Yes, he was in love.

Yes, she had the voice of an angel.

But heroin?

Hell, no.

He couldn't even bear to be in the same room as them. He always went out when they got high. And he would come back to these swimming gazes, the spaced-out smiles. And they didn't play any better, although they thought that they did. They just felt better. That was the only change: heroin had nothing to do with the music that came out. He much preferred her voice when she was clean. And the Portuguese drummer? Oh, don't even get him started. Always half a beat behind. Or a quarter-beat ahead.

No, he wasn't putting up with it any longer.

After Molde.

So far, but no longer.

He had other projects.

Many, in fact.

After all, he was Kurt Wang.

He was standing in the hall in front of the mirror after Nina and the Portuguese drummer had sneaked into the kitchen holding hands, her mouth giggling against his cheek. He studied himself, shook his head and tied his scarf around his neck. What a mess. It was a cold evening outside, but he hated the smell. Burned heroin and tinfoil. He had almost thrown up the first time the drummer flicked the lighter under the brown lump in the tinfoil.

Enough.

He lit a cigarette and felt that this time he really had made up his mind. He had had enough. No more. Too bad about the voice. And his infatuation. It would pass, wouldn't it? Five years now? Surely it would pass eventually? He would finish this rehearsal, then call Mulle. Start up the trio again. If Mulle would take his call, that is. Four months without a word. He didn't blame him. Of course he didn't.

Nina. Nina. Nina.

His friend had stormed out of the rehearsal room, practically foaming at the mouth.

Christ, it was cold. And dark. Wasn't it meant to be springtime now? Kurt Wang pulled his jumper further over his fingers and threw his cigarette onto the tarmac as a figure suddenly appeared in front of him.

'Excuse me? Aren't you . . . Kurt Wang?'

A young man the same age as him was standing in front of him, his face hidden under the big hood of his parka.

'Yes?' Kurt said, taking out his cigarette packet from his jacket pocket to light another cigarette.

How did this guy know his name?

A fan?

He smiled and felt flattered, although he had made up his mind a long time ago not to care about such things.

The music came first.

'Where's your saxophone?' the man said from under the hood, looking curiously at him.

'What do you mean?' Kurt smiled.

A fan, clearly. He shouldn't be pleased, of course, but it did him good right now, being recognized. In the street. So at least he had done something right. No, there was no going back; he had made up his mind. He could feel it now.

Enough is enough.

'It's upstairs in the rehearsal room,' Kurt said, still smiling. 'Are you after an autograph? Sorry, I'm a bit busy now, so if—'

'That's all right. I have one we can use,' the voice under the hood said.

'What do you mean?'

He didn't get any further.

Kurt felt something wet on his face.

'Don't take it personally,' said the voice, which within the space of a few seconds now seemed to come from a long way away.

What the hell . . .?

Kurt could see his cigarette clearly now, but it was no longer in his hand.

It had grown wings and was flying up to the third floor. Still burning. It knocked on the window and was let into the kitchen, where it mixed with tinfoil and became an origami pipe that looked like a hummingbird in a tree full of honey and sandpaper before it started singing at the top of its voice.

With lips speaking Portuguese.

TWO

Chapter 17

Munch was woken up by his mobile and wondered where he was. He had briefly imagined himself to be back in his old house in Røa but soon realized that it had just been a dream. He had fallen asleep on the sofa in his flat, fully dressed. He had left the office late; he hadn't even had the energy to go to bed. The clock on the wall over the kitchen counter showed a quarter past seven. How many hours of sleep had he managed? Three? His mobile stopped ringing, only to start again. The display read *Anette Goli*. Munch sat up, still half asleep, and pressed the green button to take the call.

'Are you awake?'

'Barely.' Munch coughed.

He reached for the cigarettes on the table but then remembered the promise he had made himself.

No smoking before breakfast.

He had given up giving up, but at least he could try to cut down.

'I've been talking to Wolfgang Ritter. He can see you today, preferably early.'

Anette Goli sounded as if she had been awake for a long time.

'OK.' Munch nodded, rubbing the sleep from his eyes.

'I've called Mia. She's ready. By the way, I've heard from Mikkelson.'

'Go on?'

'We can bring in as many people as we want to. He seems strangely keen to give us whatever we want.'

'Super,' Munch said, starting to surface now. 'Give Curry the people he needs to trawl through the building where Vivian Berg lived. Knock on every single door. I know that Kripos have done their rounds, but I want us to talk to everybody again, OK?'

'Will do. And Lillian Lund wants to talk to you. Please could you call her?'

'Will do. Are you at the office?'

'Yes. I didn't make it home last night.'

'I'll be right there.'

The fat investigator stretched his arms towards the ceiling. The sofa was far too hard. He was aching all over. He must try to get to bed. This was a beginner's error. A new case, working twenty-four/seven, forgetting to sleep, forgetting to eat – he ought to know better. These cases were rarely a sprint; they were pretty much always a marathon.

He gave himself time to shower and had just put on clean clothes when his mobile rang again. Munch was surprised when he saw who it was.

Miriam?

He felt it wash over him again, this instinctive paternal dart of worry. This small, dark terror somewhere inside him which refused to disappear completely.

This early?

Had something happened?

'Hi, Miriam. Are you up already? How are you?'

He waited patiently for her to reply. He knew that it took time for her to articulate the words, to get them out of her mouth properly.

'I . . . I'm . . . fine, Daddy. A— . . . And how about you?'

'I'm just great,' Munch said, reaching for a cigarette. He needed something to hold on to.

He was so proud of her and it hurt him to hear her stutter. She had fought her injuries so bravely – typical of her, the stubborn girl who would never admit how hard anything was. And it was such a relief to hear her say 'Daddy' again. There had been too many years with bad blood between them, years when she had barely spoken to him. Hatred had simmered in her eyes on the rare occasions they had met. It had been so bad that she had come close to deciding that he could never see his granddaughter. That time had passed now. Thank God. And he couldn't be happier about that. But to listen to her stammer like that? He had to steel himself.

'Did you manage your workout yesterday?'

'The phy— . . . physiotherapist . . . came here. S— . . . some good, I think. A— . . . Arms a little heavy, but my l— . . . legs are much s— . . . stronger.'

'That's wonderful,' Munch said. 'Really good, Miriam. That's great news. And is little Marion there?'

'She . . . she's asleep,' his daughter stammered.

Munch could hear the effort it cost her to speak. Most of all he wanted her to hang up so that she could rest, but it was clear she had something to tell him so he let her continue.

'S— . . . She said you were buying her a . . . h— . . . horse?'

'Yes, I promised, but it's a horse for her doll,' Munch said quickly.

'Y— . . . You . . . mustn't spoil her like that, OK? I'm t— . . . trying to raise her not to be so . . . so—'

'I'm sorry.' Munch interrupted her so she wouldn't have to expend unnecessary energy.

'Y— . . . Yes, it's quite important . . .'

'Of course, Miriam. I'll restrain myself, I promise. It's just, yes, you know that I can't say no.'

Miriam chuckled quietly. It was heart-warming. Munch smiled and lit his cigarette.

'O— . . . OK,' his daughter went on. 'B— . . . But that wasn't why I'm calling.'

'It isn't?'

Munch got another call. Ludvig Grønlie. Fortunately, he had learned how to dismiss them without cutting off the call he was already on. Holger Munch was old school and hadn't switched to a smart phone until he was forced to.

'I . . . I've decided to get married,' Miriam said calmly.

'What did you say?'

'I'm getting married,' Miriam said, more clearly this time. 'This summer.'

Miriam had once been engaged to a doctor from Sandefjord who was the father of his granddaughter, Marion. Seen from the outside, the relationship had looked fine, although Munch wouldn't have been able to say much more about it; he hadn't known the guy very well. Now they had split up and Marion lived alternately with each of her parents. Munch had actually been against this arrangement, hadn't wanted the little girl to have two homes, but his granddaughter didn't seem to mind.

Oh, Grandad, everyone has two houses these days, didn't you know?

A precocious six-year-old, evidently, just like her mother had been.

No, I didn't know that, Marion.

It's completely normal now, Grandad, and that's because then you have two birthdays and you get twice as many presents at Christmas, and it's something the king has decided.

Is that right? What a nice king.

Yes, he is, isn't he? And when he's in his palace, they raise the flag so that everyone can see he's at home and not in his cabin.

Fancy that? How clever.

Yes, the king's clever. He doesn't have a job, he just waves from the balcony and says hello to people. Please can I have a horse, Grandad?

A horse? Why would you want a horse?

Not for me, Grandad! For Barbie, because she can't wear riding clothes and not have a horse? Can she?

No, of course not. I see that.

'I . . . I'm not asking for your permission, Daddy. I'm just letting you know, OK?'

Despite her near-fatal injuries, his daughter's personality hadn't changed. No one could tell her what to do.

'Of course.' Munch coughed. 'So who is . . .?'

'Th— . . . That's why I'm calling. I . . . I want you to meet him. His name is Ziggy and he makes me very happy.'

Munch could hear that his daughter was almost out of breath.

'Congratulations, Miriam. I'm looking forward to it already.'

'You are?'

'Of course. Will you be wearing a white dress? Do I get to walk you up the aisle?'

His daughter giggled.

'W— . . . We'll have to see. W— . . . We thought we might have it at home in the garden.'

'I'll walk you up the aisle no matter where it is, Miriam.'

There was silence on the phone now.

'Thank you, Daddy. I . . . I appreciate that,' his daughter said quietly at last.

'Now you get some rest, all right?'

'All right.'

'I'm looking forward to meeting your Ziggy. I'll come and visit you as soon as I can. I'm a bit busy right now, but within a few days, OK?'

'OK, Daddy. T— . . . Take care.'

'You too, Miriam.'

Munch had only just ended the call when his mobile rang again.

'Are you at home?'

'Yes?'

'Why don't we drive up there together?'

'Sure,' Munch said. 'Are you coming over to my place?'

'I'll be there in ten minutes,' Mia said, and rang off.

Chapter 18

Thirty-six-year-old Samantha Berg had dreamed of getting married. The dream had been oh so wonderful that when she woke up and realized she was in her own bed and still single she was tempted to take yet another sleeping pill. Close her eyes. Crawl back under her warm duvet. *Go back there. To the white beach.*

Oh, how perfect everything had been. Just like she had always imagined. Barefoot on the sand. The white dress. Her veil fluttering in the wind. Background music. An arch of flowers like she had seen in American films. And he had stood underneath it. Her prince. Samantha wasn't quite sure who he had been this time, but he had looked a bit like Brad Pitt. Much younger, obviously, and smartly dressed, with blue eyes that sparkled as they waited for her. With the rings in his hand. Oh, how they had gazed at her, all the guests – admiring, envious glances. His family and friends on one side; her family and friends on the other. Laila Bekkevåg had been there too, that dreadful woman, her old schoolfriend, who always uploaded pictures of her perfect family life on Facebook and always rubbed it in whenever they met.

'Are you still single, Samantha? Oh, poor you, that must be awful, and you always wanted a husband and a family. Well, at least you have your cat.'

The others in her circle of friends were not as tactless, but she could see it in their eyes as well.

Pity. They felt sorry for her.

Oh, surely it would be her turn soon? After all, she wasn't asking for much in life.

The vicar had been an old man who had reminded her a little of her grandfather, with a gravelly voice, a big white beard and a smile that went all the way to eternity.

Samantha, do you take this man to be your lawful husband, to have and to hold from this day forward, for better, for worse, in sickness and in health, to love and to cherish, till death do you part?

She had wanted to shout it out loud. *I do, I do, I do!* But she had controlled herself, of course she had, and had just blushed a little and whispered, 'I do,' as a young woman should. She had winked slightly and seductively as he slipped a diamond ring on her slim finger. Closed her eyes as he leaned forwards through the cool summer air to kiss her. Oh, how wonderful it had been. How warm her body had felt when his strong arms embraced her, his lips against hers.

The ice-cold floor tiles in the bathroom when she opened the bathroom cabinet to get the white box of sleeping tablets had woken her up. The dream evaporated. She wouldn't be able to return to it now, no matter how hard she tried, so she just put the pills back and pottered into the kitchen to make breakfast, as usual.

Was she boring?

Was that why nobody wanted her?

She did the same thing every single day, true, but what was wrong with that? She liked her routines. They made life simpler. She could get through the days when she had a plan. Wake up at seven thirty when the alarm went off. Go to the kitchen and turn on the radio. Make breakfast, usually crispbread for her and tuna for Rebekka, her cat. Then shower and, afterwards, when she had dried herself properly, go to her bedroom to get dressed. Nothing fancy, but still presentable. She was selling the dresses, not getting married, so it was about blending in. She shouldn't stand out like someone trying to compete with the customers, yet she should still exude taste and elegance. Not easy, of course, with her small budget, but she managed somehow. There had been no complaints at her performance reviews for quite a while, and she saw that as a good sign.

Wedding Dresses Limited in Prinsensgate.

That was where she worked.

She had heard her friends whisper about it the last time they went out together, Laila Bekkevåg leaning slightly forwards with that disgusting smile of hers as Samantha returned with their drinks from the bar.

'She sells wedding dresses, but always the bridesmaid, never the bride. Isn't that a kick in the teeth?'

'Is it true that he's doing time?'

'Who?'

'The guy she was sort of engaged to?'

'God, she just has such bad luck.'

Samantha Berg got off the Metro at Jernbanetorget, wondering whether to reactivate her Møteplassen dating profile. She had tried Tinder, but it was definitely not for her. She hadn't had many matches, and the few she had had were – well, to be perfectly blunt – only after one thing.

Unlucky.

Perhaps she had just been unlucky so far?

Samantha inserted the key into the lock and switched off the alarm. A world of wedding dresses. She felt it now: she loved her job; she did. Her friends could say what they liked. She loved walking around these beautiful rooms all day, surrounded by these lovely dresses. Yes, it was a shame that it hadn't been her turn yet. But her time would come; it would. It was just a question of patience.

Perhaps she should post some new pictures of herself next time? She had taken some of herself in Frogner Park one day when she had been out walking Rebekka. They didn't show her whole body and they looked quite nice. It was about not giving up. Who dares wins. Fortune favours the brave. Wasn't that how the sayings went?

She smiled to herself, put her coat on the peg in the back and entered the shop as the bell over the door rang. The first customer of the day. A young woman with blonde hair under a green cap came in. Another bride-to-be. Samantha felt happy just thinking about it.

'Hello, how can I help you?'

The young woman looked nervously at her from under the brim of her cap.

'The thing is, I need a, well, a wedding dress.'

'Then you have come to the right place. Do you have anything particular in mind?'

The girl continued to stand there, looking rather lost.

They were always like that.

Such an abundance of choice. Of course it was difficult. She would struggle herself.

'Costing about ten thousand?' the girl said.

Samantha smiled again. Starting with the price wasn't unusual either, and she understood. She had seen enough bowed heads and disappointed faces when a woman was on her way back to the changing room once she had learned what her dream dress cost.

'That should give you quite a wide choice. Do you have any particular design in mind? Classic? More modern? We've just got some brand-new ones in from Rosa Clara, which I personally think are fantastic. Traditional, yet exciting. Very clean lines. I've always said it and I always will: the most beautiful wedding dresses come from Spain. Might you like something like that?'

Samantha guided the young woman across to the Rosa Clara section and picked a dress from the rail.

'I really like this one. It's—'

'Yes, that's great. I'll take it.'

The girl with the green baseball cap nodded quickly and continued to look out of the window.

What was it about her hair?

It looked so strange.

'Wouldn't you like to try it on first?'

'No, that won't be necessary.'

Was it a wig?

'Are you sure? I mean, isn't it important that—'

'I'll take it,' the girl said again. 'How much?'

'This one costs eight thousand four hundred kroner and the tailor will charge sixteen hundred. It may sound like a lot, perhaps, but it's important that it fits perfectly on your big day. Don't you agree?'

'I'll take it.'

'Very well,' Samantha said with a light cough. 'It certainly looks as if it would fit you. Now it would obviously be best to try it on. The changing rooms are just down there and I would be happy to help you.'

'How much, did you say?'

The girl with the wig had already gone over to the till.

'Eight thousand four hundred. But like I said—'

'Cash OK?'

'What do you mean?'

'Cash?'

The girl was looking straight at her now. Samantha had seen so many eyes in here, eyes sparkling with joy and anticipation, but she had never seen a gaze like that one.

The young woman looked almost frightened.

'So you just want me to bag it up as it is?'

'Yes, great,' the girl said, and stuck her hand into her bag.

She produced an envelope full of banknotes. Counted them with trembling hands and placed them on the counter.

'May I take your name?'

'No,' the girl said.

'I mean, in case—'

'It's fine,' the girl said as she took the big white bag from Samantha.

'You're welcome to come back if you need anything, OK? Like I said, we're happy to help with the fitting, if it needs to be altered.'

She stopped because she was only talking to herself now. The girl with the green baseball cap had already left the shop.

Samantha shook her head. Buying a wedding dress was a big deal and the woman hadn't batted an eyelid at the price. Some people. She heaved a sigh, went to the back room, poured herself a cup of coffee.

So should she do it? Now?

Create a new profile?

She wasn't supposed to be on her mobile or laptop during opening hours – they were quite strict about it – but come on, she *had* just sold a dress.

And it was only a quarter past ten.

And a Rosa Clara. Within the first hour.

Sod it, what harm could it do?

Samantha took her mobile out of her bag, returned to the counter, smiled to herself and started thinking about how to present herself this time.

Chapter 19

Blakstad psychiatric hospital. A yellow monument half an hour's drive from Oslo surrounded by trees and a park and bordering a large lake. Mia had been in a pub once a long time ago, in another lifetime, and had overheard a conversation at a neighbouring table.

'Why do psychos always get the best views? I mean, it doesn't matter where you go, same thing all over Norway. Bergen. Trondheim. Here in Oslo. Prime locations. Not that they give a toss about it – why would they? They've gone loopy. Had to be locked up. Surely it doesn't matter where they are. Imagine what we could do with those plots.'

As Mia got out of the car and followed Munch towards the imposing building, she couldn't help thinking that they might have a point. Blakstad psychiatric hospital was in a location worthy of royalty.

'So he's a consultant here, but he also has a private practice in the centre of Oslo?' Munch said, throwing away his cigarette.

'Nothing unusual about that, is there?'

'Perhaps not.'

'So Vivian Berg was a patient here?' Mia said, as they approached the magnificent building.

'The way I've understood it, no. She was one of his private patients. How much money do you think these people make?'

'What do you mean?'

'They're already being paid by the state. The director of a place like this, with a private practice as well? Is that legal? I mean, obviously it is, but even so.'

He shook his head and stuffed his hand into his duffel coat to get another cigarette. He changed his mind halfway down the path and put the cigarettes back in his pocket. A carer with a tight ponytail and a staff card around his neck let them into the big building.

Mia had imagined a stereotypical German psychiatrist, tall, bearded, wearing glasses and a tweed jacket and smoking a pipe, but Wolfgang Ritter looked nothing like his name suggested. The man across the desk was stick thin, feminine in his manner and spoke so softly that Mia had to lean forward in order to hear him. The psychiatrist was wearing a brown polo-neck jumper which might be thirty years old and the rest of his clothes and the room in general told her that this was a man more concerned with spiritual matters than material possessions. A lava lamp with pink blobs on one windowsill and a clock on the wall strongly suggested the 1970s, but they were the only elements that could be associated with Doctor LSD, if that really was how he was now known.

'A tragedy, a real tragedy,' Ritter said in his soft voice. 'Vivian was a princess. Utterly unique.'

'I'm sorry for getting straight to the point, but we have so much to do,' Mia said. 'What was Vivian's diagnosis?'

'Diagnosis, illness, normality – who can tell which is which?' Ritter mused, leaning back. 'First and foremost, we're all human beings, aren't we? Some with more baggage than others, of course, but does that mean some people need a label?'

Munch gave Mia a brief sideways glance and she knew exactly what he meant. Ritter didn't seem to be on the same planet as the rest of humankind.

'Ziprasidone and sertraline,' Munch said, pulling out a note from his pocket. 'She must have taken these for a reason. Did you suggest them?'

Munch slid the note across the messy desk. Ritter touched his glasses and looked quickly at the note before giving a small shrug and sinking back in the chair.

'We all need a little help, don't we? A diabetic needs insulin. A child takes a fluoride pill. Nature didn't give us that, did it?'

'I think you misunderstand,' Mia reassured him. 'We're not trying to stigmatize anyone here. We're just trying to get an idea of who Vivian was. A twenty-two-year-old girl doesn't take heavy medication just for the fun of it, does she?'

Wolfgang Ritter fell silent for a moment while he studied them both from behind his glasses.

'Vivian Berg had what we call a dissociative identity disorder,' he said at length. 'It was brought on by a mother who was unable to take care of her. It started when she was little, the soul's urge to disappear into another consciousness because her reality was too hard to deal with. Was that what you meant? Was that what you want to hear?'

He shook his head almost imperceptibly and looked at Mia with contempt.

I do know my job, if that was what you were wondering.

'Dissociative . . .?' Munch said.

'Identity disorder,' Ritter said. 'It's often confused with schizophrenia, which means that many patients don't get the right treatment, which obviously wasn't the case here. I like to think I know what I'm doing. She continued to improve, with almost every appointment. A tragedy, of course, that she didn't live long enough to get completely well.'

'Multiple personalities?' Mia said with interest.

'Yes, that's why the two diagnoses are so often confused. They're very similar, often presenting with the same symptoms. Reduced impulse control, emotional instability, self-harm, derealization.'

'Derea—?'

'Being unable to perceive or experience the world as real.' Ritter smiled.

Munch glanced briefly at Mia.

'She had problems knowing what was real?'

'That's right. Something which, not surprisingly, leads to problems coping with the real world. Job, friends, family.'

'So she thought she was someone else?' Mia asked.

Ritter nodded.

'Who?'

Ritter wavered for a moment.

'Listen, I know that you've been granted access to her records, but it still feels . . .'

He took off his glasses.

'. . . a bit wrong. What I'm doing, do you understand?'

'So you would rather we get someone to come here and copy the information from your computer?'

Mia briefly regretted her harsh tone, but she was tired and she didn't have the patience for this.

'Of course not. But even so . . .?'

'We understand,' Munch said. 'But it would be a great help to us, so if you could—'

'An older man,' Ritter said quietly.

'A what?'

'There were times Vivian thought she was an older man.'

'Why a man?' asked Munch.

'Good question,' Ritter said with a shrug.

The room fell silent.

'She needed someone she regarded as stronger than herself,' Mia said at length.

She was aware of Ritter's reaction, that he hadn't expected her to say that.

'It's a theory,' the psychiatrist said, sucking on one of the arms of his spectacles. 'Dissociative phenomena are thought to be a defensive response either during, or more frequently after, a traumatic experience. The most important aetiological factor is thought to be serious and ongoing sexual or physical assaults. The earlier in life the abuse occurs, the more serious the symptoms.'

'So Vivian was abused?' Munch asked.

'No, I didn't say that.'

'So why did she get this . . .?'

Munch turned to Mia.

'Dissociative personality disorder,' Mia said, and hesitated.

Ritter had challenged her to a pissing contest and she wished she hadn't been so childish as to have gone along with it, but there was something in his prudish manner that meant she just couldn't help herself.

'She wasn't abused. She developed it through association,' she said.

'What do you mean?' Munch said.

'Raymond Greger,' Mia began.

'Yes?' Munch was confused.

'My guess is that Karoline Berg was abused in some way by her stepbrother and that she involved her daughter in her grief. That's a common occurrence, isn't it, Doctor? A single mother and her daughter. The roles get mixed up. The person who was meant to be the adult can't do their job.'

If Ritter was impressed, he didn't show it, but she could feel that the mood had changed.

'Vivian Berg wasn't abused, no,' he said with a cough. 'But she grew up in an unsafe environment where it felt like she was. This happens more frequently than we think. A young child looks up to its parents in a way they don't actually deserve. A fragile young mind, if we don't take care of it, can quickly find somewhere to hide in order to feel safe. That's why I always say I don't believe in a god. If there was one, he or she wouldn't have created a race that needed looking after for twenty years before it could manage on its own and was so easy to damage. Humanity? We're delicate creatures, don't you think?'

'So people retreat into their own heads?' Munch said.

'They retreat. Disappear. Seek help.'

'But,' Munch went on, 'if she was seriously ill, why wasn't she admitted here so that she could be treated?'

'We discussed it, of course, but dancing was important to her. As long as she saw me often enough, we could keep it at bay.'

'You said she was improving?'

'Absolutely. The medication helped somewhat, but the most important thing was obviously the distance.'

'The distance?' Munch said, but understood halfway through his question. 'From her mother?'

'Yes. Now, physical distance from the problem isn't everything, of course, but it's more important than you might think.'

'Did she know that?' Mia said.

'What do you mean?'

'Vivian? When she came. Did she understand her illness?'

'Partly,' Ritter said. 'She came to me originally to get help with the symptoms, that's how it usually starts.'

'Which were?'

'Eating disorders primarily, but then again, that's very common in her profession so it took a while before I realized what was really going on.'

Mia detected a hint of pride in his voice.

'Do you treat many people with this condition?'

'I'm afraid I can't discuss other patients,' Ritter said, and smiled again with a rather superior expression.

'I didn't mean any specific individuals, but—'

'Like I said. That piece of paper you turned up with grants you access only to Vivian's medical records.'

'Did she talk much about her mother?' Munch said.

'Not to begin with. But in time, of course. Because we had to. It was difficult for her. She loved her mother more than anybody else in the whole world. That's what makes it so difficult, isn't it? To acknowledge that she's the person who has hurt you the most.'

'Did she ever mention Raymond Greger?'

'Oh yes, several times.'

'How?'

'Well, with anger, despair. She knew everything. Her mother had told her. Killing was mentioned.'

'Killing?'

'Oh yes, of course, I recommend it to all my patients.'

'What do you mean?' Munch said with a quick glance at Mia.

'Not literally, of course. But it's an important part of my therapy.'

'Killing?'

Ritter laughed briefly.

'A great way to slay the animal we can't conquer inside us, don't you think? I've had great success with this method, if I say so myself.'

101

'And how is that done, if I may ask?' Munch said with interest.

'The killing?'

'Yes?'

Ritter smiled faintly once more.

'In various ways. We do role play. Sometimes my patients write it down. Others draw pictures. It depends entirely on the individual.'

'And what did Vivian do?' Mia said.

Ritter fell quiet for a moment.

'Listen, we hadn't really got that far, but it was going to happen. She had planned a dance.'

'A death . . . dance?' Munch said, scrunching up his nose.

'You never saw her dance, did you?' Ritter said.

'No,' Munch said.

'Did you?' Mia asked.

'Oh, yes, several times. She was, well, what can I say? Unique. Sublime. Her death is a real loss to the world. She could have gone as far as she wanted to. Watching her on stage was – well, no, it almost defies description.'

Munch glanced at Mia again, and again she realized what he was insinuating.

The mobile on the table had been vibrating intermittently. Ritter finally checked it.

'I'm sorry, but I'm afraid we have to leave it there. Some of my patients – well, this can't wait, I'm sure you understand.'

'Thank you for your time,' Munch said, getting up. 'You will send us copies of all her records?'

'My secretary will see to it,' Ritter said, and shook hands with them both. 'Please ring her if there's anything else.'

'What are you thinking?' Munch said when they were back in the car park.

'That a few more pieces have just fallen into place, wouldn't you say?' Mia reached into her jacket for a lozenge.

Munch lit a cigarette as raindrops started dripping on them. The Oslo spring was reluctant to arrive.

'Raymond Greger?'

'We really need to find him.'

'I agree. I'll call Larvik police and tell them to put more people on the job. Are you hungry?'

'I wouldn't mind something to eat.'

'Great. I can't think on an empty stomach. Burger?'

'Something a little bit healthier, perhaps?'

'He saw her dance?'

'I know,' Mia said. 'Want him put under surveillance?'

'Let's think about it,' Munch said, leading the way towards the car. His mobile rang.

His face fell as he listened to the voice on the other end.

She knew what was coming long before he had ended the call.

'Where?'

'A hotel in Gamlebyen.'

'Same killer?' Mia asked, swiftly opening the car door.

Munch didn't reply. Just nodded with dark eyes and got in behind the wheel.

Chapter 20

Hotel Lundberg lay at the end of a side street in Gamlebyen with the railway tracks as its nearest neighbour. It was barely worthy of the word 'hotel'. Only the 'O' was still lit up on the old neon sign, and the handwritten note on the door – '*Cash only*' – spoke volumes about the kind of customers who normally frequented this run-down establishment. Patrol cars at the scene had blocked off the narrow street and Mia could see that the media had already descended. A crowd of eager reporters had gathered behind the cordons as Munch and she entered through the rusty door and were met by a slightly fraught Anette Goli in the shabby reception.

'Do we know who it is?' Munch said, unbuttoning his coat.

'The victim's ID says Kurt Wang. A few people have said that he's a jazz musician, but we're checking that out now.'

'Who found him?' Mia wanted to know.

'The receptionist,' Goli said, nodding towards the back room, where they could see the outline of an old man holding a cup of coffee with trembling hands.

'Many guests?'

'No. A junkie in room three and a Bosnian girl who denies being a prostitute in room five.'

'They're still here?' Munch asked.

'We're keeping both of them in their rooms for now.'

'How many rooms are there?' Mia asked.

'Ten. Our victim is in number nine,' Goli said, leading the way down the corridor.

They were met by a crime-scene technician, who nodded and issued each of them with a pair of blue latex gloves.

'Shoes?' Munch said, pointing to his feet.

'Makes no difference,' the technician muttered, and left the room.

They realized what he meant as soon as they reached the threshold. The floor had seen better days and a few more footprints across the threadbare carpet would make very little difference.

'Please could we be in the room by ourselves for a moment?' Goli requested.

The three other crime-scene technicians left.

'Oh, no,' Munch said when they had stepped inside and could see the body, which was lying on the bed.

'Same puncture wound to the chest. And the same camera.' Goli gestured towards the camera on the tripod. 'A Nikon E300. Do you think it's significant?'

This was addressed to Mia, but she wasn't listening. It was a long time since she had last attended a crime scene. She had almost forgotten what it was like. In recent years she had hidden from them, looking at crime scenes only in photographs. She had used them as a shield, but not this time. She felt it creep through her now.

The darkness.

'The mobile was on the table over there,' Anette said, pointing towards it. 'His own, programmed via Spotify to play the same song on a loop; that was what attracted the receptionist's attention. Thin walls here, clearly.'

'Which song?'

Munch was also far away now, in a fog somewhere.

'John Coltrane. "My Favorite Things".'

Mia steeled herself. She found a lozenge in her jacket pocket and put it in her mouth. It had always been a diversion tactic. A trick she had learned from a psychologist. *The taste of salt on your tongue. It protects you. It represents something good. Something beautiful. Can you feel it, Mia? Can you?*

'"My Favorite Things"?' Munch echoed.

'Yes,' Goli said. 'Does it mean anything?'

'Of course it does.' Mia coughed. 'Everything the killer does means something. Nothing here is random.'

'So the writing on the wall over there is new?'

Goli gestured towards a sentence written with a black felt-tip pen on the floral wallpaper above the bed.

WATCH WHAT I CAN DO.

'Undoubtedly,' Mia said, pulling herself together.

She had barely glanced at the bed so far, she dreaded the effect that seeing the lifeless body might have on her, but now she let her eyes rest on the victim.

A young man.

Twenty-four to twenty-five years old would be her guess.

A saxophone next to him.

Still wearing his shoes.

And his coat.

Eyes open.

An expression of terror.

Fingers clenched inside his fists.

As though he wanted to defend himself and was unable to.

'What do you think it can mean?' Goli said. 'The writing?'

'It's from *Bambi*.' Mia walked up to the camera on the tripod, which was facing the blue-and-white victim on the bed. 'Thumper the rabbit says it when he and Bambi go ice-skating.'

'But it could be . . .'

Again Munch's voice faded into the distance.

It had come to her when she went to Forensics, but she had managed to push the feeling away. A number scratched into the lens. It might just be a coincidence, mightn't it? Something that had already been there? An old, much-used lens? It didn't have to mean anything, did it?

Mia rummaged round her pocket for another lozenge as her eyes found what she was looking for but would have preferred not to see.

Another number.

Seven.

'Same blisters to the mouth,' Munch said somewhere, pointing a blue latex finger. 'Have we checked his chest? Is there a needle mark?'

106

'I thought we ought to wait for the pathologist,' Goli said, still in a fog. 'They're on their way. I've just spoken to Lund.'

'There's another number,' Mia mumbled, then pulled herself together.

The two other investigators looked at her.

'On the lens?' Munch asked, crossing the floor.

Mia nodded.

'Damn,' Munch said from behind the camera. 'Seven. Four? Seven? What the hell is that supposed to mean? What do you think, Mia?'

The filthy floor had started to move now; it mixed with the faded flowers on the wallpaper and made her dizzy.

'Not sure,' she said, chewing her lip.

'Are you OK?'

'What?'

They were both looking at her now, strange eyes somewhere out in the mist.

'I need a moment to think,' Mia said, heading for the door. 'Will you talk to the receptionist?'

'What? Yes, yes, of course. Are you off now?'

'I just need to sort something out,' Mia mumbled, and pulled off her gloves.

'Do whatever you have to do.'

Munch frowned and walked up close to the young man on the bed.

'So the mobile was playing the song on repeat?'

'Yes.' Goli nodded.

'I'll call you,' Mia murmured, and found her way to the fresh air in the street outside.

Chapter 21

'So how do we do this?' Anette Goli asked when Mia had left the room.

'What do you mean? The media?'

One of the crime-scene technicians popped his head in, but Munch asked him to wait.

'Yes. One body is one thing. Two, now that's another matter entirely. We have to say something, I think.'

'Set up a press conference.' Munch sighed. 'But we won't say anything about there being a possible link between the two deaths. Not yet. As it's an ongoing investigation and so on and so forth – you know the drill.'

'And Mikkelson?'

'Has he been hassling you?'

'What do you think?' The mobile in Goli's pocket buzzed again. 'The usual. Do we think we're dealing with a serial killer? Is Munch ready for this so soon? Is Mia mentally all there?'

'Again? When will he ever stop?'

'You know that she admitted herself?' Goli said in a quiet voice. 'To rehab?'

'I know that she feels better and looks bloody amazing, yes. What do you mean, "rehab"?'

'The Vitkoff Clinic down in Jæren,' Goli continued. 'She admitted herself just after the New Year and stayed there for a month.'

'I see. Good for her. And what about it?'

Munch was aware that he was getting irritated. Mikkelson was always like this. Whenever Mia solved cases for him and made him look like a hero in the media – well, there were never any questions about her mental health then.

'Oh, I don't know. You saw her just now, didn't you? Perhaps she's not fully recovered yet.'

'Mia will be fine,' Munch grunted, and was overcome by a strong urge for a cigarette.

'And you?' Goli asked in a friendly voice.

'Me? What about me?'

'Everyone would understand if this was too much for you, Holger. Two murders in such a short space of time. It's not that long since Miriam's accident.'

'And whose side are you on?'

'Yours, obviously, Holger, I just wanted to—'

'I'm fine. Mia is great. You can tell Mikkelson to shut his mouth unless he has something constructive to offer. We have a job to do here. So will you set up that press conference?'

'Of course, Holger.'

The impatient crime-scene technician popped his head round the door again, and this time Munch waved him in. He shook off his irritation with a cigarette under the flashing neon 'O' out in the street and went back to the room behind the reception.

'How long will I have to sit here?' the old man asked.

It was clear that the discovery of the dead young man in room nine had shocked him deeply.

'Holger Munch, special unit,' Munch said, shaking his hand.

'Jim,' the old man mumbled. 'Myhre. Jim Myhre. I'm sorry.'

A grey, thinning ponytail and round spectacles. Munch had seen this gaze before many times. A touch of nervousness in the presence of the authorities. No wonder. If this man owned and ran Hotel Lundgren, he had probably had plenty of encounters with the police over the years.

'That's quite all right, Jim,' Munch said. 'I can see that you're tired. Were you on duty all night?'

'Of course I was, or I don't make any money. I can't afford to hire anyone. I can barely make ends meet as it is.'

'I understand. So it was you who checked in Kurt Wang?'

'Who?'

'The man in room nine? You don't record the names of your guests?'

'Cash only,' Myhre muttered, rubbing his eyes. 'I don't care what they're called as long as they pay.'

'When did he arrive?'

Myhre hesitated.

'Late. It could have been around eleven.'

'And he came alone?'

'Yes.'

'There was no one else, let's say, in front of or behind him? I mean, did anyone follow him?'

'No,' Myhre said, putting the coffee cup on the table with trembling hands.

'And how did he seem? How was your conversation?'

'Conversation?'

'Yes? How did it go? "Hi, I need a room"?'

'Something like that,' Myhre said, and coughed. 'I don't know. He came in. Money in his hand. I don't remember exactly what he said.'

'Try.'

'"I need a room" – something like that. Nothing unusual. Apart from the fact that he looked high, but we're used to that here. It's not exactly the Grand, I know it isn't, but beggars can't be choosers.'

'High?'

'Staring eyes,' Myhre said, making an attempt to lift the coffee cup again. It wasn't entirely successful. 'Really high, if you ask me, but yes, like I said, we can't afford to be picky here.'

'And the saxophone?'

'What do you mean, "saxophone"? He didn't have anything with him.'

'No carry case? No bag, suitcase, anything like that?'

Myhre shook his head.

'Nope. Just the money in his hand.'

'So what happened? Why did you go to his room?'

'I never normally do that, but hell, the same song? All night? You can hear everything here. That constant howling, it was driving me crazy.'

'So you just walked straight in?'

'No, I knocked, obviously, several times. And at last, well, the door sort of just slipped open. I didn't mean to go inside.'

Myhre was lost in thought for a moment and just about managed to steer the coffee cup back to his lips. He was clearly still in deep shock.

'And he didn't talk to any of the other guests? No one else, inside or out?'

'No,' Myhre said. 'Well, that's to say . . .'

He scratched his head a couple of times.

'Who?'

'He didn't react at first, but now that I think about it—'

'What?' Munch asked impatiently.

'The guy from the cleaning company.'

'Yes?'

'We have a deal with a Vietnamese firm. And they usually send – how can I put it? – well, not young white men, if you know what I mean?'

'No, I don't.'

'They practically pay us to work here, the company hires cheap labour – do you get my drift?' Myhre said, and wrinkled his nose.

'But this time they sent a young man? A young, ethnically Norwegian man?'

'A white man, yes.' Myhre nodded. 'I thought nothing of it at the time. People need a job, no matter what they look like; I don't have a problem with that.'

'And this man spoke to Kurt Wang?'

'Yes, I saw them in the corridor.'

'What happened?'

'I don't know, I wasn't there for very long, I just saw that they spoke, that's all.'

'So this was your usual cleaning company?'

'Yes, yes. I'm very happy with them, they're cheap and reliable. We let some of their staff live here from time to time, it's part of the deal we have. You're not from the tax office, are you?'

'No. You have their name? An address?'

'Of course.' Myhre put down the cup again.

He got up, went over to a crowded cork noticeboard behind the table and returned with a business card.

'Sagene Laundry and Cleaning Services?'

'A Vietnamese family. Very nice people. Like I said, we help their staff get a roof over their heads from time to time.'

He ground to a halt and looked away.

'If you're housing illegal migrants, then that's none of my business,' Munch said.

'No, no, we—'

'Like I said, it's none of my business. But this young man – was he someone you had seen before?'

'No.'

'But he was from the cleaning company?'

'Oh yes. Turned up with all the equipment. Did a rubbish job, though. Didn't do any bloody cleaning. He made some excuse about having to go out to get something, but I never saw him again.'

'But he spoke to Wang. The man in room nine?'

'Absolutely,' Myhre nodded and blinked. 'Can I go now? I've been awake since last night.'

'I'm afraid you'll have to come to the station.' Munch got up.

'Now?'

'Yes,' Munch said, and went back out into the reception.

Anette Goli had just finished a phone call and came towards him.

'Get someone to take this man to the station. Take a full statement and get a signature, OK?'

'OK.' Goli nodded and summoned one of the police officers near the door. 'Where are you off to?'

112

'Sagene,' Munch said, sticking the business card into the pocket of his duffel coat.

'Will you be at the office later?'

'Yes.'

'OK,' Goli said as her mobile rang again.

Chapter 22

Sagene Laundry and Cleaning Services was located, not surprisingly, in the Sagene district of Oslo, near Sagene Church, an area Munch knew well. He and Marianne had lived here a long time ago in a one-bedroom flat with a tiny bedroom and the bathroom in the kitchen. He had just started as an investigator. She was still at teacher-training college. They hadn't had much money, but they had been happy. Munch felt a wave of nostalgia wash over him and allowed himself a small smile as he chucked aside a cigarette butt and walked through the glass door into the small reception area.

The company offered dry-cleaning, laundry and cleaning services. Behind the reception counter were rails of garments. He was met by a smiling, middle-aged Vietnamese woman who got up as he entered.

'Welcome. Dry-cleaning?' she said, removing a pen from behind her ear. 'Special offer on shirts today: three for the price of one and a free shirt with every suit, and another one for two suits.'

'Oslo police,' Munch said, showing her his warrant card. 'Are you the owner?'

The woman put on a pair of glasses that hung on a string around her neck and looked at him warily.

'Trouble?'

'No, no,' Munch said with a quick smile. 'Everything is fine. I just have some questions about a staff member. Are you in charge of the staff?'

'One moment,' the woman said, and disappeared behind the garment rails.

She returned shortly afterwards, closely followed by a young, well-dressed man in his mid-twenties.

'Dinh Nguyen,' he said politely, and held out his hand. 'How can I help you?'

'Are you the owner?'

'Daily manager.'

Pressed khaki trousers. White shirt under a black jumper. Nice, manicured hands with a gold watch on one wrist. Munch had a feeling he would be more at home in a clothes catalogue than behind the counter of a cleaning firm. It looked like Sagene Laundry and Cleaning Services was a lucrative business.

'I'm looking for information about one of your employees.'

'Oh?' Nguyen said with interest. 'Who?'

'He was working at Hotel Lundgren last night? Ethnic Norwegian?'

'Lundgren? We didn't have anyone down there yesterday, as far as I know. Ethnic Norwegian? Do you mean white?'

'He's said to be white, yes. Do you know if any of your staff match that description?'

'No. We're a family business – our employees are pretty much all aunts and uncles and cousins,' Nguyen said with a faint smile.

'So no outsiders?'

'No, we—'

The young man was interrupted by the woman. A short exchange between them followed in what Munch presumed to be Vietnamese.

'Oh, of course,' Nguyen said, turning back to Munch. 'I'm sorry, it could be one of our casuals.'

'Casuals?'

'We try to help people if we can.' Nguyen nodded towards a row of chairs by the window. 'We can't hire many full-time staff, but at times people turn up just to see if there's any work going.'

'And is there?'

'At times, yes.'

'You're a dry-cleaner's as well as a cleaning business?'

Nguyen nodded.

'And these casuals, how are they organized?'

'They turn up, sit there, wait, and if we have a job that needs doing, they'll get it.'

'You mean a cleaning job?'

'Yes, we have enough staff to do the dry-cleaning.'

The woman said something else, but this time Nguyen ignored her.

'And who are they?'

'The casuals?'

'Yes.'

Nguyen wavered for a moment. Munch knew why. Just like Myhre from the hotel, this young man was scared that Munch might be from Immigration or the tax office.

'Like I said—'

'Listen,' Munch said, scratching his beard. 'I don't care who they are, all right? If they're here illegally or if they don't pay their taxes. If something like that's going on, then it's someone else's job to deal with it.'

Nguyen studied him for a little while longer from under his neatly trimmed fringe and then gave in.

'Most are immigrants. It's hard for them to get a job in Norway. I mean, it's bad enough for people who are born here. Like I said, we're only trying to help.'

Munch raised a hand to pre-empt him.

'Again, I totally understand. Not my department. I just need to know if one of your casuals matches the description I gave you?'

'I think I know the man you're looking for,' he said at last.

'You do?'

Nguyen nodded.

'We don't usually hire – well, what did you call them? Ethnic Norwegians? They are few and far between here. We mostly get Afghans, Somalis, Poles. But, yes, we have had one.'

The woman protested again, but Nguyen cut her off irritably.

'What's she saying?'

'She's saying she knows who he is and that he's no longer welcome here.'

'Trouble, no, no,' the woman said, waving a crooked forefinger.

'Mum, I'm dealing with this. You said mid-twenties? White?'

'Yes?'

'We have one like that, but it's been a while since I last saw him.'

'Why?'

'We had a small disagreement.'

'About what?'

'Firstly, the casuals have no business going into my office.'

'And then?'

'And, in fact, we do require them to register with us, as it happens. I've no intention of taking the fall if they don't declare their wages. If they earn more than the taxable limit, they have to give me their tax code.'

'And this man didn't do that?'

'Karl,' the woman said, and shook her head.

'You have his details?'

'It's not much,' Dinh Nguyen said. 'I have his name, address and phone number, but he never told me his tax code.'

'Owes money,' the woman said.

'Mum, I'm dealing with this.'

'Swindle us, thousands.'

'He owes you money?'

Nguyen gave a little sigh.

'Like I said, I'm not going to take a hit for someone working cash in hand. It's bad for business. So we usually don't pay them if they can't prove that they're free to work without paying tax.'

'Too soft. Idiot,' the woman said, taking off her glasses.

'But you paid him anyway?'

Nguyen nodded.

'He promised to bring all his paperwork, but he never did.'

'And how long ago was that?'

'How long can it be now? Three weeks?'

'And you haven't seen him since?'

'No.'

'And you didn't send anyone to Hotel Lundgren yesterday?'

Nguyen shook his head.

117

'No, we didn't.'

'You said you had some information about him?'

'Hang on a moment.' Nguyen disappeared into the back room.

'Idiot,' his mother muttered. She had sat down on the chair behind the reception counter and taken out her knitting.

'Here you are,' Nguyen said, putting a piece of paper on the counter.

'Karl Overlind?'

Nguyen nodded.

'And this is his address?'

'Yes, but the phone number doesn't work, I've tried that.'

The woman shook her head and said something in Vietnamese, which, judging by the look on Nguyen's face, didn't go down well with her dapper son.

'If I send out a sketch artist, could you describe him to us?'

'Absolutely. I could pick him out anywhere. I'm only glad to be of help. Can I ask why you're looking for him?'

'I'm afraid you can't. Thank you very much for this.'

Munch held up the note before stuffing it into the pocket of his coat.

'We'll be in touch. Thanks.' He nodded goodbye to the knitting woman before going outside into the early-spring sun.

Chapter 23

Mia was standing outside her apartment building. She could feel that the fresh air had done the trick. The darkness had crept over her for a moment, but it hadn't taken root. Fortunately. It was just a little hint from her soul of what might happen if she didn't look after herself. Damn it. This was why she had booked herself a holiday. To rest. *Don't expose yourself to unnecessary stress in the near future.* Wasn't that what she had said, the therapist down at Jæren? Thirty days in rehab; she had felt like a new woman afterwards. Too late to think of that now. This investigation had already got under her skin. Just be a bit careful. She reminded herself to email the Virgin Islands, tell Viktor she wouldn't make the boat this time. She stuck her key in the door and had barely opened it when she saw an old face, a neighbour.

What was her name again? Was it Mrs Fredriksen?

The old woman was standing on the ground floor by the post-boxes, shaking her fist. A walking stick was in one hand, her wig a little askew. A strong smell of perfume, nauseating. Harshly made-up eyes. Her lips painted bright red and her voice so shrill and loud that Mia immediately wished that she was back outside in the street.

'We have to get them out of here! We need a petition! Aren't you that police officer from the second floor? This won't do! Have you seen the bins in the backyard? Are you aware how much the stairwell stinks?'

Mia shook her head lightly and slipped up the stairs to the second floor, only to be met by another expectant face outside the door to her flat.

'Hello, Mia, how are you? Ready for your big trip? My sister is thrilled about the flat. She thinks it's fabulous.'

Her neighbour gave her a thumbs-up and a big smile.

Sod it. It had completely slipped her mind.

'Sorry. I've had to change my plans; I won't be going abroad after all.'

'Oh,' the blond young man said. He looked disappointed.

'I'm sorry,' Mia said again, and unlocked her door.

Her neighbour was about to add something when he suddenly noticed what was going on down in the stairwell.

'Oh, no. Is that Mrs Vigen sounding off again?'

He sighed and shook his head in irritation.

'She's got it into her head that the Iranians on the third floor have got to leave. Typical, isn't it? The state of this country. Bloody racists everywhere. This really has to stop.'

The young man disappeared down the stairs. Mia said a silent prayer of thanks that there were still decent people left in the world and entered her flat.

However, she stopped right inside the door. *No, this was no good. She wouldn't be able to think here.* She waited in the passage until the stairwell was finally quiet again before tiptoeing down the stairs and making her way to one of her favourite pubs, Lorry.

'Hi!' A familiar face smiled, clearly surprised at seeing her again. 'The usual?'

The colourful pub at the end of Hegdehaugsveien had pretty much been her second home, but those days were long gone.

Four months sober.

'No, I'll have a cup of tea and a Farris mineral water,' Mia said, taking out the notebook from her bag.

'Coming up.' The friendly waiter winked at her and vanished as quietly as he had arrived.

Mia could barely remember the last time she had done this, lost herself in the evidence without the aid of substances, but too bad, she had to give it a try. She sat staring at the empty pages in front of her until the mumbling, distant hum of the cosy pub finally gave her the calm she needed. She put pen to paper and slipped inside her head as the world around her slowly disappeared.

Vivian Berg. Aged twenty-two. A ballet dancer. A mountain lake far from the city. Damage to her pointe shoes. Did she walk there herself? Yes? Voluntarily? Probably not. The video. Drugged? Hypnotized? Am I missing something?

Kurt Wang. Jazz musician. Twenty-something. Does his age matter? 'Watch what I can do.' *Bambi*? Bambi on ice?

Mountain lake? Ice?

Water? Purification?

The number four.

The number seven.

Mia reached for her teacup without even noticing it.

Four . . . seven?

Seven . . . four?

Forty-seven? Seventy-four?

The Brothers Lionheart.

Something is burning.

Is the fire . . .

. . . *at home?*

Number forty-seven? Number seventy-four?

She reached for her mobile almost in a trance.

'Grønlie speaking.'

'Hello, Mia here. Just a quick one. Please could you check if we have something on a fire?'

'What do you mean?'

'Sorry. A family that died in a fire – have we got anything like that?'

'It's a bit vague,' Grønlie said.

'Yes, I'm sorry. The house number could be either forty-seven or seventy-four. Please could you check if we have anything like that?'

'Absolutely.'

'Thank you.' Mia rang off as quickly as she could so as not to lose her train of thought.

Female, twenty-two.

Male, twenty-five, maybe.

Big sister?

Younger brother?

Family tragedy.

The house burned.

Who survived?

Guilt?

Was it your fault?

Antifreeze in the heart. A syringe.

Cold.

Ice.

Fire?

Heat?

Ice and fire?

Her pen flew across the sheets now. She wasn't even aware that she was smiling.

Ice and fire? That's what this is about, isn't it? Did they burn to death? Was it your fault? Antifreeze? Are you sorry? Do you want to help them? Make it colder? Make it OK again?

Is that what you want us to see?

It is, isn't it?

That you're sorry?

Are you sorry?

Do you repent?

Did you not mean to do it?

Do you want us to help you?

Find you?

'Excuse me, are you Mia Krüger?'

Mia was so startled that she almost dropped her pen. She had been so far away that her brain struggled to find its way back to reality.

'Eh, yes . . .'

'I'm sorry for intruding, but do you have two minutes?'

Black coat, white shirt, gloves, hair combed to one side. The eyes looking at her seemed familiar and yet she couldn't place him.

'And you are . . .?' Mia began.

'It won't take long. But we've reached the stage where I need to have a few words with you.'

His appearance.

His expression.

Mia could spot a police officer a hundred metres away, but she hadn't seen him before.

'Wold,' the well-dressed man said, extending a hand across the table. 'Internal Investigations.'

Her initial irritation turned to curiosity as Wold waved away the friendly waiter and focused his attention on her once more.

'I can see that you're busy, and I know why, of course. Two bodies in just a few days. I'm not going to take up much of your time, but I had to talk to you. I hope you don't mind.'

'I have a feeling that I don't have a choice,' Mia said, reaching for her teacup.

'I apologize if it feels that way,' Wold said, and glanced around the room. 'But, yes, like I said, there's something we need to talk to you about.'

Mia also glanced around the now quite busy bar, but she couldn't see anything that particularly caught her attention.

'Who is "we"? Internal Investigations? Have I done something wrong? Again?'

Wold smiled wryly.

'No, no, definitely not, Mia. It's not about you, not this time.'

He leaned across the table towards her.

'This investigation you're involved in, can I ask you a question?'

'The answer is no, obviously,' Mia said drily. 'I can't discuss an ongoing investigation with you.'

Wold smiled again and raised his hand cautiously.

'I could have gone straight to Munch, or to Mikkelson, for that matter.'

'So why don't you?'

Wold hesitated.

'You know what we do, don't you?'

'You investigate internal police matters.' Mia sighed. 'Is this a quiz? As you can see, I'm quite busy here.'

His mobile buzzed in his pocket, but he ignored it.

'OK, Mia, let me get right to it. Thomas Lorentzen?'

'Who?'

Thomas Lorentzen?

It took a few seconds before the penny dropped. The lawyer. The owner of the Mercedes in which Vivian Berg had been transported.

'What about him?' Mia was intrigued now.

'We just need to know if he's central to your investigation. Is he important? Is he a prime suspect?'

'Why?'

'Is Lorentzen involved? That's all we want to know. It's a straightforward question. I just need a straightforward answer and I'll leave you alone.'

Wold smiled, sphinx-like, and leaned back in his chair. Mia thought about it for a moment and then gave in. Internal Investigations. If Wold really wanted to know about the case, he could just call police headquarters at Grønland. No need to waste his time here. She was keen to get back to her own work. There was something there. She was on the right track. She could feel it.

'No, we're not interested in Lorentzen,' she said quickly, and picked up her pen.

'You're not curious?' Wold said, showing no sign of leaving.

'About what?'

'About why we're interested in him?'

'Of course. But I'm a bit busy now. So are we done?'

Wold looked a little hurt.

'I'm sorry, Mia, I should have approached this differently. Is it all right if I . . .'

He made to take off his coat.

'Listen,' Mia began, but he stopped her.

'The truth is, I need your help. We've hit a dead end. We've discussed at length who to talk to and we decided on you. It's that simple.'

'And who is "we"?' Mia said again, putting down her pen reluctantly.

Wold thought about it.

'This is just between us?'

'You came to me.' Mia gave another sigh. 'I didn't ask for this.'

'No,' Wold said, then looked around for a waiter. 'I think I need some coffee. Would you like anything?'

'No, thanks.'

'Like I said,' Wold went on, once the waiter had taken his order. 'We've been discussing this for a long time – it's a delicate topic, if you know what I mean – but in the end we chose you.'

'I'm honoured,' Mia said, taking a sip of her mineral water. 'So, again, who is "we"?'

'Well, let me start by telling you who Thomas Lorentzen is. Would that be all right with you?'

'OK.'

'Heroin,' Wold said, raising his cup to his lips.

'As in?'

'Importation. Distribution. And money-laundering.'

'Go on.' Mia was aware that she was starting to drop her guard.

'We don't have the full picture yet, but it's really important to us that you don't touch him right now. It would ruin an operation we've spent a lot of time on.'

'We're not interested in him,' Mia reiterated. 'It was pure co-incidence, as far as we're concerned, that his car was stolen. It could have happened to anyone.'

'Fine. Great. But it's not as simple as that.'

'No, so you said. Why me? How can I help you?'

Wold weighed up his words carefully before finally answering.

'We have reason to believe that one of our own is involved.'

'One of ours?'

'Yes.'

Wold looked around the room again and moved closer.

'We think there's a police officer high up in the drug-trafficking business that Lorentzen is a part of.'

'And you think that officer is me?'

Wold laughed briefly.

'No, definitely not. But we think you might be able to help us.'

'Because?'

'Because you know him.'

'What? You know who it is?'

'We think so. But we need proof.'

'And you want me to get that for you?'

'That's the idea, yes. Would you be comfortable with that?'

Wold leaned back in the chair and raised the coffee cup to his lips again.

'You mean you want me to snitch on a colleague?'

'"Snitching" is a strong word; I wouldn't put it like that. But, yes, that's what it boils down to. Like I said, we've hit a brick wall. We need help.'

'So this Lorentzen is involved in the importation of heroin, and you think he's got someone on the inside?'

'Yes.'

'And this is a named police officer who I know?'

'Yes.'

'You mean someone in our team? In Mariboesgate?'

'Yes.'

'No way,' Mia said, and shook her head. 'I refuse to believe it.'

'As did I to begin with.' Wold shrugged.

Mia could feel her curiosity starting to stir again.

'How can I put it?' Wold went on. 'Munch is known for picking the best, but everyone can make a mistake, can't they?'

'I still find it very hard to believe,' Mia said slowly.

'Believe what?'

'That one of our own could be involved in something like that. One of our team. We're a close-knit unit. We're practically family. Have you ever hugged a father who has just been told that his six-year-old daughter is dead?'

'No, I haven't,' he said.

'That does something to a team, do you understand?' Mia said, irritated now.

'I totally get it. Absolutely. I know what the special unit does, and we all have the greatest respect for you, but even so.'

'It's not one of ours,' Mia said firmly and reached for her teacup again. It was empty.

She looked around for the waiter but couldn't find him.

No, this was bullshit.

Heroin.

Someone in their team?

No way.

'Curry,' Wold said suddenly, as if someone had pulled the needle from an LP.

'What?'

'We think it's Jon Larsen,' Wold said gravely.

'That's ridiculous.' Mia couldn't help a brief giggle of relief. 'Curry? No, you're wrong about that. Jon is an oddball, but there's no way he would ever—'

'We're convinced it's someone from the Drugs Squad.'

'Curry isn't from the Drugs Squad.'

'He has been assigned to the Drugs Squad on several occasions. Besides, certain aspects of his private life indicate that he's in trouble.'

'Now hang on—'

'Allow me to continue, please? Some time ago, Jon Larsen's fiancée dumped him, isn't that correct? And she owned everything. The flat in which they lived? It was hers. He has nothing.'

'No, but that—'

'He rents a room now, he has no money, he's up to his eyeballs in debt. He drinks heavily and is having a casual affair with a twenty-one-year-old woman, Luna Nyvik, a bartender who has previously come to police attention because of the importation of drugs. That's how they do it. Young people who don't know any better. They're used as mules. It's how they get the drugs into Norway.'

'It's not Curry,' Mia insisted again. 'If you knew him, you would understand.'

Wold held up his hand to stop her.

'Will you help us? If nothing else, then to prove us wrong?'

His mobile buzzed in his pocket. He looked at it this time and got up from the table.

'I'm sorry, but something has come up. Please, would you at least think about it?'

'You're wrong.'

'Here's my number.' Wold handed her a business card. 'I'll call you tomorrow. Is that OK?'

Wold flashed her a quick smile, then gave her a firm handshake before moving through the crowd and disappearing. Mia picked up the pen from the table and tried to get back into her case, but the moment had passed.

An officer on the take.

Curry?

No.

Not possible.

She was about to order another cup of tea when her mobile rang.

'Hello, Holger, what is it?'

Munch sounded very odd.

'I have something you need to see,' he said quietly.

'What is it?'

Someone in the bar laughed and Mia could barely hear what Munch was saying.

'It's better if you take a look for yourself. I'll text you the address.'

'OK.' Mia stuffed her notes into her bag and ran outside to hail a taxi.

Chapter 24

Mia paid the cab driver and found Munch outside a solarium with a cigarette in his mouth and a dark look in his eyes.

'What's happening?'

Munch just shook his head.

'You know how the crime scenes were contaminated?'

'Go on?'

'The receptionist at Hotel Lundgren said that Kurt Wang had been talking to a young man before he disappeared into his room. From a cleaning company.'

'Last night?'

'Yes.'

'A cleaning company,' Mia said, feeling for a lozenge in her pocket. 'Why did we not think of that before? Hairs? Nails? Excrement? So that's how he got all those different samples. But that's brilliant, Holger.'

She felt a tingling of excitement under her jacket and smiled at Munch, who for some reason didn't seem very pleased.

'And?' Mia said, keen to know more.

'I visited the company.'

'Yes?'

'They didn't send anybody there last night.'

'But . . .?'

Mia shook her head, still unable to work out what was troubling him.

'But they knew who it was?'

Munch took a drag on his cigarette and nodded.

129

'Karl Overlind. I have an address; the mobile number they had for him has been cancelled.'

'But that's great, Holger. So what are we waiting for? What is it? What did you want to show me?'

'Bergensgata number 41.'

'What?'

'That's the address he gave them.'

Mia was so excited now she could barely stand still, but Munch continued to look miserable.

'So what's the problem? We have a name, we have an address. What are we waiting for? What did you want to show me?'

'This,' Munch said quietly.

He dropped his cigarette stub on the pavement, stuffed his hands into the pockets of his duffel coat and led the way around the corner of the tall building.

Bergensgata.

Something at the back of her mind.

Now, what was it . . .?

Munch stopped at the end of the pavement and nodded across the street.

And that was when she saw it.

The small, rust-red industrial building.

But for . . .

'Oh no, Holger!'

Munch turned to her and nodded.

'Do you see it now?'

'He gave them . . . this address?'

She felt the nausea rise in her throat.

'Oh shit, Holger. Are you sure?'

Munch nodded, his mouth closed.

'But it . . . it can't be true?'

'Should we have made the connection before? The photographs? The camera in front of the body?'

'Oh God.' Mia forced herself to look at the building again, although everything inside her told her not to.

The industrial building in Bjølsen.

Bergensgata 41.

It was where he had held them.

Where his workshop had been.

All those tools.

'Klaus Heming,' Munch muttered, and found another cigarette.

It dangled from his lips without him lighting it.

'The same address? That's not possible . . .'

Mia pulled herself together.

Eight years ago.

She was straight back there.

Klaus Heming.

The postman.

Photographs of his victims.

Sent to the families.

As if losing them wasn't enough.

The postman.

It had been one of the hardest cases she'd ever worked.

Eight years now, but she still couldn't open her own postbox without experiencing a tiny wave of nausea.

Hell.

'Bergensgata, Bjølsen,' Munch said, only now lighting his cigarette. 'I don't understand why I didn't see it at once.'

'But he's dead, isn't he?'

'He was the last time I checked.'

'So what . . .?' Mia glanced reluctantly across the road.

'A copycat?'

'You really think so? Heming never gave us anything, did he? Numbers? Messages. The bastard was just—'

'Just a thought,' Munch interrupted her. 'It has to mean something, don't you think?'

'What was the name of your guy?' Mia asked. 'From the cleaning company?'

'Karl Overlind.'

'And?'

'And what?'

Munch looked irritably at her.

The case had almost broken them.

Holger had been halfway through a round of family therapy. Two years after the split and he had pleaded with Marianne for a second chance. She had given in at last. All right, we'll try again. For Miriam's sake. Only to find that Munch didn't show up for the appointments.

Klaus Heming.

The postman.

With his own workshop.

And his own tools.

Shit.

'What do we do?' Mia said.

'I've asked Ludvig to check out all the Karl Overlinds we can find.' Munch furrowed his brow. 'We'll gather everyone in the office, and then we'll just have to . . .'

He stood there, looking gloomy.

'Organize a team briefing?'

'Why not?'

'Do you have a car?'

'I'm parked down the street.' Munch shook his head again, then tightened his beige duffel coat closely around his big body and flicked the half-smoked cigarette through the air towards the rust-red building.

Chapter 25

Curry had just raised the whisky glass to his lips when his mobile started to vibrate. He didn't hear it – it was on silent – it just buzzed on the table in front of him like an angry wasp. He watched his hand move through the air to press the green button but realized in time, fortunately, that he shouldn't take the call. It was only five o'clock in the afternoon and he was drunk already. *Shit.* It had been supposed to be a quick visit. Say hi to Luna. Clear his head. See if he could find something in his notes, which he had brought with him. Try to work the way Mia always worked. It was just an excuse, of course. He had been craving a drink. And it had turned into one too many.

His phone stopped vibrating at last. Then the text messages began. First one. Then another two. He picked up the mobile in the dim light and began reading them. Anette Goli. Munch. Something must have happened. Everyone was told to attend a meeting at the office. Shit. No, no way. Not now. He couldn't turn up in this state. He drained his whisky and waved Luna over to the table.

'Another one,' he muttered, and tapped the edge of his glass.

The young woman raised her eyebrows.

'Are you sure, Jon?'

'What do you mean?' he mumbled again, and became aware that he was slurring his words.

'Are you sure you're all right?'

She quickly ran her hand through his hair.

'Yeah, yeah. Just get me another one.'

Someone dropped a coin into the jukebox at the end of the room and an old country song started creeping up the brown walls. There was the sound of pool balls hitting one another. He was in one of the dingiest pubs in Oslo, so shabby that not even the hipsters would frequent it. Merchant navy tattoos. Biker jackets. Lonely souls in every corner, mumbling lips bent over filthy beer glasses. The two men in sports jackets sitting at the bar looked like they were in the wrong place. They had been glancing at him furtively and, at first, he hadn't understood why. A moment of paranoia: *Shit, were they cops? Were they watching him?* But halfway through his third whisky the answer had come to him. He was a pathetic sight as he sat there. They were looking at him out of pity. Yet another drunk with trembling hands.

Damn it.

When had that happened? He had always been able to control it, hadn't he? The odd drink, sure, but never like this. He was like a dry sponge, a tree in need of water. He had seen an advertisement in the newspaper some days ago and had read it with interest. Sollia Treatment Centre. *Do you know someone in need of help?* He dismissed the thought as Luna brought him another beer and a whisky chaser.

'Do you want me to ring Katrine? Ask her to cover my shift?'

She came closer and brushed his cheek with her warm fingers.

'Why?'

He tried to focus but wasn't able to make proper eye contact.

'So we can go back to yours? Is that what you want?'

Curry straightened up and waved her away.

'No, no, it's fine, I just . . .'

Sports jacket number one over by the bar looked towards them again.

'Sure?'

'You have customers,' he slurred, and attempted a smile.

'It's all right for me to leave. You just need to tell me, OK?'

'It's fine,' he said again, but she had already returned to the bar.

He raised the glass to his mouth and the tremors began to ease off, thank God. He felt warmer now, as the fortifying drink disappeared down his throat and settled in his stomach.

He hadn't eaten anything.

That was it.

That was the reason.

He could handle the alcohol – that wasn't the problem – it was just that he hadn't eaten anything.

Rehab? You, seriously?

He chuckled to himself and downed half his beer as one country song faded away and was followed by another.

He had just started drinking a little too early.

And he had forgotten to eat.

Sports jacket number one glanced in his direction again and Curry was tempted to challenge him, tell the guy to go to hell, but he didn't. He looked out of the window instead, and spotted a familiar face that made him cringe.

Allan Dahl.

Shit.

That bloody gossip from the Drugs Squad. There was a team briefing at the office and here he was, pissed out of his head. It wouldn't be long before news of his sorry state reached Munch. He ducked in the booth as Dahl crossed the street but, fortunately, Dahl didn't enter the pub. A car was waiting by the kerb. Allan Dahl got into it and it pulled away.

The driver?

Didn't he recognize his face from somewhere?

He trawled his memories but his brain was no longer working.

Never mind.

The TV behind the bar. News twenty-four/seven. The ballet dancer in the mountain lake. The young man at the hotel. The media talked of nothing else now. Two grave faces in the studio, then they cut to footage of Anette Goli. He didn't recognize her immediately because she was in uniform. It was a repeat of the press conference that had aired earlier today. Flashing cameras, eager microphones through the air. More footage. The talking heads again, and then it cut to something that looked like a live broadcast. He jolted when he saw where it was.

Shit.

He staggered up to the bar.

'Turn up the volume.'

'What?'

The sports jackets gave him a look, but he ignored them.

'The volume,' he mumbled again, pointing to the remote control.

Luna finally understood what he was talking about.

'We're outside Hedrum School in Larvik,' said a woman in a jacket with TV2's logo. 'Where the man who is alleged to be the police's prime suspect works.'

It ticked across the screen now, white letters against a red background.

Raymond Greger.

Damn.

Bloody local bobbies.

Someone had talked.

Munch would blow his top.

'What is it?' Luna said anxiously as Curry's mobile started to vibrate again somewhere far away.

'I need to get to work.' He sat down on one of the barstools, except it wasn't there.

He saw the floor come at him and tried to brace his fall, but his arms refused to help him.

'Are you OK?'

Her pretty face was above him now, and the sports jackets had got up as well.

'I need to get to work,' he slurred, and tried to stand up, but his legs wouldn't cooperate either.

'I'll call Katrine.'

A grey shadow.

A whispering voice.

From the bottom of the sea.

Before the country music suddenly disappeared and left him alone on the cold floor.

Chapter 26

Father Paul Malley was sitting in the confessional in St Olav's Cathedral, wondering whether it had been such a good idea after all. Morning Mass was over, and it had felt as if his congregation had been more preoccupied with getting to work. The big cathedral had fallen silent now. The sound of silence in this fine, spiritual space, which meant so much to him, washed over him. St Olav's Cathedral. He had no doubt that it was the most beautiful Catholic church in Norway. It was where he had been ordained as deacon five years ago and where he had served as a priest just six months later. After a brief stint as parish administrator in Lillehammer, he had been called back to Oslo, where he was now priest and the rector of the cathedral. Father Malley couldn't be more contented with the path God had chosen for him.

Traditionally, the Catholic Church in Norway couldn't compete with the Protestants, but this had changed over the last decade. Mostly thanks to immigration, weekly Masses were now said in Polish and Vietnamese, but the Norwegian parishioners had also increased in numbers. Now he led – ably aided by deacons and chaplains, of course – as many as three Masses every day of the week, at eight, eleven and four o'clock. And it was this timetable that he had decided to change last week. Not the Masses themselves – no, he was happy with their scheduling: morning Mass, lunchtime Mass, and Mass after work, so that his disciples could decide when in their busy working day it suited them to commune with the Lord.

Disciples – no, that was clearly wrong. Father Malley smiled to himself. Only Jesus had disciples; even so, at times it felt as if the flock were his own. It was rare for him not to recognize a face and, if he saw a stranger, he made a point of always introducing himself to the new arrival. After all, he was one of God's chosen ones, the gateway to the Lord, and it was important that he carried out his mission with closeness, not distance. And that was the reason he had decided to change the daily programme.

In the old system the confessional had been open for only thirty minutes every day, between a quarter past five and a quarter to six. There hadn't been much demand, and he was left with the feeling that it was primarily because the timing was wrong. Confess your sins in the afternoon? That just didn't feel right. Confess after a long day at work? No, he understood his parishioners, he really did. At that point all they wanted to do was see their family, get dinner on the table and maybe pray to the Lord in the comfort of their own home. And then it had come to him: why not offer confession after morning Mass? After all, the soul was at its loneliest in the darkness of the night. Surely the urge to confess your sins was at its strongest in the morning?

Father Malley didn't want to give up yet, but he was sorely tempted as he sat alone in the silence. He was hungry. He lifted his cassock and tied his shoelaces. He could smell the freshly washed floor and the scent of pine in the small confessional. Or did he detect a hint of lemon today? The delightful aroma made him smile, but he was obviously a little disappointed at how wrong he had been. Confession in the morning? Clearly, no one had the time or the need. He made up his mind to give it a few more minutes. After all, he had better things to do than sit here alone in the confined space, smelling the floor. He had been wrong, and it was time to admit it. Father Malley sighed and was gathering up his cassock in order to stand when he heard footsteps outside in the sonorous cathedral space.

Was there someone who . . .?

Had the Virgin decided to show him mercy?

He sat down quickly and made the sign of the cross.

Light, cautious steps on the hard floor, and they came right up to the confessional. Father Malley smiled broadly as someone opened the door and slipped into the small cubicle next to him.

He waited a few seconds until the new arrival had sat down before he opened the hatch.

'Hail Mary, full of grace. The Lord is with you. Blessed are you among women. Blessed is the fruit of your womb, Jesus. Holy Mary, Mother of God, pray for us sinners, now and at the hour of our death. Amen.'

He made the sign of the cross again as he heard the other person join in.

'Amen.'

It came tentatively. A young man. He could make him out behind the lattice, but he couldn't see him clearly, of course; that was the whole point of this box. Closeness, yet enough distance for it to feel safe to confess.

'Forgive me, Father, for I have sinned. It is . . . It is my first confession.'

His first confession?

Father Malley could feel his heart start to pound beneath his cassock; there was nothing quite like a new member of the flock.

'I have . . . well, I don't really know,' the young man said, clearly struggling to find a door to his soul.

'Take all the time you need, my son,' Father Malley said calmly. 'There's no one here but you and the Lord. He judges no one, and He will listen to you no matter what you wish to say to Him.'

'Thank you,' the penitent mumbled, and fell quiet again for a moment. Then it seemed as if he were steeling himself. 'I don't know if it's a sin because I'm not here about me but about something I might have witnessed.'

'Go on,' Father Malley said levelly. 'May I ask who this is about?'

'My brother,' the voice said at length.

The young man was now speaking so softly that Father Malley had to lean close to the small lattice.

'Your brother? Do you mean your actual brother, or is he a fellow parishioner?'

The young man seemed taken aback at the question but eventually answered directly.

'No, no. He's my actual brother. My big brother. We live together. There's just the two of us now. Our parents have passed.'

'I'm sorry to hear that,' Father Malley said kindly. 'And what is it that you have witnessed? Is it something you want to share with God?'

Again there was silence behind the lattice.

'Can I ask a question?'

'Of course, my son.'

'I don't even know why I'm here. I just needed someone to talk to. Perhaps it ought to be a therapist of some kind. I don't know if it's appropriate to come here. I don't want to take someone else's space or anything—'

Father Malley had never interrupted anyone during confession, and yet now he felt it was the right thing to do.

'My son. Big things or small things – it doesn't matter. If you have come here to talk, then you're welcome. You don't need to feel shame or guilt in here. You're pure and I'm happy to listen.'

'Thank you.' The young man sounded relieved.

'So, your brother? What have you witnessed?'

'I'm scared of him.'

'Scared, how?'

'He's changed. I'm scared that he . . . does things.'

'What kind of things are you talking about?'

Father Malley was becoming intrigued.

'He hardly talks to me any more. He goes out at night. He locks his door when he comes home. He won't let me into his room. I think he's hiding something in there.'

'I see. May I ask how old he is?'

'Twenty-eight.'

'And what does he do for a living?'

'Oh no, he doesn't work. He's been ill, you see.'

The stranger paused again. Father Malley could hear him squirm on the wooden seat. It was clear that the young man was feeling uncomfortable.

'Ill? In what way?'

'I don't know if I should be saying any of this, Father. I feel I'm letting him down. That I—'

'This is about you and God,' Father Malley interrupted calmly. 'You're not letting anyone down. God is father to us all.'

'No, it's no good. It was a mistake. I'm too scared.'

Father Malley was struggling to sit still.

'What are you scared of, my son?'

'He's dangerous.'

'What do you mean?'

'My brother. He's dangerous.'

'Are you afraid that he might . . . hurt you?'

There was total silence in the other cubicle now. Then Father Malley thought he could hear soft weeping.

'My son, listen to me.'

'No,' the young man said, getting up. 'I don't dare. It's too evil. I'm sorry for disturbing you, Father.'

Father Malley heard the small handle being turned and quickly made up his mind.

'Son,' he said, some gravity in his voice this time. 'I have a suggestion. Please, would you listen to it?'

That worked.

The stranger sat down hesitantly.

'I think you should go home, I do, but not before you and I and God have made a deal. It's clear that you're carrying a burden, and I can see that it's difficult for you. But you've been here today and you know who I am. Now go home and think about it, and then come back when you feel the time is right. Tomorrow, in a few days, it makes no difference, but I want us to promise one another that we will meet again. Can we do that?'

There was a long pause. Father Malley could almost hear how the young man suffered in there, how he was being pulled in different directions, but he finally opened his mouth.

'OK, Father. I'll be back. Will you be here?'

'Of course,' Father Malley said warmly. 'I'll be here for you. Every morning. I want you to know that. You come back to me when you're ready.'

Thank you.' The young man sounded relieved. 'I really appreciate that. Thank you so much.'

'Until we meet again,' Father Malley said.

'Until we meet again, Father. Thank you so much.'

Father Malley smiled to himself as the footsteps disappeared across the cathedral floor and faded away.

So it had been a good idea, after all, offering confession in the morning.

He thought of the Virgin with gratitude before he left the confessional, folded his hands across his chest and walked calmly up towards the sacristy.

Chapter 27

Gabriel Mørk had slept on the sofa in the break room and was woken by Ludvig Grønlie, who had come to get himself a cup of coffee.

'What's happening?'

'Kripos are here. Munch is doing a briefing now. I don't think you need to be there. It's pretty much the stuff we went over a few hours ago.'

'I'm on my way,' Gabriel said, stifling a yawn.

He had had such a strange dream. He had been a postman. On a sailboat. On his way to deliver a large, important letter. It said *Tove and Emilie* on the envelope. He had spied an island in the distance but, no matter how hard he tried to get the boat to sail towards it, he couldn't get any closer, he just drifted further away. A glimpse of sad faces. The letter grew bigger and bigger until it eventually dragged him into the waves.

A subtle hint, perhaps?

His mother had always been obsessed with dreams and their significance. How they meant much more than we thought they did: which images symbolized what in real life, and so on. She had become very New Age in recent years. Gabriel had never been into any of that – he would just nod and say, 'Is that right?' whenever his mother held forth about what she had experienced during the night, but now he got a feeling that his unconscious might be trying to tell him something important.

He had been working so hard these last few days he had barely had time to reply to his girlfriend's text messages. *Don't turn into Munch*, he had been thinking when the call from Goli came.

The Fraud Squad had been a calm place to work. Regular hours. A desk job. He and Tove had eaten breakfast and dinner together, curled up next to one another every night.

And now?

Well, not any more.

Gabriel rubbed the sleep from his eyes and realized that he was clammy under his collar.

The postman.

He had been a teenager in those days, but he still remembered him, of course he did.

Klaus Heming.

A man who had imprisoned his victims, played with them as though they were dolls and then sent pictures to their families.

It had been a national trauma. People had refused to believe that it was true; they had been in collective denial in front of their TV screens when the details of the gruesome case were presented to them.

Naive Norway.

It had happened right in the centre of Oslo.

No, it couldn't be true.

No one could be that cruel.

It must be somewhere in the US.

In the world out there.

Not one of ours.

Not here at home.

His mother had retreated into what he later concluded must be a kind of depression. The neighbours, too. Glum faces in the stairwell, bowed heads, people almost too scared to open their postboxes in case they had received one of his packages, in case they were about to learn that he had someone they loved as his next prisoner.

Time dulls the memory.

It had passed.

Normality slowly returned.

It's so typically Norwegian.

We forgive.

We choose to believe in goodness.

But the darkness was back now. He had seen it in every member of the team throughout the night; even Munch, who was generally a big teddy bear, had walked the corridors with a deep, dark look and a furrowed brow.

Call home.

Gabriel stifled another yawn, took a can of cola from the small fridge and stretched his stiff body as he headed down the corridor.

Munch was already by the screen when he entered the incident room.

'Gabriel Mørk,' Munch said quickly. 'Tech, databases, social media.'

Gabriel returned the nods he received from the three people he hadn't met before and found a seat at the back next to Mia.

Kripos officers. Tactical investigators. Two men and one woman. There had been muttering in the corridors throughout the night, a short but loud exchange between Anette and Munch as well, but now Munch was acting as if he thought it was a great idea that they had been joined by Kripos, even though it was Mikkelson who had organized it.

More people?

Why not?

Gabriel couldn't see what the problem was.

Were they fighting over who would be top dog?

Now?

He had almost said something but had decided against it.

'Would you say something about the name, Mia?' Munch asked.

'Karl Overlind.' Mia Krüger remained sitting. 'I was a bit slow, I'm sorry, but take away the v, the e, the r and the d.'

The three Kripos officers turned to her with raised eyebrows.

'Karl Olin . . .' The woman sounded confused.

'Karl Lion,' Mia said, seeming strangely alert despite her tired face. 'My mistake. I should have spotted it at once.'

'OK,' one of the Kripos investigators said.

Blond hair. Moustache.

A man of nondescript appearance, like these people always were.

'So yet another link to *The Brothers Lionheart*?' the second Kripos officer said.

Dark hair. Beard.

Again, he could be anyone.

Perhaps that was why they got the job. The ability to blend into any crowd without being noticed.

'Yes.' Mia nodded. 'Jonathan and Karl Lion. We weren't sure to begin with, but there's little doubt now that the killer is doing this deliberately to play with us.'

'Remind me who Karl was again,' the woman said.

'The younger brother, who survives,' Munch said. 'Jonathan saves him but dies while doing so. Young Karl lives on with the feeling that the world around him would prefer that he had died instead.'

'So there's no Karl Overlind in real life?' the blond Kripos officer asked, addressing Munch this time.

'Not in Oslo,' Ludvig Grønlie interjected, checking his notes. 'We had one in Stavanger but, as we said, no one here in Oslo, as far as we can see.'

'What about Raymond Greger?' The Kripos woman was now addressing Munch.

'We're still looking.' Munch sighed. 'It's obviously very unfortunate that some idiot from Larvik police leaked the name to the press, but never mind. Perhaps it'll prove to be a blessing in disguise. The more people who know his name, the more eyes will be looking for him. We'll have to view it like that.'

'But you're working on a theory that the murders are about Klaus Heming?'

It was the dark-haired Kripos officer this time.

'We're not sure,' Munch said, raking a hand through his beard.

Eyes on Mia again.

'The cameras pointing at the bodies,' Mia said. 'The address in Bergensgata, which he gave the cleaning company. I've been mulling it over and I think there are two ways of looking at it.'

Silence in the room now while everybody waited for her to continue.

'Either Klaus Heming is still alive—'

'Impossible,' Munch said. 'I saw the post-mortem report myself.'

'Or the killer wants us to know that he's like Heming.'

'Is like him how?' the man with the blond moustache wanted to know.

'That he compares himself to Heming.'

A new silence in the room as Mia's words sank in.

'Heming had no next of kin, did he?'

The Kripos woman this time.

'No,' Munch said. 'No wife, girlfriend, children, not even siblings.'

'And we're quite sure that he's dead?'

The man with the blond moustache again. His question lingered in the room like a gust of something that no one really wanted to deal with.

Klaus Heming.

Alive?

No, it . . .

He wasn't in favour of the death penalty, definitely not, but even so, all of Norway had drawn a collective sigh of relief when the news broke that Klaus Heming had taken his own life. Hanged himself with his own shoelaces in the psychiatric ward.

Justice.

It had felt like justice.

'According to the Norwegian government and everyone I've spoken to, Klaus Heming is dead and buried in Our Saviour's Cemetery,' Munch said.

'But—' the dark-haired Kripos officer began.

'We'll stick with theory number two,' Munch interrupted him sternly. 'The killer is using the idea of Heming to tell us something. To make it clear to us how serious he is.'

'Yes, but . . .' the blond officer continued.

Munch ignored him and flicked through the notes in front of him. He drew his hand across his forehead, suddenly looking a little lost.

'The cleaning company,' Mia prompted him.

'Yes, that's it, exactly,' Munch said. 'The mysterious Karl Overlind did casual work for them. If this escalates and there are more victims, it might be that they're picked from locations where he has worked. In one way, it looks like it, but no, it doesn't feel right.'

He pondered it.

'Perhaps the victims aren't picked that way, but somehow the locations are relevant.'

'A mountain lake and a cleaning company?' the dark-haired Kripos officer said, sounding sceptical.

'We were thinking more about the Opera,' Munch said.

'Have they ever cleaned at the Opera? We haven't checked that, have we, Holger?'

'We certainly will now,' Holger mumbled, rubbing his eyes.

'We know that Hotel Lundgren was one of their customers. Perhaps the Opera was too? Other venues? Can we prevent there being any more potential victims?'

Mia glanced at the dark-haired officer, who nodded.

'I'm on it, absolutely.'

'Great,' Munch said, looking across the room. 'Ludvig?'

'I'm working to get an artist's impression of Karl Overlind from Hotel Lundgren and the cleaning company.'

'Great. Ylva?'

Munch looked about him, but she wasn't there.

'She's asleep,' Anette Goli said. 'But I've told her to check all the CCTV. We must be able to find something. I mean, he can't be a ghost.'

'Good,' Munch said. 'Gabriel?'

'I've checked Kurt Wang's mobile and computer and Vivian Berg's social-media activity.'

Munch seemed very tired now; he had barely taken on board what Gabriel said.

'OK, good. Jon?'

Another silence.

'We haven't heard from Curry for a while,' Anette said. 'I don't know where he is. I'll try him again.'

'OK. I need a cigarette. Anette will be the coordinator. Everything we find must go through her to me, understood?'

There was nodding throughout the group as everybody got up.

Gabriel returned to his office and was about to close the door when Mia quickly slipped in behind him.

'I need your help.'

'Of course. What is it?'

'The psychiatrist. Ritter. I need access to his computer.'

'Could you be more specific?'

Mia lowered her voice and looked briefly over her shoulder.

'Everything he has. Everyone else. All his other patients. Can you do it?'

'You mean, can I hack his computer?'

'Yes.'

'I don't know,' Gabriel said, as a visibly exhausted Munch passed them, a cigarette dangling from the corner of his mouth. 'Hack Blakstad psychiatric hospital? Eh, hello? I think that breaks every rule of the Data Protection Act, plus I'll probably lose my job and go to prison for ten years, not to mention that Munch will kill me. Can't we just apply for a warrant?'

'You really think that we would get it?'

'No.'

'And it's not the hospital. I wouldn't ask you to do that.'

'It isn't? Then what is it?'

'He has a private practice up at Ullevaal Stadium. Only those patients.'

Mia smiled and tilted her head.

'Sure, but really, Mia—'

'Thank you.' Mia winked and stroked his arm.

'Will you call me when you have it?'

'Of course, but I really can't—' Gabriel began, but Mia had already taken her mobile from her leather jacket and was heading out of his office.

Chapter 28

Ellen Iversen was sitting in her car outside Morellbakken School, regretting having invited so many guests. Turning forty? Was that really something to celebrate? She glanced quickly at herself in the rear-view mirror and felt exhausted. She looked exhausted as well: bags under her eyes, her skin sallow, her eyes rather red around the rims. She looked like she hadn't slept for a week. *Shit, why had she got herself mixed up in this? After all, she was happy, wasn't she?*

She had met him in the shop. One of the teachers from the school. She hadn't thought anything of it: another day, another customer.

'How can I help you?'

'I'm looking for some dining chairs.'

'Do you have anything particular in mind?'

'Arne Jacobsen, perhaps. Do you stock those?'

'We do.'

'By the way, that chair I saw in the window, who made that?'

'I designed it myself, as it happens.'

'Did you now?'

Flattery. Was it that simple? He had liked her chairs. And the dining table she had made. And the lamps. He had bought practically her entire collection. On a teacher's salary. That had been her first thought, she had to admit it: the things she made were not cheap. But then he told her that he had inherited some money from his mother and she felt bad for having been so judgemental.

Stop it now.

Enough.

This won't end well for anyone.

150

Ellen Iversen glanced at the time on her mobile and realized that she was starting to get annoyed. It was twenty minutes to two. The dental appointment was in twenty minutes and it took at least fifteen minutes to drive there. Hadn't they agreed to meet at half past? She tried calling him. Again. Still no reply. How many messages had she sent now? Fifty? Had he replied to any of them? No.

Teenagers.

Ruben, her son, had just turned fourteen. He had pestered her for the latest, overpriced mobile, but could he be bothered to pick up when she rang? No. Did he remember to charge it so that she could get hold of him? No. Was he able to pay the bill himself, like they had agreed? No. Was he at least able to tidy his room, help out at home, take the bin out, do something so that she didn't feel like an idiot when she gave him the money? No.

She shook her head and tried his phone again, but there was still no reply.

Teenagers.

The dentist. Why couldn't he make his own way to the dentist?

'How was your dental appointment today, Ruben?'

'What appointment?'

Same conversation two weeks later.

'How was your dental appointment today, Ruben?'

'Er, what do you mean?'

I'll take time off work.

I'll pick you up from school.

You'll meet me at one thirty.

Is that clear?

Do you want me to write it on your hand?

Ellen Iversen sighed and took out a lipstick from her bag. Was that a grey hair she spied in the mirror? Another one? Did she have to go to the hairdresser's again? She had only just been. Now what was all that about? Surely she didn't care about a few grey hairs? It was OK. Completely natural. The lipstick as well. She tended not to wear lipstick. Her lips were perfectly fine as they were. She saw the irony in it. I'm sitting outside my son's school waiting to pick him up, but am I tarting myself up because *he* works there? It's not like you, Ellen. You're married. You're a happily married woman.

Well, there's happy and there's happy. Ellen Iversen got out of the car and started walking towards the school entrance. She wasn't unhappy, no, but something was vexing her. Boredom? Was it that simple?

Her entire life had become so . . . practical.

She missed the spark, the tension.

It started to rain as she walked across the playground and knocked on the school secretary's door.

'Hi, can I help you?'

'I'm looking for my son, Ruben Iversen.'

'What year is he in?'

'Year nine.'

'Let me have a look. English with Heidi Laukvang in 104.'

Ellen Iversen thanked her and walked down the corridor to the classroom. She knocked on the glass pane in the door and waved quickly. The teacher came over and opened the door a crack.

'Hi, how can I help you?'

'Is Ruben here? He has a dental appointment, only I think he has forgotten.'

Heidi Laukvang frowned.

'No, Ruben didn't come to school today.'

'He didn't?'

Ellen Iversen felt the rage surge with such force that she had to clench her teeth.

That arrogant little brat.

Skiving off?

She had had her suspicions, but even so . . .

Today?

When they were going to the dentist, and she had taken time off work?

Who did he think he was?

No, enough was enough . . .

She spotted Martin behind the glass.

'Please could I have a quick word with Martin?'

Laukvang summoned him, and the slouching teenager shuffled out into the corridor. He was barely able to keep upright.

'I thought Ruben slept over at your house last night?' Ellen Iversen said through clenched teeth.

'Yes, only he never showed up—'

'Is that true, Martin?' Ellen said, putting her hand gently on his shoulder.

Heidi Laukvang returned to the classroom, closing the door behind her.

'Yeah . . . of course it is. Why would I lie about that?'

'But Ruben and you had arranged that he would stay over at your house last night, hadn't you?'

The lad nodded.

'So that bit was true?'

'It's all true,' Martin said, throwing up his hands. 'I've no idea where he is.'

'He hasn't called you?'

'No, I swear it. You have to believe me.'

'And you've had no contact with him?'

'I've tried Facebook and texting, but he hasn't replied, so I thought that perhaps—'

'What did you think?'

'That perhaps you had changed your mind and said that he couldn't go after all. You know.'

'Know what?'

'No, I mean, you're cool, but his dad can be—'

'Thank you, Martin, I'm sorry. It's clearly not your fault.'

Ellen Iversen managed to calm herself down and produce a genuine smile this time.

'So you don't know where he is?'

'No idea,' the teenager said with a shrug.

'OK, but where do you think he might have gone if he and you – how shall I put it? – decided to take some time off school one day?'

The boy looked at her warily.

'Storo, maybe?' he muttered eventually.

'The shopping centre?'

'Yes. But I don't know for sure.'

'Thank you, Martin, if you do hear from him, please would you tell him I'm looking for him?'

'OK, Mrs I.' The gangly teenager nodded and disappeared back inside the classroom.

Storo shopping centre. God help us all.

On a school day.

He was in big trouble now.

Ellen Iversen felt the rage well up inside her again as she stomped down the corridor and half ran back through the rain to her car.

Chapter 29

By the time he reached the office block by Ullevaal Stadium, Gabriel Mørk was starting to wish that he had worn some kind of disguise. He was also wondering whether perhaps he should have told Munch about the trip after all. Typical Mia, this. Rules and regulations were for other people. Of course he should have said no and talked to his bosses. Anette, the police lawyer, for one. She would have filed a request for a warrant. Access to psychiatrist Wolfgang Ritter's files. And the response? No way. Not a chance. Of course not. And fair enough. How many patients were they talking about? Twenty years of people pouring out their hearts. A thousand? As many as two thousand? Well, there was your answer. It didn't matter how important it was. For all he knew, the judge could be one of Ritter's patients.

He felt a tingling under his collar as he entered the building and took the lift to the third floor. Shared consulting rooms. Dentist. Gynaecologist. And Ritter. A receptionist behind the glass door. Gabriel quickly scanned his surroundings. There would appear to be a shared waiting area a little further down a corridor. Some chairs. A small sofa. He took a deep breath, opened the glass door and smiled at the receptionist, an old woman with white curls and glasses far down her nose. Just act normal. Once again, he wished he had something to hide behind as he coughed lightly and headed for the waiting area. A man with a hat on his lap. A stack of magazines on the table. Posters on the walls. A stand with leaflets near one wall. He nodded to the man, who ignored him, and took his MacBook out of his bag. He sat down with it on his lap and tried to blend in. Whatever that meant.

He had debated various ways of doing it but had concluded that this was his only option. In order to get into Ritter's computer, he needed access to a network. It boiled down to three options: Ritter's home? Oh, no. Follow Ritter and hope he connected to an open network? He didn't have time for that. Ritter's private practice was his only option. He turned on the Mac and looked around quickly. The man with the hat continued to ignore him. The receptionist glanced briefly in his direction, but then looked back at her desk without appearing to think anything was amiss. And why would she? Gynaecologist. Dentist. Psychiatrist. People came and went all the time.

He waited for a few seconds.

Wi-Fi. Searching for network . . .

A long list came up. That was the problem, obviously, with being in an office building. His laptop picked up every network on the floors above and below him. He scanned the list and found the one he thought it must be. *Shared3*. A shared network for all the offices on the third floor? Excellent. Nothing could be better. Plenty of traffic. Less risk of anyone discovering that he had been in there. He opened a program he had downloaded on his way out of the office.

John the Ripper.

He wondered if people knew that these programs existed. Open access online for anyone who might be interested. The ability to hack without having any skill at all; it was just a question of turning it on. Connect it to a network, press the button and it did the work for you. It would take a little time, of course, and he began to feel nervous as the receptionist glanced at him again over the rim of her glasses.

The logo in yellow on red, with a drawing of Jack the Ripper in the background. Macabre, perhaps, but it would do the job. He was about to double-click on the icon when it occurred to him that there might be a simpler way of doing it. The Ripper was great, but no programs could do this in just a few seconds; it would take at least ten minutes.

He quickly made up his mind, put the Mac on the table and went up to the receptionist.

'Excuse me.' He cleared his throat and put on his most innocent expression. 'I'm waiting for my girlfriend. Would I be able to log on to your network?'

'Of course.' The receptionist smiled and scribbled something on a piece of paper.

Kindness personified.

'It's Shared3.'

A yellow Post-it note across the counter.

'We've had a few problems with it, but I think it's OK now.'

'Thank you so much,' Gabriel said, and almost felt a little guilty.

Such a nice woman and there he was lying right to her face.

But it couldn't be helped.

The end justifies the means, wasn't that what they said?

He walked back to the sofa as calmly as he could and entered the code.

Shared3.

JgFrPh45

At least they had had the sense to pick a password that was difficult to crack. If only they didn't give it out to just anybody.

He dismissed the thought and couldn't help smiling when the Wi-Fi icon on the screen showed him that he was logged on. The excitement from the old days returned. He couldn't put his finger on what it was, but it had always fascinated him. He didn't want to destroy anything, that had never been his thing; it was purely the knowledge that he could do it. Get into places where he shouldn't be. Use his head to outwit them. The thrill. He was startled when someone came through the door. A mother with her child. He was used to the safety of his basement; this was completely new. Suddenly he felt strangely vulnerable as he downloaded the connection protocol. Five machines were logged onto the network, including his. He wondered whether he should have made more of an effort to hide, to make himself completely invisible, but it was too late now. It would take a professional to see that he had been there, and even then it would be very difficult to find him again.

The signs on the doors.

Marit Eng, gynaecologist.

Mrit_Eng.

Gert Oversjø Vik, dentist.

Gover_V.

Wolfgang Ritter, psychiatrist.

Wolf_Ritt.

He double-clicked on John the Ripper and entered the information the program needed.

Thirty minutes later he was back in the street with his MacBook in his bag and his heart pounding under his jumper.

He glanced up at the third-floor windows one last time before pulling his hood over his head. He found Mia's number on his mobile and walked briskly towards the cab rank.

THREE

Chapter 30

Early morning. Not even six o'clock yet. It might be the most boring route in the world, but thirty-two-year-old Jonas Olsen was behind the wheel and grinning from ear to ear. Thinking about last night still made him feel warm all over. He could barely believe it was true. That it had gone so well.

It seemed almost unreal.

April. Spring was really happening now; it was still dark outside, but even so he could just about make out the green leaves on the trees. Normally it made him sad, triggering a feeling of loneliness. It always seemed to get worse at this time of the year. Funny when you thought about it. Surely it should be the other way round and the dark winter should be the hardest time of the year? But no, he didn't think it was like that. He had read about it in an article online. There were more than six hundred suicides in Norway every year, and most of them occurred in the spring. He hadn't completely understood the article, but it was about how, during the winter, everyone was depressed and you only realized you were different when the sun came out. Once it got light outside, you discovered that the darkness was inside you, or something along those lines.

Jonas Olsen leaned forwards and turned on the radio as dawn began to break around him. The route that included Kjelsås, Grefsen and Maridalen was regarded as a job for older security guards. Great if you were the lazy type; it was a cushy job with only a few places to check and quite a distance between them, at least where he was going. Camp Skar. A former army camp, now a further-education facility. It always felt like an unnecessary trip.

It was far from town. Off the beaten track. He couldn't imagine that anyone would be bothered to go all the way out there to nick pens and a few outdated computers. But this was what he was paid to do and today it didn't matter anyway. He found a radio station that was playing a song he liked and sat humming to himself and drumming the steering wheel with happy fingers.

He had given up hope of getting himself a girlfriend. He was too odd. Too shy. Too awkward. He cringed when he remembered his schooldays. His budding attempts to attract the opposite sex had been pretty disastrous. He had spent most of his time at home, his nose in books. But then? No, he could hardly believe it. Linda. A temp in reception. The usual one had been on maternity leave. There had been something about her, something he couldn't put his finger on. And he had known that her time with the company would come to an end, that the usual receptionist would soon be back. He had wanted to stop the calendar in the break room. Stop the days from passing. As long as time stood still, she wouldn't be going anywhere.

But then, quite out of the blue, she had said:

Fancy going for a coffee sometime?

He had been so flustered he had barely been able to open his mouth.

Yes . . . why not?

Or dinner, if you fancy it? On Saturday? Is that convenient? Or perhaps you're busy?

Busy? No, absolutely not. Saturday would be great.

And then her smiling eyes looked at him as she slid a note across the counter. Her phone number.

In the car afterwards he almost couldn't get the key in the ignition. His initial joy, however, was soon replaced by his usual fear. It just came over him; it was like drowning slowly in ice-cold water. No, no, no. What had he just let himself in for? It would be a disaster. He had to cancel. What would he say? She would start to hate him when she realized how stupid he was. Nervous. Frightened. Unable to string a sentence together. Only nonsense came out of his mouth. He had heard it so many times before: the laughter, the whispering behind his back when he passed someone in the school corridor, or at work, for that matter.

But she had liked him.

'I really like you, Jonas.'

Linda.

'Do you fancy doing something tomorrow as well?'

He couldn't believe his luck.

And as if the world had decided to send him yet another little token of joy, the sun suddenly rose and erased the darkness from the forests around Lake Maridalen. Another morning in the kingdom of spring. Strong, glorious colours all around him now. What a difference it made, he thought to himself as he drove towards the car park at Camp Skar. Nature in the dark. Nature in the light. Life on your own. Life with . . . He didn't dare complete that last thought. They had only had one evening together. The chance that he would make a fool of himself again was great. It was about not having expectations. Enjoying the moment, this lovely feeling in his body.

From the Camp Skar car park you could walk through the forest up to Øyungen. Feed the ducks. Perhaps put up a tent for the night and see the fish wake up. A car was parked, its engine running, and he felt himself getting irritated. Was it really necessary? Why couldn't people be considerate? Jonas Olsen got out of his car and went to check the gate into the camp itself. The chain was still in place. The lock was untouched. He scanned the camp area. No sign that anything was amiss. Everything was as it should be. He was about to get back in his car and drive off when he spotted something that made him stop in his tracks. The parked car with its engine idling. It was . . . odd, wasn't it? He took a few hesitant steps across the car park. After all, he was the security guard, it was his responsibility to make sure everything was as it should be. Now what was that . . .?

He didn't see it properly until he was very close, the smoke seeping out from the open window on the passenger side. Not a lot, just a thin, grey column, but it was there.

'Hello?'

Jonas Olsen knocked on the windscreen, but there was no one in the car.

'You shouldn't leave the engine idling. Please would you . . .?'

He couldn't see anyone inside who could answer him. How strange. He knocked on the windscreen yet again.

'Hello?'

There was no reply. He was a security guard. Was it his responsibility? Yes, it was. Olsen knocked on the windscreen a third time before opening the door and seeing two empty seats filled only by grey smoke.

'Hello?'

That was when he saw it.

Something was burning.

On the back seat.

A doll's house?

'Is anyone here?'

Jonas Olsen could feel it coming now. The fear. The dark water. He quickly withdrew his head from the car, retreated a little, his fingers on the buttons of the radio attached to his breast pocket.

'Central, this is JO, route KGM. I'm at Skar. Do you copy, over?'

He retreated further from the car; he could feel his heart hammering under his shirt.

'Central? This is JO. Can you hear me? Over?'

He hadn't seen it before, but he saw it now. The small gap. The boot. It wasn't closed properly.

He didn't want to, but he couldn't help himself.

No.

Jonas Olsen was practically watching his hands from the outside. It was as if it weren't him who opened the boot.

'Central? Do you . . .?'

There was a boy in the boot.

'Central?'

His eyes wide open.

'Hello?'

And then it became too much for him.

By the time the voice from the radio finally replied, Jonas Olsen had passed out.

Chapter 31

Mia Krüger was woken up by her mobile. She hadn't even realized she had been asleep. She had been tossing and turning on her mattress all night, getting up several times. There were images of Vivian Berg on her retina. The delicate, white body half covered by the dark water. Karoline Berg's desperate eyes, an ocean of grief that had yet to surface. The writing on the wall. The terror in Kurt Wang's eyes.

Come, Mia, come.

Images of her sister running through a field of yellow wheat. Again.

They had left her alone for a long time, but now they were back.

She had gone into the room which held the cardboard boxes. Considered opening one of them.

Mia's album.

Have a look at her grandmother.

That usually made her feel better.

Granny, who had howled at the moon at night, whom the neighbours had called a witch, but to Mia she was the only person who had seemed normal in this crazy world.

You're not listening, are you?

To yourself?

I thought you were going on holiday?

You know that you're not well, don't you, Mia?

Dark thoughts at night and a body that wouldn't stop shaking. In the end she had been tempted to go to Lorry; it was open until 3 a.m.

Two beers and a Jägermeister would get her to sleep.

Or Charlie Brun's transvestite club in Tøyen, which was always open.

Some pills just so she could rest.

She had managed to resist, evidently, without quite knowing how. The time on the mobile on her bedside table showed just after seven thirty.

'Yes?'

'Awake?'

It was Anette Goli.

The brilliant police lawyer was driven like no one Mia had ever met; and seemed to need neither food nor sleep in order to exist.

'I am now.' Mia yawned. 'What's happening?'

'We have another one.'

'Where?' Mia got up from her bed and realized that she was already dressed.

She had got dressed, hadn't she?

So that she could nip down to Charlie's in Tøyen?

Damn.

'Maridalen,' Anette said. 'In a boot. Looks like another stolen car.'

'A girl?' Mia asked as she headed to the bathroom.

'No. A teenage boy.'

Had she gone down there?

No, she had gone to bed sober.

It had been close, but she had resisted.

'Needle mark to his chest.'

Mia quickly splashed cold water on her face and felt herself slowly returning to life.

'Fourteen years old. Ruben Iversen.'

'We know his identity already?'

'Yes. His clothes were found in a bag in the front of the car. Mobile and bank card. He was lying undressed in the boot, wearing only swimming trunks.'

'Say that again?'

Mia took her jacket from the peg.

'He was lying almost naked in the boot, wearing only swimming trunks, and there was something burning inside the car.'

'What was burning?' Mia asked, putting on her shoes.

'A doll's house. Are you on your way?'

'Where are you?'

'Maridalen. The car park outside Camp Skar.'

'Has his family been told?'

'His mother reported him missing late last night. We're trying to contact her now.'

'I'm on my way,' Mia said, and rang off.

Chapter 32

The journalist Erik Rønning was standing some distance behind the cordons up at Camp Skar, regretting not having put on a thick jumper under his camel coat. Spring? It was supposed to be spring, wasn't it? Well, clearly not. He didn't normally work on stories like this one. He was a feature journalist and most comfortable indoors, preferably in front of the fireplace, back in his flat in Frogner, ideally with a glass of brandy and a cigar by the keyboard. Rønning had won a SKUP award some years ago for a series of articles about the homeless in Oslo, although he had rarely stepped outside to write it. That was the reason he now found himself up here. His boss, Geir Grung, editor of *Aftenposten*, had summoned him to his office some months ago, to find out if the rumours going round the office were true, if he had really just sent a photographer out to take pictures of destitute people and then invented the stories. Were the interviews fake? Were those tear-jerking stories which the paper had run as a series in its weekend edition pure fiction?

Erik Rønning had neither admitted nor denied anything – that was his specialty. He could have been a politician if he had been interested in other people, but he wasn't. The twenty-seven-year-old reporter knew perfectly well that if it came out that he had made up the stories, it would seriously damage the newspaper's credibility, so he hadn't worried all that much. He had banked on them wanting to save their own skins, and he had been right. Nevertheless, as a punishment of sorts, he had been dispatched to cover stories like this. Bodies turning up in mountain lakes dressed in ballet costumes. In sleazy hotel rooms. Was there a link? The police had said no, but you couldn't trust them. Now there was a third body in a car park at one of Oslo's most popular beauty spots. They hadn't been told who it was yet. A junkie, presumably. Someone killed by a jealous boyfriend. Erik Rønning didn't really care.

Unless . . .

He tightened the coat around himself. He should have worn a woolly hat too. He had thought about it at home in front of the mirror but had decided against it. Hats always ruined his hair. He had opted for a thin, grey cashmere jumper with a roll-neck which went well with the camel coat and a pair of brown shearling gloves that were short enough to show off the Breitling watch he had recently bought himself. It was the one advertised by Leonardo DiCaprio. He was rather proud of it. Fortunately, he had been smart enough to wear a pair of thin, wool long johns under his suit trousers. After all, he lived in Norway. For now. Maybe Monaco one day? It had been at the back of his mind when he bought some shares some months earlier. Across the street, he saw a small woman get out of a car.

Mia Krüger?

That would mean Munch was up here too. The big guns? Perhaps the body in the car park wasn't just some drunk who had frozen to death or a student who had taken their own life. Mia and Munch? First the ballet dancer, then the jazz musician and now this? Were the three deaths connected after all? Rønning smiled to himself and felt mildly intrigued. Was there really a . . . *serial killer* at large? Now that would be worth covering. A proper story for a journalist of his calibre. Maybe his luck hadn't deserted him after all. Rønning ploughed his way through the crowd and found Ole Lund, a reporter from *VG*.

'What's happening?' Rønning asked.

'We don't know very much yet,' Lund said, 'but there's a rumour that it's a teenage boy.'

Rønning took out a packet of cigarettes from his pocket.

'A student?'

'Don't know,' Lund said. 'It might be.'

'What's happening?' a new arrival wanted to know.

She was from *Dagbladet*. Vibeke something or other. Rønning couldn't remember exactly, but she was a babe. He had tried it on once with her at the hotel bar of the Grand. He had liked the way her dress looked from the back.

'A student,' Rønning lied. 'Suicide, most likely.'

'Really?' Vibeke the babe said. 'They didn't say anything about that on the police radio.'

'What did they say, then?' Lund asked eagerly.

'That he was fourteen years old.' Vibeke looked at Rønning. 'Isn't that what you have?'

'No idea. I've only just arrived.' Rønning grinned and lit his cigarette.

'Wanker.'

Vibeke shook her head and walked on towards the cordons.

'Do we have a name yet?'

'Ruben Iversen, they say, but it hasn't been confirmed yet. Fourteen years old.'

Another new arrival, a young man with glasses.

He was from *Dagsavisen*.

'Who told you that?' Lund asked.

'I have my sources.' The young man grinned.

Rønning took out his mobile and sent a quick text message.

Victim probably a Ruben Iversen, fourteen. Find his school? Send someone there? Family, fellow students, teachers, etc.?

Suddenly the crowd of reporters stirred.

'Goli!'

'Anette!'

A black car heading out through the cordons. Flashlights and eager hands, panting tongues, shoulders carrying TV cameras.

'Goli!'

'Anette!'

'Is this connected to the other victims?'

Bingo.

So he wasn't alone in thinking there was a possible link.

Great. A challenge. Time to show them what he was made of. He wasn't prepared to stand here prostituting himself like just another hack.

Erik Rønning retreated to a place where he had a better view. He might be lazy, but he wasn't stupid. There was a reason why he had been the person closest to the editor. Grung's favourite. He had enjoyed it, he really had, and it had hurt a little, the look Grung had given him when the old newspaperman realized that his award-winning star pupil had hoodwinked them all.

Get over it. Now was not the time to sulk. Now was the time to think outside the box. He walked a little further away to see if there was another route up to the car park. Munch and Mia, oh yes, they were pros, but the rest of them? The police officers attending the scene? Nothing but jumped-up shopping-centre security guards, the lot of them. Rønning doubted they had managed to secure the crime scene already. The sheep were still clustered in front of the cordons and looking up the road.

Amateurs.

They would never get anywhere.

Erik Rønning smiled to himself, discarded his cigarette and started walking.

Chapter 33

Mia arrived at the car park outside Camp Skar and was met by a worried-looking Munch.

'Haven't you slept?'

'What do you mean?'

'You look like shit.'

'Gee, thanks,' Mia said.

'Sorry, I didn't mean it like that. Is everything OK?'

'I'm fine. What have we got?'

'Another car.' Munch nodded to the far end of the car park. 'Stolen. Belongs to a family from Økern. They came back from holiday and their car was gone.'

'And why are we standing here?'

'The pathologist wanted to finish first.'

'Is that the new one?'

Mia indicated a dark-haired woman, standing next to the open boot, who was gesturing eagerly and issuing orders to her team.

'Lillian Lund,' Munch said.

'Hard taskmaster?'

'She seems OK.'

'Anette said there was a needle mark?'

'Yes.'

Mia could see another camera on a tripod facing the back of the car.

'Have you checked the camera?'

'Thirteen,' Munch said quietly.

Mia swore.

'Does that mean anything to you?'

He turned to her and lit his cigarette.

'Four, seven, thirteen?'

'You're the mathematician,' Mia said, rubbing the sleep from her eyes.

'Lottery numbers?' Munch said.

'What do you mean?'

'Oh, nothing. It just bugs me.'

'What does?'

'Well, everything, to be honest. These numbers. I hate that he plays games with us.

'Who found him?' Mia asked.

'A security guard. Olsen. He's in shock. I've sent him down to police headquarters. Anette will interview him.'

'A long time ago?'

'A couple of hours. Why?'

Mia nodded in the direction of the road.

'The press got here very quickly.'

Munch shrugged.

'The sharks can smell blood,' Mia remarked.

A crime-scene technician crossed the car park. She pulled down her face mask and sighed at Munch.

'Did you approve of this?'

'What do you mean?'

'That we won't get access until the pathologist has finished?'

'She probably won't be long.'

'Yes, but—'

'Have you searched the forest?' Mia asked.

'Oh yes, we're doing that now. And we were about to start on the car.'

'You carry on working the area around here,' Munch said. 'We'll get access once they've finished.'

The crime-scene technician shook her head and muttered something they couldn't hear as she put her face mask back on and went to join the other technicians.

'So, a doll's house?' Mia said eagerly.

'According to the security guard. It was burning on the back seat when he arrived.'

'Have you had a look at it?'

'Yes, I think it might be very easy to trace.'

'Why?'

'It looks handmade. Not something mass-produced from Toys "R" Us. I've seen quite a few of those.'

He flashed a smile.

Of course he had. Marion, his granddaughter, had him wrapped around her little finger.

'Are we looking into it?'

'Grønlie is on it.'

Munch took a drag on his cigarette as another technician came towards them. He was about to open his mouth, but Munch beat him to it.

'We'll wait,' he said brusquely. 'They won't be long.'

'Have we cordoned off the whole area?' Mia asked.

'I hope so. And, by the way, Ludvig didn't find anything. He asked me to tell you.'

'About what?'

'You asked him to look up cases involving a burning house? Number forty-seven? Seventy-four?'

'Yes?'

'Nothing, as far as he could see.'

'Worth a try.'

'It was a good idea,' Munch said.

'It was an obvious lead to follow. *The Brothers Lionheart*? Their house burned down.'

'It looks like you're onto something.' Munch nodded towards the car.

'So it was still burning when the security guard arrived?'

'I think so. Like I said just now, he's very shaken up.'

'So what are we talking in terms of timing?'

'He believes he arrived here around a quarter past six.'

'And how long would something like that burn for?'

'It's impossible to say. If the killer used an accelerant, a couple of hours, perhaps?'

'So somewhere between three and four in the morning?'

'Might even have been later.'

'Right under our noses.'

'I know,' Munch said, stubbing out his cigarette.

'How did he get here?'

'No idea.'

'Any buses this early?'

'No, the first one has just driven past.'

'So he has his own car?'

'It's possible.' Munch looked like he was considering lighting another cigarette straightaway, but decided against it. 'But then who drove that one?'

'He brought a bicycle?'

Munch shrugged.

'There may be some cameras further down the road. There's a Co-op not far away. We're on it.'

'Naked?'

'Dressed only in swimming trunks. His clothes were in a bag in the front of the car.'

'He undressed him up here? But, Holger, it—'

'I know.' Munch decided to light another cigarette after all. 'I'm starting to think you might be wrong.'

'About what?'

'That the victims are randomly chosen. I think he knows exactly who he wants. And what he wants to do to them.'

Munch frowned and his expression grew darker as his mobile rang. He shook his head and walked away to answer it.

'Mia Krüger?'

'Yes?'

A dark-haired woman the same age as Munch came towards her, pulled down her face mask and shook Mia's hand.

'Lillian Lund. Pathologist. We're ready to take him away now.'

'Was it you who examined Vivian Berg?'

'Yes.' Lund nodded.

'And Kurt Wang?'

'Yes.'

'Are you sure we're talking about the same man?'

'The method is the same, yes. I don't know if it's a man. Evidence of a needle to the heart. No obvious injuries anywhere, something I find strange.'

'Why?'

Lund gave her a puzzled look.

'No evidence of a struggle? No resistance? Why not? Isn't that strange? Not on any of them?'

'No nail scrapings?'

The pathologist shrugged.

'We have to check in the lab to be a hundred per cent sure, but not as far as I can see. It's just like the others.'

'Any injuries to his mouth?'

'Was it you who first spotted it?'

'Yes.'

'Good catch. We have the same thing here. Under the tape this time.'

'Tape?'

'Yes. Over his mouth. Do you want to have a look at him before we take the body away?'

'Yes, please,' Mia said reluctantly as Munch came rushing back.

'Holger.' Lillian Lund smiled.

'Hello, Lillian.'

'What's going on?' Mia asked.

'They've found him,' Munch whispered eagerly.

'Who?'

'Raymond Greger. He's on his way up from Larvik.'

'Do you want me to interview him?'

'We'll do it together. And there's no hurry. He's asked for a lawyer.'

'Shall we?' Lillian Lund asked again, pulling her face mask back on.

'Absolutely.' Mia followed the new pathologist over to the open boot.

Chapter 34

Munch was standing behind the mirror with Anette Goli; he had decided to let Mia start the interview on her own after all. Sometimes it was more effective. Less intimidating. They were short of evidence against Raymond Greger. They had only hearsay to work with, an old story from Bodø. No forensic evidence. No witnesses who could place him near any of the crime scenes. No mobile-phone traffic, no pings from any masts. There was a family connection, but that wouldn't help them much if they couldn't get him to talk.

He turned to Anette as Mia began the interview.

'Please would you turn up the volume?'

Anette nodded and adjusted the button on the panel by the door.

'The time is twelve fourteen,' Mia said, leaning closer to the microphone. 'First interview of Raymond Greger. Present in the room are Raymond Greger, his lawyer Albert H. Wiik, and homicide investigator Mia Krüger.'

Her voice was soft and gentle. She had smiled nicely to both men as they entered. Well played. He had seen her lose control several times in there, letting her emotions take over, but not today.

'Let me start by putting on record that my client is baffled as to why you're holding him,' the lawyer said, adjusting the knot in his tie. 'If you're not going to charge him, we ask that he's released immediately, and may I also advise you that we're considering suing the police for releasing my client's name to the press.'

Lawyers.

Munch shook his head and undid a button on his coat.

'We're not charging your client with anything,' Mia said, still with a hint of a smile on her lips. 'And I'm sorry about what happened. As I'm sure you're aware, we have forty-eight hours now to question your client, but we obviously hope to get this sorted out as quickly as possible. If you work with us, tell us what we need to know, you'll soon be able to leave. That's how we look at it. You were at your cabin, right? On sick leave?'

Greger glanced briefly at his lawyer, who nodded.

'Recently, it started to get to me. The workload, I mean. I wanted to carry on teaching, I really did, but my doctor thought I needed a few weeks' peace and quiet.'

'I understand,' Mia said. 'And that's why you didn't know what had happened, your niece being found dead?'

'No, sadly not,' Greger said, appearing genuinely upset. 'It's not my cabin. It belongs to a friend who lets me use it. He likes simple living, as they call it, no Internet or television, just power from a small solar panel.'

'So when the police turned up, you were completely surprised?'

A neighbour in the archipelago had called them after Greger's name had been broadcast on TV2.

'That's right, I knew nothing. Poor girl. What a tragedy.'

'You're Karoline Berg's brother, is that right?' Mia said, flicking through the notes in front of her.

Again, it was just an act. She knew precisely what they contained.

'Stepbrother. My mother remarried. Her father. And I was part of the deal, so to speak.'

'What happened to the two girls in 2007?' Mia said out of the blue.

Greger jumped in his chair. His lawyer also looked taken aback. Munch enjoyed the sight and took off his coat.

'What do you mean?' Greger asked.

Idiot.

Munch shook his head.

Greger must have known they would find out about this, even if it wasn't on the official record.

'I advise my client not to—' the lawyer began, but the middle-aged teacher stopped him.

178

He took off his glasses and rubbed his face.

'It wasn't me,' Greger said at length, shaking his head slightly.

'Not you?' Mia flicked through her notes again. 'Camilla was seven. Hege was nine. You picked them both up when they were on their way home from school, on separate occasions. You persuaded them to get into your car. You held them captive for several hours. You like little girls, don't you? You like to play?'

'I really think—' the lawyer mumbled, slightly red-faced now, but Greger interrupted him again.

'It wasn't me,' he said in a surly voice.

'You didn't do it?'

'Yes, but it wasn't *me*.'

'I think you're going to have to explain that.' Mia put her friendly smile back on. 'Two young girls? Taken during the day, against their will?'

'Listen,' Greger said. 'I was . . . I had . . . It was a bad time for me. My wife had left me. She lied about everything, do you understand? The judge sided with her. She got full custody of my daughter, and I haven't seen my daughter since.'

Mia glanced almost imperceptibly over her shoulder towards the mirror.

'He has a daughter?' Munch said, addressing Anette.

'Sorry, we didn't know. My mistake,' his colleague mumbled. 'I'm on it.'

She took her mobile quickly out of her pocket and left the room.

'Your daughter?' Mia asked. 'How old are you?'

'Fifty-seven.'

'And how old is she?'

'Her name is Nina,' Greger said. 'She'll turn thirteen this summer.'

'So in 2007 she was seven years old?'

Munch could hear the irritation in Mia's voice and he understood her only too well. She had gone into the interview without being fully briefed. It was on his head. It was amateurish.

'So what—?' Mia began, but Greger cut her off.

'I'm not excusing what I did. It was wrong of me. I know it. Of course I do, it was just, well, like I said, it was a difficult time.

Everything I had built was suddenly snatched away from under my feet. Nina, she was, she is, yes . . .'

Greger took off his glasses again and wiped away something that would appear to be a tear.

Play-acting?

Munch couldn't tell from where he was standing.

'So you missed your daughter and decided to find someone else to play with?' Mia said, her voice devoid of warmth now.

'Yes.' Greger stared down at the table.

The lawyer sat with his jaw hanging open and didn't say a word. He looked as if he felt just as wrong-footed as Mia.

'You do know what this sounds like, don't you? Two little girls? Kidnapped?'

'I know. *I know*. I wasn't myself. I didn't hurt them. We just—' Greger buried his head in his hands.

'Played?' Mia said archly.

'I actually asked to be punished,' Greger said quickly. 'I didn't want to hurt them. Lock me up, that's what I told them.'

The door opened again and Anette appeared at Holger's side.

'A daughter. Aged thirteen. His wife divorced him in 2007, got full custody, no visitation rights. Accusations of physical and mental abuse on both sides. I tried to find the judge who dealt with the case, but I couldn't get hold of her, I just spoke to someone in the archives.'

Mia glanced at the mirror again.

Help me out here, would you?

'So why didn't you get to see Nina?'

'My wife lied,' was all Greger said.

'About what?'

The lawyer had given up now; he was just leaning back in his chair and watching it all play out.

'She said I treated them both badly.'

'And did you?'

'Listen, I'm not perfect, I'm not, but then again . . .'

Munch's phone pinged. He quickly took it out of his coat. A text message from Ludvig Grønlie.

We have found where the doll's house came from! Send Curry?

'What do we do?' Anette said. 'Is he our guy?'

Munch shook his head.

'We don't have anything on him, do we?'

'There's nothing to suggest it right now.'

'No contact with Vivian?'

'No, not according to Gabriel.'

'Get her out of there,' Munch said, and shook his head.

Mia threw up her hands when she entered the room behind the mirror.

'What the hell, Holger?'

'I know,' Munch said. 'Blame me.'

'Do you want me to explore his relationship to Karoline Berg?'

'Do you think it's him?'

'We don't have anything on him, do we?' Mia said with a look at Anette, who shook her head.

'But even so, playing with little girls?' Mia went on, looking at Greger through the mirror.

'We'll keep him,' Munch said. 'See if we can get him to say anything else, but I think we can cross him off the list for now.'

'Do you want me to do it?' Anette offered.

'You don't want me to continue?' Mia asked.

'We've found the shop where the doll's house was bought,' Munch said.

'So quickly?'

'Yes. Ludvig found it. Curry is on his way. You go with him, all right?'

'Is Curry at the office?'

'I think so.'

'Creepy guy,' Mia said, still facing the interview room.

'Anette will deal with it,' Munch said, gesturing to Goli, who nodded. 'Will you call me afterwards?'

'OK,' Mia mumbled, and glanced through the mirror one last time before zipping up her leather jacket and leaving the room.

Chapter 35

Erik Rønning had ordered tempura crayfish with kimchi and tarragon and a glass of Petit Chablis, but what he really fancied was a cola. He had a slight hangover after over-indulging last night, but a cola obviously wouldn't do, not here at the legendary Grand Café. The waiter disappeared with the menus and Rønning could feel that he had butterflies in his stomach. He was back in his boss's good books. That hadn't taken long.

Grung, on the other side of the table, could barely contain his excitement.

'So where is it?' the old newspaper editor whispered, looking around the room.

Erik Rønning smiled and tapped his mobile.

'And it shows the whole killing?' Grung said, wide-eyed.

Rønning nodded.

Oh, how fortune had favoured him.

He had had a flash of inspiration by the crime scene, hadn't he?

'May I see it?' Grung asked nervously, reaching for the mobile.

'Not here,' Rønning said. He winked and quickly slipped his mobile back into the pocket of his suit jacket.

Fortunately, he had been home to change first. The trip up to Maridalen was proving lucrative, but his outfit had paid the price. Would he be seen at the Grand with mud stains on his trousers and dirt on his shoes? Not bloody likely. He had chosen a dark-blue Ermenegildo Zegna suit with a simple, black Armani tie and brown Mantellassi shoes.

'So tell me again,' Grung said as the waiter brought their food.

Grung had wanted to see the footage immediately; of course he had.

What are you telling me?

Come to the office, now!

But Rønning had had other plans. The office? Out of the question. Before he knew it the others would want a piece of the action. Silje Olsen. Or that idiot Ellingsrud. No, he wanted Grung to himself. And why not make an occasion of it? Celebrate? After all, he had had to spend his whole morning in the middle of nowhere with a bunch of idiots. Rønning raised the wine glass to his lips and felt almost drunk already. Grung hadn't looked at him like this for a long time. His boss was bordering on awestruck.

'OK, so here I am standing by the cordons,' Rønning began.

Grung had heard most of the story on the phone yet he listened patiently. His phone continued to vibrate in his pocket, but the editor showed no signs of wanting to answer it.

'They were all there, you know – Lund, Vikhammer, the usual suspects.'

'Of course.' Grung nodded.

'But then I had an idea,' Rønning went on, pleased with himself. 'Why hang around down there? We can't see anything here. And they couldn't possibly have managed to cordon off the whole area already, could they?'

'Good thinking.' Grung smiled.

'It was, wasn't it? The message had gone out about an hour earlier. A surprising number of people had turned up, I must say. NRK and TV2 had outside-broadcasting vans there already.'

'The ballet dancer.' Grung prodded his steak tartare. 'Everyone is on full alert.'

'It turned out that they had actually cordoned off the whole area,' Rønning said with a shrug. 'Still, the trip up there turned out not to be wasted after all. It was almost as if . . .'

He took another sip of his wine and tapped his nose.

'. . . you know when it just feels meant to be?'

Grung reached for his glass now.

'I don't quite understand,' the editor said, unable to rein in his impatience any longer. 'What did any of this have to do with prostitutes?'

'I think I need to start at the beginning,' Rønning said, signalling for another glass of wine. 'I recognized a face up there. In the crowd.'

'Among the onlookers?'

'I could tell from his face straightaway,' Rønning said triumphantly. 'He wasn't there to watch. He was there to take down the cameras.'

Grung shook his head.

'Cameras? Slow down, will you? What did you say his name was?'

'Pål Amundsen.'

'And who is he?'

'Do you remember one of our old stories?' Rønning said in a low voice, leaning across the table. 'That tip-off we got some months ago about men looking for prostitutes, picking up girls in the city centre and driving up there in order to, well, complete their business?'

'You put up cameras?' Grung said sternly, and wrinkled his nose.

'No, no, not officially, but yes, I was tipped off about a guy who might be able to help me with such things. Have you heard of those motion-sensitive cameras people use for making wildlife films?'

'You know we can't do that, Erik. What the hell were you thinking?' Grung shook his head irritably.

'And we didn't. There's nothing that can link me to this guy Amundsen. Relax.'

His boss looked as if he were about to say something, but he decided against it.

'We dropped the story,' Rønning went on. 'We didn't get any results, as you remember, but I, yes, I could see it in his face . . .'

'He hadn't taken the cameras down?'

'Dirty old sod.' Rønning laughed drily. 'He was probably hoping to get something he could enjoy in private. I could tell straightaway. The man reeked of guilty conscience. It took me only ten seconds to get him to admit it.'

The waiter returned with more wine. Rønning let him finish pouring before he continued his story.

'Twenty minutes later we're in the guy's home, on his computer, and there it was.'

He grinned and put his mobile back on the table.

'Unbelievable,' Grung said, shaking his head. 'And you've seen it?'

'Of course.'

'And it . . . well?'

'The whole show.'

'Right from? Do you see the . . .?'

'Everything.'

'May I?'

Rønning smiled, sliding his mobile across the white tablecloth.

'Be my guest.'

'Thank you.' Grung slipped the mobile into the pocket of his suit jacket.

'My pleasure.'

Grung looked around the room nervously, as if he were half expecting the security service to have followed them or an armed response unit to storm the café, before getting up carefully and calmly making his way to the Gents.

Chapter 36

Curry was already waiting by the lift when Mia arrived. The compact bulldog pressed the button and clutched his head.

'What a bloody awful day,' he mumbled.

'Yes, for all of us,' Mia said, looking at him. 'Where have you been? Have you been drinking?'

'Just a quick one, that's all. Nothing to worry about.'

Curry gave her a look, which she interpreted as meaning that he didn't want her to probe.

His shoulders were hunched. He had dark rings around his eyes. There was something in his gaze she couldn't fathom.

Mia couldn't help being reminded of what Wold had told her in Lorry, but she didn't have the energy to go there now. Three murders. It would have to wait.

'Where are we going?' she asked when they had reached the underground car park.

'Kalle's Toys in Torshov,' Curry said, and clicked to unlock the car.

'I'll drive,' Mia said, taking the keys from him.

'Are you sure?' the bulldog barked.

'Yes,' Mia said, getting behind the wheel.

Curry sighed and put on his seatbelt. It looked as if keeping his head on his shoulders was something of a challenge.

'How did we find the place so soon?' Mia asked as she drove out of the car park.

'Grønlie emailed everyone he could find. Toyshops, importers, wholesalers – absolutely everyone – and received a reply almost immediately that Kalle might be our man.'

'You've already talked to him?'

186

'Sort of. He was asleep. He said he would come over as soon as he could.'

'The shop wasn't open?'

Curry sighed again and clutched his head in his hands.

'Eh, no, it appears to be some sort of alternative place. Proper toys. Handmade. Using materials that don't harm poor kids in developing nations, that kind of thing. Unconventional opening hours. But he's on his way there now.'

Curry produced a box of chewing tobacco from his inside pocket and, after a few attempts, managed to slip a wad under his lip.

'You wouldn't happen to have some water, would you?'

Mia had to laugh.

'What do you mean? Do I look as if I have a tap in my pocket?'

'What the hell would I know?' Curry clutched his head again. 'These days everyone carries a water bottle. Oh God, I feel awful.'

'Sorry,' Mia said, taking the route to Torshov.

'Paracetamol, then?'

'No.' She smiled compassionately. 'Would you like me to stop somewhere?'

'Could you?'

Mia pulled up at the kerb and waited while Curry ran into a 7-Eleven.

'Thank you,' the bulldog mumbled when he was back in the car and had washed down four pills with practically a whole bottle of water.

Mia thought it wisest to stay quiet for the rest of the drive.

They parked and had just noticed a homemade shop sign when a middle-aged man with long hair and a big beard came strolling down the pavement towards them.

'Are you the guy who rang?' the man said, producing a clattering bunch of keys from a large anorak.

'Jon Larsen,' Curry said, shaking his hand.

'Thomas Lange,' the bearded man said. 'But everyone calls me Big Tom.'

'So you're not called Kalle?' Mia asked, nodding to the sign above the door.

The man smiled.

'*Kalle's Climbing Tree*? Ever heard of that? The children's TV show?'

'Is he the one who lies in a tree all day watching the clouds?' Curry said.

'That's me.' Lange smiled and unlocked the door.

Curry sang the theme tune, missing practically every single note. 'You don't remember it? Kalle sits in the tree pondering life while his grandad sits on the grass reading the newspaper.'

'Yes, sure,' Mia nodded.

'Amazing programme. Why does all the good stuff come from Sweden? *Emil. Tjorven, Bill Bergson, Master Detective, The White Stone*. Can you think of any good Norwegian children's stuff? Nope, everything is from Sweden.'

'Shall we?' Mia said, indicating the open door.

'And there's *Ronia the Robber's Daughter* and *Alfie Atkins*—'

'After you,' Mia said, following Curry over the threshold.

'Don't I know you from somewhere?' Lange said once they were inside the shop.

'Mia Krüger,' Mia said, holding out her hand.

'Ah.' Lange took off his long, colourful scarf and put it on the counter. 'I thought there was something familiar about you. Can I offer you anything?'

'No, thank you.'

'We just need to know if you sold this,' Curry said, producing a photograph from his inside pocket.

Lange took it and scrunched up his nose.

'That's my work, yes, but who burned my house down?'

'That's what we're trying to find out,' Mia said. 'Have you sold many of them?'

'No. I only sold one, and that was it. Not much demand for quality goods these days. It's a pity. I made quite a few. I thought they were nice.'

Lange returned the photograph to Curry and disappeared into the back room. He reappeared with a white doll's house, an exact copy of the one they had found at Camp Skar.

'Bamboo,' Lange said, placing the house on the counter. 'The world's most environmentally friendly material. It grows quickly. Uses few resources. We should make everything from bamboo. I believe that somewhere—'

'Did you sell it recently?' Mia asked.

'I did, as it happens. To a very nice girl. She looked a bit like you, come to think of it, only blonde.'

'A girl?' Mia said.

'Girl, woman, lady, I don't know what you prefer, but a young woman. Twenty-something, I would guess. Very nice. We chatted for a long time. She wanted to travel to Goa. Have you ever been there?'

'Angola?' Curry said.

'No, Goa, India. Or paradise, as I call it. I usually spend the winter there, but not this year, sadly. Business hasn't been as good as it usually is. Everybody wants shiny plastic now, don't they? We no longer care, do we, that the planet goes to hell in a hand-cart and all our children will inherit is rubbish? And now these fighter planes? I ask you. Hundreds of millions of kroner. People are starving, kids don't have school books, old people sit in their nappies with no one looking after them in care homes, and yet we can afford to buy American fighter planes. This country will go to the dogs if we don't get someone with their head screwed on properly at the helm soon.'

'A young woman?' Mia repeated, sounding surprised and glancing at Curry, who shrugged.

'Yes, it was a good day.' Lange smiled. 'It's nice when people appreciate your craftsmanship, isn't it? Handmade, right down to the smallest detail.'

'You wouldn't happen to have a camera in here, would you?' Mia asked.

'Big Brother watching you? No, thanks.'

'Or a mailing list or something? You didn't get her name?' Curry said.

'A mailing list?' Lange snorted with contempt. 'Intrude on people's privacy? Do you know how much global capital knows

189

about you these days? Big data? Do you think they want your phone number and your email so that they can be helpful? Shorter working days? Better pay? Oh no, buy more, buy more. Of course I don't have a mailing list. But I have a small jar where people who want to can make a donation to a school in Rwanda. My girlfriend and I sponsor it. Can either of you spare some change for the people who need it the most?'

Curry looked at the almost empty jar Lange was holding out to him, and reluctantly produced a fifty-krone note from his trouser pocket.

'Anything else you can tell us about this girl?' Mia said.

'Well, like I said, she was very nice. Twenty-something, perhaps, slim. Long hair, green baseball cap, looked like a chav, as you would say if you lived up west.'

Lange smiled ironically and gestured westwards.

'But no name or address?'

'Big Brother,' Lange said again, and shook his head. 'I wouldn't dream of it.'

'Please would you give us a call if she turns up again?' Mia took out a business card from her inside pocket.

'Of course. Are you sure you don't want anything? I have really good Darjeeling and honey directly from Svartlamon in Trondheim. The real deal. It'll warm you up, seeing as spring is keeping us waiting.' The bearded man nodded to the foggy cityscape outside. 'Nature is fighting back. Soon we'll all freeze to solid ice and I guess that's what we deserve.'

'Would you mind if we sent a sketch artist up here?'

'An artist? To do my picture?' Lange winked.

'To produce a sketch of the woman who bought the doll's house?'

'I knew that,' he said. 'Again, twenty-something, long blonde hair, green baseball cap, but you're welcome to send one along. I'm always here. Or nearby, at any rate.'

'Great. Thank you for your help so far. Please call if you remember anything else,' Mia said, and followed Curry out of the shop.

She stopped for a moment on the damp pavement.

'There, there and there,' she said, and pointed.

'What?'

'Cameras. Please would you get the footage?'

'Me?'

'Yes.'

'Where are you going?'

'I have to check something. Are you all right?'

'Why?'

'Are you?'

'Yes, yes, don't worry about it.' The compact bulldog coughed and replaced his chewing tobacco with a fresh piece. 'I'll take a cab back. See you at the office.'

'Fine,' Mia said, and got in behind the wheel.

Chapter 37

Gabriel Mørk was sitting in his office, wondering what to do with the enormous amount of information now on his MacBook when Ylva popped her head round the door.

'It's an emergency.'

'What?'

'Everyone is on their way.'

'Why?'

'A reporter from *Aftenposten* thinks he has the murder on film.'

'What? Which one?'

'Ruben Iversen.'

'You're kidding me? How is that possible?'

'Don't ask me,' Ylva said, and disappeared down the corridor.

'OK, before we begin,' Munch said when they were all gathered in the incident room, 'we've just received the artist's sketches of the young man who worked for the cleaning company and was seen at Hotel Lundgren.'

'Karl Overlind?' Curry said.

Munch nodded.

'Before we watch the footage,' he said, once he had finally got the screen behind him to work, 'I think it's important that we take a look at them.'

Two artist's sketches. There was murmuring across the room when those gathered saw them.

'That's not the same man,' Ylva burst out. Gabriel had been thinking the exact same thing. The two sketches were completely different. The man on the left had short hair. The man on the right had a Beatles-style haircut with a fringe and he was wearing glasses.

'Are we looking for two different men?' Curry wondered out loud. 'Are they in it together?'

'I have a hunch he's messing with us,' said Mia, who was leaning against the back wall.

'Why?' Ylva asked.

'Just look at this.' Mia pointed to the screen. 'The eyes. Same size. The noses, quite similar. The chins, practically identical. These are features that are hard to camouflage, don't you think?'

She turned to the others.

'So he disguises himself?' Goli said.

'I think so,' Mia said.

'Seriously?' Curry exclaimed.

'I agree with Mia,' Munch said. 'And that's why we've been having problems finding him on the CCTV footage.'

'He changes his appearance?'

'If it's the same man,' Munch said, nodding towards the screen, 'then, yes, we have reason to think so. And if he changes his face like that, who knows what else he might change. Up until now—'

'Everything has been a diversion tactic,' Mia interrupted him. 'The contamination of the crime scenes. The wrong address. It's as if he wants to send us on a wild-goose chase, waste our resources.'

'While he carries out the next phase of his plan?' Goli wondered out loud.

'It certainly feels like it,' Mia said.

There was murmuring across the room again.

'So there will be more?' Ylva said anxiously.

'Listen,' Munch said. 'We can't be sure of any of it, it's just a theory, but it's worth bearing in mind.'

'What if they're siblings?' Gabriel ventured cautiously.

He rarely opened his mouth during such meetings, but this time he couldn't help himself.

Munch looked at Mia.

'I mean,' Gabriel went on, 'both sketches might be right, but there are two of them? As you just said, those are features that aren't easy to disguise – the eyes, the nose – maybe there are two of them and they really do look like one another?'

He could feel his face getting a little flushed as Munch turned to Mia again.

'It's possible,' Mia said at length. 'In fact, that's not a bad idea. Good thinking, Gabriel.'

'Brothers?' Munch said.

It was clear that their bosses had only just seen the sketches themselves and hadn't had time to discuss them.

'But back to the film,' Curry said again. 'Is it true?'

'Is what true?' Munch said.

'That it shows the murder? The one up at Camp Skar? How did they get it? It sounds unlikely. I mean, how could they know that a murder would happen right there? Were they tipped off or something?'

Munch looked at Anette.

'The newspaper insists on protecting its sources,' Goli said irritably, 'but I've put a couple of our lawyers on it. I can't imagine that their refusal to cooperate will impress the judge, but it'll take time to resolve.'

'Will we be charging anyone from the newspaper?' Grønlie asked.

'We could always try that.' Anette glanced at Munch. 'But there are still procedures that we have to follow.'

'There's nothing to indicate that they knew about the murder in advance,' Munch said. 'I know Grung. I trust him. He's a good man. I can't imagine he would sanction something like this. Of course he wouldn't. If they had known a crime would be committed, they would have informed us.'

'But what about the journalist?' Curry said. 'Erik Rønning? He's a prat, isn't he? A show-off? Did he discover it? Or is he the victim of a hoax?'

'Like I said, finding out where that film is from is going to be an uphill struggle,' Munch went on. 'In the meantime, we should just be grateful that we have it – regardless of how callous that might sound. It's not every day we get such detailed evidence of a crime, where we get to be a fly on the wall.'

'So what are we waiting for?' Curry said, flinging out his arms.

He seemed under the influence of something and was slurring his words a little.

'Completely different appearance again.' Munch nodded towards the screen once more. 'And the reason I want you to keep that in mind is that this time we see the killer.'

'He's on the film?' Ylva said.

'Yes,' Munch nodded. 'But this time—'

'Don't tell me that he has changed his appearance again.' Curry sighed impatiently, oblivious to the fact that he had just hit the nail on the head.

Munch looked at Mia and then at Anette.

'He has?' Curry said, surprised. 'We have a third man?'

'The film isn't top quality, so I'm going to talk you through it before I show it to you,' Munch said. 'The camera is mounted quite far away, it's a little grainy, but we can still see things that I regard as useful. The car arrives. Ruben Iversen is sitting in the back. We can't see the driver's face. Iversen gets out of the car and starts undressing right away. He puts his clothes in a bag and stands for a moment, naked, in the car park before putting on his swimming trunks and going behind the car. And it's at that point—'

'The killer gets out, takes the bag, places it on the ground in front of the car, and that's when we see him,' Goli said.

'And?' Curry said.

'Third disguise,' Munch said gravely. 'A moustache this time.'

'Surely we're not dealing with three brothers?' Curry again slurred his words. 'He's obviously some kind of – well, what do you call them, impersonator? Can't you just show us the film?'

'Damn,' Mia said, still not wholly present in the room.

'What is it?' Munch asked.

'Can you get me a screenshot?' Mia said eagerly, addressing Ludvig Grønlie.

'Of what?'

'The face? On the film?'

'Yes, of course. Do you mean right now?'

'Yes,' Mia said, putting on her jacket.

'Sure.' Grønlie nodded.

'I need to check something,' Mia mumbled, and followed the grey-haired investigator out of the room.

Chapter 38

Susanne Hval was waiting at the foot of the steps to the National Theatre, between the statues of Bjørnstjerne Bjørnson and Henrik Ibsen, when Mia came rushing across the square. She had mixed feelings about this meeting. It was good to see her again; of course it was. Her old friend from Åsgårdstrand. But Susanne had always felt that their friendship was mostly on Mia's terms. She had tried to contact her for months without any success. Mia Krüger. Homicide investigator. It felt as if her friend always had priorities other than her.

And then Mia had called her out of the blue.

I need a favour.

Stupid, perhaps, that she was like this. Saying yes to everything, to everyone, all the time, although it wasn't always reciprocated. Well, it was too late now. It had sounded important.

'Hi, Susanne,' Mia said, and gave her a long hug. 'I'm sorry I didn't get back to you, but you know how it is.'

'Forget it.' Susanne smiled. 'Everything all right with you?'

Mia looked very well. The last time they had met Mia had looked like a ghost. Skinny. Exhausted. Like a skeleton on the verge of collapse. She was a changed woman now. Herself again. Almost like the old days.

'I'm fine,' Mia said. 'Did you manage it? Did you get hold of him?'

'We have several,' Susanne smiled. 'But I got hold of one of them, yes. Is it really that urgent?'

'It's an ongoing investigation,' Mia said, glancing up the steps. 'Something I need to confirm. Or disprove. Is he in there?'

'Why don't we go for coffee first?' Susanne said. 'Or lunch? I'm between production meetings today. We're doing *The Metamorphosis* by Franz Kafka. Gísli Örn Garðarsson? The Icelandic director? It sold out last year and is being revived on the main stage this autumn.'

'I'm not hungry,' Mia said. She seemed to be preoccupied. 'So he knows about this?' Mia pointed to her own face. 'Masks. How you change your appearance, and so on?'

'Sure.' Susanne smiled and swallowed her disappointment. 'In here people can do most things.'

She ushered her friend up the steps.

'He understands that this is police work?' Mia asked as they made their way to the wardrobe department.

'Well, I've only had a quick word with him,' Susanne said, grabbing the door handle. 'If you had given me a little more warning—'

'He can't tell anyone about what I'm going to show him,' Mia interrupted her. 'OK? And neither can you.'

'Understood.' Susanne nodded and opened the door.

Ishmael was sitting at his worktable and got up when they entered.

'Mia Krüger,' Susanne said. 'This is . . .'

'Ishmael Malik,' the young make-up artist said, unable to hide the fact that he knew who she was.

It happened all the time. Mia Krüger. Homicide investigator. Celebrity. Susanne had always been a little jealous – no, not that, not jealous, mostly proud, but yes, a little envious, she had to admit.

'Hi, Ishmael.' Mia nodded and took something from her bag. 'Sorry to spring this on you, but I need you to look at something for me. Do you mind?'

'Of course not.' The young Afghan smiled and cleared his table. 'Happy to help. What is it?'

'These three,' Mia said, placing three pieces of paper on the table.

Two drawings and one photograph.

Susanne was no fool. She realized immediately that the pictures related to the murders the whole country was talking about. It was everywhere now, no matter which TV channel you watched. She had seen the press conferences. The blonde police lawyer, who kept brushing aside all the questions, seemed calm. *No need to worry.* Despite that, everyone at the theatre and everyone else she met had started looking over their shoulders. A serial killer at large in Oslo? Even her mother had called earlier today. *Are you quite sure you don't want to come home to Åsgårdstrand, Susanne?*

'What am I looking at?'

'This needs to stay between us, understand?' Mia placed her hand on his shoulder for a moment.

Ishmael nodded, still gazing at her as if he couldn't quite believe she was really here.

'Is this the same man?' Mia wanted to know.

'It's hard to say.' Ishmael studied the three images on the table in front of him. 'Two of them are sketches, so yes, but . . .'

He held up the photograph to the light.

'The fringe,' Mia pointed. 'And as you can see, we have a moustache here and a pair of spectacles there. Is it that simple? To change your appearance, I mean?'

'Like I said,' Ishmael added, putting down the photograph, 'these two are just sketches, but no, I don't think it would be that difficult.'

'No?'

'Absolutely not. It could be the same man, if that's what you're asking me.'

'We've been wondering if we're dealing with several people here.'

'I see,' Ishmael said, still with flushed cheeks. 'Now that's possible, of course. But I would have said not.'

'Are you sure?'

'Like I said, it's possible. And again, these two are just sketches, but there are structural similarities here.'

'Yes? You mean the nose?'

'No, no,' the young man said, warming to his subject now. 'Some things are easy to change. The nose, the forehead, the ears, the chin – I can turn you into a fat old man in a matter of hours, say. What you need to look out for is the eyes.'

'Go on?'

'Look at them. You can't change the eyes.'

'So you're saying it's the same man?'

'Again—'

'Except that two of the pictures are only sketches. Yes, I know.'

Susanne could feel it returning now, the sting of disappointment. She had been trying to contact Mia for so long. Not for any special reason, just so that they could hang out together.

She dismissed the feeling and plastered on a smile. But there was no need; neither Mia nor Ishmael was aware that she was still in the room.

'So, as far as you're concerned,' Mia said, 'this is the same man?'

Ishmael studied the images again.

'I would say so, yes. Look. These lines. Here. If the sketch artist or the people who told him what to draw have got this right, then that's a feature which is hard to disguise.'

Susanne rummaged around in her pocket for her mobile, just to have something to do.

'Thank you so much. Ishmael, was it?'

'Yes, and you're welcome.' The young man nodded, an almost bashful smile at the corners of his mouth.

'You're a brick, Susanne.'

And she was off. Mia gave her a quick hug and zipped up her leather jacket.

'Don't mention it. How about lunch or maybe a drink one evening?'

'Absolutely. I'll call you,' Mia said, and gave her a peck on the cheek before running down the steps and disappearing into the crowd in front of the Spikersuppa ice-skating rink.

Chapter 39

Erik Rønning had just had his make-up done and thought he looked rather orange, but he had been on TV before and knew that it was necessary. It would make him look better in the studio lights. He had arrived at TV2's studios just over half an hour ago and been welcomed like – well, like a hero, he would say. Ever since the news of the film from Camp Skar had come out his phone hadn't stopped ringing. He had briefly discussed with Grung whether he should talk exclusively to *Aftenposten*, but they had agreed that the newspaper would receive even more exposure if he agreed to be interviewed by other media outlets, and Erik Rønning didn't mind in the least. In addition to all the newspapers, he had done the rounds of the TV stations, NRK TV and NRK Dagsnytt 18, and had now been invited to be the expert commentator on TV2's news channel. Open doors. Smiles in the corridors. Eager hands pressing his.

Welcome, Erik.

Brilliant, what a scoop.

How did you do it?

Delighted you could make it!

How about a drink later tonight?

'Are we ready in here?'

An elegantly dressed young woman with a set of headphones around her neck popped her head in and looked at him with warm, curious eyes.

'I'm good to go,' Erik said with a nod.

'Great,' the producer said. 'We'll have a commercial break soon, then you're on straight afterwards.'

'I'll be there. I just need the little boys' room.' Rønning winked and got up from the make-up chair.

The woman with the headset giggled.

'Now don't get lost.'

'I'll try not to.' Rønning smiled and went to the Gents.

Mi-mi-mi-mi.

Mo-mo-mo-mo.

Ki-ka-ko-ka-ki-ko.

Vrr-brr-vrr-brr-vrr.

He did the voice warm-ups he had been taught during his year at Romerike Adult Education College back when he thought he wanted to become an actor and looked in the mirror again. He had brought out the big guns. He wore the dark-blue suit he had had made specially at Brooks Brothers in Manhattan. It was a little tight now – he didn't work out as often as he should – but he still looked very good in it. A simple, red Armani tie and Salvatore Ferragamo shoes. He checked that he didn't have anything in his teeth, washed his hands and returned to Make-up. Back to the big mirror now; an important politician, that was what he looked like. Maybe that would suit him, Erik Rønning, Member of Parliament? Erik Rønning, Foreign Minister? He laughed to himself and ran his hand over his hair, smoothing his fringe to the left. He liked it like that, hard and smooth. He thought of his hopeless colleagues who saw themselves as artists, who wore their hair long and pretty much turned up for work in Crocs, if you could believe it. Erik Rønning, Prime Minister? He ran his hand over the red tie and tightened the knot slightly. Red ties. The colour always worn by conservative politicians when they wanted to be seen as warm and trust-worthy, as having a heart. Rønning had briefly dated a stylist who worked for a PR company and that had been her job. To make the idiots look human. Likeable on TV. Because that was what it was all about, wasn't it?

'You're on after the commercial break. Are you ready?'

'I was born ready.' Rønning winked again and followed the producer into the studio.

He nodded to the news anchors and sat down in the chair indicated. The studio was small. It could almost have been his living room. It never ceased to surprise him, the reality of television compared to your expectations.

'Microphone check,' a young man said. He, too, was wearing a headset.

Erik Rønning said, 'One-two,' and got a thumbs-up.

'Twenty seconds,' the producer said as Rønning turned to the female news anchor and got a smile back.

Now what was her name again?

Mossfjord?

Mossberg?

Veronica Mossberg, that was it.

He had seen her at various events and she had never deigned to look at him, but today was different.

'Ten seconds.' The producer held up a hand in the air. 'Five.'

Outstretched fingers. She closed them one after the other in silence as the commercial break came to an end.

Vignette. Imposing and action-packed. The producer closed her hand and swung her arm through the air towards Mossberg.

'Welcome back,' the pretty presenter said. 'Tonight we have a guest in the studio, Erik Rønning from *Aftenposten*. He's the journalist who managed to capture this morning's terrible incident on film, but first a summary for those of you who have just joined us. Roger?'

Rønning cleared his throat and took a sip of water. Roger. A short guy with a reddish, speckled face, Rønning had played poker with him some months ago and hadn't taken to him.

'Is there a serial killer at large in Oslo?' Roger asked in a grave, slightly affected voice. 'That's the question everyone in Norway is asking after the third victim in just a few days was found this morning in the boot of a car in Maridalen. Lars Ellingsen has the story.'

The producer appeared and indicated that they were off air. A pre-recorded report was shown on a small screen behind them, the volume on mute. Rønning had seen it earlier today.

Vivian Berg, the ballet dancer. Blah-blah. Kurt Wang, the jazz musician. Found in a hotel. Ruben Iversen, the teenager. Same killer? Blah-blah. Was this really necessary? When they had him right here? He shook his head and hoped they would notice. Took another sip of water from the glass in front of him and cleaned his teeth with his tongue.

The producer stepped out beside the camera and repeated her countdown as the report neared its ending.

Three-two . . .

'As I was just saying, we have Erik Rønning from *Aftenposten* with us. Welcome,' Roger said, nodding towards him when they were live again.

'Thank you,' Rønning said solemnly.

'You've managed to get hold of footage which shows the actual murder of Ruben Iversen, is that correct?'

'That's correct.' Rønning nodded and folded his hands in front of him.

'Tell us how that happened? Was it coincidence? Or was it, as some unpleasant rumours have it, that the killer gave you advance notice?'

'I would like to deny this immediately, Roger.' Rønning cleared his throat. 'The footage is the result of another feature we were working on, and yes, whether we were extremely skilful or just lucky, that's for others to decide, but fortunately, fortunately . . .'

At this point, he looked straight into the camera in order to make contact with the viewers.

'. . . we were able to produce evidence which has been absolutely essential for the police in this case. They are very grateful.'

'Is it the case . . . ?'

It was Veronica Mossberg now, in a completely different tone of voice. She sounded impressed, whereas Roger was simply envious. Wasn't that always the case in this business? Rønning couldn't help chuckling to himself when the female news anchor practically ate him up with her eyes.

'. . . that the footage will never be shown to the public? Don't you think that we all have a right to know?'

'Well, Veronica,' Erik Rønning said, and cleared his throat again, 'as you know, in cases such as this one it's important to protect not just the victims and their families but also – well, the whole nation, I would say.'

'But—' Roger began.

'This is . . .' Rønning smiled and made a conciliatory gesture '. . . obviously not something which I alone, or we from *Aftenposten*'s editorial team, have decided. We're working very closely with the police and the authorities, as you would expect, and when you think about it, Roger, the answer is clear, isn't it? Would you like your son's murder streamed live on national television? I don't think so.'

Rønning winked at Mossberg and took another sip of water.

'But what do you think,' Mossberg continued, 'of the prospect that we who live in a small country like Norway may now be dealing with a second serial killer in less than a year? What's going on in our country?'

'Well, Veronica,' Rønning began, but was interrupted by Roger pressing a finger against his ear plug.

'We have to interrupt you there. We're going live to Stockholm, to Sweden's most highly regarded expert in this field, the crime novelist and professor of criminology Joakim Persson. Professor Persson, welcome and thank you for joining us.'

The bearded, middle-aged Swede appeared on the screen in front of them.

'My pleasure.'

Rønning shook his head and drank some more water.

What was this?

Was it really necessary?

He had better things to do than be messed about by TV2.

In fact, he had many other things to do; they should count themselves lucky he had even deigned to come here. And then to cut him off for a bloody Swede?

'Here in Norway,' Roger continued, 'we're not used to this phenomenon, a thrill killer who appears to pick his victims at random. Are you, as an expert, able to tell us what that means?'

A thrill killer? Someone who kills for pleasure?

Where the hell did he get that expression from?

It sounded really professional, damn it.

'Well, it's early days yet,' Persson said. 'And I don't know what the police know, so I can only go on the information in the media, but saying that, I have no doubt that we're now faced with a perpetrator who could kill again at any time.'

'And what do you base that on?' Roger asked.

'It all seems planned,' Persson continued. 'The method is the same and the crime scenes appear staged. It's typical in such cases that . . .'

Rønning zoned out from the suit and wondered whether to start using the term as well.

Thrill killer?

He would be posting a new article online in a few hours. They were updating the story constantly now; the paper wrote of little else. They had people in the field talking to the boy's school, to his neighbours and friends. Ruben Iversen was said to have been on his way to a sleepover at a friend's house but had disappeared after filling up his moped at a petrol station.

What was the link between the two first victims and a teenage boy? No one had found one so far and yet it seemed as if all the murders were planned, although the police continued to deny it.

The Swede held forth about serial killers and why they did the things they did.

Ted Bundy.

David Berkowitz.

Jeffrey Dahmer.

Edmund Kemper.

Blah-blah.

Rønning had heard it all before.

Was it possible that Roger had actually stumbled across something? That the killer really did pick his victims at random? Killed people just because . . . he felt like it?

Now that was something.

He could use that.

Because there was no link, was there? It was just brutal chance.

Was there a sexual motive?

Random killings?

A thrill killer?

He had to phone Grung. Rønning could feel an itching under his collar when the Swede signed off and the producer with the headset raised her hand to count them down to another commercial break.

Chapter 40

Munch had just stepped out on to the smoking balcony when his mobile rang. He checked the display and decided to take the call.

'Hi, Marianne, how are you?'

'I could ask you the same.'

He had heard that voice so many times before. His ex-wife trying not to sound anxious, and failing.

'Busy,' Munch said. 'And Miriam?'

'Better and better. The physiotherapist said yesterday how well she was doing.'

'Great.' Munch lit a cigarette while he waited for what he presumed was coming.

'So you've heard?' his ex-wife said.

'Heard what?'

'About the wedding?'

'She called me.' Munch slightly regretted having answered the call. Just then, the clouds that had lain across the town all day finally allowed the sun to peek out for a moment.

He didn't really have time for this. Not now.

'What do you think?' Marianne asked, the touch of anxiety still in her voice.

'I don't see anything wrong with it.'

'Have you met him?'

'No, have you?'

'Briefly.'

'And?'

He could see Grønlie waving to him through the window. Munch nodded and pointed to his mobile.

208

'Well, he seems like a nice enough guy. I think she calls him Ziggy. They didn't come in, stayed outside the front door. I don't think she wants Marion to meet him yet. And I can see her point, but even so, getting married? So soon? It's a bit quick, don't you think?'

'Yes,' Munch said. He wasn't really listening.

He had to redirect his troops, restructure his investigation. They had to prioritize the Iversen family. And follow up the interviews with the people who knew Kurt Wang. The jazz band. Something about the Portuguese man having a criminal record.

'. . . do we do?' Marianne said.

'Pardon?'

'Do we think it's OK?'

'Well, she's an adult.' Grønlie appeared at Munch's window again. 'I don't see that it's any of our business.'

'But what about our grandchild?' His ex-wife's voice had taken on a slightly different tone now. 'We should be able to give advice, don't you think?'

'Marion is tough. Surely the most important thing is that Miriam is happy, don't you agree? After everything she's been through?'

Grønlie disappeared again, as did the sun. This spring that refused to come. Munch tightened his duffel coat around him as a beeping told him he had a call waiting.

'But that's my point. How long has it been? Less than six months? She still can't talk properly. And it's a big decision. Don't you think she ought to wait until she's well? Until she's herself again?'

'I have to run,' Munch said as the beeping stopped. 'I'm in the middle of something. I've promised I'll walk her up the aisle. I think she deserves it.'

There was silence for a moment while his ex-wife seemed to brace herself to say something more.

'So do we need to worry?'

'Like I said, if that's her choice, then I'll support her.'

'No, that's not what I meant. What we're seeing on TV – I'm guessing that's what's keeping you busy right now. All these terrible murders?'

'You know I can't talk about my work, Marianne.'

'I know, Holger, but even so?'

'There's nothing to worry about,' Munch said, hoping he had managed to sound convincing as the beeping started again.

'You would give me a hint, wouldn't you? Do we need to be careful? Should I take Marion out of school?'

'No, no,' Munch said as Grønlie popped his head out on the balcony.

'Please could you take a call from Mia? I've tried to tell her that you're on another call.'

'Two seconds,' Munch whispered.

'Are you there, Holger?'

'Listen, Marianne.' Munch took another drag on his cigarette. 'How about we let Miriam decide for herself, eh? And, as far as the other matter is concerned, just carry on with your life as normal. There's no need to worry. OK? I have to go now. I'll call you later. Give them both my love.'

He ended the call before she had a chance to say anything else and pressed to speak to Mia.

'Have you stopped taking my calls?' Mia snapped at him.

'I'm here now.'

'I think it's the same man.'

'Based on what?'

'I spoke to a make-up artist at the theatre. He says that the eyes are the same.'

'Based on the sketch artist's drawings?'

'And the still from the footage. They could be brothers,' Mia said, without listening to him. '*The Brothers Lionheart*, and all that, but yes, I think we should continue working on the theory that it's the same man.'

'OK. Will you be coming down to the office?'

'No, I need time to think. I might turn off my phone. It's annoying me. Might get a new one.'

'Keep it switched on, would you?' Munch said, but Mia had already gone.

Munch was stubbing out his cigarette in the overflowing ashtray when his mobile rang again, an unknown number this time.

'Munch speaking.'

'Hello, Holger,' a friendly voice said. 'It's Lillian Lund. The forensic pathologist. I hope it's all right to ring you directly?'

'Yes, of course. What can I do for you?'

'Two things, really. Number one, I wanted to tell you that the cause of death is the same for all three victims. Ethylene glycol. A slightly higher dose this time, but there's no doubt. I found nothing on the body. No signs of a struggle, nothing under the nails – well, you know the score. It was the same with Ruben Iversen as it was with Vivian Berg and the young man at the hotel.'

'OK.' Munch lit another cigarette. 'Have you found out anything about the sores on their mouths?'

'Yes.' Lund hesitated. 'I've just had the test results.'

'And?'

'That's the second thing. I think I know,' Lund said quietly.

'Know what?'

'Why they didn't resist.'

'Really?'

'Listen.' Lund cleared her throat. 'I know this isn't strictly by the book, but do you think we could meet? I would prefer not to do this over the phone.'

'Absolutely.'

'How about a bite to eat? I was going to meet a friend, but she called it off at the last minute. I've booked a table, but I don't like eating alone. Would you like to join me?'

'Of course. When and where?'

'Do you eat sushi?'

'Not really, but I can make an exception.'

'Great,' Lund said warmly. 'Alex Sushi? On Tjuvholmen? In just under an hour?'

'I'll see you there,' Munch said, and rang off.

Chapter 41

Lillian Lund was already seated at a window table but got up when he arrived. He barely recognized her in civilian clothing. Gone were the surgical cap and mask. Her dark hair flowed loosely over her shoulders, and her white scrubs had been replaced with a yellow dress with a short, grey wool jacket on top.

'Hello, Holger.' She smiled. 'I'm sorry about this.'

'Oh, don't be,' Munch said, unbuttoning his duffel coat.

'Well, it's just that, eating on my own? I can't do it. It feels all wrong. Do you feel the same way?'

'I can't say that I do.' Munch smiled and sat down. 'When it comes to food, some people might say that I have too few problems.'

He laughed as a Japanese waitress discreetly approached their table and placed two menus in front of them.

'I can recommend the maki.' Lund smiled again. 'You haven't eaten maki if you haven't tried the one they do here. I mean, everyone says so, but I didn't know why until the first time I tried it. Are you allergic to anything?'

'What? No.' Munch coughed and got the feeling that it might have been wise to have nipped home first. Was he wearing yesterday's clothes or those from two days ago? He was afraid to raise his arms in case the smell disturbed the other diners. Well, it couldn't be helped. He was keen to find out what was so sensitive that she couldn't tell him on the phone.

'Do you mind if I order for both of us?' Lund said, summoning the waitress.

'Absolutely not.'

212

'Great.' Lund said something to the young woman without looking at the menu.

'So?' Munch said when they were alone by themselves at the table once more.

Lund placed her napkin on her lap. 'Again, I'm sorry, but I thought it was best if we did this in person.'

'And, like I said, it's quite all right,' Munch said, trying not to seem too eager.

'The tests,' Lund said, taking a sip of the water in front of her. 'To be quite honest, it was exactly as I had feared.'

'Go on.'

'Or no, that's wrong, "feared" may be too strong a word, but yes, they . . .' She glanced out of the window. 'Scopolamine, hyoscyamine and atropine,' the attractive pathologist said, and caught his eye again.

'And what does that mean?'

'Have you heard of scopolamine before?'

'It doesn't ring any bells.'

'Devil's tongue.'

'Devil's . . .?'

'Tongue.' Lund nodded. 'That's what they call it. Scopolamine. There's a lot of uncertainty about this substance. Many people regard it as a myth.'

She cleared her throat before continuing.

'There have been reports, mainly from South and Latin America, of criminals using it to gain complete control over their victims. It's not on the list of banned substances in Norway, but it's said to be so strong that it takes effect immediately. A tiny prick is enough – skin contact, for example, through a quick handshake.'

'And that's what we're dealing with here?'

'Yes. There's no doubt, unfortunately.'

'Scolo—?'

'Scopolamine. In Norway the substance is found in a plant called a thorn apple. You can find it in the botanical gardens, if you know what you're looking for, of course. It induces extreme

213

hypnotic intoxication. Strange, really, that it isn't better known. Or good, I guess you could say.'

She proffered him another quick glance and another smile.

'And you can find it here in Norway?'

'Yes, easily. Some people grow it, I believe.'

'And you think . . .?'

'The blisters to their mouths,' Lund said, leaning towards him. 'Because of them I double-checked the samples. I think they might have had a reaction.'

'Seriously?'

'Yes, it's a toxin, don't forget. It's potentially lethal, if you overdose on it. I think we're dealing with direct exposure here and that someone must have – well, squirted it into their mouths or something. I don't know.'

'Why haven't I heard of it before?'

'Like I said, it's not terribly well known.' Lund tucked her hair behind her ear. 'The effect is said to be a form of brain paralysis. There are very few scientific studies, but there are examples of people meeting strangers in the street and then acting as if they're in a trance the next moment. The attacker – or whatever term you would use – then follows the victim home. Clears out their house. Walks the victim to a cashpoint, empties their bank account. People have woken up several days later without any of their possessions or any recollection of what happened to them. Do you understand? It's as if they were awake but not present at all? It's really creepy.'

'And you're quite sure that's what they were given?'

'Yes.'

'Why?'

'The mixture. Scopolamine, hyoscyamine and atropine. It's datura. Or thorn apple in Norwegian.'

'But, for God's sake,' Munch mumbled, 'why would anyone want to grow this?'

'To get high,' Lund said, and raised her eyebrows. 'It has almost the same hallucinogenic properties as LSD, only it's much stronger.'

'But why . . .?'

214

'Why didn't I want to tell you that over the phone?'

'That wasn't what I was about to say, but go on.'

Lund cleared her throat again and looked out of the window before taking another sip of the water in front of her.

'Do you have children?'

'A daughter, why?'

'I have a son,' Lund said. 'Benjamin. Twenty-six years old. He is – well, how do I put it? Different. Struggling to find his place in the world, if you know what I mean.'

'I certainly do.'

'Benjamin.' Lund coughed before she went on. 'Well, like I said, he has had some problems adjusting to real life, if I can put it like that. He has always been creative by nature, you see. I'm sorry if this is getting a little too personal.'

'Oh no, not at all.'

'Thank you,' Lund smiled and continued. 'He went to Trondheim. To study Anthropology at NTNU. A random choice, I think, but who knows? Up there he shared a flat with some rather "alternative" people, I guess you could say. People who played in a band, and so on? They had heard the rumours, gone to a botanical garden there and found the plant. Stupid, of course, but that's what they did. The boys didn't come round until several days later, and in a completely different part of the town with absolutely no idea what they had done in between. He told me that he hadn't tried it himself, but well, you know. I imagine he wanted to spare his mother the worry.'

Munch was unable to hide his smile.

'What is it?' Lund asked with a frown.

'I'm sorry. I didn't know what to expect when you said you didn't want to discuss it on the phone.'

'Was it silly?' Lund said with a faint smile. 'It's just that, in my profession . . . You get it.'

'Sensitive information. Your own child. I understand.' Munch nodded as the waitress appeared with their order.

'So that's what we're dealing with,' Lund said, unwrapping her chopsticks. 'Devil's tongue.'

'If you're right, it would answer many of our questions. I just can't believe I haven't heard about it before.'

'Latin America and South America. Like I said, there are few or no studies, but its use is spreading, if Internet reports are to be believed.'

'And it's not illegal?'

'Not currently, but it can only be a matter of time. By the way, you don't have to eat with chopsticks.'

'Are you sure?'

Lund giggled.

'Not if you don't want to. In Japan many people eat with their fingers. It's so typically Norwegian – we're so terrified of making a mistake. The green stuff is wasabi. You can mix it with the soy sauce.'

'OK.'

'Oh, sorry. I forgot to ask if you wanted a beer or something.'

'I don't drink alcohol.'

'You don't?'

'No.'

'Never?'

'No. I tried it once. Not for me.'

'Good heavens. A man after my own heart.' The dark-haired pathologist winked and raised her water glass in a toast.

Chapter 42

Mia glanced through the windows of Lorry and changed her mind. Her usual booth was taken and there were too many people at the bar. Darkness had descended upon the streets of Oslo, but she still hadn't been able to sleep. She had gone home to try again, but the circus in her stairwell just wouldn't stop. The old lady was ranting away. Something about a pet that had gone missing this time. Have you seen my cat? Her neighbour on his way out of his flat, his eyes indicating that he hadn't given up hope yet. *So how about your holiday?* She had seen the question form on his lips and just made it into her flat before it came. Her head hitting the pillow the next second, still dressed. Thumping from upstairs. A man's voice complaining and a woman responding in the same tone. The banality of everyday life. She had pressed her eyes shut, but her mind refused to let her rest. She couldn't shut out the world. All those people. It had always been her responsibility to keep them safe. So they could look for their cat. Help their sister. Argue with their husband. It was up to her. To make sure they didn't end up in a mountain lake in a ballet costume. In beds in dubious hotels. Alone and undressed in a car park in the middle of the night, unable to defend themselves.

Your work is making you sick.

You know that, don't you?

That you should be doing something completely different?

Yet another well-meaning psychologist, and she had dismissed it, but it came creeping over her now as she crossed the street and found another place to hide. Kunstnernes Pub. A dive. A bearded man at the bar over a drink and a sketch pad. Three quiet faces at a chessboard, coarse hands around lukewarm beer glasses. She had found a table in the corner as her phone rang. It was Gabriel. She set down her bag on the chair and went back out into the street to answer the call.

'Do you have two minutes?'

'Of course, Gabriel. How did it go?'

'I have everything,' her young colleague said. 'What do you want me to do with it?'

'How much is there?'

'A lot. I'm almost scared to look at it. It's a bit private, if you know what I mean.'

'Is there any way to search it?'

'What do you mean?'

'The files – can you type in a word or something?'

Gabriel laughed.

'No. There's no database. Just thousands of documents. Scanned PDFs of his own notes. You can't search that.'

'But Ritter must have had some kind of system?'

'Well, he already knows everyone's name, and then it's not difficult. If you give me a name, it'll take me ten seconds; or a date of birth, an address – something like that.'

'Not to worry,' Mia said. 'Like I said, it was just an idea I had up there.'

'You don't have a name or anything?'

'No, unless it says "Karl Overlind" anywhere.'

'I did try that, but no. It was just an alias, wasn't it?'

'Leave it for now. We'll find something we can link it to eventually.'

'OK. Did you talk to Munch? This drug they found? Scopolamine? It explains why Vivian Berg walked to the lake herself, and why none of the victims fought back?'

'It seems like it,' Mia mumbled impatiently.

She wanted to get back to processing the clues in her mind.

'Creepy stuff,' Gabriel said, 'to know that he can take any one of us, at any time, without us being able to defend ourselves, don't you think?'

'Listen, I'm a bit busy right now, Gabriel. I'll call you if I think of anything, OK?'

'OK,' Gabriel said, and rang off.

Mia would have given anything to be able to sleep, but she shook off her irritation about it. Ordered a cup of coffee and a Farris mineral water and took her papers out of the bag. Avoided the temptation of the taps behind the bar. It would have been much simpler, wouldn't it? Shut out the world with a beer and a Jäger. Cowardly, of course, but it would have been welcome now, she had to admit it.

The coffee tasted of dishwater, but she drank it anyway. She put pen to paper in front of her.

A burning doll's house?

Same type of clue, wasn't it?

The Brothers Lionheart?

A house in flames?

Bamboo?

Handmade?

Irrelevant.

The numbers?

Four? Seven? Thirteen?

A date of birth?

No.

Fourth of the seventh, thirteen.

Made no sense.

Or did it?

She moved them around the paper, but they didn't turn into anything. 7 April, 4 July, 13 something? 74?

Was she onto something?

Thirteen, new victim, 1974?

She took another sip of the disgusting coffee.

Damn.

One beer wouldn't hurt, surely?

Just to loosen up her thoughts?

She overcame the urge again and opted for more mineral water.

Swimming trunks.

Same theme again, wasn't it?

Water.

Ice.

Watch what I can do.

What if she was wrong? What if it had nothing to do with *Bambi*, because, why would it? There could be a million other reasons.

Do you see me?

I'm laughing right in your face.

Can you see what I'm doing?

And there's nothing you can do to stop me.

Watch what I can do.

Her pen moved more swiftly across the paper now.

Victim 1.

Vivian Berg.

Ballet clothes.

Costume?

Why?

This is important, isn't it?

Victim 2.

Kurt Wang.

Music on his mobile?

'My Favorite Things'.

What was . . . his costume?

The saxophone? The whole scene?

This is important.

She could feel it coming now.

She was onto something.

Victim 3.

Ruben Iversen.

Age? Did his age matter?

Swimming trunks?

Not symbolic?

No?

No water?

More concrete?

Look at . . . what he was wearing?
A new costume?
A mind game?
Her fingers flew more eagerly across the paper now.
Wolfgang Ritter?
The psychiatrist?
A dance of death . . .
Shit, she had almost forgotten that.
Wolfgang Ritter.
They would have to talk to him again.
There had to be more to it.
She underlined his name and chewed her pen.
Klaus Heming?
Is he still alive?
No, impossible.

Mia hadn't noticed that the door had opened, didn't notice him until he was standing next to her table. A face far away in the fog.

'Isn't your phone working?' the deep voice said, and the man sank into the chair in front of her.

Chapter 43

Erik Rønning hadn't bought a single drink all night and now yet another one was placed on his table, followed by a new face with the same expression they had all had. Fifty per cent jealousy, fifty per cent curiosity. Yet another scruffy colleague pushed his way forward and slumped down beside him in the hope of extracting the latest news. Someone from *Nettavisen*. Now what was his name again? Rønning couldn't remember. Not that it mattered. He raised the gin and tonic with a small smile and turned his attention back to Veronica Mossberg, who looked even more attractive after – was it six drinks he had had? He had lost count.

They were at Stopp Pressen. Not a bar he went to very often; it was a little too proletarian for his taste. For the people. Editors rarely frequented it, so he saw no reason to waste his time here, but Mossberg had suggested it.

'So how did you really get that film?' Mossberg asked, her eyes swimming with the alcohol.

Was that another button undone on her blouse? It was, wasn't it? He had turned away for just a moment to say hello in response to yet another hand in the air. He blinked and smiled, sphinx-like, over his drink, moving a little closer to her.

'Ah, you know,' he said, putting his arm on the back of the sofa. 'I have a nose for it. Hard work.'

Mossberg giggled and shook her head.

'No. Seriously, Erik, I'm curious. Go on, tell me.'

'My lips are sealed.' He grinned and trailed a finger across his mouth.

'Oh, please, it's just the two of us here.' Mossberg winked at him.

'So it is,' Erik said, flashing his teeth at her.

He had had them bleached only a few days ago. At the dentist's on Rådhusplassen. He was tempted to have them capped. It was a real faff, keeping them shiny white, so why not opt for a more permanent solution? If he was going to be appearing more frequently on TV – and that was definitely on the cards now – then it was important to have a dazzling smile. But he had put it off for the time being. He had been at a dinner party a week ago with some investors, something about a hotel in Dubai, and the wife of one of them – or was it the mistress? It was hard to tell – anyway, she had looked like a horse with her new teeth, so perhaps he should just stick with what he had.

He moved even closer to Mossberg, his lips brushing her soft cheek. He could smell her perfume now.

'I know a quiet little place,' he whispered.

'Do you indeed?' Mossberg giggled again and stuck a drinking straw into her mouth.

Someone else appeared in the background, probably about to offer him another drink. More curious well-wishers. It had been like that the whole day. Bloody fools. Did they really think he would reveal how they had caught the killing on film? No way.

'Oh, hi,' Mossberg said, and stood up.

She kissed the new arrival.

'Erik, this is my husband, Konrad. You haven't met, have you?'

Husband?

Rønning gulped and suppressed a burp. Got up reluctantly to shake the guy's hand.

'Konrad Larsen,' the man introduced himself.

Suit jacket, open shirt. A dense moustache and glasses.

'Delighted,' Rønning muttered as the man sat down.

Shit.

He could feel it now.

Was it six or seven?

He struggled to find his way back to the seat.

'That's what I call a scoop,' Larsen said, stroking Mossberg's shoulder. 'So did you just get lucky or what?'

Where had this guy come from, and why now?

What a pain.

He plastered a smile on his face, mumbled a reply and made his excuses. He found his way to the Gents and spent a long time looking at himself in the mirror. What a bloody waste of time. Sitting there flirting. He had given away some of his drinks, too. And all for some silly cow. He turned on the taps and splashed water onto his face. The bar at the Grand, perhaps? A glass of champagne?

He staggered back and was thinking about leaving when he noticed a pair of eyes staring at him from the bar. Red lips over a cocktail. Blonde hair. A tight dress that didn't hide much. His age, possibly a little younger. He didn't see the point of the green baseball cap, but hell, why not? Maybe she was going for the sporty look?

He adjusted his tie and made a beeline for the bar.

'What's your poison?' He grinned, nodding at her glass.

'I'm all out,' the young woman flirted back.

'Oh,' Rønning winked. 'We can't have that.'

He tried and failed to get the bartender's attention.

Didn't he know who he was?

'It's a bit crowded here, isn't it?'

'Sorry?' Rønning said, turning back to her.

'Too many people.'

'Absolutely.' Rønning smiled and moved closer to her. 'So what would you suggest?'

'It's a shame I live so far away. How about you?'

Score.

'I live just round the corner.' He grinned and trailed his fingers tentatively down her naked arm.

'And what are you offering?' The young woman giggled.

'Oh, you know. Whatever takes your fancy,' Rønning leered.

'Hang on two minutes.'

The girl in the green baseball cap touched his hand lightly before winking at him again and moving graciously across the floor towards the Ladies.

Chapter 44

'I'm sorry,' John Wold said. 'I can see that you're working, but I've tried calling you. Have you thought further about our conversation?'

He unbuttoned his coat, took off his leather gloves and placed them on the table.

'Listen . . .' Mia was frustrated.

She had been on the right track. She had been onto something. She had almost grasped it.

'I understand,' Wold said, holding up his hands in a placatory gesture. 'You're busy. But it's important.'

'Don't you read the newspapers?' Mia snapped, and stared him down.

'Of course I do. And I wouldn't be here if I didn't think it was necessary. Can I get you anything? Another cup of coffee? A beer?'

'Nothing,' Mia said, shaking her head. 'And listen—'

'I know, I know. Five minutes and I'll be out of your hair. Only I have to know whether you're in or out. I know that this might be against your principles, Mia. Your own team. And a friend, too, for all I know – I get it, but we're talking about a main importer here. Of heroin that ends up on the streets. And I, well, I too am risking my reputation here, do you understand? Mia Krüger? Can we trust her? Isn't she . . .?'

He smiled faintly.

'Go on?' Mia said. 'Isn't she what?'

'You know,' Wold said. 'Your file? You're not exactly a model citizen, are you?'

'What do you mean?' Mia asked icily.

'I'm just repeating what I've read,' Wold said in a conciliatory voice. 'What the others are thinking. I mean, shooting a suspect? Being repeatedly suspended from work? What was it he wrote about you . . .?'

'Who?'

'Mikkelson? He's not your biggest fan, is he?'

'Now listen—'

'Mia,' Wold said in a voice designed to calm her down. 'Not my words, OK? I was the one who suggested you, don't forget. Don't take it out on me. This is very hush-hush, even internally. Tell Mia Krüger what we're doing? Take that chance? Tell her that one of her closest colleagues might be bent? I'm running a big risk here, I hope you realize that.'

Suddenly Mia fancied that beer after all.

'OK.' She sighed and took a sip of her mineral water. 'So what do you want from me?'

'Curry.'

He summoned the waitress and ordered a cup of coffee.

'I think you're wrong. Is that what you wanted to know?'

'No. I wanted to know if you might be willing to work with us. To prove us wrong, if nothing else.'

'Didn't you hear me the last time?' Mia sighed. 'It's not Curry. He's a police officer through and through. He would never sell his soul for anything.'

'The old Curry, perhaps,' Wold said. 'But what about the new one? How has he been lately? On time? Sober?'

Wold raised the cup to his lips and pulled a face when he tasted the coffee.

'Have you met his new girlfriend?'

Mia shook her head.

'Luna Nyvik? Twenty-one? Dreadlocks? Bartender?'

'Like I said, no.'

Wold stuck a hand into his coat and slid a photograph across the table towards her.

'Oslo Airport last summer. Newly arrived from Bangkok. We let her through in the hope that she would take us to someone higher up the food chain, but we lost her, unfortunately.'

'So Curry has got himself a girlfriend, so what?' Mia said, pushing the picture back. 'Coincidence. Doesn't sound like you have much of a case.'

'I wouldn't have come to you if we weren't sure, would I now? We're very close, we really are. Lorentzen, the lawyer. He's involved, there's no doubt about it. He launders money. Has a company on the Cayman Islands. We could have picked him up a long time ago, but the top brass wants the man on the inside. A police officer responsible for the streets overflowing with heroin? It doesn't look good for any of us, does it?'

'I'm busy enough as it is. And I don't think it's Curry, OK? You have to find somebody else. So, no. Can't we just leave it at that?'

The handsome agent grew silent for a moment. He seemed to be weighing his words very carefully before finally making up his mind and opening his mouth again.

'Yes, of course we could pick somebody else. But there's another reason for choosing you, Mia. Do you know what I'm referring to?'

'No.'

'Heroin?' Wold said, leaning close to her now.

She could almost smell him. It reminded her of something. Summer. A rock. An old boyfriend.

'What do you mean?'

'Seriously?'

'Seriously, I've absolutely no idea what you're talking about.'

Wold stroked his chin. Looked at her sideways. The eyes were similar as well. A kind of warm curiosity. She had been wearing a swimming costume. Giggling under a towel in the roasting sun out in the archipelago. Now what was his name?

'Listen. The others were against it; they said we should have picked one of the others. Grønlie. Goli. You were my choice. Asking you, I mean.'

'Wow. I'm impressed. Thank you so much,' Mia said sarcastically.

'I didn't mean it like that. It's just that – well, I thought you would be the right one. Because you're already involved.'

'How?'

'You haven't been told? About your sister?' Wold said, sounding genuinely surprised.

An animal crawled up from her stomach.

'No?' said her dry mouth while the room around them suddenly contracted.

The chess players got up and left.

The artist at the bar turned to her.

Come, Mia, come.

'Mia? Are you OK?'

'Yes,' Mia mumbled, and drained the Farris bottle.

'Can I get you anything? Are you all right?'

'I'm fine.'

'You didn't know?'

'Know what?'

'We have reason to think that she was one of the first,' Wold said, folding his hands in front of him on the table.

'First what?'

'Mules,' Wold said. 'That's why. Do you understand now?'

'Why you picked me?'

'Yes.'

'I don't believe you.'

'It's up to you, of course.' Wold smiled. 'But think about it. Why did she die, Sigrid? Did she really inject herself with an overdose?'

Mia glanced at the taps.

'Markus Skog? She imported drugs for him. We think it's all connected. I thought you knew. That was why I came to you.'

A beer.

'No,' Mia said. 'I didn't know.'

He glanced at her bracelet.

'Nothing? I mean . . .?'

A Jäger.

She needed something now.

'What is it?' Mia asked.

228

'Your bracelet?'

'Yes?' Mia said quietly, lifting her hand from the table.

She could feel the bracelet tickle her skin.

A heart, an anchor and an initial.

You take mine and I'll have yours?

'This?'

'Yes.'

'What about it?'

'There's a rumour,' Wold said gravely. 'One of the other mules, a middle-aged woman. Her name is Cecilie. They say she was there.'

'Where?'

'When your sister died. They say she walked around town with a bracelet like yours.'

Wold nodded towards her wrist.

'Looking for something. Wanting money for it – I'm not sure.'

'What was her name again?' Mia said, and she felt the room disappear around her.

'Cecilie. They call her Cisse. We don't know her surname. A junkie. Coming up to forty. Blonde hair. Red puffa jacket. That's all we know, I'm afraid. I still can't believe they haven't . . .'

Pills.

Anaesthetic.

Anything.

It made no difference now.

She needed to feel nothing, just for a little bit.

Mia raised a hand and gave him a disarming smile.

'It's OK. Thank you. And if you could leave now, that would be great.'

'Of course.' Wold nodded and got up. 'But are you in?'

'Absolutely.'

Anything to get him to leave.

'You have my number?'

'I do.'

'And you'll call me?'

'As soon as I have something.'

'Thank you. I really appreciate it. I'm glad you're in. I really am.'

'Super,' Mia said, taking the hand that came through the air in front of her.

Wold put on his coat, raised two fingers to his forehead and headed for the door.

Mia waited until he was completely out of sight.

Then, with trembling fingers, she took her mobile out of her leather jacket.

And found the number for Charlie Brun at his bar.

FOUR

Chapter 45

Father Paul Malley had finished morning Mass and couldn't wait to get to the confessional. He had rushed there yesterday as well but had ended up sitting all on his own for two hours. The young man hadn't come back, not that Father Malley was going to give up that easily. Admittedly, he had been a little disappointed. The other day had been so good. He had had this idea about extended confession hours and not only had someone seized the opportunity to come but someone who really needed him had turned up. A new member of the flock. Someone who hadn't been to confession before.

It's about my brother.

Father Malley was well prepared. He had sat up late last night reading the Scriptures again, finding quotes about brothers. About loving your neighbour. About sacrificing yourself for other people. The desperate young voice had followed him in his dreams. He had woken up with the sun on his face and a strange feeling that someone was talking to him. Was it God? It wasn't entirely clear, but it could have been. The Lord had praised him for what he had done, encouraging this poor lamb in need of divine guidance, and the Virgin had sat on a cloud with a harp and a big smile on her face, so he couldn't have been properly awake because, not long afterwards, his alarm had gone off, but as he lay with his head resting on the white pillow, he had felt born again. He had barely been able to eat his breakfast, he had been that excited.

But no one had come.

I'm here for you. Every morning. I want you to know that.
You come back to me when you're ready.

What about the next day? Why hadn't he come?

Yes, he had been disappointed, he had to admit it.

He had managed to conduct today's morning Mass well, although his focus had been elsewhere.

The young man, would he turn up today?

And then a less Christian thought occurred to him:

If he doesn't turn up today, how long do I wait?

He pushed up the sleeve of his cassock and checked his watch.

Maybe it was a silly idea, making such a grandiose promise.

Father Malley heaved a sigh and drummed his fingers lightly against his thigh. The wooden seat was hard and uncomfortable and he was hungry too; after all, he had been sitting there for almost an hour now. The forty-three-year-old priest had decided that enough was enough when he suddenly heard footsteps on the church floor and a figure slipped in on the other side of the lattice.

'Father,' the young man mumbled, and closed the door carefully behind him.

Jubilant trumpets and bassoons.

He was back.

'My son,' Father Malley said in his deepest, most priestly voice. 'You found your way back?'

There was silence for a moment behind the lattice.

'I really wasn't sure. But I think I'm doing the right thing, Father. I want to thank you for convincing me to come here.'

Thank him?

Father Malley smiled to himself and felt warm in his chest.

'Thank the Lord and the Virgin,' he said softly. 'We are all mere servants of the divine. I'm no one. I'm just here for you.'

'Thank you anyway,' the young man said. 'I've given it a lot of thought. And I've made up my mind.'

'Yes?' Father Malley said cautiously.

'I will tell you everything.'

'You can trust me,' Father Malley said calmly. 'In this room, only the eyes of the Lord will judge.'

'Judge?'

Father Malley cleared his throat.

'I didn't mean "judge", I meant "see". That was what I meant: in here, only the Lord sees us.'

'What if the Lord doesn't like what he sees?'

'Listen,' Father Malley said, moving a little closer to the lattice. 'No one is judging you. It came out the wrong way. There's only you and me here. No one else.'

He leaned back a little and waited in tense anticipation.

'Yes, that's fine, Father,' the unknown voice said at length. 'I think I need to tell someone. I hope it's not a mistake. And that no one gets hurt.'

'The Lord is pleased to hear you,' Father Malley said, hoping he didn't sound too keen. 'And He wants you to know that, no matter what troubles you, He will receive it with compassion and understanding.'

There was another silence on the other side, but at last it came.

'Forgive me, Father, for I have sinned. I know things that I haven't told to anyone, and I can't bear it any more. My heart is so heavy, I have to tell someone.'

Father Malley couldn't be sure, but he thought he could hear soft weeping behind the lattice.

'I'm glad you came,' he said calmly. 'The Lord is willing to listen to what you have to say. A dark burden is heavy for a light heart.'

He couldn't remember if the last line was a quote from the Scriptures, but it felt like the right thing to say.

'Yes, Father, in our house everything is dark,' the stranger said in a whisper. 'But that's not my fault, is it?'

Definite tears now. Sobbing behind trembling lips.

'Absolutely not, my son.' Father Malley shifted still closer to the lattice.

He was sorely tempted to open the lattice and give the brave young man a big hug, make him realize that he wasn't alone, but he hoped that the warmth of his nearby voice would have the same effect.

Poor lad.

'How much time do I have?' the voice stuttered beneath the tears.

'As long as you need. I have all the time in the world.'

'Thank you,' the young man sniffled, then grew quiet again.

'I don't really know where to start,' he said eventually. 'It's quite horrible.'

'What's horrible?'

'Talking about it. About my brother. I feel that I'm letting him down after all these years, but I can't go on. Do you understand, Father?'

'Of course.'

'Where should I begin?'

'Where do you think you ought to begin?'

Another silence behind the wooden lattice while the stranger steeled himself.

'The fire, perhaps,' the voice said.

'Go on?' Father Malley said, and felt his heart beat a little faster under his cassock.

'Or perhaps the deer,' the young man said tentatively. 'I don't know . . .'

'Take as long as you need, my son. What fire are we talking about?'

'We all died that day, but some of us are still alive. Can I trust you, Father? Can I tell you everything?'

'Of course, my son.'

And he shifted yet closer to the lattice.

Chapter 46

First he was at home. Then he wasn't at home after all. First the girl with the green baseball cap was there. Then she turned into . . . a monkey? Erik Rønning switched off the TV, only he wasn't holding the remote control, but a . . . banana? The girl in the green baseball cap had turned into a monkey and she was giving him a banana. The walls around him suddenly changed colour. His flat became a glitter ball. No, that was wrong. He wasn't at home. He was somewhere else. Yes, he was at home, but it wasn't his home now. It had been his home a long time ago. It was 1999. He was only fourteen years old. There was a Backstreet Boys poster on the wall. Nick, Kevin, AJ, Howie and Brian. His lungs hurt. He must be ill. The girl with the green baseball cap was gone. She had left his flat waving her magic wand, Hermione Granger from *Harry Potter*. Abracadabra. Was his mum in? Was it his mum making that noise in the kitchen? Was it his mum sitting with a balaclava over her head at the end of his bed? With a scout's knife? The one Uncle Tore had given him? *Quit playing games with my heart.* It was club night down at the youth centre in Asker this Friday. Dancing. Why did he feel so nervous? Why was everything around him so blurred, like a movie playing at a crazy speed and turning everything upside down? Was that why his mum had tied him up? So he wouldn't fall off? Because his bed was on the ceiling? He tried to speak, but the big sailboat from the jetty below the house where he would often dive into the water was taped to his mouth.

Erik Rønning opened his eyes.

A man wearing a balaclava was sitting at the foot of his bed.

'Are you awake?'

'What?' Rønning said, but no sound came out.

Tape covering his mouth.

He didn't realize it at first.

What was going on?

Which explained why he wasn't scared.

But then . . . *it came*.

'Are you awake?' the man in the balaclava said again and poked something into the sole of his foot.

Oh, God . . .

He could barely cope with the pain.

He was using all his energy to keep his panic at bay.

Shit . . .

Oh, please God, no . . .

Someone had tied him to his bed. Bound his hands and feet. He was naked except for his boxer shorts. Tape covered his mouth. The soles of his feet were facing a man in a balaclava who had a big knife in one hand.

'Can you hear me?' the dark eyes wanted to know, pricking his foot again.

The agony . . .

He howled so loudly that his head almost burst, but still not a sound came out of his mouth.

'Are you awake now?' A third time.

Rønning nodded.

'Good,' the eyes said, the voice calm. 'So you like talking, do you? You like attention?'

The man made a small puppet with his hand and chatted away to it.

'Look at me. I'm on TV. I know secrets. I think I'm special.'

He was in deep shit now.

'Do you know what we used to do in Afghanistan? To people who liked chatting?'

Rønning felt the tip of the knife against the sole of his foot again. His body jerked as the room started spinning.

Arrgghh.

238

He must have blacked out for a moment, because when he opened his eyes the man in a balaclava was bent over him.

He recognized the smell.

Of the glove that had slapped him so hard that he woke up.

And something acidic.

'Now don't you go disappearing from me, OK?'

The balaclava was back at the foot of the bed.

Dark eyes through the holes.

'Nod if you understand me.'

Rønning nodded again.

As if his life depended on it.

'Good. You're not going to doze off again, are you?'

Rønning shook his head frantically.

'Good. You're a little bitch, aren't you? You swan around in fancy clothes on TV and steal all the attention?'

Rønning nodded eagerly.

He could feel his own stench.

His fear turned into the smell under his armpits.

Oh, please God.

Shit, shit, shit.

'Good.' The man in the balaclava nodded. 'But you're my bitch now. I *can* improvise, you know. I like planning, that's my strength, but I can improvise when I want to, do you understand?'

Rønning didn't know if he was meant to answer the last part of the question, but he nodded all the same. The light from the ceiling lamp stung his eyes. He was experiencing a level of physical sensitivity he'd never had before. He thought he could still feel the cold blade against his foot, although he could clearly see that the man was holding the knife up in the air.

'Are you my bitch?'

Rønning nodded desperately as his own smell grew stronger, making him nauseous.

'Good,' the eyes said. 'Normally, I would just have killed you, but then I thought perhaps I can use this bitch for something. I can improvise. Clever, isn't it?'

Something that resembled a smile formed in the hole at the bottom of the balaclava.

Rønning nodded for dear life.

'I know,' the man said. 'I'm clever. They thought they would get away with it, didn't they? Well, it doesn't look like that now, does it?'

Rønning's brain was working overtime, but it was like wading through treacle.

Afghanistan?

Get away?

With what?

He shook his head, just to be on the safe side.

'Lashkar Gah,' the voice said quietly. 'Do you know where that is?'

Rønning shook his head feverishly.

'No, you don't, do you?' the man in the balaclava said with a light shrug. 'You sacrifice your life for your country, and what thanks do you get? Am I on the news, with medals on my chest? Have you seen any parades? Children waving flags and brass bands? No. I guess they were hoping everyone would forget. I mean, they hid me away in a basement. They pretended nothing had happened.'

The man narrowed his eyes again and spat demonstratively on the floor.

'No. It's my time now.'

He stuck his gloved hand into the pocket of an army jacket and held up a piece of paper.

'Do you see this?'

Rønning couldn't see what it said, but he nodded all the same.

'You'll give them this from me, OK? And I don't mean the people you work for. The top brass. Go right to the top. Do you understand?'

Rønning nodded again and felt that yesterday's alcohol intake was on its way up from his stomach now.

'Good.' The mouth grinned in the hole and the man stood up.

He turned quickly to the wall and rammed his knife through the piece of paper.

Erik Rønning could see the handle quiver against the wallpaper. The man in the balaclava came towards him and untied one arm from the bed. Rønning's ears just about registered that his front door slammed shut somewhere far away before he ripped the tape from his mouth with trembling fingers, leaned over the edge of his bed.

And threw up all over the floor.

Chapter 47

Gabriel was sitting in the incident room with Ylva and Ludvig, impressed at how much information the old investigator had managed to put up on the walls in such a short space of time. Lots of photographs, each with a name underneath and arranged to highlight their connection to one another. And therein lay the problem, the problem they had been working to solve since yesterday afternoon without getting very far.

The connections.

There just didn't seem to be any.

'It has to be random.' Ylva sighed and took off her glasses. She rubbed her eyes and suppressed a yawn.

'I'm tempted to agree with you,' Grønlie said, and looked once more at the colourful wall. 'And that's the only connection we've been able to find, isn't it?'

He pointed to the red line connecting Vivian Berg to Raymond Greger.

'Remind me who the people around Kurt Wang are again?' Ylva said.

'His band,' Grønlie said. 'The vocalist, Nina Wilkins. And the drummer, a Portuguese man named Danilo Costa.'

'Sorry.' Ylva rubbed her eyes again. 'I've been staring at this so long my brain feels as if it's full of dust.'

None of them had been home. Ylva had been napping in her chair in front of her computer. Gabriel had dozed briefly on the sofa in the break room. He wouldn't call it sleep. Just dreamy, restless thoughts, photographs and incidents that refused to make sense.

Munch entered with a cup of coffee; his hair was tousled and he didn't look as if he had had very much sleep either.

'How are you doing?' he said, and flopped onto one of the office chairs. 'Any connections? Anywhere? Anything?'

'We're still looking,' Grønlie said, chewing his lip, 'but nothing has come up.'

'OK,' Munch said, scratching his beard. 'Talk me through what you have so far.'

'Victims, crime scenes, anyone with a relationship to the victims,' Grønlie pointed. 'Then we have a timeline over there. Here, on this wall, we have everyone's electronic footprints. Mobiles, computers, places we can prove they have been.'

'By the way, has anyone seen Mia?' Munch yawned. 'Or Curry?'

'Not since yesterday,' Grønlie said.

'Sorry for the interruption. Please go on,' Munch said, taking a sip of his coffee.

'Nothing on their mobiles or social media.' Ylva pointed. 'We found all Vivian Berg's devices in her home, so no signals from them since the afternoon she left her flat. Kurt Wang's mobile pinged off masts in Grünerløkka and down to Gamlebyen. The times correspond to when he disappeared until he was found.'

'He went missing from a rehearsal, isn't that right?' Munch said, stifling another yawn.

Ylva nodded.

'But of no use to us?'

'No, nothing from when he was last seen.'

'What about Iversen?'

'CCTV from Storo shopping centre tells us that he wasn't there, or at least he isn't on the footage we've viewed so far. His text messages confirm that he was planning a sleepover with his friend. He went missing on the way there.'

'And do we know where?' Munch asked.

Grønlie walked up to the big map near the door.

'The last time his phone was picked up he was here. Grefsen.'

'So not very far from home?'

243

'His house is here. His friend lives there. I can't remember his name.'

'Martin,' Gabriel said.

'OK, so our theory stands up?'

'Yes, as far as we can see.' Ludvig nodded. 'It looks like he really was heading out for a sleepover – we have him on his moped at this Statoil petrol station – but yes, after that it looks like someone waylaid him on the way there.'

'We don't have any cameras?'

'It's a residential area,' Grønlie said, shaking his head. 'I doubt we'll find anything.'

'So Berg was picked up at her home. Wang was picked up during a break at a rehearsal. Iversen was stopped and picked up on the street. No similarities. No connections.'

'No.' Ludvig sighed.

This was the conclusion they had reached some time ago, but Munch didn't seem willing to accept it yet. Gabriel hadn't been with the special unit very long, but even he could work out why. Random victims? It was every investigator's worst nightmare.

'Social media? Still nothing?' Munch took another sip of his coffee.

'Vivian Berg, fairly low profile,' Gabriel said. 'Few friends. Posted very little. Kurt Wang was slightly more active. He runs a Facebook page for the band, which has quite a few followers.'

'And the boy?'

'Like most teenagers, he was very active, especially on Snapchat. Not so much on Facebook and Instagram – those are more for older users,' Gabriel said.

'Snap—?' Munch said.

'You take a picture and send it to someone, and they can look at it for just a few moments, and then it's gone,' Ylva explained.

'Gone?' Munch echoed.

'Yes.'

'So what's the point of that? The point of the picture?'

Gabriel concealed a smile as Ylva started to explain, but Munch just waved a hand dismissively.

'OK, good, so Snap—?'

'He has been very active, lots of streaks with plenty of people.'

Munch looked as if he was about to ask another question but decided against it.

'But there's still nothing to suggest that any of these people know one another? They haven't met somewhere? Online or in real life?'

'Not so far, I'm afraid,' Grønlie said.

'Sports? Hobbies? Political involvement? Do they shop on the same website? Have you checked their search histories?'

'I've been through the browser histories of all three of them quite carefully,' Gabriel said, 'as well as all their Google searches in the past few weeks, but the only common denominator is NRK TV.'

'And?' Munch said, sounding optimistic.

'Berg and Wang looked at the news. Iversen watched a youth programme. That's all, I'm afraid.'

'By the way,' Ludvig said, 'Ruben Iversen's uncle called me this morning.'

'Did he now? And?'

'He was wondering if we could help them. Their house is besieged by journalists. They ring the family round the clock. It's the same with the boy's school; they won't leave the students alone.'

Munch sighed.

'That's not something we can do anything about, unfortunately.'

'I know.' Grønlie nodded. 'That's what I told him.'

'Those poor people,' Munch said, and shook his head as the door suddenly opened and a breathless Anette Goli rushed into the room.

'Why aren't you picking up your phone?'

The normally composed police lawyer was wide-eyed and almost ashen-faced.

'It's in my jacket,' Munch said. 'What's happened?'

Goli glanced at the other three.

'Your office. Now.'

'We're in the middle—'

'No. Now. Right now,' Goli ordered him, and half ran ahead of him down the corridor.

Chapter 48

'So what's happened?' Munch wanted to know when Anette had closed the door behind them.

'I've just had a phone call from the top,' Goli said when she had got her breath back.

'Mikkelson?'

The police lawyer shook her head.

'The top top. The office of the Justice Minister. I'm guessing it was really FST, but it was presented as such.'

'FST?'

'Army intelligence. You know that journalist?' Goli said. 'Rønning?'

'Yes?'

'He had a visitor last night. They think he's our man.'

'What?' Munch said, glancing at the clock on the wall, which was showing twelve thirty already. 'Last night? And we haven't heard about it until now?'

'That's the last thing we need to worry about, Holger,' Goli said.

'Our man? How the hell can they know that?'

'Holger,' Goli said.

'Bloody idiots.'

'Holger,' Goli said again, holding up a hand towards him. 'There's a list.'

'What are you saying?'

Anette grew quiet for a moment. It was almost as if she were bracing herself for what she was about to say.

'A list of names.'

'What names?'

'A kill list.'

'What the . . .?'

'Fifty names,' Goli whispered. 'Vivian Berg. Kurt Wang. Ruben Iversen. As you know, we haven't published the numbers of any of the victims, but they're all on the list. I've just had the phone call from the Ministry.'

'But this has got to be a hoax. It's—' Munch began, but Anette interrupted him again, a look of urgency in her eyes that he hadn't seen before.

'The Prime Minister has raised the threat level to five. They're talking about evacuating the royal family.'

'But for God's sake,' Munch mumbled under his breath.

'Fifty random people,' Goli said, and shook her head.

'Do we have the list?'

'No, it's classified.'

'What? Then how are we supposed to . . .?'

Munch looked at her and could see it now. There was something she wasn't telling him.

'What?' he said again as she looked away. 'We're out, is that it? They're taking over the investigation?'

'No, no,' Goli said, and started chewing her lip. 'We're in, or . . .'

'Or . . .?'

'It's just you and me,' Anette said reluctantly. 'People with the highest levels of security clearance. They're putting together a management group as we speak. They'll be calling me back within the hour.'

'But, that's outrageous, Anette. So no . . . Mia?'

'What would you have done? In their position?' Anette said with a shrug. 'You know her history? Her many problems? They don't trust her. She hasn't got clearance. I mean, fifty people? Random victims? Imagine if it were made public.'

'So who is in?'

'You and me. Everyone else will keep the wheels turning but it's just you and me at the top table.'

'Yes, but who are the other members of this management group?'

'Like I said, FST, and I'm guessing PST, the security service, as well as civil servants from the Ministry of Justice.'

'Mikkelson?'

'No idea,' Goli said. 'Not as far as I'm aware.'

'And definitely no . . . Mia?'

'Definitely not.' Anette's phone rang. 'Do you want to tell her? Or shall I?'

'No, no, I'll do it.' Munch sighed as her mobile rang again.

'Goli speaking,' the blonde police lawyer said, and left his office.

Chapter 49

Forty-two-year-old Jon Ivar Salem was a plumber by trade, but that was obviously not his claim to fame in Ullersmo prison. He was serving a maximum sentence of twenty-one years and was one of the longest-serving inmates on the wing. That alone earned him enough respect for the other inmates to leave him alone. Until a group of Kosovo Albanians had arrived. Those bloody idiots hadn't read the newspapers or watched the telly and thought they could mess with the system. Play at being king. Take over the kitchen and the phone, decide who would be doing what. Jon Ivar Salem had decided it was time to teach them a lesson.

Normally, he didn't give a toss. He tended not to get involved in the internal discipline of the prison for the simple reason that the other inmates rarely dared raise a finger to him or deny him anything. It might be hard for outsiders to understand that grown men, covered in tattoos, could fight over something as petty as a packet of sausages or access to the shower, but that was life on the inside. He had served seven years and had fourteen left. He could apply to be released on licence once he had served two thirds of his sentence, so there was no reason to be a good boy.

Not yet.

It would be burning soon and he couldn't wait.

He was older than most of the men in here and regarded himself as a kind of father figure to them all. The prison food was as bad as you would expect; they were lucky if they got stew or something vaguely reminiscent of fish. Usually, they were given food that tasted as if it had come out of a camel's arse. Fortunately, they also had the opportunity to order their own food, paid for with their own money, obviously, and he had taken the initiative and put himself in charge. Got together a group of his closest friends, taken over the kitchen and now felt almost like a chef with his own restaurant. While he wouldn't call it fine dining, at least he offered edible meals every day and his fellow inmates handed over their cash almost voluntarily.

Oh, the flames.
Like a man in the desert.
Many years without water.
But soon he would be quenching his thirst again.

The Kosovo Albanians. There were just the three of them, convicted of importing cocaine and heroin, and the idiots who ran this dump had placed them in the same wing. They were big kids, really. Twenty-something-year-olds, tough gangster types with the obligatory tattoos. Just having your girlfriend's name on your forearm was no longer enough these days – no, it had to be skulls and teardrops, preferably in the middle of your face or all over your throat, and something on your knuckles, LOVE-HATE, KILL-FUCK. To begin with, Salem had ignored them, as he did with all the newbies in here, those doing less than ten long ones, but then they had attacked a couple of young inmates down in the basement. Beaten them senseless with their fists and cans of tuna in socks, taken over the showers, the kitchen, and now the time had come to put them in their place.

The flames.
He was itching all over.
His toes were tingling.
Up through his groin.
He hadn't slept for days.

The Kosovo Albanians could have saved themselves a lot of bother if they had only watched TV. Then they would have known who he was. They might even have lived to see thirty. But they hadn't. Probably because they didn't speak Norwegian, but more importantly because, in 2006, while it had been at its worst, these boys had been only thirteen or fourteen years old. He could feel a smile spread across his face now and had to check himself to remain calm.

Oh, it would be wonderful.

The flames.

Finally.

He could barely breathe.

He was woken up by the squeaking of the post trolley as a smiling Muffins, one of his closest friends on the inside, came down the corridor. He was a tattooed guy from Trøndelag who was serving time for the same reason most of the young men were in here: drugs, violence; usually both.

'For me?' Salem said, surprised, and looked at the parcel Muffins had just handed him.

'Yes.' Muffins smiled and picked his teeth with a filthy finger. 'Got yourself a girlfriend?'

'Not as far as I know.' Salem grinned back and felt his curiosity stir.

He hadn't been sent anything from the outside for as long as he could remember.

The parcel had been opened, obviously, but he couldn't see what it contained. The guards had resealed it and written the usual wording – CHECKED – in glossy blue letters on the brown paper.

'I tell you, they were scratching their heads in the post room.' Muffins looked up and down the corridor.

'Were they now?'

'Ha-ha, yeah. They were discussing whether or not they were going to let you have it, I think.'

'Really? What is it?'

'How would I know? Do you think they would let me see? I'm just the delivery guy. Are we on, by the way?'

The latter was whispered through tight lips as he glanced over his shoulder. Not that he needed to; there were no guards around. There rarely were at this end of the wing, unless it was time to let the prisoners out of their cells or back into them, or if someone needed the loo after lights-out.

Norway's resources were spent elsewhere.

Open season in here.

It couldn't have suited him better.

They had to get them now.

The time had come.

Flames over skin.

'Yes, absolutely,' Salem said, and nodded, not taking his eyes off the parcel.

'After lunch? In the basement?'

'Yep. The Kosovo Albanians are playing basketball until one o'clock. We'll get them just after that.'

'Ker-pow! That'll be fun. How far do we go? Will we be sent to Solitary?'

Salem looked sternly up at the young man.

'All the way, of course.'

'Come on, Jon. I only have sixteen months left. I can't kill anyone. You see that, don't you?'

'Who said anything about you doing it?'

The young drug dealer's eyes widened.

'So you'll do it?'

'You keep a lookout, I'll handle it.'

'Awesome.' Muffins grinned and raised his hand in something which was probably meant to be a high-five or another equally idiotic greeting the kids used these days, but Salem left him hanging.

'You'll get a few days in Solitary, max.'

'I can cope with that, no worries.'

'Oi, Muffins, are the two of you getting married or what? Get a bloody move on!'

Impatient cries from further down the corridor. For most of this wing, the rattling trolley was as exciting as Christmas.

'Take it easy, I'm coming. Keep your hair on.'

Muffins sighed, winked one last time and rolled on with the trolley to the waiting inmates.

A parcel?

Salem closed the door to his cell and sat down eagerly on the chair by the small desk. He opened the parcel carefully but was none the wiser when he saw the contents. A gold ring and a short note.

252

Dear Jon Ivar Salem. You don't know me, and yet I'm asking you to do me a favour. Take care of this ring; someone will come for it soon. You will be rewarded. Thank you for your help.

No signature.

What the hell was this? How odd. If the note hadn't had his name on it, he would have been convinced the sender had made a mistake. Salem picked up the ring from the small box; it glistened faintly in the light from the desk lamp. He examined the paper it had been wrapped in, but there was nothing else. Bizarre, but whatever. He could look after some ring. And be rewarded for it as well? No problem.

It will burn soon.

Tomorrow morning.

Jon Ivar Salem smiled to himself, stuffed the gold ring under his pillow and lay down on his bunk to rest.

Chapter 50

Mia was woken up by a familiar singing voice and staggered from the strange bed and into the kitchen as she yawned.

'Moonbeam.' Charlie Brun smiled and gave her a big hug. 'Someone's had a long sleep. Breakfast?'

'What the hell did you give me?' Mia yawned again and sat down, dazed, on a chair.

Charlie was in his element. He was wearing a billowing green dress today beneath an apron which read 'Kiss the Chef'.

'Eggs? Bacon?' The charming man beamed and waved a frying pan.

'No, thank you,' Mia mumbled. 'What time is it?'

'You don't want any food? But you have to eat. You're nothing but skin and bones.'

Charlie danced across the floor and filled her plate.

'There are sausages as well. Would you like some?'

'For breakfast?' Mia yawned.

'Why not? The Brits love it. Did I tell you I was in London two weeks ago? Saw a musical. *The Lion King*. Completely lived up to the hype. Absolutely wonderful. I cried my eyes out. Isn't it funny how these things can move us?'

'What is?' Mia said, popping a rasher of bacon into her mouth.

'Grown men sobbing at something originally written for children.'

'Nothing about you surprises me, Charlie.' Mia smiled and felt herself slowly starting to return to reality.

Something to sleep on.

She had stumbled through the door of his club, desperate for oblivion, a drink, anything, and he had calmly talked her down.

Thank God.

Not one drop of alcohol.

Just a sleeping pill.

She reached her arms towards the ceiling and glanced around the small, cosy flat.

'Have you redecorated?'

'Yes,' Charlie said with a big smile. 'Everything is new. The carpet, the furniture, new colour on the walls. Feng shui. You need to change your surroundings from time to time; otherwise you die, you know?'

Charlie jabbed his temple as he opened the door to the fridge.

'What would you like to drink? Let me see. I have juice, a smoothie?'

'Just some water, thank you. Unless you have coffee?'

'Coffee? Do I have coffee? I have a brand-new machine. State of the art. Me and George Clooney, you know? Now there's a man for me. Did you know that he likes dressing up as well? No, really, he does.'

Charlie winked and presented her with a board of capsules.

'Arabica? Linizio? Kazaar?'

'Something strong.'

'Ristretto. With a combination of the best South American Arabica beans and a hint of Robusta for extra intensity.'

He presented the capsule to her with an extravagant gesture and pursed his lips.

'You sell them?' Mia smiled and slipped a slice of bread under her fried egg.

'I'm the new face of Nespresso.' Charlie tilted his head. 'What do you think?'

'I think you're perfect.' Mia giggled.

'George and me,' Charlie said, raising his eyebrows seductively.

'You were just making it up, weren't you?'

'Making what up?'

'That he, too, likes dressing up in women's clothes?'

'In my dreams, Mia.' Charlie winked and pressed a button on the coffee maker. 'Though I don't mind – I love him just the way he is. Did you say you wanted a glass of water?'

'Yes, please.'

Her mouth was dry. There was also a veil behind her eyes, but it was starting to lift.

He had talked her out of it.

You just need something to make you sleep.

Thank God for Charlie Brun.

He was nothing less than a living saint.

'I see you put the family up,' Mia said as he brought her coffee.

'Yes,' Charlie said somewhat wistfully, and gazed at the wall behind her. 'It hasn't been easy for them, all this. Their little Charlie, who was such a promising boy. Did you know I used to play ice hockey?'

'Did you now?'

'Indeed I did, for Storhamar. Forward. And I was good at it, too.'

Four photographs, neatly framed. Smiling adult faces, a short, round boy between them from a time that no longer existed.

'Good memories,' Charlie said, sounding a little glum.

'You're still not in contact with your dad?'

'I wrote a letter to him some time ago. He's an old man now, you know. So he likes to get things in the post. Or at least I think so – I'm guessing here. Not that I would know, of course. It's been a few years now.'

'And?'

'No reply, sadly.' Charlie sighed. 'Oh, well, it was worth a try. How's your coffee?'

'Perfect,' Mia said, then she spotted the clock above the cooker. 'Oh, no.'

'What is it?'

'It's almost one thirty in the afternoon.'

'Yes?'

'I'm seriously late.' Mia leapt up and patted her trouser pocket, but it wasn't there.

'My mobile?'

'I've got it,' Charlie said, and disappeared.

Yikes.

Had she really slept that long?

Mia drained her coffee cup standing up as Charlie returned.

'Busy these days?'

'I'm afraid so.'

A dozen missed calls.

Most of them from Munch.

She rang him back.

'Mia?' she heard him grunt through his beard on the other end. 'Where are you?'

'Sorry,' Mia said. 'I overslept. I'm on my way to the office now.'

'No, no,' Munch said. 'I'll meet you.'

'Why?'

'I'll come and meet you,' Munch said again, in a strange tone of voice. 'Where are you?'

'What's your address?' Mia said to Charlie, putting her hand over the phone.

'Tøyenbekken 9.'

'Tøyenbekken 9,' Mia said.

'Is that close to Grønlandsleiret?'

'Yes. I'll meet you there. Has something happened?'

Munch didn't reply.

'Holger?'

'I'm on my way, OK?'

'OK.'

'I'm leaving now,' Munch said, and rang off.

'Are you leaving so soon? But you've hardly touched your food.'

'Got to go,' Mia said, and slipped her mobile into her pocket.

'Promise you won't leave it so long next time.' Charlie took her lightly by the shoulders and kissed both her cheeks. 'Are you all right, Moonbeam? You know that I'm always here for you if you need anything?' He looked rather anxiously at her now, wouldn't quite let her go.

'I'm fine. Thank you so much for all this, Charlie. You're worth your weight in gold, did you know that?'

'Oh, we try.'

'Where's my jacket?'

'It's in the hall. You will call me, won't you? And be careful out there.'

'Yes, Mum, and thank you so much.' Mia smiled and gave him another big hug before spinning round and running down the stairs.

Chapter 51

Munch felt like an idiot, but it was just too bad. He shook his head and pulled the Audi up alongside the kerb. A bright and breezy Mia got in and put on her seatbelt.

'Where are we going?'

Munch sighed and decided he might as well cut straight to the chase.

'What?' Mia said, scrunching up her nose.

She could tell from one look at him. They had worked together for so long.

'Do you still fancy a holiday?'

'I beg your pardon?'

'Sorry,' Munch mumbled, and ran a hand across his face. 'Orders from the top.'

'About what?'

'FST is now involved in the investigation. They've taken over.'

'Taken over? What do you mean?'

'It's not our case any more—' he began, but she cut him off.

'Eh? But what the hell, Holger?'

'I know. I—'

'I don't bloody believe it!' Mia raged. 'Seriously, are you kidding me? Army intelligence? How the hell did they get involved?'

'It's a long story.' Munch sighed and scratched his beard. 'Something happened last night. Listen, I did my best, but, like I said . . .'

He could see that she had worked out what he was trying to tell her. The expression in her eyes went from brightly inquisitive to darkly aggressive in less than a second.

'I'm . . . *out*?'

'Just for the time being,' Munch said, trying to placate her. 'Just until we're back on our feet.'

'But what the hell?' Mia grunted. 'And who the hell are "we"?'

'They're putting together a management group now with FST and PST.'

'So no one from our unit? What's happening, Holger?'

'Anette and I are part of it,' Munch said quickly. 'Like I said, it's just for the time being, until we—'

'But for fuck's sake, Holger.' Mia shook her head in despair. 'How many days is it since you dragged me down to Justisen? Asked me to look at the case? I had booked plane tickets, for God's sake. There was a yacht waiting for me.'

'Can you still use them?' Munch tried, but regretted it immediately.

Mia turned away from him; she was practically foaming at the mouth now.

'Sorry,' Munch said. 'I was only—'

'And why not me?'

Her sharp eyes speared him. It was a question to which she already knew the answer, but she was going to make him say it out loud.

'Security clearance,' Munch croaked.

'Because I'm an unstable psycho?'

'Mia—'

'Someone you can use when it suits you, but not where it really matters – is that what you're saying?'

'Listen, Mia . . . If it had been up to me, well, you know . . .'

'Bloody pen-pushers,' Mia hissed, unclicking her seatbelt and reaching for the door handle.

'They found a list,' Munch interjected before she had time to open the door.

'What kind of list?'

Munch decided he didn't give a toss about orders from the top. His primary responsibility was to his staff. The Ministry could go to hell; he was fed up. He had been for a long time, frankly.

Fed up with the way Mia had been treated in recent years. Warnings, suspensions – only for them to let her back inside when it suited them. Hell no, enough was enough.

'Rønning had a visitor early this morning,' he said quickly.

'The journalist?'

'Yes. From a former soldier. They think he's an Afghanistan veteran.'

'Where?'

'He came to his home. I haven't got all the details, but I think Rønning was assaulted. He was given a list. Of the victims. They're working on a theory that this is some sort of revenge action.'

'Revenge for what?'

'We don't know that yet. Something must have happened in Afghanistan, maybe he's angry with the government, I don't know, but listen—'

'A list?'

'A kill list. Of random victims.'

'What? How many?' Mia asked, shocked.

'Fifty.'

'Oh, Christ.'

'So they're keeping it under wraps. Do you understand?'

'He fits the profile?'

She turned to him and at least looked less angry now. A milder face with her gaze starting to turn inwards.

'He's the right age.'

'The numbers?'

'Vivian Berg was number four on the list,' Munch said. 'That's all I know for now. They're keeping their cards very close to their chest.'

'So, random victims?' Mia stared out of the windscreen.

'Selected randomly from a list of fifty, it would seem.'

'Shit,' Mia mumbled, as she did her mental arithmetic.

He had done the same.

The profile. The numbers. The random victims.

'Have you seen it? The list?'

Munch shook his head.

'We're waiting by the phone now. Anette is in contact with them. The threat level has gone up. They're talking about taking the government, even the royal family, to a safe place.'

'Seriously?'

'Like I said, they're sparse with the details, but Anette thought so.'

'But they can't do that! How can they justify that to the general public? The king has gone underground, but there's no need to worry, you just carry on with your lives as normal. Idiots.'

'I don't think it'll get that far but, even so, the army, the home guard, the territorial army – I'm guessing they're putting them all on alert now, as discreetly as possible. That's why they—'

'Want to keep all the nutters away?' Mia fulminated. She looked as if she was strongly tempted to spit on the floor.

'Listen, Mia—' Munch began, but she stopped him with a raised hand.

'Can I give you a lift anywhere?'

Mia shook her head and grabbed the door handle firmly.

'I'll keep you posted, OK?' he called after her when she was outside.

Mia gave him a last, resigned look before slamming the door shut and disappearing along the pavement without looking back.

Bollocks.

He really wanted to go after her, but then his mobile rang in his pocket.

'Yes?'

'We're about to start,' Anette said.

'Where?'

'Bankplassen in twenty minutes.'

'I'm on my way,' Munch said, and turned the key in the ignition.

Chapter 52

Mia wandered the streets, irritated, furious, shocked; she didn't know how to process her conflicting emotions. She was in turmoil. She had started the day thinking *What if he's setting me up? What if he's full of crap?* John Wold in the pub the night before. He had seen the incredulity in her eyes, hadn't he? Damn it, she had put him straight. *It's not Curry. I've no intention of helping you with anything.* Clever of him, wasn't it? To invent some bullshit story he knew would get her hooked. Make her doubt. Make her switch sides. *There's a junkie out there. Your sister is mixed up in this.* Sigrid. *Bastard.* Because it had worked. Of course it had. Her grief at her loss. Her yearning. He had played on her most private feelings, hadn't he? Just to make her say yes.

Mia muttered curses and crossed the street again. She didn't care where she went as long as her legs were moving. That was what had happened, wasn't it? He had tricked her. Cisse? A red puffa jacket? That description could fit so many people. She should have seen through him immediately, but he had caught her off guard. She stroked the bracelet on her wrist then came to a halt as a taxi sounded its horn and brushed her thigh.

She jumped back from the road.

Shit.

And she had had such a good start to the day. Waking up in Charlie Brun's lovely guest room, feeling completely clear-headed. And Curry? Of course Curry wasn't on the take. Mia had known him for ten years. He might look like a thug, but behind the tough façade was a soul that couldn't hurt a fly.

No, no, it had to be someone else.

A police officer.

It could be anyone.

And now this?

She had started to cross at a junction when a hand grabbed her leather jacket and pulled her back. Pointed to the red light as another hooting car rushed by. She nodded a quick thank-you to the friendly face and stuffed her hand into her pocket, searching for a lozenge.

Fifty people?

One of those?

The woman in the yellow coat out walking her dog?

The boy on his skateboard?

Hell.

She began to calm down as the lights changed to green and the crowd calmly crossed the street. On their way home. On their way to work. Going home from school. Smiling, happy, tired. Grocery bags bashing against prams, a completely normal day in quiet little Oslo with spring just around the corner.

Fuck.

She couldn't help it. She knew it was just a story but she had to check.

Of course she did.

Mia stopped at a street corner and pulled her mobile out of her pocket.

OK.

Sort your head out.

Cisse?

Cecilie?

A junkie wearing a red puffa jacket?

It should be a straightforward matter.

Having it checked out.

Confirming that it was all a ruse.

Oslo was a small town, a village, really, and Mia knew exactly who to call.

'The Prindsen Centre.'

'Yes, hello, my name is Mia Krüger. Please can I speak to Mildrid Lind?'

'Just a moment.'

She was put on hold.

A young man with tattoos emerged from a building near her, took a big, jangling bunch of keys from his trouser pocket and stuck a key in the door to lock it. He was heading out to lunch. Just another day.

'She's on the phone, but I don't think she'll be very long. Shall I ask her to call you back?'

'Yes, please. Thank you.'

Mia stuffed the mobile back into her leather jacket and was about to start moving again when she noticed something in the window right in front of her.

But what the . . .?

A tattoo parlour.

Rows of pictures behind the filthy glass.

What the . . .?

Bragging pictures. A Motörhead logo on a bicep. A big eagle on a chest. Red and yellow flames up a thin shin.

And there.

In the middle of a row.

Surely not . . .?

Mia stood, her mouth hanging open, then shuffled closer to the window.

What?

Her?

A naked, pale back. Long, dark hair between the shoulder blades. Blue eyes.

No, it couldn't be . . .

Oh, shit, it was.

In there. Among the hearts and the peace doves and the burning skulls.

A tattoo of her face.

What the . . .?

A sound from far away, vibration in her pocket.

'Mildrid Lind speaking. You called me?'

Chapter 53

Rumours had long been circulating about this new, top-secret situation room. The world was changing. It was no longer East versus West, generals with fingers on expensive red buttons; the enemy was now terror attacks carried out with homemade nail bombs, hijacked planes, stolen trucks. Civilian targets, unthinkable just a few years ago and almost impossible to defend yourself against. Although, so far, Norway had been spared these religiously motivated actions, the attack on the government quarter had made even naive Norwegian politicians realize the seriousness of these threats. Munch had never really believed that they had done anything about it. He had assumed that there would be the usual debate, action plans drawn up by cross-party committees in Parliament, but when he and Anette stepped out of the lift and into the hypermodern operation room, he had to admit he had been wrong.

He was deep in the basement under the Ministry of Defence offices in Myntgata number 1. It had security measures the like of which he had never seen before. If he hadn't been as inherently sceptical about the top brass as he was, he might have been willing to admit that he was impressed. Lifts with long codes. Checkpoints with body searches. Doors with more codes, metal detectors wielded by young soldiers in uniform. They finally reached a big metal door where they were told to hand over their mobile phones, something that Munch found irritating, but there was nothing for it other than to obey orders. The well-dressed young man entered a new code on a panel which now flashed green, and they had finally arrived at their destination.

A large oval table. Men with serious faces, some in uniforms, most wearing suits and neutral ties over white or pale-blue shirts. Munch scanned the room to see if he recognized anyone, but he didn't.

'General Edvardsen,' a tall, distinguished-looking man with grey hair introduced himself as he came towards them.

A large hand through the air and a firm handshake.

'So you're Munch? And you must be Goli?'

Munch nodded. As did Anette Goli. If being the only woman in the room made her uncomfortable, she didn't show it. Women tended to be well represented in senior positions in Norway, but equality clearly hadn't reached this basement. The general nodded quickly around the table and introduced the others before returning his attention to the huge screen which covered the whole of the wall behind him. FST and PST agents. A representative from the Prime Minister's office. Several high-ranking officers from various branches of the military. Munch suddenly felt a little shabby as he stood there. His corduroy trousers were stained and his duffel coat was well past its prime.

'Gentlemen,' Edvardsen said as the light was dimmed in the large room. 'You all know why you are here. Some of you know more than others, and – for the most part – that's how it will stay; all information in this investigation is strictly NTK. If you have any questions, we will deal with them at the end; first, I want us to review the incident as it unfolded today, and then run through the various initiatives we have employed.'

There was nodding around the table.

A picture appeared on the screen.

'Today, just after eleven hundred hours, we had a call from this man, Erik Rønning, a journalist from *Aftenposten*. Fortunately for us, Rønning kept a cool head and contacted the Ministry directly, and in subsequent interviews he has told us that he hasn't shared the information with his superiors at the newspaper. As a result, we believe that, so far, we're in control. I don't have to stress that this is of the utmost importance. It is, as I said, NTK, and we will do everything in our power to keep the public out of it. What they don't know won't hurt them. The last thing we need now is panic on the streets.'

'NTK?' Munch whispered, leaning towards Goli.

'Need to know,' Goli mumbled, without looking at him.

'Rønning was visited by what we have reason to believe was one of our men – a soldier – and was given a list of fifty names.'

Another image appeared on the screen and there was stirring around the table as papers were circulated. Munch looked at the screen and down at the list now lying in front of him. He quickly checked for any names he might recognize but couldn't find any, thank God. Miriam Munch. Marion Munch. It was selfish and unprofessional, perhaps, but his reaction had been instinctive.

'As you're all aware, the events of the past week support the authenticity of this list. Our friends from the special unit in Mariboesgate know this better than anyone, and that's obviously why they're here, in case anyone in this room was wondering why Oslo police is represented.'

Quick glances towards them. Munch nodded back out of politeness.

'Perhaps you could give us a brief overview for the benefit of everyone here who doesn't know the details of these murders?'

Edvardsen looked briefly towards them.

'Yes,' Munch said, and coughed.

He considered getting up for a moment but stayed put; the general up at the screen seemed impatient enough as it was.

'We have three victims. Vivian Berg. Aged twenty-two, a ballet dancer. Found in a mountain lake a few hours' drive from Oslo.'

'Along with a number, is that correct?'

'That's correct,' Munch said. 'The number four, scratched into a—'

'As we can see,' Edvardsen cut him off, 'Vivian Berg is number four on the list.'

'Er, yes,' Munch said. 'The second victim was Kurt Wang.'

'Number seven on the list.' Edvardsen nodded. 'And the last one?'

'Ruben Iversen, aged fourteen. Found in the boot of a car up by Camp Skar.'

'With a number?'

'Thirteen.' Munch nodded.

'Which also fits with the list Rønning was given.' Edvardsen indicated the screen. 'Have you found anything that links the victims?'

'No,' Anette Goli said. 'And that's been our biggest headache. The apparent randomness. That is, until we, well . . .'

She nodded at the piece of paper in front of her.

'Fifty names,' Edvardsen said firmly. 'Random civilian Norwegians. Three of them have already been killed so there's no reason to think that this threat is anything other than real, and we have orders from the Prime Minister's office to respond accordingly.'

The general took a sip of water from a glass on the table before continuing.

'According to Rønning, the killer was dressed partly in army clothes, he mentioned Lashkar Gah in Afghanistan, and the motive seems clear. This is most likely a revenge action. I'll return to the reason for this shortly, but I'm pleased to be able to tell you that we have already identified the suspect.'

Edvardsen turned as another picture appeared on the screen.

A suspect?

So soon?

Munch turned to Goli, who raised her eyebrows. He had little time for the others who were present, but on this occasion he had to take his hat off to them. Rønning's encounter with the killer had happened only hours ago.

'May I remind you once again that we're dealing with extremely sensitive information. I am not at liberty to divulge how we found our man, but I can tell you what we know about him. This is top secret at the highest level, not to be made available to any members of the public. Under no circumstances, I repeat, *under no circumstances* can what you're about to hear leave this room.'

Edvardsen didn't look at them directly, but there could be no doubt as to who he had in mind.

'Do we have active forces in Afghanistan? Officially, no. Our men are merely taking part in humanitarian UN-supported operations. Unofficially? Of course we do. We don't sit on the fence when our allies are at war. And again, what you're about to hear will not leave this room. Do you understand?'

Edvardsen looked up now to make sure they understood that this was serious. Goli nodded back and eventually Munch did the same, albeit reluctantly.

'Good,' the general grunted as another picture appeared on the screen.

A young man in uniform, squinting slightly at the photographer. Armed to the teeth. A desert landscape in the background.

'We think this is our man,' Edvardsen said.

Another picture. The same soldier, an archive picture this time.

'His name is Ivan Horowitz.' Edvardsen looked at them again. 'Born in 1988 in Gjøvik. Started his army career with the Telemark Battalion and was later recruited to Alfa. For those of you who don't know Alfa, let me put it this way: they're the best of the best. The Americans have their Green Berets, the Russians have Spetsnaz, and we have Alfa.'

The general was unable to hide the pride in his voice as he clicked and another picture appeared on the screen.

'Afghanistan. Northern region. The Americans had undertaken a large-scale operation called Endurance, and we contributed a group of six soldiers, all Alfa. One of these was our man, Ivan Horowitz. I won't go into detail – as I said earlier, this is NTK – but we have reason to believe that what happened next was the trigger for what we're now dealing with. A revenge action, some kind of hatred of the Norwegian government, or whatever you want to call it; anyway, you're about to see why we're quite sure that we have our man.'

Edvardsen took another sip of water.

More desert. Scorched mountaintops.

'Spring 2010. Alfa was engaged in something that should have been a routine job when they were ambushed. We lost five men.

Ivan Horowitz was the only survivor. It's still unclear exactly what happened but, according to Horowitz, he regained consciousness after the explosion, in which he sustained shrapnel injuries to his chest and abdomen and a broken leg. Horowitz spends the next ten days in a mountain cave. He drinks his own urine. He eats – well, we don't know what he ate. In any case, he eventually manages to drag himself to a nearby road, where he's picked up by a patrol.'

Edvardsen looked gravely across the gathering before continuing.

'After being treated and debriefed in a field hospital, Horowitz is returned to Norway, his active army career now over. We give him a medal and try to help him with the transition to civilian life, we offer him a desk job, but Horowitz is no longer himself. He wants to go public: what happened out there wasn't right, he lost his best friends, people need to know what's going on. Yes, I'm sure you get the picture. In the end we had no choice but to let him go. We follow him closely so that we can help him, of course, but also to keep an eye on him.'

Edvardsen clicked again.

'2011. Horowitz is admitted to Blakstad psychiatric hospital. He's discharged in early 2012. And there the trail goes cold. He didn't take any money out of his bank account. There's no evidence of electronic activity. It's as if Ivan Horowitz has ceased to exist. We presume that he has killed himself but that his body has yet to be found. We close the file. But now this.'

'A new identity?'

A dry voice over a blue tie.

'Most likely.' Edvardsen nodded.

'And his hatred is real?'

Another calm voice, this time with a grey tie.

'I'm afraid so,' Edvardsen said. 'The reports from our own psychologists state that, shortly after his homecoming, Horowitz showed signs of what we call, well, negative behaviour that caused concern.'

'The clock is ticking,' an older man at the end of the table suddenly said, and nodded almost imperceptibly towards Munch and Goli.

'Yes,' Edvardsen confirmed. 'Munch and Goli, is that right?'
Munch nodded.

'We've initiated a major hunt for Ivan Horowitz, obviously, and now we want you to do the following.'

His voice changed; it was an order now. Munch didn't like it, but he said nothing.

'We're going to tell the media about Horowitz. We'll get you pictures and anything else you may need. He's your prime suspect now, but you won't mention his army background.'

'Listen—' Munch began, but he was cut off.

'Good,' said a mouth over another tie. 'Surely someone must have seen him, even if he's hiding? No one can be completely invisible. I mean, maybe he got a new job, friends, neighbours?'

'Exactly,' said Edvardsen. 'What we're hoping for is exactly that, that someone will recognize him. If we're lucky, they will do so soon, before Horowitz has time to – well, has time to pick another name from the list.'

'Are we offering any of these people protection?' asked a man with glasses, holding up the list.

'We've talked about it, of course,' Edvardsen said. 'But as you can see, most of these names are quite common. Nils Olsen, Janne Andersen – how many potential victims are we talking about? We don't have the capacity, unfortunately. It's simply not feasible.'

The latter was spoken with something which for the first time sounded like humanity.

'So,' the general continued with a glance towards Munch and Goli, 'Ivan Horowitz is now officially your suspect. That's the best angle we can pursue now, without causing concern. A suspect in a triple homicide. That's why we're looking for him. We think this story will stand up. And, hopefully, it'll be enough for us to find him. We have also allocated plenty of our own resources to the case, but I'll get to that in a moment.'

'But—' Munch said, but was interrupted again.

'I'm sorry. Goli, was it?'

Anette Goli nodded.

'We'll send you what you need. Apart from that, it's business as usual, OK?'

'Are you telling me not to brief my team about any of this?' Munch said.

'Only that Horowitz is a suspect.'

'But how do I—?'

'You'll find a way,' Edvardsen said. He was clearly keen to move on to the next point on his agenda.

The young man who had escorted them down had returned discreetly.

'I'll see you out.' He smiled politely and nodded towards the big, open door.

Chapter 54

Mia was standing outside the cream-coloured brick building in Storgata, feeling apprehensive about going inside. She had been there before, but it was a long time ago now. The old days. In another life. Seeing the building brought back memories she would rather forget. The Prindsen Centre. A service for addicts run by Oslo city council. A bed for the night. Shooting galleries. Doctors offering health care. Psychologists. Nurses. Dentists. Money and support to go back home. That was why she had come here originally. To pick up Sigrid.

She was starting to feel really bad.

Her sister had been huddled in a corner, hugging herself, looking so very small.

Sorry, Mia.

Don't worry about it, Sigrid. Of course I don't mind you calling me.

I didn't want to bother you.

You're not bothering me, Sigrid. Of course I'll help you. What happened?

Friendly but guarded faces. Going in and out of one chilly room after another. Papers to be signed.

I'm not feeling too good, Mia.

How about coming home? You could live with me.

Would that be all right, do you think?

Of course it would, Sigrid.

I won't get in your way, I promise.

You're never in the way, Sigrid.

New people. New forms. Her twin sister's practically transparent body on the passenger seat in the car, wrapped in a blanket.

Mia was snapped out of her memories as a tram rattled by close behind her. She pulled herself together. She entered through the black, cast-iron gate and made her way to the reception.

'Hello, how can I help you?'

A gentle but tired face behind the glass pane.

'Mia Krüger. I'm meeting Mildrid Lind.'

'OK. If you take a seat over there she'll be right with you.'

'Thank you.'

Mia had only just sat down when the door opened and a middle-aged social worker appeared.

'Hello, Mia. It's been a long time. Nice to see you again.'

'Thank you. Likewise.'

'Why don't we go to my office? I think it's best if we speak there.'

Mia followed her down the corridor and out across the gravel square. A small office with a desk and posters on the walls. Offers of help.

Mildrid Lind pushed her glasses up her nose and sat down.

'The people who come here are a bit wary of the police, you know, but I have managed to talk to some of them. Your info was a little vague.'

'I know,' Mia said apologetically, 'but it was all that I had. Cecilie. Cisse. A red puffa jacket. Aged around forty.'

'I've been asking around the centre and I think I've found someone who can help you.'

'Really?' Mia was surprised. 'She exists?'

'What do you mean?'

'Oh, it's nothing, I just . . .'

'Like I said, our clients don't trust the police. For obvious reasons.'

'This is a private matter,' Mia interjected quickly. 'I'm not here on police business. There's no investigation. Nobody is accused of anything. I'm just trying to find her.'

'I understand.' Lind nodded. 'And that was the impression I got when we spoke earlier. I'm not a big fan of the police myself, to be quite honest, but I know you.'

'Thank you. I appreciate you saying that.'

Lind picked up her phone.

'Hi, it's Mildrid here. Is Synne around? Great. Please would you ask if she could join me in a moment? It's about our earlier conversation? OK, thank you.'

They waited in silence in the small office until there was a knock on the door.

'Hi, Synne. Do come in. Are you all right?'

'Er, yeah,' said a young woman, throwing a quick glance at Mia.

'This is Mia Krüger,' Lind said.

'Oh, OK,' the skinny woman said, but she continued to linger in the doorway, unsure of what to do with herself.

'Why don't you have a seat here?' Mildred said, getting up. 'I just have to do something. Do you mind? Will the two of you manage without me?'

'It's fine.' Mia smiled. 'Or it is with me. Is it all right with you?'

'She's not in trouble, is she?' the young woman asked.

'Who?' Mia said.

'Cisse?'

'Oh, no. This has nothing to do with the police. She's just, well, important to me. Does that make sense?'

Mildrid Lind smiled and disappeared out of the door.

'I don't know,' the skinny woman said. 'Why is she important to you?'

'I believe she has something that belongs to me.'

The skinny woman sat down, still wondering whether she was being tricked into something.

'What?'

'This,' Mia said, reaching out her arm. 'Or rather, one very like it.'

Synne glanced at the silver bracelet and smiled faintly.

'I had one of those once.'

'Did you?'

'Yes, or not exactly like it, but with three boats. Sailing boats. My brother gave it to me before he went to war.'

'Your brother is a soldier?'

The skinny girl wrapped her scruffy wool jacket more tightly around herself and nodded cautiously. She twirled from side to side on the office chair. Looked nervously out of the window at the courtyard.

'That's a long time ago now.'

'Which branch of the military is he in?'

'I don't know, he joined – now, what do you call it? – the foreign legion?'

Mia nodded.

'He wanted to be a tough guy, I think, but we never heard from him again. My mum tried to get someone to help us, but it turns out there's not a lot you can do if someone has joined up voluntarily, if you know what I mean. Have you ever been to Lofoten?'

'I'm afraid not.'

'The mountains back home dive straight from the sky and into the sea,' the young woman said, and a hint of a smile emerged.

'That sounds very beautiful.'

'It is.'

'So you know her? Cisse?'

'Yes,' she said at length. 'But I think she's gone.'

'Gone. How?'

'Dead. That's what they say. But I don't know. People talk a lot, don't they? You never know who you can trust in this town.'

'So you haven't seen her for a while?'

'No, not since . . . probably before Christmas, I guess.'

'Did you know her well?'

'Quite well, or that's to say we hung out a lot. She was nice. She would always share a hit; she was never stingy like that. And she would lend you money if she had any.'

'And you just know her as Cisse? You don't know any more? Her surname? Or where she lived?'

'I don't think she lived anywhere,' Synne said. 'And I don't know her surname, no. Have you talked to Kevin?'

'Who?'

'Kevin? They were always together. I used to think she was his mum, but I don't think so now, I think they were just close friends. Whatever, if you find Kevin, he'll probably know more.'

Synne coughed lightly and tightened the wool jacket around herself even more.

'And how do I find Kevin?'

'I don't know. He's everywhere and nowhere. Just like the rest of us.'

'You don't know where he is most of the time? Or if he has a mobile?'

'No, no idea,' the young woman said.

'How old is he? What does he look like?'

'He's not that old. A little older than me, perhaps. Last time I saw him he was wearing that yellow beanie of his, but maybe that won't help you. He could have lost it, I wouldn't know.'

'Yes, of course, but even so, I'll look out for a yellow beanie,' Mia said as the door opened behind them and Mildrid Lind popped her head round.

'Synne, the doctor can see you now. Would you like that?'

'Yes, I would.' The young woman nodded and got up.

Lind looked at Mia, who nodded back.

'Oh, by the way,' Synne said in the doorway, 'his eyebrows are strange.'

'Whose? Kevin's?'

'Yes. They're bit like – it's almost as if they're not there, if you know what I mean. I think there's something wrong with them.'

'He has no eyebrows?'

'He does, but it's almost as if they're not there.'

'I think we had better go now. Lots of people want to see the doctor today.' Mildrid Lind smiled amicably.

'Of course,' Mia said, and got up.

'I hope you find what you're looking for.'

'Thank you for your help, Synne.'

The young woman smiled briefly and raised her hand in a cautious goodbye before hugging herself and following Lind down the corridor.

Chapter 55

Kevin was sitting in the back room of a 7-Eleven in Hegdehaugs-veien, nursing a bump to his head, not because someone had hit him but because he had been hungry. Normally, he could go for days without eating. It was like that when he was on heroin – he needed nothing else; a little water, perhaps – but he hadn't had a fix for days and he had a sudden craving for a Snickers bar.

'Bloody junkie, he's in here all the time,' said a female voice far away.

Kevin tried focusing his eyes on the speaker, but he couldn't do it.

And no wonder.

He had thought this might happen, hadn't he? He hadn't had enough money for a proper fix and he'd been unable to get any more. He'd been overtired. Sick, almost. He'd had no energy for anything and so they had shot up something else instead, him and Jimmy. Crushed pills that they had liquefied. Ritalin and Rohypnol. An upper and a downer. Jimmy had heard they made a good sub-stitute for heroin, but Kevin had had his doubts just as the needle went into his skin.

And no wonder.

From that point onwards he couldn't remember very much.

'Oi, zombie?' another voice said, someone taking hold of his shoulders and shaking them.

'Eh?' Kevin said, and opened his eyes, not sure if the words had actually left his mouth.

'Are you asleep?' the man said, turning into a security guard, and Kevin was wide awake. He almost jumped in the chair before the switch was flicked inside his brain and he floated away once more.

And no wonder.

Rumour had it Jimmy was a former maths professor who had gone loopy and ended up in the gutter, that he knew all sorts of things about how the world worked, but this had been a really big mistake.

How long ago was it now?

He had retched a lot on an empty stomach, only bile coming up. And this theory that minus and plus equalled zero, or whatever the hell it was Jimmy had hoped to achieve when he mixed an upper and a downer, hadn't worked as it was meant to. One moment Kevin was wide awake, thinking he could run all the way to the moon if he wanted to, the next he was completely out of it, totally zonked.

He was coming down now.

Another downer, but this time less horrific. It was almost over now. He just had to hold out a bit longer. He remembered that he had felt hungry. He had found a 7-Eleven and seen the Snickers bar. That was the good news. But then he had run straight into a post and blacked out and had now woken up in this room. That was the bad news, but the theft was no big deal. It was just a bar of chocolate. The most important thing was that it would soon be over.

What a shit trip.

'And look here,' the girl said, pointing to the table.

Kevin was awake now, but he still couldn't understand what she meant.

'He stole money?' the security guard asked.

'From the till. There was at least twenty thousand kroner there, and now only half of it is left.'

'Do you have any money on you?' The security guard shook Kevin's shoulders again.

'Snickers,' Kevin mumbled, and felt how dry his mouth was, but at least his voice was coming back.

'So all you took was a bar of chocolate?'

Kevin wanted to nod, but he was scared that his head might fall off so he sat very still.

'He's lying to you.' The girl pointed at the till again. 'I caught him red-handed. He's been here before. Look, nearly all the money is gone.'

Kevin felt better now. He was able to see and hear what was going on. What a relief. He had been so scared of dying just then – or had that been earlier today?

'Where's the money?'

The security guard grabbed him hard by the shoulder now.

'If you don't give it back to us, we'll have to call the police.'

'What money?' Kevin mumbled in his confusion.

'The money from the till,' the girl said, pointing to it for a third time, as if the first two hadn't been enough. 'There was at least twenty thousand kroner there and now only half of it is left.'

It was over now. Thank God. Oh, no, it was coming back. Kevin clung to the edge of the chair, terrified of what was happening, but it was a false alarm. He was still here. No more ups or downs. He smiled to himself. Jimmy was a moron. He was never doing that again. He had to talk to Lotte. They had to have a serious chat. They were a couple. They were supposed to do things together and have no secrets from one another.

'I'll be back in a week.'

'Where are you going?'

'I can't tell you.'

'Why not?'

'Please don't ask, Kevin. You just have to trust me, OK?'

'Sure, but, seriously, just a hint?'

'I'm going to get something.'

'What?'

'Please don't ask any more. I promise. When I'm back, we'll get out of here, the two of us, OK?'

'Get out of here? And go where?'

'Away from here. From this shithole. You and me. Doesn't that sound great?'

Of course it sounded great. Kevin felt himself coming round now. It was time to move on. He had lost his mobile. No wonder he hadn't heard from Lotte. He would have to get himself a new one.

'So where is it?' the security guard demanded to know. He seemed angry now.

'Where's what?'

'The money? From the till?'

'I only took the Snickers,' Kevin ventured cautiously.

The security guard looked at the girl, who shook her head. It took a few seconds before Kevin worked out what was going on. There was something in the eyes of the girl wearing the 7-Eleven uniform. That cunning bitch. She had had her hand in the till. Seized her moment as he sat in there. He saw it now. A comatose junkie. The perfect crime. Take the money. Blame him.

'Then we'll just have to sit here until the police turn up,' the security guard said.

Two officers turned up. Police community support officers. Those who hadn't made it to the academy but still felt the need to wield power. After nearly six years on the streets of Oslo, Kevin had met most of them. In shopping centres. Multistorey car parks. Stairwells. They were everywhere you tried to find a little warmth and a roof over your head.

'It's total chaos in the city centre. Something must have happened. No one else is going to turn up,' the first officer said to the second.

'But it needs to be reported,' said Little Miss Hand-in-the-Till, and folded her arms across her T-shirt.

Listen, everyone. Hello? No wonder you didn't make it to the police academy. Ready cash? Add one junkie? Why would I leave half of it behind, if I were the thief? Ten thousand? Why would I leave ten thousand kroner behind? Kevin smiled at his own cleverness and was just about to open his mouth when there was a screeching sound in the street outside the store. Squealing metal wheels followed by an ear-splitting human cry.

'What the hell?'

Police community support officer number two stuck his head out of the door and his eyes widened.

'Oh, shit.'

'Someone got knocked over by the tram.'

Mayhem ensued. Kevin found himself between police community support officers one and two, with his face pressed against the window and looking out at the street, where an old man was lying on the ground. Then that moment where nobody knows what to do next happened. It's not in the script. You're walking down the street. You're minding your own business. Suddenly there's a bang. A man lies dying right in front of you. Someone faints. Others hug one another. There's crying. Someone calls an ambulance. Someone takes out their mobile and films everything. Someone tries to help. Puts their hands on the injured man's chest. Tries mouth-to-mouth resuscitation. Tries to stop the bleeding. Kevin did none of these things. He walked calmly to the back room, stuffed the remaining ten thousand kroner into his pocket.

And legged it to the city centre.

Chapter 56

Hege Anita was only seven years old, but she understood much more than the grown-ups believed. Take social services – they were dangerous people. They stole little girls from their mummies. Whenever they turned up, it was important to be as quiet as a mouse and not open the door, no matter how many times they rang the doorbell. If it became too scary, as it sometimes did, she would stick her fingers in her ears and think about nice things, like the white cat that often sat in the playground outside their block of flats, or perhaps sing a song to herself. 'Twinkle, Twinkle, Little Star' or 'Rudolph the Red-nosed Reindeer', although Christmas was a long way away and they would be spending it with Granny; her mum had promised that last Christmas as well, only it hadn't happened.

A teacher had kept her back after school today. He had asked her questions, but Hege Anita had learned what to say by now so, fortunately, it had gone well this time too. Her teacher's name was Tore and he had some sort of disease because his hair grew only over his ears and not on top of his head, but he was very nice. Hege Anita didn't think it was right to lie, but you couldn't always get what you wanted in this world, she had learned that at a very early age, so it was just a matter of getting it over with.

Please would you tell your mum that we would like to talk to her?

Nod, smile nicely and say yes.

She hasn't been to parents' evenings, you see, and she doesn't pick up the phone when we ring.

More nodding, maybe scratch her leg, think of something else, perhaps the other children on their way home outside the windows of her classroom, to homes where they lived with their mummy *and* their daddy, who weren't away all the time and didn't sleep in the middle of the day.

Did you give her the letter I gave you to take home?

Squirm on her chair, maybe pretend that she needed the loo. That usually worked.

Hege Anita took the key that was hanging around her neck and let herself into the flat.

'Hello?'

Not a sound.

But her mum's shoes were there and the jacket she always wore was on the floor and Hege Anita felt happy.

Her mummy was home.

Hurrah! she wanted to shout, but not too loudly, obviously; her mum didn't like being woken up if she was asleep, something she often was when she wasn't out working. She didn't have a job but she would do things and bring home money so it was sort of like having a job.

There had been an open day at her school recently and some of the other mums had talked about their jobs. One was a doctor who saved sick children. One was a dentist who helped children if they had cavities. One worked with computers, and another looked after her family, and she had thought that woman was almost like her mum. And that her mum could have been there, although her mum had said no and practically laughed at Hege Anita when she had asked.

'Hello?' she whispered cautiously, and kicked off her boots. She half ran down the passage and into the living room, but no one was there.

The door to the bedroom was closed.

Do not disturb.

She knew not to, but even so, today? Perhaps it was OK today, given all the good things that had happened.

Tore had praised her. Held up her drawing to the whole class and said nice things about it, and she had gone red in the face. She had drawn a picture of her grandad in the car with Granny next to

286

im. And the dog, of course, and in the background she had drawn a fishing boat and a seagull. She hadn't really thought much about it until he had come over to her desk.

A gold star.

She could hardly believe it.

Everyone else in her class had praised it as well.

'Wow, that's really good.'

'Wow, you're great at drawing.'

'Wow, can you teach me to draw like you?'

In the break afterwards everyone wanted to play with her, which was so different from how it usually was. She had been allowed to go first when they played Simon Says and been picked as the captain of one of the rounders teams.

What a great day!

The drawing was in her school bag.

Hege Anita took it out carefully and positioned herself in front of the door to her mum's bedroom again.

This is for you, Mum.

But she didn't.

It was probably for the best.

Hege Anita put the drawing back in her school bag and went to the kitchen. Her face lit up when she saw what was on the counter. Honey Cheerios. And milk in the fridge as well. Her mum must have got money again, probably from the man in the army jacket who never came in but just stood in the doorway. No wonder she was tired. Hege Anita carried the milk and the cereal into the living room and turned on the TV.

NRK Super was her favourite channel, but it wasn't on Channel 3 where it normally was.

'Breaking News,' it said at the top of the screen.

Hege Anita poured milk into the bowl and turned up the volume.

'Police have today released pictures of the prime suspect in the triple homicide . . .'

A picture of a man appeared on the screen.

The Odd Squad was her favourite programme. And the cartoon about the girls who had their own horses.

No horses now, only a picture of a man with a gun and a helmet on his head.

She opened the cereal box and scattered Cheerios onto the milk. She preferred to eat it like that because she could dunk the cereal hoops and pretend they were little boats with people who she could then save with her mouth.

Hege Anita had stuck her spoon into the bowl when another picture appeared on the screen and her eyes widened.

'Police are also looking for this woman . . .'

What?

The TV showed a picture of . . .

Her mum?

No . . .

First one.

Then another.

Yes, it was her . . .

Leaving a shop.

Wearing her green baseball cap.

The woman on the TV was still talking, but Hege Anita was no longer listening.

A drawing now.

And then another photograph.

Mum?

But why . . .?

Hege Anita got up and ran as fast as her little legs would carry her across the slippery floor. She waited in front of the door for a moment, her heart pounding under her jumper, before she made up her mind and started banging her fists on the closed bedroom door.

FIVE

Chapter 57

Holger Munch was in Freddy Fuego Burrito Bar in Hausmannsgate, eating a late breakfast. He had slept badly and was feeling grouchy. It hadn't helped that the benches in here were narrow and rock hard either, but at least he was getting something to eat. He had considered Starbucks, as it was nearer, but he couldn't cope with all those people. Not today. He had left the meeting in the situation room with a bad feeling, and it had only worsened during the evening. Arrogant know-it-alls – how could they be so sure that they had found the right man? It had troubled him throughout the night. He had got up several times, chain-smoked out the window like an old chimney, then woken up feeling sick and in a thoroughly foul mood.

He scrunched up the wrapper and drained the rest of his cola as Anette Goli entered the café. He hadn't spoken to her since yesterday afternoon and he needed her to help him straighten out his thinking. Mia was his usual sounding board, but she wasn't taking his calls. For obvious reasons.

'Hello?' Anette said, looking around, somewhat confused.

'I know,' Munch said, wiping his mouth with a napkin. 'I had to get out of the office. I've convinced myself that they hear and see everything we do down there.'

'Who?' Goli asked, sitting down.

'Oh, you know,' Munch mumbled. 'The generals.'

Anette smiled faintly and tucked her hair behind her ear. He knew that she had been working non-stop since the meeting yesterday but, if she was tired, she was hiding it well.

'Coffee?' Munch said. 'Burrito?'

'No, thank you. I have to get back as soon as possible.'

They had set up a temporary call centre down at police head quarters in Grønland. Twenty manned telephone lines. After they had gone public with the suspect, the response had, predictably been overwhelming.

'How is it going down there?'

'Oh, you know.' Anette sighed. 'The phones haven't stopped ringing. It's not easy to stay on top of all the calls, but we're sifting through them as best we can.'

'Any proper leads yet?'

'It's hard to say. We don't have the capacity to check even half of them out. Someone saw him in the house next door. Someone saw him on Gran Canaria. On the metro. Roller-skating up by Lake Sognsvann. We even had a caller who insisted he had to be his daughter's football coach, and no, he didn't look much like the man in the pictures but he had a military bearing.'

'I see.'

'So what did you want to talk to me about?' Anette said, ignoring her phone.

'This.' Munch opened the file on the table in front of him.

He pulled out the sketch artist's drawings of Karl Overlind and placed them next to the photograph of Ivan Horowitz.

'What's your point?'

'Do we seriously think that this is the same man?'

Goli glanced at the pictures.

'Holger—'

'Just take a look at them.'

'I know you don't like it. Them taking charge. I don't like it very much myself, but what can we do?'

'No, seriously. I agree there are similarities, but are there enough of them? Enough for us to jettison everything we already have. Jump when they say jump?'

'True, but the two drawings aren't identical either, are they?'

She put her fingers on the two drawings.

'But we've already established that he disguises himself, dresses up, or whatever it is he does.'

Her mobile rang again. She glanced quickly at the screen.

'Mikkelson. I have to take this call.'

'He can wait,' Munch grunted. 'So do you think the similarity is strong enough for us to let them take control?'

'These are just sketches—'

'I know.' Munch nodded. 'But I've sent Curry off.'

'Sent him where?'

'Off to talk to the people who actually did see him. In the flesh.'

'The hotel in Gamlebyen?'

'And Sagene Cleaning Services.'

'That was a good idea,' Goli said. 'Although I could do with him down at police headquarters.'

'If nothing else just to have it confirmed.'

'That it's the same guy?'

'Yes.'

Anette began to smile.

'Absolutely, Holger. That's up to you, although I—'

'You trust them?'

'I see no reason not to. Why would they point us in the direction of the wrong man? Share classified information with us unless there's a reason. I mean, you saw for yourself what they have. We don't have a fraction of their resources. I almost had the feeling that the CIA was watching us as well when we were down there. How long did it take them to find Horowitz? Twenty minutes?'

'True, true.'

'This is obviously up to you, Holger. But if you want my opinion, then we're on the right track. Remember that the photographs of Horowitz are three years old. And again—'

'They're just sketches, I know,' Munch mumbled. 'I just want to be sure.'

'Of course,' Anette said, and got up.

'There's one more thing.' Munch gestured for her to sit down again. 'You noticed that they didn't let us keep the list with the fifty names?'

'Classified.' Anette nodded. '"NTK", wasn't that how they put it?'

'NKT my arse.' Munch took another piece of paper from the file.

'You took it with you?' Anette was shocked. 'How?'

Munch shrugged it off.

'Of course I did. There have to be limits. And look at this.'

He pointed to some of the names on the list.

'What's your point?'

'Ann-Helen Undergård.'

'Yes?'

'Tom-Erik Wangseter.'

'I don't follow.'

'They said the names were too common, that we don't have the capacity, didn't they? To protect all these poor people? Or at least warn them, if nothing else.'

'Holger,' Anette said, shaking her head slightly.

'I'm serious. How many people are called that? Anton Birger Lundamo. I accept that there could be many different people on the list who share the same name, but some of them are rare. How many? Why not do something for them at least?'

'Holger,' Anette said again.

'I'm thinking about assigning some of my people to it.'

'To contact them?'

'Yes.'

'No, no,' Goli said.

'Why not?'

She leaned forwards across the table towards him now, glancing furtively over her shoulder before whispering:

'And say what? There's a madman at large who kills random people, and your name is on his list? How long do you think it'll be before that hits the news? It'll be pandemonium. And anyway it's classified, what if it gets back to them that it was us?'

'Yes, but for pity's sake, Anette, what if one of your loved ones was on this list?'

'Who would you assign to the job then? Gabriel? Ylva? Kripos are already busy. As is everyone at police headquarters. Pretty much every single traffic officer is out following up leads. This is much bigger than us now, Holger. It's about what's in the country's best interests. Reassuring the public and all that. Not to mention that they'll sack you on the spot. Before you know it, you'll be counting polar bears on Svalbard.'

'I don't give a toss about that.'

'Don't you? What about Miriam and Marion? I'm sure they do. Anyway, you must do what you think is best,' Anette said as her incredibly irritating mobile vibrated again. 'I trust that they have made the right decisions. The Prime Minister's office. The Ministry of Justice. There's a reason they have those jobs. As for Ivan Horowitz, I'm convinced that somebody out there knows something; it's just a question of filtering out all the crackpots. We're close. Something has to happen soon. I can almost feel it. I have to get back now, OK?'

Anette rose and picked up her bag from the table.

'I hope you're right.' Munch put the papers back in the file. 'Will you let me know straightaway if anything happens?'

'You're at the top of my list, Holger.' Goli smiled and half ran towards the exit as her mobile rang again.

Chapter 58

Curry opened the door to Sagene Cleaning Services and jumped slightly when a tinny bell announced his arrival. His nerves hadn't settled down yet. Three beers and a small whisky last night, that was all. He had felt almost proud of himself, but his body begged to differ.

'Yes?' a middle-aged Vietnamese woman said as she looked up at him from behind the counter without putting down her knitting.

'Police,' Curry said, producing his warrant card. 'Special unit. Can I speak to the manager, please?'

'Already,' the woman said, showing no signs of getting up.

'Eh?'

'Already been here,' the woman said again as a young Vietnamese man appeared from the back room.

'She says that the police have already been here.' The young, well-dressed man smiled and placed his hands on the counter. 'Can I help you with anything?'

'Jon Larsen, special unit,' Curry said, holding up his warrant card again. 'Am I right in thinking that you had an employee called Karl Overlind?'

The Vietnamese woman rolled her eyes and mumbled something.

'He wasn't employed here,' the young man said. 'He was a casual. What's it about this time?'

'This,' Curry said, and stuck his hand inside his jacket.

Three, no more.

Or was it four?

No, three. He had been pretty sober, hadn't he?

Three beers and just the one whisky – or was it two?

He couldn't quite remember slipping under the duvet with Luna, but at least she had smiled to him from the pillow when he woke up.

He had been pretty sober.

'This is the drawing you produced with the sketch artist, isn't it?'

He put the crumpled piece of paper on the counter and smoothed it out.

'Yes, that's correct. What about it? Has something else happened?'

'And what about this one?' Curry had to rummage around in his pockets before he found the photograph of Horowitz.

'Who is this?' the young Vietnamese man asked as he peered at the picture.

'Is this the man who worked for you?'

'Hmm, I'm . . .'

He frowned and studied the picture more closely. The woman with the knitting shook her head again and said something Curry didn't understand.

'What did she say?'

The young man smiled apologetically.

'She says he's put on weight.'

'But is it the same man? The one who was employed . . . I mean . . . who worked here?'

'As a casual,' the Vietnamese man emphasized, and had another look at the picture. 'He looks younger, but yes, this is Karl Overlind. Yes, I would say so.'

'Are you sure?'

The knitting woman shook her head again and mumbled something else.

'Same person, yes, as far as I can see.'

'That's great, thank you.' Curry put the pictures back in his jacket pocket.

Sagene Bar.

Wasn't that just round the corner?

Just a small beer?

To straighten out his thoughts?

'Let me know if there's anything more we can do. Glad to be of help.'

'You've been more than helpful. Thank you again.' Curry opened the door more carefully this time to avoid the racket of the bell.

Ivan Horowitz.

Karl Overlind.

Same man.

Munch had been in a foul mood right from the morning. It had been a long time since Curry had last seen him so cross, but at least this had now been resolved.

A soldier.

A veteran from Afghanistan.

He had no idea how this suspect had been identified, but whatever. He had had it confirmed. It was the same man. He had been feeling like he was on the sidelines recently and thought that this would definitely help him get back on the right side of Munch. He needed it. He had struggled to explain the cut to his forehead and his absence from work.

Sagene Bar.

Just a quick one?

Call Munch first.

Give him the good news.

He took his mobile out of his pocket and was about to make the call when it started to ring.

When he saw the name on the display he was so stunned that he almost forgot to answer the call.

'Hi, Mia?' Curry said when he finally managed to move his fingers. 'How are you? They're looking for you.'

'To your right. Fifty metres. Just by the church. Grey Subaru. Do you see it?'

'Eh?'

'Blue jacket. Do you see him?'

'Er, yes.'

'Across the street. Outside the 7-Eleven. Woman on the phone. Grey coat. Brown ankle boots. Do you see her?'

'What are you talking about?' Curry said, turning around.

'Act normally. Start walking.'

'What's going on?'

'Leave now. Don't let them see that you have noticed them. Walk towards the park.'

Noticed them?

Curry had no idea what was going on yet he did as he was told. His feet started moving along the pavement.

'What's happening?'

'The two red telephone booths, do you see them?'

'Er, yes?'

'The bench, do you see it?'

Curry was even more confused now. He glanced at the woman in the grey coat outside the 7-Eleven again and realized she was looking at him. Not for long. Only for a brief second before she turned her attention back to the window.

'Mia? What's going on?'

'Just listen to me, Jon. And do as I say.'

'OK?' Curry mumbled, and let his legs carry him further down the road.

'The bench. Take a seat on the side facing the church.'

For the third time Curry glanced at the woman in the grey coat. She had turned towards him and was watching him.

'You're there now. Sit down.'

The Subaru by the kerb. The man in the blue jacket was getting out of the car.

'Feel underneath.'

He was on autopilot now. A hand under the seat where something had been attached. A piece of paper.

'In one hour, OK?'

'I don't understand—' Curry began as the woman in the grey coat calmly crossed the street, only to stop in front of another shop very close to him.

'Go inside the 7-Eleven. Show them your warrant card. They have a back door. You found the note?'

The man in the blue jacket was heading into the park now.

'Yes?'

'Turn off your mobile. I'll see you in one hour.'

And then she was gone.

Chapter 59

Dolores Di Santi was convinced that she had been possessed by the devil. She had grown up on Sardinia in the small coastal village of Portoscuso, the daughter of the local butcher and a very God-fearing woman. Her mother had started every day by making the sign of the cross and mumbling the words *Non oggi né Dio*; 'Not today either, God.' When Dolores was a little girl, she had always rolled her eyes at this, her mother's exaggerated belief in Heaven and Hell, but she did it herself now as she sat on the cold pew in St Olav's Cathedral. *Non oggi né Dio*. Although she was convinced that it was already too late.

When she was young she had dreamed of becoming an architect, but it hadn't worked out that way. He had turned up in a sailboat and swept her off her feet. Salvatore Di Santi. The son of a rich family from Milan. After that the years had just flown by; she couldn't even be sure where they had gone. First a daughter, then a son. Her mother had been a housewife and Dolores had promised herself never to follow suit, yet she had ended up doing exactly that.

But it was a comfortable life really; she mustn't grumble. Both her daughter and her son had got a good education; she was a doctor now, he an engineer. Salvatore Di Santi had always had political ambitions and he had achieved them. They had spent five years in South Africa, he as Italy's ambassador, she as the ambassador's wife, and that was where it had happened, the episode which had now convinced her that the devil had taken over her life. An innocent affair, really. He had been young. Much younger than her. An embassy employee.

L'introduzione del diavolo.
The devil enters.

Dolores crossed herself as the congregation stood up. Mid-morning Mass was over. She looked around for Father Malley but couldn't see him anywhere. It was another priest saying Mass today, which was a little disappointing; she had come to speak to Father Malley. She had to confess her sins. It was the only way. She would have to put an end to her wretchedness. It couldn't go on.

South Africa had been hot. Colourful. Vibrant. This outpost they had now been sent to was the exact opposite. Italy's ambassador to Norway. She had been so cold during the winter that she almost couldn't bear it. The light that never came. Eternal darkness. The calendar said it was spring, but spring refused to come, to give her the warmth she so sorely needed. *Il diavolo.* He was everywhere around her and she had to confess her sins once and for all. Then go home to Italy. She couldn't take any more of this icy country.

She made her way tentatively to the sacristy and approached a priest.

'Pater Malley?'

'We haven't seen him for a while,' the young man said in his broken language she didn't understand. 'He might be ill. We haven't been able to contact him, I'm afraid.'

'Pater Malley?' she tried again, but he didn't seem to understand her.

'I'm sure he'll turn up again soon.' The priest smiled, but she didn't understand a word of what he had said either.

That was why she had to talk to Father Malley. He spoke a little Italian. He had studied in Rome. She spoke a little English. Together they could communicate. Malley had explained to her that he had extended the hours for confession. She was welcome in the morning, midday – any time, really; it was just a question of turning up.

She walked slowly down to the confessional at the end of the church – perhaps that was what he had meant, the new priest – and sat down on a pew to wait. Twenty minutes later she had had enough. It didn't look like he was coming. She picked up her bag from the cold floor and was about to get up when she noticed a small gap in the wooden door.

Was he there after all?

Was that what the priest had said?

Just go right in?

Dolores walked slowly towards the ornate box.

'*Scusa?*

'Pater Malley?'

Chapter 60

Curry went into Café Mistral in Majorstua and found Mia sitting at a table in the far corner.

'So why the cloak-and-dagger stuff?' the bulldog snapped, and flopped down heavily on the chair opposite her.

'Did you lose them?' Mia wanted to know. Her blue eyes gave him a look he couldn't gauge.

Mia seemed on edge. She struggled to keep her hands still, she kept drumming her fingernails on her coffee cup and she was constantly scanning the room. If he hadn't known better, he would have said she was on something.

'I think so,' Curry mumbled. 'What the hell is going on? Have you completely lost the plot?'

'Did you turn off your phone?'

'Yes.'

'Good. They track us, don't they? GPS. They know where we are at any given moment. It occurred to me that that's how they've been doing it. Watching you.'

'Watching me? What are you talking about?'

'Sorry.' Mia put her hand briefly on his. 'I should have come to you sooner. But I'm here now, all right?'

An old man was being served a beer over at the bar. Curry felt the temptation in his throat but pushed it away.

'And who are those bloody people?'

'Internal Investigations. Long story,' Mia said, sweeping her hair behind her ear. 'Whatever, I should have spoken to you immediately, and I'm sorry, OK?'

'Internal Investigations? The police? Why are they after me? What the hell have I done?'

'Listen,' Mia said, leaning closer. 'A few days ago I was contacted by an agent by the name of Wold. Do you remember the lawyer? Lorentzen?'

'No.'

'He owned the car that was stolen. The Mercedes that was used to take Vivian Berg to the mountains. But what Wold wanted to know was whether Lorentzen was of interest to us.'

'Why?'

'Heroin.' Mia took a sip of her coffee. 'They think they've found a major importer and that Lorentzen is involved.'

'Drugs?' Curry shook his head in exasperation. 'But what does any of that have to do with me?'

'They think the traffickers have someone on the inside,' Mia said quietly.

'What?'

'A police officer. One of us. And they wanted me to help them prove it.'

Slowly he began to take on board what she meant. And the rage surged in him.

'Me?' he hissed so loudly that the old man at the bar turned around.

'Shhh.'

'Me?' Curry hissed again, more quietly this time.

Mia nodded.

'For real?'

'I know.'

'What the hell gave them that idea?'

'It's a long story,' Mia said again, and tried to calm him down, but he was consumed with outrage now.

'What the hell am I supposed to have done?'

He slammed the palm of his hand so hard against the table that her cup clattered. The bartender startled behind the counter and looked nervously in their direction.

'Calm down,' Mia said. 'It doesn't matter, does it? I've told them it's not you. Repeatedly. It's not you, is it, Jon?'

She tilted her head and looked at him. He could see how tired she was now.

'Of course not,' he fumed. 'Why the hell would I do something like that?'

'There you go.' Mia smiled. 'Then you have nothing to worry about.'

'But, fuck,' Curry mumbled, then ground to a halt, unable to finish his sentence.

Heroin?

Him?

'I need your help,' Mia said, leaning even closer.

'What the . . .?' Curry muttered under his breath, still struggling to make sense of it all.

Someone on the inside?

Trafficking drugs?

How the hell could anyone have thought . . .?

'Earth to Curry?' Mia said, bringing his attention back.

He saw it clearly now.

Shit.

He had mistaken it for alertness. He could not have been more wrong. It was the exact opposite. His frail colleague was so tired she struggled to sit upright on the chair.

'Are you OK? Mia?'

She took a breath, closed her eyes and looked as if staying awake was a struggle.

'Mia?'

'I'm fine. I'm just . . .'

'You haven't slept?'

She shook her head.

'For how long?'

'Nearly twenty-four hours. Nothing to worry about,' she said, and dismissed it with a wave of her hand.

'What the hell is going on?' Curry leaned across the table now. 'Internal Investigations think I'm bent? You look as if you've seen a ghost. Why haven't you slept? What have you been doing?'

'Trawling the streets,' Mia mumbled, and rubbed her eyes. 'I've been all over town.'

'Why?'

'Listen,' Mia said, pulling herself together. 'I need your help and I don't know who else to ask.'

'Of course, Mia. Anything.'

He could see the gratitude in her eyes now as she pushed her hair behind her ear again and flashed him a tired smile.

Christ, she really wasn't OK.

'It's about Sigrid,' Mia said at last.

'Your sister?'

'Yes. I . . .'

'But she is . . .?'

Mia closed her eyes again and Curry began to fear that she might pass out altogether, just collapse across the table right before his eyes.

'I need your help in finding someone.'

'Sure, Mia. Who?'

'You know the scene, don't you? You were on the Drugs Squad for a long time?'

'Of course. Who are you looking for?'

'His name is Kevin,' Mia said quietly. 'I went all over town last night, but I just . . .'

'A junkie?'

Mia nodded.

'Here in Oslo?'

Her head flopped forwards again, and this time she almost couldn't pull it up from her chest.

'Of course I'll help you,' Curry said quickly, and gently put his hand on hers. 'Do you know anything else about the guy? Is his name all you've got?'

'Cisse,' Mia mumbled.

'Cisse?'

'Kevin and Cisse. One or, better still, both of them. Will you help me?'

'Definitely,' Curry said. 'Can I ask why, or is it . . .?'

Mia blinked and ran a hand over her weary face.

'She has something that belongs to me.'

'This other junkie? Cisse?'

'Yes.'

'I'm on it. Damn, Mia, of course. If you promise me one thing?'

'What is it?'

'That you go home and get some shut-eye, OK?'

Mia smiled wearily at him.

'No, that—'

'I mean it, Mia. Kevin and Cisse? Leave it with me. And don't you worry. But you have to get some sleep now, OK?'

A long silence ensued.

'OK,' said Mia after a while.

'Good.' Curry took his mobile out of his pocket.

Chapter 61

Munch crossed the cordons, walked up the steps to St Olav's Cathedral and was met by Torgeir Bekk, the head of the response unit, a police officer he already knew. They had played chess before and after only a few games Munch had been forced to acknowledge that he still had a lot to learn.

'Pathology is already here,' Bekk said.

'What about the crime-scene technicians?'

'They're on their way. Have you any idea what's going on?'

'What do you mean?' Munch stubbed out his cigarette.

'It's total chaos everywhere, I can't get hold of anyone,' Bekk said, scratching his head.

'It's all about finding Ivan Horowitz now.'

'I know, but even so, the *whole* police force?'

Munch ignored this and entered through the big door. The cathedral was dimly lit. His footsteps echoed in the cavernous space. He could see Lillian and her team working over by the confessional.

'Who found him?'

'An Italian woman. She's in the priest's office. Shocked. Can't stop crying. There's an attaché from the Italian Embassy with her now. I believe she's the wife of the Italian ambassador.'

'Right.'

'Do we need to detain her?'

'Have you interviewed her?'

'To some extent. She came here for confession. Thought the priest was sitting in there. Which, in a sense, he was.' Bekk raised his eyebrows.

'Get her contact details, then let her go,' Munch said, and made his way towards Lillian Lund.

'Hi, Holger.' Lund smiled and removed her face mask.

'What have we got?'

An unnecessary question, really. He could see right into the confessional now, where the priest sat slumped backwards in a cubicle with a terrified expression in his eyes.

'There's a camera in there.' Lund pointed.

'In the other cubicle?'

She nodded.

'It looks as if the killer confessed his sins. Gave the priest the dose through the lattice most likely. Then the killer switched to the other side and did what he was there to do.'

'Have you looked in?'

'I couldn't help it.'

'And?'

'Twenty-nine.'

'What the hell.'

'It certainly looks like hell in there,' Lund said, no hint of irony in her voice.

'Any damage to his mouth?'

'Not as far as I can see, but that doesn't necessarily mean anything. Not everyone reacts in the same way.'

'But there is a needle mark?'

'Yes, in the same place.' Lund nodded and pulled the mask back over her face as Anette Goli came rushing across the echoing floor.

'What have we got?' she said as soon as she had got her breath back.

'Number twenty-nine,' Munch said quietly.

He produced the list from the pocket of his duffel coat.

'Paul Malley. Priest.'

'Oh, no,' Anette mumbled, taking the piece of paper.

'Do you still disagree?' Munch looked at her.

'About what?'

'Paul Malley? Perhaps we should start warning people.'

Anette Goli chewed her lip but made no reply. Munch shook his head in irritation, thrust his hands into his pockets and walked towards the crowd that had gathered around the altar.

Chapter 62

The call came in a matter of hours. Luna had looked strangely at him several times, but Curry had been adamant.

'So no beer?'

'No, just coffee.'

He could tell from her smile that she didn't mind at all. The room was quiet, only some old regulars who were sitting over by the jukebox, but even so Curry had felt paranoid.

Were they watching him?

Were they undercover . . .?

Of course they weren't police officers. He had seen the men in here several times so thoroughly wasted they could barely stand up. *Hell.* He couldn't help it. His pride. It hurt a little – no, it hurt a lot. How could anyone think he was on the take? What the hell had *he* done? And how many people were thinking this, people he knew? And how long had it been going on? Now that he had calmed down and thought about it, it was starting to make sense. The guys in the sports jackets by the bar that afternoon when he had been unlucky, drunk too much and forgotten to eat. They had looked out of place; he had thought that at the time, hadn't he? What a mess.

An unknown number showed up on his mobile, which was lying in front of him.

Don't answer it. Wait a few minutes then call back on another number.

Jimbo.

Curry didn't know why but that was how Jimbo wanted to be contacted. When Curry had realized what Mia was after he had known exactly who to call.

Jimbo Monsen.

He had known the talented police officer since their time at the academy. They had worked together on the Drugs Squad, but then Jimbo had gone undercover and stayed there. While the others from their year had risen up the ranks, Jimbo had chosen to stay on the streets. Curry had asked him why over a beer some years ago but he hadn't got a clear answer.

Jimbo had merely said, 'I like it,' with a shrug, and they had spoken no more about it.

Jimbo Monsen.

The obvious choice.

And now he had made contact.

He waited until he thought enough time had passed and entered the number he had been sent earlier that day.

'Curry?' the deep voice said.

'How did it go?' Curry was tense.

'Bingo. Kevin, wasn't it? Young guy? Funny eyebrows?'

'Yes. And Cisse.'

'I couldn't find her. I know who you mean, but they say she's gone. OD'ed on H.'

The years undercover had not only changed his appearance but also his language. The last time they met, Curry had barely recognized him. He had thought he was a vagrant and had almost gestured for him to go away.

'She's dead?'

'I'm not one hundred per cent, but that's what they say.'

'But this Kevin? Do you know where he is?'

'I just said I did, didn't I? You want to meet the guy?'

'Yes, please. Is that possible?'

'Anything is possible.' Jimbo coughed. 'Got any readies?'

'Readies?'

'I can set up a meeting, but I doubt that he'll turn up unless he gets a few quid out of it, if you know what I mean. Talking to the cops is a quick way to earn a bad name for yourself for guys like him.'

'Yes, yes, sure. How much are we talking about?'

'A grand should do it.'

'A thousand kroner?'

'Let's make it two – that way he can get high for a few days. We have to help where we can, don't you think?'

'Whatever,' Curry said. 'So how do we do it?'

'I'll call you,' said Jimbo, and rang off.

'Refill?'

A smiling Luna came over with the coffee pot in her hand. Curry nodded and wondered whether to ring Mia straightaway. No. Better to wait. Let her sleep. It was a long time since he had last seen her looking so exhausted.

What a bloody mess.

And what was really going on?

Why hadn't he seen this coming?

It was all because of the booze.

He blamed the booze.

He was outraged.

Him, bent?

No way.

He was a bloody good cop, he really was.

Bloody brilliant, really.

A fresh start.

And this time he meant it.

Curry muttered curses under his breath then raised the coffee cup to his lips as he stared out of the filthy window.

Chapter 63

Gabriel Mørk was sitting in the incident room with his laptop, unable to think straight. The wall facing him was almost completely covered now. Ludvig Grønlie's collage. Photographs, pieces of paper and notes in various colours. And on the wall by the door, all on its own:

Ivan Horowitz.

Munch had been vague, Goli rather evasive. The morning briefing had been a strange experience, yet he had spent the day doing what he had been told to do. The new suspect. Ivan Horowitz. Vanished without a trace in 2012, but could he possibly have left a footprint on the Internet?

He hadn't found much. Nothing, really, and nothing recent. Just an old Facebook page. A few pictures of Horowitz in uniform, squinting against the sun and holding an automatic rifle. Last posting in the spring of 2011. *Home on leave soon*, smiley face. *See you, Ivan!* Only one comment, someone called Caroline whom he had phoned every now and then, but she appeared to be just as ignorant as the rest of the world. Haven't seen him. Sorry. No idea. It hadn't seemed as if she cared very much, except for claiming the bragging rights, the excitement, something to tell her friends. *I know Ivan, we were friends. You know that serial killer they're hunting for? The police called me. I'm important.*

Gabriel had developed a bad taste in his mouth halfway through the conversation and simply rung off.

Ivan Horowitz.

Born in Gjøvik, 21 November 1988.

A man about his own age. Gabriel shook his head and carried on reading the notes.

Mother: Eva Horowitz, died 2007 (car crash)

Father: Anatol Horowitz, died 2007 (same)

Siblings: None

Education: Gjøvik College, 2006 to 2008

The army, Telemark Battalion, 2008 to 2010

Medically discharged from the army in 2010.

Admitted to Blakstad psychiatric hospital, 2011 to?

And that had got his attention. Blakstad psychiatric hospital. Horowitz had been a patient there? Gabriel could still remember how nervous and twitchy he had been when he'd visited the office building near Ullevaal Stadium, only to be told now to ignore the information he had gathered.

He had been a little disappointed, he had to admit. All that work for nothing. True, he hadn't been able to find a way of searching the files but, even so, to be told to just drop it? He had been tempted to ask Mia if they shouldn't do a little digging anyway. Sit down together, perhaps, see if there was something in there after all, but it hadn't worked out that way. He hadn't seen her for a while. She didn't turn up for meetings. She was nowhere to be seen. Mia had suddenly disappeared and neither Munch nor any of the others seemed to care. It was strange, but then again everything at the office had been weird ever since this new prime suspect had appeared, completely out of the blue, out of nowhere. Neither Munch nor Anette had given them any explanation; all they knew was that this was the man they were looking for. One hundred per cent of their focus on him. Sources deep within military intelligence, they were told. Don't ask any questions.

The media talked of nothing but the hunt for Horowitz.

The soldier.

The serial killer.

Who was still at large in the streets of Oslo.

Gabriel had been home for a quick visit earlier that day and could almost see it in people's faces. Rushing from A to B, their arms wrapped protectively around their children. Neighbours he would normally stop to have a chat with had avoided him, practically run to safety behind their front doors.

He couldn't blame them.

He had sent Tove and Emilie up to stay with Tove's mother in Hadeland.

'Are you serious, Gabriel?'

'I'm sure you'll be fine, but please, for my sake?'

'Yes, of course, and I know she'll be pleased to see us.'

He had kissed them quickly as they left and felt a sense of relief as he saw the red rear lights of the Volvo disappear.

'Well, this is exciting.'

An ironic Ylva entered the room with her laptop and flopped down on a chair next to him.

'Heard anything new?'

'Not since the last time.'

'There has to be something we can do other than just sit here?'

The young Icelandic woman sighed and rubbed her eyes. Gabriel knew what she meant. The office, which was normally teeming with life, phones ringing off the hook, people running up and down the corridors, had been turned into a lunar land-scape, just the two of them left now. Ludvig was down at police headquarters in Grønland. Munch and Anette were up at the cathedral – another victim, a priest this time. Gabriel had been hoping they might stop by, have another briefing meeting, a fresh update, but no, it seemed that they had better things to do. And, of course, he hadn't seen hide nor hair of Mia for a long time.

'So when were you going to tell me?' Ylva said, nudging his shoulder.

'What do you mean?'

'Oh, you can't fool me.' She smiled.

'What?'

'Your little mission,' Ylva teased. 'Come on! I can see right through you. What were you doing for Mia?'

'What do you mean?' Gabriel said again, aware that his cheeks were growing hot.

'OK, so that's how we're playing it,' she said, affronted. 'A secret mission? And you won't tell me anything? Oh, come on! What did you do?'

Gabriel Mørk sighed now. He realized it no longer mattered. Munch didn't seem to care any more. And they weren't going to use the information anyway.

'I hacked Wolfgang Ritter's database.'

'You're kidding me? Without a warrant?'

'Depends how you look at it,' Gabriel mumbled. 'It was at Mia's request.'

'Bloody hell.' Ylva chuckled. 'So how did you do it? You went to his office? You accessed his computer?'

'I sat in the waiting room,' Gabriel said, cringing somewhat in the chair. 'Do you think I shouldn't have done it?'

'Idiot, of course you should have. What did you find? Is it in there?'

She moved her chair a little closer and nodded eagerly towards his laptop.

'It's useless to us but, funnily enough, I was just thinking about it. You know Horowitz?'

He nodded towards Ludvig's notes. 'He was admitted to Blakstad as a psychiatric patient.'

'So why can't you use it?' Ylva wanted to know. 'What if Ivan Horowitz was one of Ritter's patients? Perhaps we might find a link there?'

'I've already checked,' Gabriel said, and shook his head. 'He isn't there.'

'How do you know that?'

'I've already checked,' Gabriel said again.

'I just thought you said it was useless?'

'What we have are Ritter's handwritten notes scanned as PDF files, do you see? So you can't run a search. Not of the documents.'

'What do you mean?'

'They were handwritten and then scanned. Do you see the problem?'

318

But Ylva looked as if she still couldn't follow him.

'Say that I want to search for the word "fire", OK? Or *The Brothers Lionheart*? There's no way the computer can search for them; you need a method to recognize the symbols. If I want to search his notes, I need to teach the computer his handwriting – A looks like this, B looks like that, and so on, but it would still be tricky. How one character is written when the handwriting is joined up, L to K, M next to N. Do you understand?'

'Oh,' Ylva said as the penny finally dropped.

'I mean, I'm sure there's a way of doing it,' Gabriel went on. 'But it could take weeks . . .'

'But how . . .?' Ylva began, and pushed her spectacles further up her nose.

'How what?'

'How can you be so sure Horowitz isn't in there?'

'Titles, file names. Take a look at this,' Gabriel continued, and opened one of the documents. 'Ritter has used the patient's name and date of birth to identify them. And that I can search, of course, that's not the problem. As I can search all the other files I have here.'

'But what if . . .?' Ylva said as an idea began to take shape in her mind.

'If what?'

'Well, we know his age, don't we?'

'What do you mean?'

'We can search his date of birth? Can't we? I mean, it's right there?'

'Yes, but I just told you, he's not one of the patients. His name isn't listed.'

'So how about Karl Overlind?'

'Not there either. I've checked.'

'OK, but look up there.'

Ylva pointed to the wall in front of them.

'The artist's sketches? You can see they're different, can't you?'

'Where are you going with—?'

'The killer is clearly – well, I don't know what, but he seems very calculating, doesn't he? None of this is random. He wears glasses there, a different hairstyle in that picture. What if Horowitz is in the files after all, under another name?'

'But that makes no sense,' Gabriel objected. 'Why would he see a psychiatrist under a false name? And is that even possible? Don't they check? No, that's a non-starter, I'm afraid.'

'No, you're right,' Ylva said, taking off her glasses. 'Why would he?'

'That's what I just said.'

'No, why on earth would he want to do that?'

She rubbed her eyes again and put her glasses back on.

'Ah, well.'

They sat in silence, staring at the colourful wall.

'Unless . . .' Ylva said.

'What?'

'No, it still makes no sense,' she said, cradling her head in her hands. 'Damn it. It would have been so cool to be able to show the old-timers a thing or two. I mean, they've just dumped us in here like spare parts. I hate not being able to contribute.'

'I know exactly what you mean.' Gabriel nodded.

'But Blakstad? A psychiatric hospital? You had the same thought, didn't you? He must have found his victims somewhere. I mean, come on, completely at random? Something must have triggered him. And Vivian Berg? She was the first one, wasn't she?'

'Yes . . .?'

'Vivian Berg was Ritter's patient, wasn't she? And you know what Mia is like,' Ylva said, getting up, excited now. 'Why would she ask you to hack Ritter's files unless she had a hunch? Did she say what they had talked about up there?'

'When?'

'When they interviewed him? Ritter, I mean.'

'No.'

'Come on, Gabriel. There must have been something, surely?'

'Of course, but what?'

'I'll be damned if I know. What about this, we know Horowitz's age, don't we?'

'Twenty-five.'

'Right, let's add a couple of years either side.'

'What do you mean?'

'Well, look at the cameras. The sketches. The descriptions from people who have actually seen him. Let's make it . . . twenty-three to . . . say, twenty-seven?'

'I don't understand where you're going with this.'

'You said date of birth, didn't you?'

Ylva bent over and placed her finger on his screen.

'Which would make it? 19 . . . 86 to 1990? Try that.'

Gabriel entered the numbers.

'How many hits?'

'Two hundred and seventy-five.'

'There you go.' Ylva smiled and punched him happily on the shoulder.

'You want us to read two hundred and seventy-five files? Have you any idea how long that will take us?'

'So what? Do you have anything better to do?'

A sudden silence filled the room. Gabriel could hear the cars in the street far away, the hum of the air conditioning, which, up until now, he had never even noticed.

'Sure. Why not?'

'Good.' Ylva smiled and punched his shoulder again. 'I'll take A to . . . what's halfway through the alphabet?'

'N.'

'Great. And you take the rest. Would you email me the files, please?'

Ylva seemed just like a schoolgirl now as she clapped her hands eagerly and grinned from ear to ear.

'Let's meet up here when we've been through them, all right? Or if we find anything?'

'It could take several days.' Gabriel sighed.

'Well, that's just too bad. So will you send me those files?'

'They're on their way,' Gabriel said, and dragged the files into an email addressed to her.

Chapter 64

Mia was existing in a vacuum somewhere between dream and reality. She just couldn't settle. Her body was shattered, but her brain continued to work overtime. She had declined Charlie's magic sleeping potion for now; she didn't dare risk crashing out completely. Curry might ring at any time; she had to be awake, present, so she could crack this. Munch had called her several times as she made her way to Charlie's flat, but she had ignored his calls. They couldn't treat her like this. Damn them, the whole lot of them. She had glanced quickly at the text message he had sent her. *New victim, Paul Malley, priest. Another camera, number 29.* The words had followed her down onto the soft pillow, mixing quietly with her body's need for rest.

The numbers. Four, seven, thirteen, twenty-nine. A kill list? A little too simple, wasn't it? What was the point of the camera, then? Scratch the number into the lens? A new one at every crime scene? Surely there were hundreds of other ways of doing it, weren't there? Indicating a number. You could write on the wall. On the body. Wouldn't that somehow also be more appropriate? Why the camera? She was missing something important here, wasn't she? The numbers are . . . on the camera. OK. No, no, no; *focus now*. The numbers are *inside* the camera. Big difference. On the lens. Not outside. Forget the camera. The photograph. Hold that thought, Mia; don't disappear now. This is important. If you press the shutter release, the number will become . . . a part of the picture?

She must have dozed off anyway because suddenly Sigrid was there, in the streets of Oslo in front of her. A faceless shadow, that was all, but it was her, her bracelet clunking heavily on her skinny wrist as she beckoned Mia across the dark, wet tarmac. *Come, Mia, come.* A boy with a yellow beanie appeared then, bent over a woman in a red puffa jacket, but they disappeared again, swallowed up by the mist. She lost Sigrid for a moment. Mia stood with her heart in her throat and a voice that wouldn't leave her mouth. Sudden glimpses of her mother, then of her father standing in front of their graves at the cemetery. Weeping, mournful shadows, nothing more, as Sigrid reappeared in front of her and she realized where she was. In the basement. The mattress on the floor. The dump where they had found her. Her sister lay down carefully and tightened the rubber strap around her emaciated arm. Mia desperately wanted to run to her, fling her arms around her to protect her, but her body didn't work. Her legs were stuck. She couldn't move. Now her sister picked up the syringe from the floor and looked at her. Mia wanted to shout, howl, scream, but she had no voice. There was a figure behind her now; there were more people in the basement. Arms grabbing her, holding her back, a stranger's hand covering her eyes. Panic as her sister pressed the needle against her skin and smiled wistfully through the fog.

Death isn't dangerous, Mia.

Are you coming?

Mia sat up abruptly in the bed and gasped for air. The sweat was pouring from her face. She got up and walked barefoot across the floor. Stumbled into the kitchen, the dream still sitting heavily in her body. *Hell.* She opened the cupboard door in a daze, then poured herself a glass of water and drained it. Refilled it and stood trembling by the sink while reality slowly came back. She let herself flop softly onto a chair and finally opened her eyes properly.

She was in Charlie Brun's kitchen. OK. Good. A safe place. She had been so tired. She shouldn't have allowed her body to go to sleep. *The numbers.* The camera. *Pointing at the victim.* Scratched into the lens. Look, Mia, God damn it, look properly! Look through the camera? What do you see, Mia?

Do you get it now?

She glanced at the family photos on the wall above the kitchen table. Poor Charlie. Memories of a life which hadn't been that simple.

No, it couldn't be . . .?

She nearly dropped the glass on the floor.

Surely there was no way . . .?

Yes, God damn it . . .

Four.

A ballet dancer.

Seven.

A jazz musician.

Thirteen.

A boy in swimming trunks.

Twenty-nine . . .

No, please, no, it . . .

Mia got up so quickly she bashed her knee against the table, but she didn't even feel the pain shooting through her as she ran back to the bedroom and frantically pulled on her clothes. She couldn't remember where she had left Charlie's keys, but that was just too bad. She put on her jacket as she ran down the steps and left the front door open behind her.

Out.

People.

A taxi . . .?

There.

She threw herself into the back seat while still putting on her other ankle boot.

'Take me to Sofies Plass number 3.'

'That's in Bislett, isn't it?'

'Just drive. It's . . . important.'

'Are you in a hurry?'

'Just drive, will you? Drive . . . quickly.'

'OK,' said the voice behind the wheel.

And at last the taxi pulled away from the kerb.

Chapter 65

Curry glanced up at the flat as the rain started drumming on the windscreen. Bloody weather. It had been a hard, dark winter and now spring refused to come. He found a pouch of chewing tobacco in his pocket, stuffed a wad under his upper lip and looked out of the windscreen again. Kyrre Greppsgate. He had been here before, hadn't he? He hadn't realized it at first. Jimbo's text message. *Kevin will meet you at 15, Kyrre Greppsgate. Second floor, flat C, 6 o'clock. Bring the readies.*

He had half run from the office in Mariboesgate, expecting all sorts of questions from Munch about why he needed a car, but luckily the place had been practically deserted. Only Ylva and Gabriel had been there, both of them hunched over a computer in the incident room. He had snatched a set of keys from the wall without them even realizing he had been there. Just as well. He didn't have the energy to explain himself right now. He looked up at the second-floor flat again. He and Allan Dahl had sat in a car on a surveillance job outside this address not very long ago when the news had come in that the special unit was back. Lotte. That was her name, wasn't it? The junkie who lived in the flat; he hadn't been able to work out why they were wasting time watching her. He took out his mobile and tried Mia again, but she still didn't reply. The time on the dashboard was getting dangerously close to six. Should he just head up to the flat alone?

No, he should wait for her. Shouldn't he? After all, he had no idea what questions to ask this Kevin. Well, there was the bracelet; he could start with that. He pressed Mia's number again, but there was no response. Bugger. Hmm. What to do? What to do?

The rain was drumming even harder on the windscreen now; the wipers could barely keep up as the clock in front of him rolled over to six. A brief window of opportunity. Would Kevin be on time? Or would he just not bother, float off on another cloud? Curry tried Mia again, but there was still no reply, just the same generic voicemail.

You have reached the voicemail of . . .

He stuffed his mobile back in his pocket and made a decision. He opened the car door quickly, pulled his jacket over his head and ran across the street as the water splashed off the tarmac around him.

Bloody weather.

He shook off the raindrops and looked at the row of doorbells.

Second-floor flat.

Call Mia again?

No, she could thank him later.

He smiled faintly to himself and pressed the bell labelled 2C.

Chapter 66

Mia gave the taxi driver all the cash she had and ignored the stunned look on his face as she unlocked the door to her apartment building with trembling fingers and ran up the stairs. No one in the stairwell, thank God – not that it would have made a difference now, another key moving through the air. She unlocked her own front door, ran to the spare bedroom and tried to get her breath back as she stood in front of one of the cardboard boxes.

She slashed the tape with the key, took the photo album out of the box and dropped to the floor.

Mia's album.

Her hands were still trembling, as was her body, when she carefully opened it and started to count.

Page one.

Page two.

Page three.

She could barely suppress her emotions when she saw the picture.

There.

On page four.

Sigrid in her ballet costume. Young, barely five years old. Next to her, little, insecure Mia, squinting at the camera.

In the middle.

Their ballet teacher.

A young woman in her early twenties. In full costume, pointe shoes, pearl studs in her ears, her arms wrapped around them both with a big smile in honour of the photographer.

No . . .

Her hands shook violently, but she managed to turn the pages.

Page seven.

Their father. With her on his lap. An open-air concert. Smiling at the camera, giving a thumbs-up. In the background someone on a stage, a jazz saxophonist. Her mother's cursive handwriting underneath.

Daddy's favourite song. 'My Favorite Things'.

No, it couldn't be . . .

She forced herself to carry on.

Page thirteen.

Some rocks in Åsgårdstrand. Summer. Mia in a swimming costume, squinting at the sun, barely fourteen years old. A young lad from the neighbourhood with them. In swimming trunks. Beads of water on his skinny body. Sigrid waving in the background, wrapped in a towel.

The sun is out at last. The kids are having fun.

Mia carried on flicking through the album, on autopilot now.

Page twenty-nine.

Inside a church. The twins wearing identical white dresses, Sigrid with a big grin, Mia with her lips pressed shut, ashamed of her braces, refusing to smile at the photographer. In the middle, the priest.

Proud confirmands!

Four.

Seven.

Thirteen.

Twenty-nine.

A camera on a tripod. The number scratched into the lens. *Look, Mia. Look through the camera.*

But why the hell . . .?

It began to rise now, the black nausea that had been building up inside her.

She staggered to the bathroom and knelt in front of the lavatory bowl, but her stomach was empty. She got up, moved to the sink and splashed cold water over her face.

Her.

There was no kill list.

Mia's photo album.

It was all about her.

She wiped her face and rushed back to the room with the boxes and squatted down on the floor while she tried to get her brain to work.

Shit.

OK.

Pictures.

In my own family album.

She carefully turned the pages back to the first photograph.

And that was when she noticed it. Someone had disturbed it. Taken it out. And then glued it back in place. The edges were different. Her fingers still wouldn't obey her properly but eventually she managed to ease it out. She turned it over carefully.

Someone had written on the back of it.

Curly letters written with a blue pen.

Congratulations.

She steeled herself, flicked a few more pages forward.

Next picture. Page seven.

How clever you are.

Onwards, again on autopilot, teenagers on the rocks; she turned over the picture quickly this time.

Would you like a final hint?

Her hands were shaking badly now. She could barely turn the pages. The priest smiling at the camera, Sigrid and Mia in their white confirmation dresses.

Same handwriting.

Blue pen against the knobbly reverse side.

Salem.

Of course.

Oh, shit.

Mia left the album lying open on the floor, stood up in a daze and started running around the flat, looking for her leather jacket, before realizing she was already wearing it.

Salem.

329

Jon Ivar Salem.

The Brothers Lionheart.

The burning house.

She struggled to get her mobile out of her jacket pocket and found Ludvig Grønlie's number.

'Mia? Where are you? Munch has—'

'The arsonist,' Mia interrupted him, feeling the room around her swing from side to side.

'Who?'

'Jon Ivar Salem? Do you remember him?'

'Yes, of course I do,' Grønlie said from somewhere far away.

'Please would you look him up for me, Ludvig? Now? Where is he? Which prison?'

'Are you OK, Mia?'

'I'm great, Ludvig. Would you look him up? Please?'

'Of course, hang on . . .'

In the distance she could hear his fingers on the keyboard.

'Ullersmo prison,' Grønlie said, coming back to her.

'Are you sure?'

'Yes, I'm sure. What's going on, Mia?'

She didn't take the time to answer; she just ended the call and ran to the hallway.

The keys to her dad's old Jaguar.

Now where had she put them?

Oh, there they were.

She snatched them from the hook in the hallway, then failed to shut the door to her flat behind her as she ran as fast as she could down the stairs.

Chapter 67

Curry had just pressed the doorbell outside the second-floor flat when it occurred to him that something didn't add up. The information rose slowly through his brain but it surfaced eventually from a long way away. There had been a car parked on the other side of the street. He recognized it from somewhere, didn't he? And it was the same flat. That was too much of a coincidence, wasn't it? Him and Allan Dahl? Out on their totally unnecessary surveillance job? And where had he seen that car before?

The door opened and a face appeared cagily in the gap.

'Yes?'

'Kevin?'

'Yes?'

'Jon Larsen. We're supposed to be meeting? Jimbo set it up?'

'Mmm, yeah, all right,' said the young lad. He could barely be more than twenty.

He took off the security chain and let Curry into the flat.

What funny eyebrows. It was almost as if they weren't there.

He had the right guy.

All Kevin was missing was the yellow beanie; otherwise, he fitted Mia's description perfectly.

'Do you have the cash?' the junkie mumbled, hugging his skinny body.

'I do.'

Curry glanced around the flat and his expectations were confirmed. It wasn't somewhere any normal person would call home. Rubbish littered the hallway and spilled towards the mattresses on the floor. A green 1970s lamp by a window. A filthy sheet nailed in front of it.

'Two thousand – that was what we agreed, wasn't it?' Curry said, stuffing a hand in his pocket.

'Er, yes, sure.' Kevin glanced furtively over his shoulder.

The car in the street.

Arrrghh, why was this taking so long?

He had seen the same car outside the window of the pub where Luna worked, when he had crouched down, scared that someone might see him.

Money passing through the air towards skinny, blue, outstretched hands. His body acting before his brain had time to tell it to stop.

Allan Dahl.

It was like wading through treacle as the thought slowly formed.

A police officer?

On the take?

The man behind the steering wheel. He knew he had seen that face before. It was the lawyer, Lorentzen.

Shit.

Of course.

He could see it in the eyes of the junkie now as he slowly took the money and shifted his nervous gaze towards someone who had suddenly appeared behind Curry.

Oh no . . .

Curry raised his arms above his head, trying instinctively to defend himself against the blow he knew was coming, but it was too late.

A man stepped out from the shadows.

Metal hitting his temple.

Curry had blacked out long before his body hit the floor.

Chapter 68

An icy shower had washed the car park clean, but Mia didn't even notice that it had stopped raining when she stumbled out of the big gate of Ullersmo prison. Jon Ivar Salem. He had seemed just as surprised as she was. They had brought him up from Solitary – something about an attack on some fellow inmates; she hadn't caught all the details. *Damn.* What had she been thinking? Had it been like this all along? Nothing but red herrings. Raymond Greger. Klaus Heming. She had screamed at Salem in the small room; she had been emotional, unprofessional, the adrenaline pumping through her. *Did you pay someone? To kill? Because I caught you? Was that why? My pictures? My album? Who went to my flat?* He had stared at her with a deep frown. As if she were the patient and he the doctor. *Shit.*

Norway's most notorious arsonist. Jon Ivar Salem. This revolting man had ravaged Østlandet for almost fifteen years. House after house, apparently picked at random. He had set them alight at night. Not with petrol cans and a lighter – oh no, he was cynical and much more devious. A plumber by trade, but familiar with electrical installations. During his trial it was revealed that he had worked in every single house at some point or other. A leaking pipe. A blocked lavatory. A new boiler. And he had been patience itself. Waited until he would no longer be on the list of suspects. A break-in at night. An incorrectly wired electrical circuit, often helped along with some old clothing or rags he found in the basements of the houses. And then he would sit in his car. Watching the flames. Twenty-four detached houses. Twenty-four families.

Thirteen fatalities. And no one had spotted the connection until a young and inexperienced Mia Krüger was one day assigned to the case.

She had seen it in his face in the courtroom. More curiosity than hatred, really, as he kept turning towards her. Who was this person who, after fifteen years, had finally managed to catch him?

Jon Ivar Salem.

It's burning.

Of course.

But even so . . .

It didn't make any sense . . .

Because Jon Ivar Salem had had absolutely no idea about what was going on.

'Someone just sent me a ring,' he had muttered at last. 'I was promised a reward.'

His leery smile across the table as the prison guard went to his cell to fetch it.

'Who sent it?'

'Well, I don't know. I was just promised something. Do you have it? My reward?'

A gold ring.

She had stuffed it into her pocket. He had protested vociferously, but the prison guard had dealt with him. He had handcuffed him and escorted him back down to Solitary.

A gold ring?

The afternoon sun crept out behind a cloud and gazed at its own reflection in a puddle in the car park. Mia stuffed her hand into her pocket, found a lozenge and tried to clear her head.

OK, deep breath now, Mia.

The pictures. In the album. Mia's album. All the murders are in there. They were reconstructions.

Congratulations!

How clever you are.

Salem.

Mia was so absorbed in her own thoughts she was unaware that someone was coming up behind her. Out of the corner of her

e she finally noticed him: a prison guard; nothing unusual about
at. Ullersmo prison housed some of Norway's worst criminals
nd there were strong security measures both inside and out.

'Can I help you?' the voice said as it came close.

A bundle of keys jangled. A big torch not yet turned on; dark-
ss was still some hours away.

'Sorry, I'm a police officer,' Mia mumbled, pulling her warrant
rd from her inside pocket and holding it up in the air.

Salem?

Jon Ivar Salem.

What the hell was his part in all this?

The security guard took her warrant card, studied it and
turned it to her.

'How clever you are.'

'What . . .?'

She turned, still lost in a world of her own.

'How clever you are, Mia.'

What the hell . . .?

She found herself staring into a young, smiling face. An out-
retched, gloved hand moved through the air towards her again;
wasn't holding a torch after all but *a small spray can.*

Feet trying to run, fingers curling into her palms as her brain
alized what was happening, but by then it was already too late.

'We'll take your car. It's such a nice car.'

A key in the ignition and her arms somewhere far away, a last
tempt to control her movements, but all she was able to take in
as that it had started to rain again.

Gentle drops falling softly on the windscreen as the car pulled
t slowly from the car park.

SIX

Chapter 69

Munch had just parked in the underground car park in Mariboesgate when his mobile rang. He was hoping the display would read *Mia*; he had tried calling her several times, but she still refused to pick up.

'Hi, it's Anette,' Goli said. 'We've got him.'

'Who?'

'Ivan Horowitz.'

'So soon?'

'Three independent tip-offs saying the same thing.' Goli sounded out of breath. 'I've passed them on to Edvardsen. They're on their way now.'

'On their way? Who? Where?'

'He has a cabin,' Goli continued. 'Not very far from where we found Vivian Berg. It's about an hour into the forest in the opposite direction.'

'Horowitz?'

'Yes, like I just told you, three independent callers all with the same information. He moved into the cabin a long time ago. Said he'd had enough of people. Wanted to live alone in nature. And no one has seen him since.'

Munch swore and started running back to his car. 'So who is on their way there now?'

'The army. They've dispatched Alfa, the elite force they mentioned. Edvardsen wants us to come down there.'

'To the situation room?'

'Yes?'

'Why?'

'Don't ask me.' Goli sighed. 'So that he can boast? Show how they're so much better than us? I don't know. It doesn't matter, w have him now. It'll soon be over. Thank God.'

Munch could hear the relief in her tired voice.

'Will you be joining us?'

'I'm on my way,' Munch said, and quickly got back into his ca

Chapter 70

ia Krüger woke up and didn't know where she was. It felt as if
e were still dreaming. Diffuse images slipped in and out of her
ind. She couldn't work out which ones were real. She was in a
bin. She could see a wooden wall. A small window which some-
e had covered up. Her grandmother was sitting at the foot of
r bed. She smiled and wrapped a blanket around Mia. Then her
andmother was gone. Her arm was tied to a bedpost. As was one
her feet. She could smell trees. And birds. Her forehead felt hot.
er mother was sitting at the end of the bed. She had a tray with
uash and a cold flannel. Then her mother was gone. Her father
is outside. He had just come home from work. He had fixed the
r, the old jade Jaguar that used to be his father's, the one she
uld one day inherit. Sigrid was sitting at the end of her bed,
itching a photo album. Mia wanted to reach out for her. Hold
r tight. So tight that she would never disappear again.

Death isn't dangerous.

Her grandmother came back.

Sigrid smiled at her.

Are you coming, Mia?

Mia opened her eyes and gasped.

What the hell?

She tried to get up but couldn't. She could feel herself starting to
nic but she forced it back.

Calm down now, Mia. Easy does it.

Concentrate. Her arm was tied to a bedpost. As was one foot.
ere was nothing covering her mouth. She scanned her surround-
s, still disoriented, but she could distinguish what was real now.

341

The wooden walls. A door leading to another room. A wardrobe against one wall. Old-fashioned design. A cabin. A covered window. A ceiling lamp. She took a deep breath and tried to free her hand. No luck. Not her foot either. OK.

Don't panic, Mia.

He has caught you, but he hasn't killed you.

That must mean something, surely?

She felt the bile rise from her stomach as the sequence of events slowly came back to her. The camera. The pictures. The images rather than the camera itself, were what really mattered. The pictures on the walls in Charlie Brun's home. The page numbers in Mia's album. The murders were all about her. Salem. In Ullersmo prison. The gold ring.

She got no further.

The door opened and a smiling face appeared; its owner was holding something.

Something that was on fire.

Candles?

A cake?

'Many happy returns, darling. I know it's not your birthday, of course I do, but I thought we ought to celebrate. Would you like me to blow out the candles? Or would you rather do it yourself?'

Chapter 71

Curry had never thought about how he would die. It wasn't something that had ever crossed his mind. From old age, possibly. Sometime in the distant future, on a veranda with a sea view. Certainly not in a place like this, in a filthy flat, ambushed and tied to a chair with a hood over his head.

He tried to move again, but it was as if he were glued to the hard spindle-back chair. The rope cut into his wrists. The pain made him want to howl, but he pressed his lips together. His head was throbbing. He could feel dried blood on his neck. They had beaten the living daylights out of him. His brain was no longer working.

Jimbo?

No, not Jimbo.

Jimbo had set up a meeting. With Kevin, the junkie. Who was the boyfriend of someone called Lotte. And she was Allan Dahl's drug mule. That had to be the connection. It explained why they had been watching her flat that morning. Dahl had been there to watch his girl. Watch his heroin. His money.

And now Curry was tied to a chair.

With a hood over his head.

Betrayed by that bastard Dahl who was supposed to be on his side.

Fuck.

No, that wasn't how he had imagined the end.

He could no longer hear any noise coming from the next room. There had been frantic activity for a while. Raised voices in broken English. The odd word in Norwegian. He had heard him.

That bastard Dahl.

'What do we do with him?'

And Dahl had replied.

Kill him?

Or had he said: 'We're leaving'?

Curry hadn't been able to tell.

He tried the rope yet again but only managed to force it deeper into his wrists. He sat upright in the chair and felt his heart pound under the sweaty, bloodstained shirt.

Oh, shit.

Footsteps.

Someone was out there.

He heard the door handle moving.

Shit.

A sharp flash of light washed over him; it was so bright he could even sense it through the hood. A figure in the doorway. A big, black shadow. He heard the sound of a weapon, the safety catch being flicked off.

Shit.

He bowed his head instinctively.

OK.

So it was going to be this way.

He pressed his eyes shut. He could feel himself trembling now and mumbled a few last words between his dry lips.

Sorry, everyone.

Chapter 72

Munch was sitting at the end of the oval table. He could feel the charged atmosphere in the room. The general had tried to hide it, but Munch had seen his smug face. Goli had been right. They were here purely to watch. He had noticed it during their first visit. The condescending glances. Wooden-tops. Civilians. Now they would see who was really running this country. Who took charge when national security was at stake.

'Every single image is a live video feed from a soldier's helmet.'

Edvardsen was almost like a little kid now, wielding the remote control.

'We can move the images up to the main screen as we see fit.'

A little kid playing a video game. One costing millions of kroner would be his guess. Munch felt vaguely disgusted, but it no longer mattered. Ivan Horowitz. The serial killer. In a cabin in a forest. Soon it would all be over.

They could have dispatched Delta, the armed-response unit. But Edvardsen had favoured his own, obviously. And he needed to prove to the politicians in the room that the taxpayers' money was well spent. Perhaps they could even add a few extra millions to next year's budget? Oh, grow up, Munch ordered himself. He had to stop it now. The only thing that mattered was that this sick individual was captured once and for all. Munch had been a sceptic about the involvement of the higher ranks, but the death of the priest had convinced him that they needed the extra firepower. Paul Malley. Number twenty-nine on the list.

A crackling sound came from the screen.

'One, three, target in sight, over.'

345

'Three, one, await orders, over.'

The cameras moved through the forest as if in a video game, which was almost what it was. Soldier number one. Light mist between dense tree trunks. Soldier number two. A glimpse of a cabin further ahead. The barrel of an automatic rifle. Soldier number three. Running across the heather, then down behind a tree, the cabin no longer quite so far away.

'One, four, ready to enter, over.'

'Four, one, await go, over.'

Digital warfare. Live from the forest. Munch realized he was unable to peel his eyes away from the screen. Several soldiers were now approaching the grey door to the cabin.

'Team, this is one. Radio silence, wait for go.'

Suddenly there was total silence in the situation room. A thumbs-up in front of a camera very close to the grey door.

New arm movements.

One masked soldier swapping places with another.

Two men at the door now, the others covering separate windows.

A cabin.

Deep in the forest.

Ivan Horowitz.

It would soon be over.

At last.

'GO!'

And the scene in front of him exploded. Smoke grenades. The door splintering. Glass breaking. The first soldier ran inside the cabin, his camera, now with a light, looking around desperately. Another one entered through the window. Smoke. Chaos. They could no longer see what was going on until the radio silence was suddenly breached and the smoke began to settle.

'We have him.'

'Oh, fuck.'

A glove through the air towards a lifeless body hanging from the ceiling.

'One, three, we have him. But he has been here a long time.'

'Three, one, ID?'

346

Same glove reaching for the throat of the badly decomposed body. A military dog tag appeared.

'One, three, this is our man. Horowitz. But, as you can see, there's no way he could have done any of this. He's been dead a long time.'

The camera pointed at the floor; the smell of the dead body hanging inside the cabin had caused the soldier to throw up.

'This is Eagle,' Edvardsen said gravely.

'Eagle, come in.'

'Are we sure?'

'Repeat, Eagle?'

'Are you sure the dead man is Horowitz?' Edvardsen said, clearly stressed now.

'Two, one, double-check ID.'

Another soldier pinched his nose and walked up to the body to check the tag around its neck.

'Horowitz,' the soldier said.

'Eagle, we have the right man. But he's not your killer.'

'Damn it,' Edvardsen said, his face going bright red as he turned to the other people in the room.

'So do you think we can have our mobiles back now?' Munch grunted irritably then got up and left.

Chapter 73

'I didn't think you would ever wake up,' the smiling face said 'I've been waiting for so long and now, finally, the day has arrived Aren't you happy?'

Mia couldn't get the images on her retina to make any sense.

Alexander?

Her neighbour?

What the hell . . .?

The blond young man got up to fetch something from a small table 'There you go.'

A hand behind her head. A glass of water held to her lips. Hal of it went down her throat, the rest all over her jumper, but wha she managed to swallow tasted heavenly.

'Why . . .?' Mia croaked, but her voice faltered.

'I'm sure you've been wondering about this a lot, and I've beer waiting so long to tell you,' the big, smiling eyes said. 'So let's star at the beginning, shall we? We don't have much time before we need to leave.'

Alexander caressed her cheek softly. Mia flinched instinctively and felt the pain in her wrist as the knot tightened.

'Or would you rather guess? You worked it out, you did, bu perhaps you don't realize why?'

'You killed all those people just because of . . . me?'

Her voice sounded as if it were coming from another planet.

'The pictures in your album. Elegant, wasn't it?'

Alexander grinned and raised the glass to her lips again.

Mia scanned the room.

A door. Open. Leading to a room.

Noises in there. Crackling.

A radio. No, a police radio. No, several.

But no voices on any of the channels.

Shit.

They were far away from civilization.

Really far away.

'Watching you has been fun.' The young man smiled. 'Very exciting. I started bugging your phone a long time ago. You look so sweet when you're asleep, did you know that?'

He got up eagerly, left the room and returned with her lozenges. Pushed one of them in between her lips.

'There you go – some salt; that will help. Poor old you. Are you starting to feel a little better?'

He trailed a finger down her cheek and let it linger over her lips for a moment.

'It's fate. How many years have we known one another, Mia? And then suddenly I see it one day. The flat right next to yours is . . . for sale. The chance to be your neighbour? Have you any idea how happy it made me? But then . . .'

He shook his head sadly.

'Barely a hello. I mean, after all these years? Disappointing, Mia. Very selfish of you. If it hadn't been the two of us for ever, I would almost have said that it was . . .'

The young man smiled to himself and placed a cold flannel on her forehead.

'You went into my flat?' Mia spluttered.

She scanned the room again but saw only shadows now. Her eyes began to close but he nudged her.

'Oh, no. Wakey, wakey, darling. Remember, we don't have very much time left.'

He took her gently by her jaw and shook her.

'The great investigator Mia Krüger!' the young man shouted, and stood up. 'Does she notice her true love when he's standing right in front of her? No! So how will this poor rejected lover ever win her favour? What does she really care about, this great investigator? There's only one thing!'

349

He stuck a finger into the air and grinned from ear to ear. Mia felt like she was witnessing some sort of sick circus act.

His eyes.

His smile.

He wasn't really here.

This young man was somewhere completely different.

'Well, you've noticed me now, haven't you, Mia?'

Alexander smiled and flung out his arms.

'I'm not invisible any longer, am I? What? No? Yes? You can see me now, can't you?'

He burst out laughing.

'Genius, isn't it? You have to admit it. Oh yes. I've read everything. Seen everything. I know everything about you, Mia. The pictures. Your diary. Isn't it strange how beautiful such things can be?'

He grinned again and returned to the bed. Put his hand on her cheek once more.

'And isn't it amazing how well you can get to know another person, even though you never speak to them?'

'Why . . .?' Mia mumbled as the darkness slipped over her eyes again.

'You saved my life,' the young man said, and suddenly grew serious. 'Well, not in that sense, but yes, I would say so. Because you caught him, didn't you? Salem? The arsonist.'

Mia shook her head, or maybe she nodded. She was no longer sure. She couldn't feel her arms or her legs.

'The house was full of smoke.' The young man got up again.

The circus act resumed, only this time the mood was sombre.

'There was smoke in my room. That's the last thing I remember. When I woke up again, they were dead. My dad. Kyrre, my brother. Both of them. Eaten by the flames, as was our house in Fredrikstad. And if that wasn't bad enough, then my mum thought I had done it. Me, Mia? She thought I was to blame.'

A fire.

The Brothers Lionheart.

A dead big brother.

She had been right.

'I had been playing with matches, Mia, hadn't I?'

The young man tilted his head, a smile on his lips, but his eyes were elsewhere.

Mia wanted to say something but she was unable to.

'After that,' Alexander continued eagerly, as if this were a rehearsed speech which he had waited a long time to deliver. 'She didn't want anything to do with me. As if I had the mark of Cain on my forehead. As if I were the spawn of the devil. Didn't want to look at me. Shut me in the basement. She let me out so that I could go to school, but that was all. A television and an old video recorder. With one movie. Over and over again. *Bambi*. Just me. And this movie. What do you think that does to a child, Mia?'

A serious gaze now above the thin lips, but his eyes were no longer looking at her; he was far away.

'But then, one day, Mia, "Would you like to go to the cabin, Alexander?" she said. Have you any idea, Mia, how happy it made me? To go somewhere with my mum? I remember how nice it was, sitting in the car listening to the radio. A log fire. The smell of food from the kitchen. It was the middle of winter. Then my mum took something from the wall and tied it round my head. Antlers. She pointed to the frozen lake outside. The glossy ice. *Bambi is down there*. That was what she said, Mia. *Bambi is down there, Alexander, and if you walk out on the ice with the antlers on your head, you'll get to see him for yourself . . .*'

Mia pulled her foot slowly towards her and felt some leeway. If only she could free her arm . . .

'Are you listening, Mia?' the wistful eyes said.

'I'm listening,' Mia croaked and attempted a smile. 'You went out on the ice to see—'

'Bambi,' the young man smiled. 'I was ten years old and I was going to see Bambi, do you understand? Because I loved Bambi. So I sat on the ice. For hours. Until I turned blue. But Bambi never came. And when I finally gave up and fought my way through the snow back to the cabin, there was no one there.'

'What?' Mia mumbled.

351

'My mum. She was gone.'

The young man fell silent for a moment.

'But then you came. Mia Krüger. Out of nowhere. It was an arsonist, Mum. It wasn't me. It was an arsonist. Oh, Mia, you should have seen the look on her face in the hospital bed when I showed her the newspapers all those years later. Do you remember? The front pages?'

A vague memory.

VG and *Dagbladet*.

Right after she had caught him.

'She understood, Mia. She looked at me with such love in her eyes, Mia, do you understand? Right before she died. Her eyes. She stroked my hand, Mia. I could see she was sorry for all the hurt, for neglecting me, for letting me be raised in care while she served her time in jail. For leaving me out there, for not being a mother to me. She finally *understood*. Now do you see?'

The young man smiled and stroked his cheek.

'Mum . . .'

Mia had begun to carefully retract her foot again when Alexander became mentally present in the room once more.

'And that was when it happened, of course it was. Mia Krüger. Fate. My true love. You and me for ever. It was no coincidence was it, Mia? That you saved me?'

'Thank you,' Mia said, finally managing to produce something that looked like a smile.

'And now we'll travel together,' the young man said. He seemed calmer now. 'But first . . .'

He ran out of the room and returned with something a moment later.

A . . . *wedding dress*?

'Do you think it'll fit you? You and me, darling? Before we go.'

He held up the wedding dress so that she could see it and smiled again.

'Where . . . are we going?' Mia asked with a hesitant smile.

'What do you mean?' Alexander sounded rather surprised.

'You said "travel"? Where are we . . .?'

He looked at her strangely.

'To join Kyrre, of course. And Sigrid. Isn't that what you want? To put all this behind you? For you and me to go to Nangiyala?'

Nangiyala.

The Brothers Lionheart.

In the story, it was the magic land.

She finally realized what he was talking about and her thoughts became instantly lucid. Her diaries in the boxes. The notes she had made after those endless sessions with the psychologists.

Her suicidal thoughts.

Her twin sister walking slowly through a field of yellow wheat.

Come, Mia, come.

'Oh, I almost forgot.' The young man smiled and clapped his hands.

He ran eagerly back out into the living room and returned with his hands behind his back.

'Look.' He smiled again, holding up a shiny piece of jewellery in front of her face.

She could see the initial but her brain refused to take it in.

M.

M for Mia.

It was . . . Sigrid's bracelet?

What the . . .?

'For you, darling.' Alexander, still smiling, carefully placed the bracelet next to her on the bed.

Chapter 74

'Clear. No one here.'

Curry returned to the land of the living as someone pulled off his hood. The light grew even brighter now and stung his eyes.

Stampeding boots across the floor.

'Clear. It's empty. They're gone.'

A hand under his chin, pulling up his head.

'My name is John Wold. Are you Larsen? Curry?'

He could barely open his mouth.

'Dahl? The lawyer? Lorentzen? Were they here?'

Curry nodded slowly.

'Did they leave a long time ago?'

A police radio crackled somewhere.

'I . . .' Curry began, but his voice failed.

'They're gone,' said the voice belonging to Wold as he turned to someone Curry couldn't see. 'Issue a wanted notice. They can't have got far.'

Dear God.

He was still trembling. He couldn't stop.

'Untie him,' another voice said.

Hands on his legs. Arms. He felt the blood return to his hands.

'No one here?'

'No one except this guy.'

More boots across the hard floor.

'Shit. OK.'

More voices outside, further away this time.

'Get the message out. Close everything.'

Then Wold again, far away in the fog.
'Are you OK? Are you able to stand up?'
Hands helping him, his legs refusing to carry him.
And then Curry passed out.

Chapter 75

Mia resurfaced once more, this time in front of a mirror. She must have passed out again. He had moved her. Was he still drugging her? A chair. In the living room. Handcuffs now. Nothing round her legs.

'It's a great fit, don't you think, darling?'

A smile in the mirror as she felt something in her hair.

A hairbrush.

He was brushing her hair.

Her face.

He had put make-up on her face.

Something around her finger.

A gold ring.

And a strange garment on her body.

A wedding dress.

He had dressed her.

Applied make-up.

Fuck.

Mia felt an instinctive urge to get up and rid herself of it all, but she was unable to move. His face in the mirror came into focus as her brain slowly grew more lucid.

'How do you want your hair, darling?'

She felt his disgusting fingers in her hair.

'Up?'

Alexander smiled and moved his face close to hers in the mirror.

'Or down? I think you look best with it down, but perhaps I should put it up, given that today is a special day? What do you think?'

Play for time.

Finally, she managed to think straight.

'Up, perhaps,' she mumbled, plastering what she hoped was a smile across her face.

'Yes, I agree, I do.' The young man took a step back.

Get him to talk about something.

'How?' her dry mouth began.

'What, darling?'

Another finger across her cheek.

'The bracelet? How did you get it?'

'Oh, by chance. It was meant for you. A friend of your sister. Cisse. She left it on the door to our building, but you didn't find it. I did. She hung around our neighbourhood quite a lot. She was spying on you.'

He laughed a little and let the brush glide through her hair again.

'You were right, by the way.'

His voice was now suddenly very close to her ear.

'Markus Skog. The guy you shot? He did kill Sigrid. I invited Cisse in. You know what junkies are like. Gave her some money so that she could get herself a fix. She told me everything that happened.'

'Why . . .?'

Mia could feel herself fading away again.

'Oh, it was the same old story, as far as I could work out. Sigrid was a drug mule, bringing in heroin, then she went to rehab and wanted out.'

Mia could no longer speak.

'Oh yes, she cleaned up her act. She was ready to start a new life. I think she even hinted that, unless they left her alone, she would tell everything. Markus Skog and some lawyer decided they couldn't let her do that, now could they?'

Darkness coming over her.

'But this junkie overheard them – Cisse. She was shooting up on a sofa, yet she seems to have been paying attention nevertheless. An overdose, and Sigrid was gone. They carried her body to a basement nearby. Another dead junkie – who would suspect anything was amiss?'

The young man smiled and pressed his cheek against Mia's once more.

'Are you sure you like it up? Why don't we just leave it loose? It's more natural.'

Mia was close to fainting.

No.

Please, no.

She pulled herself together again.

'How?' she mumbled. 'Ivan . . . Horowitz?'

With her last strength Mia raised her head and managed to fix Alexander's eyes in the mirror.

'Oh, yes, that was clever, wasn't it?'

Alexander put down the hairbrush.

'We were at Blakstad together. Six months. We got to know one another quite well. He had been to war. He was a total wreck. And I was – well, I'm me, aren't I?'

He laughed briefly.

'I couldn't have all these people getting in our way, now could I? It was just going to be you and me, that was the whole point. It was a brilliant plan, wasn't it? Send them all on a wild-goose chase? A kill list? Fifty random people?'

Alexander laughed out loud, cocked his head and picked up the hairbrush again.

'No, I think up, don't you? I mean, it's a big day today.'

The little strength Mia had managed to summon disappeared once more. She could barely keep her head upright.

Sigrid?

No . . .

She couldn't take any more.

Leave.

Why not?

A world of evil.

Her sister running through the field.

This image that would never leave her.

Come, Mia, come.

Death.

To Nangiyala.
'Or would you rather have it down?'
Fuck it all.
She was done with it.
'You do what you like,' Mia said.
And slowly closed her eyes in front of the mirror.

Chapter 76

They had barely got back out on the street again before thei
mobiles started to ring. Munch answered his and saw Anette d
the same.

'Where have you been, Holger?'

It was Gabriel Mørk.

'Listen, I'm a bit busy right now, Gabriel,' Munch said. 'W
have a situation here, I'll have to call you back.'

'Haven't you heard?' Gabriel panted.

'Heard what?'

'It's not him.'

'Who?'

'Horowitz. It's not him. We've found him. It's her neighbou
His name is Alexander Sørli.'

'How . . .?'

'We went through the files,' the young hacker continued eagerl
'Ylva and I. We found something. He was one of Ritter's patient
He's obsessed with Mia. He lost his brother in a fire. I'm guessin
he met her through Ritter. The first victim. Vivian Berg.'

'Easy now,' Munch said, completely forgetting to light his ciga
ette. 'What are you saying? What files?'

'Mia's neighbour.' Gabriel was practically shouting now. 'We'v
sent people to the flat already. Where have you been?'

'You have . . .?'

Anette had finished her call and was waving to him, signallin
for him to ring off.

'Ludvig organized it. There are people over there. So are yo
coming?' Gabriel continued.

'Organized what?'

'A search of the flat belonging to the guy who lives next to Mia. Alexander Sørli. He's the killer. We've found photos on the walls. Pictures of different disguises. False teeth. Wigs. Glasses. He has pictures of her everywhere, even by his bed. Are you coming?'

'Pictures of . . . who?' Munch asked as Anette gestured urgently to him again.

'Mia. It's all about Mia . . .'

Anette came up to him, nodding eagerly.

'They've found the young woman.'

'Who?' Munch said, putting his hand over the microphone.

'The young woman with the green baseball cap. Her daughter phoned us. Saw her mother on TV. She's being interviewed down at police headquarters right now. We were sent on a wild-goose chase, Holger. His name is Sørli. Alexander Sørli.'

Shit.

Munch resumed his conversation with Gabriel.

'You've been there?'

'We're here now. You need to see his flat, it's completely . . . And Mia's front door is open . . .'

'Stay where you are, Gabriel, I'm on my way,' Munch said, and threw his cigarette down on the tarmac.

Chapter 77

Hair up. A big white wedding dress. A gold ring on her finger. Nothing on her feet, but Mia didn't notice; she felt nothing as he led her out of the cabin and through the forest. Pistols pressed into her back. Two of them.

Glocks.

You like them, Mia.

They're just like the ones you have, aren't they?

The wind whispered softly in her face as he lifted a branch and steered her further down towards the water.

It was all the same to her now.

She had been good, hadn't she?

No alcohol.

No pills.

A good girl.

So positive.

She could let go now.

The pills on the table.

On the Trøndelag coast.

In Hitra.

The house she had bought purely so she could disappear.

He had disturbed her.

Munch.

Turned up with a file.

A dead girl.

Six years old.

Hanging from a tree with a sign around her neck.

I'm travelling alone.

A cold case. And she had put it off. She had put death off.

Let them use her as they always did.

Damn them all to hell.

The young man nudged her onwards through the forest, right down to the water's edge.

This darkness.

Evil everywhere.

She couldn't take it any more.

She wanted to leave this world behind.

Come, Mia, come.

She wanted to join Sigrid.

The young man led the way into the water, still holding the pistols.

'This was the place, Mia.'

She could barely hear his voice now.

'It was this lake. Except there was ice on it back then, of course.'

A smile spread across his young face.

'I sat here. With antlers on my head. Waiting for Bambi, only he never came, did he?'

Mia opened her eyes again as the young man pointed the pistols at her.

'Time to go?'

The wind through the trees.

A gentle breeze.

'Together? To Nangiyala?'

The birds.

Wing strokes across the water.

Come, Mia, come.

Mia Krüger opened her eyes and suddenly felt wide awake. The smiling face at the water's edge. He was a stalker. He was nothing but a pathetic stalker who had got it into his head that she was an angel. Who had killed in her name. She had seen so many of them before. Those quiet children no one ever noticed. Evil hiding behind masks of innocence. Was she really going to die like this?

Not bloody likely.

Not like this.

'No.'

'What?' the young man said. He sounded surprised and cocked his head slightly. 'You don't want to?'

'No,' Mia said gravely.

'Are you sure?' The young man took a step further out into the water.

'Yes.'

'You don't want to come with me?'

'No.'

The wind in the trees.

'You want to live?'

She nodded slowly to the figure in the water.

'OK.' The young man smiled and stuck out his hand towards her. The Glock.

One of them.

'I'm happy to hear that, Mia.' His disgusting mouth smiled as he took a few more steps out into the cold water. 'But will you do me a favour?'

'What is it?'

'Shoot me.'

He smiled again.

'You'll do that for me, won't you?'

She wasn't ready for the bang that followed.

The birds taking off from the trees.

'Shoot me.' The young man curled his finger around the trigger a second time.

It hurt this time.

The bullet brushed her thigh before hitting the stones behind her.

And then.

Another.

This time the bullet went right through the wedding dress near her hip. She could see blood on the white fabric.

'Shoot me, Mia.'

The boy took another step out into the water and pressed the trigger again.

The bullet grazed her leg.

Mia pointed the Glock at his smiling face.

'Alexander,' she warned him.

'You or me?'

A ripple now in the dark water.

'I love you, Mia.' The young man raised his gun again, this time aiming straight at her face, his finger on the trigger.

Mia quickly made up her mind.

SEVEN

JUNE 2013

Chapter 78

The sun was high in the sky, a welcome warmth Munch hadn't felt for a long time as he stood with a cigarette in his mouth under the green trees in the garden in Røa and saw Marianne's big smile as she came towards him.

'Isn't it time you gave up?'

'What do you mean?'

His ex-wife walked right up to him and gave him a big hug.

'Give up smoking, Holger.'

'Yes, I'm giving up today.' Munch smiled and chucked away the cigarette stub as another smartly dressed couple entered through the gate.

'Hi.' The young woman smiled and shook his hand. 'I'm Kathy. We're friends of Ziggy.'

'Welcome.' Munch smiled. 'Drinks are through there. The ceremony will begin in a few minutes.'

The couple nodded in the sunshine and walked up the steps and into the house.

'It's our daughter's wedding day,' Marianne said, taking his hand.

'Yes, indeed it is.'

'Are you happy? Are you OK, Holger?'

Munch squeezed her hand and smiled.

'Yes, Marianne. I'm very well.'

'Good,' his ex-wife said as yet another couple came up the gravel path.

'In there. Drinks on the table.' Munch smiled at the new arrivals as Mia entered through the gate.

'Congratulations.' His blue-eyed colleague smiled too and hugged Marianne. 'Where can I leave my present?'

'They didn't want any presents,' Munch said.

'Yes, isn't that what they always say? Is she in there?'

'They're in the living room.'

'OK, I had better go and say hello. I'll see you later.'

Mia gave Marianne another quick hug before disappearing into the house.

'Grandad!'

Little feet across the gravel and Marion, dressed up to the nines, threw her arms around him.

'Hello, sweetheart, how are you doing? Can you remember everything you have to do?'

'Oh, Grandad,' the little girl said, putting on a serious face. 'I'm not five years old any more. How hard do you think it is? I have a basket of flowers. I look lovely and I throw the flowers on the ground as they walk. Hello? Grandad, you asked me the exact same question yesterday.'

'Good, Marion. I just wanted to check.'

Marianne smiled and squeezed his hand again.

'But listen, Grandad?' Marion said, and looked at him.

'Yes?'

'Barbie isn't very happy with her horse.'

'Isn't she?'

The little girl lifted her pink dress and scratched her leg.

'No, or that's to say, yes, but it's so very lonely . . .'

'The horse is lonely?'

'Yes, Grandad. It's all on its own. Poor horse. It eats hay and jumps over hurdles, but still it's all alone.'

Marianne looked at him and shook her head.

'So what you're telling me is that it needs a friend?'

'Yes! Grandad, it needs a friend. Please could we look for another horse? A black one this time, and we can name it Arrow and it can run so quickly that the other horse will be really happy?'

'We'll see about that, Marion.'

'Brilliant, Grandad. Today?'

'No, Marion, your mum is getting married today.'

'Tomorrow?'

'Soon.' Munch smiled as the gate opened again.

'Hello,' Curry mumbled. He looked uncomfortable in the suit he was wearing. 'This is Luna.'

'Welcome, Luna.' Munch nodded and shook her outstretched hand. 'Drinks in there. The ceremony will be taking place in the back garden in – well, it'll be very soon now.'

'Thank you for inviting us,' Curry said politely, and ushered his girlfriend up the steps.

Munch was easing a cigarette packet out of his pocket as his mobile pinged.

A text message from Lillian.

Congratulations on your daughter's wedding, Holger! And thank you so much for last Saturday's date. How about another one? I have tickets for the concert hall on Thursday. We could have dinner first?

Munch quickly texted her back.

Absolutely, Lillian. I look forward to it. I really do.

A slightly fraught face appeared on the steps, one of Miriam's friends who was acting as the wedding planner.

'We're starting now. The band is playing. The bride is about to walk down the aisle. It's all happening. Are you coming?'

'Of course we are.'

'We're coming.' Marianne smiled and squeezed his hand again before running in front of him up the steps and into the white house.

Chapter 79

Mia Krüger got out of the car and carried the flowers up through the beautiful cemetery. She knelt down and removed the withered ones in front of the grave. She placed the new bouquet in the vase and caressed the letters on the stone.

Sigrid Krüger
Sister, friend and daughter
Born 11 November 1979. Died 18 April 2002.
Much loved. Deeply missed.

Her twin sister in a field of yellow wheat.

Beckoning her.

Come, Mia, come.

'No, Sigrid.'

Mia stuck her hand into her jacket pocket. She cradled the silver bracelet in the palm of her hand for a moment then took off the one she wore around her wrist.

M for Mia.

S for Sigrid.

A hole in the brown earth and both bracelets were gone. Her sister's pleading voice somewhere deep inside her.

'No, Sigrid,' Mia said. 'I have to try now. Be myself. Live Because I want to. Do you understand?'

She stood up to the answer of nothing in front of the white stone.

'OK?'

Not a sound.

Just the wind.

'I've left my job. I'm going away.'

Mia lingered in front of the grave.

Her sister in a field of yellow wheat.

A blurred face turning towards her for a brief moment.

And then she was gone.

Mia tightened her jacket around her and walked down the gravel path. She glanced up at the white stone one last time then got into the jade-green Jaguar.

And pulled out on to the narrow road.

I'm Travelling Alone

Samuel Bjork

The first in the Munch and Krüger series.

When the body of a young girl is found hanging from a tree, the only clue the police have is an airline tag around her neck. It reads 'I'm travelling alone'.

In response, police investigator Holger Munch is charged with assembling a special homicide unit. But to complete the team, he must track down his former partner, Mia Krüger – a brilliant but troubled detective – who has retreated to a solitary island with plans to kill herself.

Reviewing the file, Mia finds something new – a thin line carved into the dead girl's fingernail: the number 1. This is only the beginning. To save other children from the same fate, she must find a way to cast aside her own demons and stop this murderer from becoming a serial killer.

'Terrific . . . Intelligent and gripping . . . May well propel [Bjork] to deserved international fame'
THE TIMES

'Samuel Bjork's formidable *I'm Travelling Alone* is despatched with real élan . . . Mia's confrontation with both her own demons and a very human one is mesmerising fare'
INDEPENDENT